EYES OF THE INNOCENT

ALSO BY BRAD PARKS

Faces of the Gone

EYES OF THE INNOCENT

Brad Parks

MINOTAUR BOOKS
A Thomas Dunne Book
New York

A THOMAS DUNNE BOOK FOR MINOTAUR BOOKS.
An imprint of St. Martin's Publishing Group.

Library of Congress Cataloging-in-Publication Data

Parks, Brad, 1974–
Eyes of the innocent : a mystery / Brad Parks.—1st ed.
p. cm.
"A Thomas Dunne book."
Sequel to: Faces of the gone.
ISBN 978-0-312-57478-9
1. Reporters and reporting—Fiction. 2. Children—Crimes against—Fiction. 3. Real estate investment—Fiction. 4. Political corruption—Fiction. 5. Newark (N.J.)—Fiction. I. Title.
PS3616.A7553E94 2011
813'.6—dc22

2010039029

First Edition: February 2011

10 9 8 7 6 5 4 3 2 1

This will always make me think of a little girl who, while snuggled against her daddy's chest in a Baby Bjorn, was the first person to hear the following book read aloud.

Put her to sleep every time.

EYES OF THE INNOCENT

The electrician patted his breast pocket for the tenth time and, once again, exhaled noisily: the envelope—Primo's envelope—was still there.

It was the weight of the thing that threw him. He thought $10,000 ought to have more heft to it. In his hometown of Belem, Brazil, $10,000 was a substantial sum, enough for a down payment on a house—a brick house in a decent neighborhood, not one of those shanties in the slums. There was a time when if you converted 10,000 American greenbacks into cruzeiros, you needed a wheelbarrow to haul it.

Here in the States, meted out in hundred-dollar bills, it could be bound in paper bands and slipped into an envelope. And it weighed, well, not enough to stop the electrician from constantly checking the pocket of his winter coat.

His errand was simple enough. Or at least it should have been. He picked up the money at Primo's office, a small warehouse in a swampy section of Newark, New Jersey—the industrial part that runs alongside the New Jersey Turnpike. He dropped it off at a storefront office on Springfield Avenue, in the heart of the Central Ward. It was a route the electrician had come to know well.

He had done this, what, fifteen times? Twenty? He was starting to lose count. But every time, it made him feel as if he had scorpions in his underwear. It was only a matter of time until he got stung.

Cash. Why did it always have to be cash? And why did it have to be delivered personally? Why couldn't Primo just write a check and slip it in the mail?

The electrician brought his hand to his pocket one last time. Still there. He parked his truck and braced himself for the worst part: the twenty feet from the curb to the storefront, where he had to wait to be buzzed in—all the while feeling as if that cash brick were a signal flare to every punk, thug, and stickup artist for five blocks.

He glanced around to see no one was coming, made his twenty-foot dash, then mashed the buzzer four times in rapid succession. After what seemed like forever but was really just ten seconds, the door buzzed open. Relieved, he burst through it. The scorpions had decided not to sting him. Not this time.

A thickset, round-shouldered black man looked up from behind his desk.

"Damn, boy, where the fire at?"

It had been the same man receiving the money every time, but they had never bothered with introductions or niceties. They were simply doing the bidding of their powerful bosses. Names didn't matter. Banter accomplished nothing.

"Ten?" the man asked.

"Ten."

The electrician handed the man a piece of paper. The man scowled.

"You Spanish guys got to learn to write English. The last letter on the last name . . . That a a *or a* o*?"*

The electrician swallowed the insult. The name wasn't his. And he didn't bother to inform this ignoramus that the name was Portuguese, not Spanish, and that they used the same alphabet—which happened to be Roman.

"Ronaldo. With an o*," he said.*

The man scribbled for a few more seconds, then handed the electrician a receipt. Not another word passed between them.

CHAPTER 1

I made at least four mistakes that Monday morning, the first of which was going into the office in the first place. There's an old saying among newspaper reporters that news never breaks in the newsroom. So if you're not currently working on a story, you ought to be out finding one. If you hang around the newsroom with nothing to do, you put yourself at extreme risk of being assigned something to do by an editor. And—ask any writer, anywhere—editors are approximately ninety-eight percent full of stupid ideas.

Which leads to my second mistake: wandering by the open office door of my editor, Sal Szanto. I'm an investigative reporter for the *Newark Eagle-Examiner,* New Jersey's largest newspaper. My last story had been what we in the business call BBI. Boring But Important. It was a piece about patronage hiring in a nearby county government. (My suggested headline, "County Keeps Nepotism in the Family," was rejected as being too cheeky.) The thirteen people who actually bothered to read it—the same thirteen people who read all our BBI's—were very impressed. To everyone else who picked up our Sunday paper, I suspect it was merely an impediment on the way to sudoku.

Either way, it was now yesterday's news, making me an investigative reporter momentarily lacking anything to investigate.

And so we arrive at my third mistake: not feigning deafness when Szanto croaked out my name.

"Crrrtrrsss!"

That's "Carter Ross," for those who don't understand the peculiar dialect of my fifty-something, chain-smoking, antacid-devouring, coffee-guzzling editor. Szanto has difficulty pronouncing vowels when he's upset, stressed, or tired—which, with the way newspapers have been going the last few years, is most of the time. It usually takes him a couple of sentences to lift his vocal cords out of the gravel and start speaking coherently.

"Hvvsstt."

I took that to mean "Have a seat." So I did. Szanto cleared his throat.

"You read the fire story this morning?" he growled. "The thing with the two kids?"

A fast-moving fire at about nine o'clock the night before had swept through a house on Littleton Avenue in Newark, killing two little boys, Alonzo and Antoine Harris, ages four and six. The Newark Fire Department was offering no theories about what started it. The whereabouts of the mother, Akilah Harris, was unknown as of press time—which did not exactly speak well of her custodial abilities.

We had given the story the usual tragedy treatment, with a large photo of the blackened house along with smaller headshots of the little boys—smiling school portraits—along with a story gang-written by the herd of semisupervised interns we have working on the weekends. During my eight years at the paper, we had probably written variations of the story fifty times—albeit with changed names, dates, and places—so maybe I should be more callous about it by now. But it still rips my guts out.

"Yeah, I read it," I said. "What about it?"

Szanto had this look on his face I couldn't quite place. Just like Eskimos have fifty different words for snow, Szanto has at least that many pained expressions. Parsing them takes a certain amount of expertise. The difference between "I'm pained because an intern just handed me a story that might as well be in Farsi" and "I'm pained because I ate hot wings for lunch" could be as subtle as a slight lowering of the lip or an extra furrowing of the brow.

In this case, it was neither.

"Brodie wants a space heater story," he said.

Now it was my turn for a pained expression. Brodie is Harold Brodie, a living newspaper legend who had presided over our newsroom as executive editor for the last quarter century. Now in his late sixties, he was basically a nice man, with a high-pitched voice and eyebrows that could use some serious manscaping. He was small and fragile in a way that sort of reminded everyone of their grandfather. As a leader, he was the most benign of dictators. And, more or less, everyone loved him.

But he was still an editor, and as such he was as prone to stupid ideas as any other editor. Plus, he had this tendency to get fixated on certain subjects.

Space heaters was one of them. Like many of the nation's more depressed cities, Newark had its share of unimaginably horrid slum buildings where the heat may or may not be working—thanks to busted boilers, pilfered pipes, or landlords who decided the best way to combat the high cost of heating oil was to abstain from buying any.

One of the ways tenants survive this injustice is to plug space heaters into their already overloaded electrical sockets and leave them on 24-7. Fire-safetywise, you'd do just as well tossing an unsupervised ten-year-old into a room with oily rags, lighter fluid, and matches.

As a result, we write about the perils of space heaters at least once every winter. The only surprise was that December and January had been so mild we made it all the way to February without running our annual offering.

"Did a space heater have anything to do with it?" I asked.

"How the hell should I know?"

"But—" I started.

"I don't care," Szanto snapped. "Brodie asked for a space heater story, so write him a damn space heater story. You know how he gets."

I did. Some editors cajoled writers into doing stories with threats or loud demands. Brodie went more for the Chinese water torture approach, drip-dropping in on you until you just gave in. Sometimes, when he approached you from behind, he jingled the change in his pocket just so you knew he was there. Most longtime *Eagle-Examiner* reporters, trained by years of Brodie jingling, stiffened reflexively when they heard nickels and quarters banging together.

"Can't we just reprint one of the old space heater stories?" I asked. "I seem to recall from the archives the nineteen eighty-eight space heater story was a classic—fruity yet full-bodied, with hints of singed circuit breaker."

Szanto hit me with pained look No. 28—upturned lip, creased forehead—and I gave in.

"Fine," I huffed. "A space heater story."

I went to lift myself out of the chair.

"I want you to work with Sweet Thang," he said.

I sat back down. Sweet Thang was what Szanto—and most of the other cave-dwelling editors in the building—called our newest intern, a honey-haired twenty-two-year-old Vanderbilt graduate whose real name was Lauren Somethingorother.

Between her button nose, bright blue eyes, and a torso that rather nicely filled out a sweater set, she hadn't lacked for mentoring from some of the men in the office.

The only problem was, there was a rumor out she had gotten the job because her father and Brodie golfed together at their country club. So while working with her would improve the scenery, it did come with certain dangers.

"Do I have to?" I asked.

"Just make her feel like she's doing something important, then when it comes time to write, make sure she's in a different county from your keyboard," Szanto said.

"Fine. Whatever."

It was only a stupid space heater story. I could knock it off in a few hours and then move back to real journalism. As I left Szanto's office, I told myself it would be simple enough.

That, it turns out, was my fourth mistake.

With something short of my usual zeal, I moseyed across the newsroom and found Sweet Thang sitting in the area occupied by an ever-changing cast of interns. Newspaper economics have been so bad so long that our place, like most places, has a hiring freeze that is now old enough to enroll in the third grade. There have been buyouts, some more voluntary than others, and the threat of layoff is constant. The only people left behind are the foolish (people like me, who love the business too much to leave) and the desperate (people who can't find anything else and cling to the newspaper like bilge rats to driftwood).

Whenever a full-time staff member leaves, taking their high-five-figure or low-six-figure salary with them, they are replaced by an intern who is paid wages that would shame an Indonesian sweatshop. Really, they ought to do these kids a favor and tuck food stamps in with their paychecks each week. Still, the kids keep on coming to us, in ever-increasing numbers, to soak in all the valuable news-gathering "experience"—read: overwork—we provide them.

Given their low lot in life, I always go out of my way to be friendly to the interns. If nothing else, they're good for entertainment.

"Hi, Lauren," I said, as I walked up to her.

She looked startled.

"Oh, my goodness, you know my name?"

"Yeah, I'm—"

"You're Carter Ross!" she said, flashing a smile that surely weakened the knees of many a Vanderbilt frat boy. "You're, like, the reason I wanted to come to work here. When I read your Ludlow Street story, I told my dad, 'Dad, I totally have to work at the *Eagle-Examiner.*' Oh, my goodness. I even tweeted about your story so all my friends would know about it. And they all retweeted it. And we looked for you on Twitter, but you're not there, so we just tweeted round and round until we were tweeted out."

"Lauren?" I said, mostly to stop the river of words spouting from her mouth. Instead, I only diverted it.

"You can call me 'Sweet Thang' if you want to. I know that's what everyone calls me behind my back. I'm okay with it. I mean, it's not, like, flattering or anything—I don't *think* of myself as a Sweet Thang. I actually took courses in women's studies and stuff. All I'm saying is, it's not like I'm going to Human Resources or anything, because it's like my dad told me, 'A newsroom is still a man's world. You have to have a tough skin.' But then he also told me if anything got really bad, we could just tell Uncle Hal—sorry, Mr. Brodie—and he would take care of it. But I don't think being called Sweet Thang is like an insult or anything, it's more like—"

"Lauren," I said again.

"Oh, sorry," she said, looking downward. "I only babble when I get nervous. I'm so sorry. I'll stop. Oh no, now I'm babbling again. Okay. That's it. Stop."

She put her hand over her mouth and looked up at me.

"Szanto wants us to work together on a story."

"You and me? Together?"

I nodded.

"Oh, my goodness, that's so perfect," she gushed. "Oh, my goodness, teach me *everything.* I want to learn. I want to write just like you. You're totally my favorite writer at the paper, you don't even understand. The only writer I ever liked as much as you was Judy Blume, but that was when I was nine after I read *Freckle*

Juice, and it was a totally different thing. Oh, my goodness, I have to shut up. So what story are we working on?"

The words were coming so fast it took me a second or two to realize she had, somewhere in there, formed a question I was expected to answer.

"It's a follow-up to the fire story today," I said.

"Oh, my goodness, that story was like the saddest thing ever. Can you believe those two poor little boys dying like that? I just about cried when I saw their pictures. Did you see their eyes? They were just beautiful little boys. I mean, I would have almost cried even if they were ugly. I don't want you to think I'm superficial or anything. I'm just saying—"

I held up my hand like a crossing guard halting traffic.

"Sorry," she said.

"Anyhow, it's supposed to be a story about the dangers of space heaters."

She tilted her head.

"Space heaters?"

"That's right."

"What do space heaters have to do with the little boys?"

"At the moment, nothing," I said.

"No one from the fire department mentioned anything about space heaters."

"I know."

"So how are we going to . . . ?"

"I don't know," I snapped. "Stop asking so many questions."

The bright blue gaze dropped down to the desk. The heart-melting smile vanished. Even the bouncy, honeyed hair seemed to droop. I felt like I had kicked a puppy.

"I didn't mean . . . look, it's just . . ." I said, groping for the right words. "See, sometimes, Brodie—uhh, Uncle Hal—he gets these ideas in his head that a story exists whether or not it actually does. But because he calls the shots around here, we sort of have to humor him."

"Well," she said, considering this new information carefully, "I don't think Uncle Hal would have us write a story that isn't true."

"Oh, me neither," I said, hoping she wouldn't hear the irony in my voice.

"Cool. So what do we do now? Where do we start?"

She looked up at me expectantly. The bright blue eyes were shining again. She plopped her elbows on top of her desk, leaned over and rested her chin in her palms, treating me to a rather unfettered view down her scoop-necked top.

I sat down to remove myself from temptation. Had I not resolved to maintain a perfectly professional demeanor around her, I might have enjoyed that vista. There was no denying the young lady was rather fetching—I mean, if you like shapely twenty-two-year-old blondes, that is—and she had a wholesomeness about her that put certain unwholesome thoughts in my head. As a tall, nearly broad-shouldered, thirty-two-year-old single guy with a reasonable body mass index and no facial disfigurement, I could entertain the thought she wasn't repulsed by me.

But while there's no official policy at the *Eagle-Examiner* against fraternizing with the interns, there were at least three factors to consider. One, Uncle Hal might decide his paper needed one less investigative reporter if I made a play for his buddy's little girl. Two, I had some unresolved romantic issues with Tina Thompson, our city editor, and I suspected she would not be impressed if I summited Mount Intern. Three, I was getting exhausted just trying to listen to her for five minutes; an entire evening's worth of conversation and flirtation might make me slip into a coma.

All in all, it seemed like enough reason to leave Sweet Thang to the Sigma Alpha Epsilons.

"Do you want me to call the fire department?" she asked. "Or find a national expert on space heaters? Maybe there's a space heater awareness group out there? Or a space heater safety nonprofit or something? I want to do this story exactly how you would do it. How would you start?"

I was tempted to tell her I planned to start like any self-respecting reporter approached a story in which he has absolutely no interest: waste time chatting with colleagues, return several lengthy personal e-mails, take an extended lunch, check in with old sources on completely unrelated matters, then start making phone calls around three o'clock when there was absolutely nothing better to do.

But that didn't seem like the kind of example I should be setting for an impressionable young person.

"Well," I said. "I like to get a feel for what I'm writing about first. Visit the scene. Take in the sights. Talk to some neighbors. So what do you say we make a little trip out to Littleton Avenue?"

The question was barely even formed and she was already grabbing a notebook and her car keys.

"Can I drive?" she asked.

"That depends. What kind of car do you have?"

"It's the cutest little BMW. My dad got it for me for graduation. It's red. I call him Walter. He's got an iPod dock and everything. I just love him."

I immediately got this image of Sweet Thang bopping through the hood in her shiny red BMW, blasting Taylor Swift on Walter's speakers. The carjackers would play rock-paper-scissors to determine who got dibs.

"No," I said. "Better let me drive."

My car is a five-year-old Chevy Malibu. It has traveled some undetermined distance beyond a hundred thousand miles: dead speedometers tell no tales. I bought it for a suspiciously low price from a used car dealer in Newark. I'm not saying the guy was unscrupulous, but the title work looked like it had eraser marks on it.

It wasn't exactly a chick magnet. But the Malibu had certain benefits that were practical—no, essential—when operating in a rugged city like Newark. You didn't have to worry about it getting beaten up by the potholes because it was already beaten up. You could leave it unlocked with the motor running outside a chop shop and not have to worry about it being there when you got back. And when it comes to blending into the hood, it does just fine.

Which is good, because in most Newark neighborhoods, I don't exactly blend. It's not just that I'm white. It's that I'm a peculiar subset of the white race, one that disappeared from Newark long ago: a purebred, stiff-upper-lipped, can't-dance-a-lick WASP. I've got carefully parted brown hair, blue eyes, and a way of walking and talking most inner-city black people just find funny. I wear well-pressed shirts—usually white or blue—with pleated slacks and a tie with a half-Windsor knot. Even white people tease me about how white I am.

So I'm perfectly aware, when I enter many parts of Newark, that I create a little bit of a scene. Some people, assuming I'm lost, will approach and ask if I need directions. Most merely stare like the Stay Puft Marshmallow Man just went past.

People have suggested to me that if I acted like I have some street in me—wear hip-hop clothes, drop certain colloquialisms into my vocabulary, get a haircut that didn't look so *Leave It to Beaver*—black folks might open up to me more easily.

But I don't believe that. You can only hide who you are for so long. The simple truth is, I grew up in Millburn, a proper New Jersey suburb that is only a few miles away from Newark geographically but a full country away demographically. From the time I grew out of onesies, my mother dressed me in collared shirts. My upbringing featured things like tennis camp, Broadway musicals, and trips to Europe. I went to Amherst, a small, expensive, exclusive liberal arts college that doesn't exactly do much for one's street cred. I'm pretty much what black folks refer to as The Man. If I pretended otherwise, I'd come off as a fraud. And no one—of any race, gender, or creed—wants to talk to a fraud.

Besides, I *like* half-Windsor knots.

And, funny as it may sound to my fellow WASPs, I like Newark, too. And not just because of the gentrification that is slowly (very slowly) taking root or because of the new, shiny stuff being built downtown. I like the old parts of the city, too—the old neighborhoods, the old churches, the old stories that seem to be lurking around every corner. Say what you will about Newark, but it's got character. And heart. Two things we could all use more of.

So I didn't mind that as Sweet Thang and I pulled up to the scene of the fire on Littleton Avenue, two old guys on a nearby porch openly gawked at us. The Man—now with a bubbly blonde anchor in tow—tends to have that effect.

The air was still acrid from the fire, with that wonderful aroma of burned plastic and toasted toxin wafting about. Even if I didn't have the address, my nose could have led me there.

The house wasn't at all what I expected. Usually, when fatal fires broke out in Newark, they were in nasty, tottering, ninety-year-old tenements, the kind of places that had been fire traps for so long you wondered how they hadn't burned down sooner.

But this one was a relatively new construction, one of those architecturally challenged boxes that started popping up around Newark at the turn of the new century. It had been quite a moment for a long-depressed city. Real estate developers had finally discovered that, for all its ills, Newark is still just a twenty-minute train ride from Manhattan. Soon, builders were falling over themselves to snatch up the abundance of empty lots and toss up one- and two-family houses.

At the peak of the boom, new two-family houses were going for more than $400,000, an astounding number to Newark residents who remembered the not-so-distant time when they couldn't even give away their houses. Then the bubble popped, the foreclosures began hitting in waves, and it was back to reality.

Still, the city's housing stock had been at least partially transformed. And most folks figured it would take a few years before the new construction started looking—and burning—like the old tenements.

"Well, I'll be damned," I said out loud.

"What?" Sweet Thang asked. She had been yammering non-stop on the way out—can't for the life of me remember about what—but had been quiet since we left the car.

"Check this place out," I said. "It's nice."

Sweet Thang looked at me, looked at the house—with its soot-streaked siding, blackened window frames, and scorched roof—then looked back at me like she couldn't believe she had placed me next to Judy Blume in the writing pantheon.

"Well, okay, maybe *nice* is no longer the right adjective," I said. "But it used to be nice. It couldn't be more than a few years old. It's got its own driveway, a garage, this nice sturdy gate here."

I shook the gate for emphasis. She whipped out a pad and started taking notes. I could get used to having my own stenographer.

"Look at the landscaping," I said, gesturing to some well-manicured shrubs. "At one point, someone cared about the way this place looked. I bet there used to be border flowers planted in front, maybe some impatiens. No, no, make that marigolds. Too much sun for impatiens."

Sweet Thang wrote down every word, like I was dictating the next coming of *Ulysses*. I unlatched the gate and walked closer, with Sweet Thang trailing behind, still scribbling madly. The front door was . . . well, there was no front door. The firemen must have busted it off its hinges.

"Come on, let's go in," I said, walking up the front steps.

She halted.

"Are we allowed?"

"You're not in homeroom. We don't have to raise our hands and ask for a hall pass to use the bathroom," I said. "Besides, I don't see anyone here telling us not to. As far as I'm concerned, an open door is an invitation."

Sweet Thang bit her lower lip and let out a whiny "But couldn't we get in trouble?"

"In trouble?" I asked. "For all we know, there's a melted space heater in one of those kid's rooms. That space heater is our smoking gun, literally and figuratively. Can't you just see it? With the charred teddy bear leaning up against it? Isn't that the perfect start to our story? It could be. But I guess we'll just have to go back to the office and tell Uncle Hal we're not sure if a space heater had anything to do with this fire because we were afraid we could get *in trouble.*"

"Fine," she huffed and charged past me up the steps.

Interns, I chuckled to myself. So easily goaded.

I pulled a pad out of my pocket and began jotting down a few notes when, from inside the house, I heard a loud thud.

Then Sweet Thang screamed.

I took the porch steps in two leaps and barreled inside the house to find Sweet Thang with a long kitchen knife at her throat.

The person holding said knife—a wiry, dark-skinned black woman—looked like she knew what she was doing with it. And when she saw me, her eyes opened wide and she pressed the blade even tighter against Sweet Thang's neck.

"Step back," she yelled, then took a fistful of bouncy blond curls and tilted back Sweet Thang's head. "I'll cut your little girlfriend here."

Sweet Thang had gone stiff and silent. I suppose she didn't feel like she was in a position to negotiate, so I did the talking.

"Take it easy," I said, trying to keep my voice steady. "We're reporters with the *Eagle-Examiner.* We're just here working on a story."

You could see the woman's mind whirring, trying to decide whether to believe me. Sweet Thang was holding up remarkably well under the circumstances.

"My name is Carter Ross," I continued. "This is my partner Lauren."

"It's Lauren McMillan, but people call me 'Sweet Thang,'" she squeaked.

Now the woman looked downright perplexed.

"Sweet Thang?" she said derisively.

Her brow furrowed deeper.

"Y'all messing with me?"

"Here's my card," I said, digging it out and inching toward her, holding it at arm's length. When I got just close enough, she released Sweet Thang's hair and snatched my card. She barely bothered to look at it.

"That don't mean nothing. Anyone could fake that."

"How about I give you my phone and you call information and get a number for the *Eagle-Examiner.* Ask whoever answers if a guy named Carter Ross works there."

She removed the knife from Sweet Thang's throat and pushed her at me, which brought us together in an awkward half hug.

"Don't matter," she said. "Ain't no scrawny white boy and his shorty gonna give me no trouble anyway."

Sweet Thang rubbed her neck, which didn't appear to have blood on it. I was guessing this was the first time anyone had held a knife to daddy's little girl's throat. I was just grateful I didn't have to explain to Uncle Hal how his buddy's kid had been decapitated while in my care.

"You must be Akilah Harris," Sweet Thang asked.

The woman eyed her.

"I'm very sorry for your loss," Sweet Thang continued. "Those little boys were just so precious. I'm very, very sorry. I want you to know I said a prayer this morning for Alonzo and Antoine."

What happened next has to go down in journalism history as the fastest anyone has gone from homicidal to hysterical. The mention of those boys' names instantly caused this woman, who was evidently Akilah Harris, to crumble. She dropped the knife, brought her hands to her face, and started sobbing. And not just little sobs, either—big, gulping-for-breath, snot-everywhere sobs.

"They was . . . they was my little angels," Akilah said between gasps.

Sweet Thang rushed to Akilah's side, enveloping her in an embrace. Soon, Akilah was hugging her back and they were *both* crying. It was hard to make out who was saying what amid all the blubbering, but it was something along the lines of Akilah repeatedly saying "my babies" and "my angels" and Sweet Thang saying "I know" and "I'm so sorry."

I suppose somewhere there was some tweedy journalism professor who would have said that what Sweet Thang was doing—dropping that wall between reporter and source, allowing herself to connect emotionally with Akilah's pain—was a Very Bad Thing. But then there's also a reason why those tweedy journalism professors fled to academia in the first place: they were sucky reporters.

You've got to get your sources treating you like a fellow member of the species, not an alien with a notepad. Legions of kids come out of J-school each year having been drilled endlessly about objectivity, balance, and other semiuseful subjects—much to their detriment. Some of them unlearn it quickly enough. But for others, the inability to get real with sources becomes a crippling affliction they carry throughout their journalism careers.

Should we teach kids about balance? Of course. Getting both sides of a story is one of the foundations of what we do. There are many areas—politics, court trials, business disputes, and so on—where we're absolutely obligated to play it down the middle.

But there are also stories where, frankly, there is no middle. A mother's pain over losing her children in a fire would be one of those stories. There's no "other side" to tell. There's just one woman and her profound tragedy. I believe telling that story in a sensitive, compassionate way makes the news—and all those who read it—a little more human.

They finally released their embrace.

"I'm sorry I almost cut you," Akilah said, sniffling.

"It's okay," Sweet Thang cooed. "You thought someone was breaking into your house. I would have done the same thing if I were you."

Now there's an image: Sweet Thang threatening someone with a knife. I'm sure they taught all the Vanderbilt debutantes proper throat-slashing technique just in time for their cotillions.

"I wish I could invite you in for some coffee or something," Akilah said. "But they cut off the electricity."

"That's okay," Sweet Thang said.

"And I'm sorry the place is such a mess," Akilah added.

It was such a perfectly absurd thing to say under the circumstances, we all laughed. From knife-wielding to crying to laughing, all in about ten minutes. At least this job isn't boring.

My keen reporter's instincts told me Akilah was in the mood to unburden herself of her story. And as the good little scribes we were, Sweet Thang and I were not opposed to letting her do so.

But while this was the time, it was not the place. Too much debris. Too much smell. Too much death.

I made the suggestion we head to African Flavah, a hole-in-the-wall diner on Springfield Avenue that just happened to serve the best breakfast in the city. Akilah was unsure for a moment until I sealed the deal by making it clear the *Eagle-Examiner* would be more than happy to pick up the check.

Akilah asked for a few moments alone in the house to collect herself. I told her we'd be waiting for her out in the car.

The fresh air felt good and smelled better. As I fired up the Malibu to get the heat going, Sweet Thang flopped down heavily in the passenger seat.

"I'm so sorry," Sweet Thang said.

"What for?"

"For crying."

"Yeah, so . . . ?"

Obviously, there had been at least one tweedy journalism professor in her past.

"Isn't that . . . unprofessional?" she asked, biting her lower lip in a way that still managed to be coquettish.

"No, I'd say it was great. You made a connection and now a grieving mother wants to talk to us—to you, I should say. That's pretty much the definition of a good human interest story right there. How did you know she was the boys' mother anyway?"

"I spent all morning looking at their pictures in the paper. They both look like her. The younger one could be her little clone."

"Good catch."

"Thanks," she said. She leaned back in her seat and, because she apparently abhorred silence, asked, "So when do we ask her about the space heater?"

"Space heater?" I said.

"I thought we were doing a story about a space heater."

"No. Oh, hell no. Lump the space heater story."

"But what about—"

"Lump it."

"But we're supposed to—"

"Lump it."

"But Uncle Hal—"

"Even Uncle Hal will realize this is much better than a space heater story. If we do this right, this could go on page one tomorrow," I said. "Hang on, I'm just going to run inside and check on Akilah."

Sweet Thang grabbed my wrist.

"Wait a second," she said.

Her hand felt soft and warm and lovely. And for the briefest moment, I started imagining what it might feel like to have that hand situated elsewhere on my person.

"What is it?" I asked, reminding myself I was old enough to

be her . . . well, her older brother, for sure. Perhaps even her youthful uncle.

"You're going to do the interview, right?" she asked with big, imploring blue eyes.

"No. You are. You're the one she obviously trusts. At this point, I'm just the guy driving the car."

"But what do I doooo?" she whined.

"You'll be fine," I said, trying not to look at her. "When we sit down, just ask her what happened and then let the conversation flow. Be understanding. Make sure she realizes you're not judging her. Cry all you want to. It'll be perfect."

"Oh, my goodness, thank you so much," Sweet Thang gushed, and touched me again, this time on the shoulder. "I knew working with you was going to be the best thing ever."

"Well," I said, gradually trying to inch away but finding the Malibu had restricted my westward movement. "I'm sure we'll have fun."

"I *know* we'll have fun," she said, fixing me with a serious look, placing her hand back on my forearm and giving my arm a pat.

Thankfully I saw Akilah coming out of the front door, which I used as an excuse to get out of the Malibu and wave for her. The air was cool on my face and I realized I was flushed. Carter Ross, star investigative reporter for the mighty *Newark Eagle-Examiner*, reduced to a blushing teenager by the wiles of one blond coed.

Akilah climbed into the backseat and soon we were pulling up alongside African Flavah. Granted, I'm probably not real typical of the clientele at African Flavah—and I have a hard time saying the name without sounding ridiculously Caucasian—but the restaurant's owner, a guy named Khalid, was a buddy of mine and a real inspiration. Back in the mid-1990s, Khalid and his wife, Patty, had opened their diner in a row of burned-out, empty storefronts on a part of Springfield Avenue that still hadn't recovered from Newark's 1967 riots.

But their diner flourished. And soon, so did the neighborhood around it. A clothing store moved in a few doors up. A bodega and a barbershop opened a few doors down. Then came a small electronics store and a furniture store. It was a regular renaissance.

Along the way, Khalid and Patty's diner became a local institution, one so revered that in all the years they had been in business, Khalid proudly told me, they had never been robbed once. It helped that Khalid treated all his customers with respect and dignity, which wasn't always the case with business owners in the hood. The matching bulletproof security cameras—one inside, one outside—might also have something to do with it.

As we entered, Khalid and I exchanged greetings and before long we were seated in a booth along the wall with a pot full of coffee. Akilah attacked it like it was planning to run off.

In this different light—when she wasn't threatening my colleague with a very large knife—she looked younger than I originally thought. Younger and prettier. Her body was slim but not without curves in the right places. Her hair was straight and pulled back into a no-nonsense ponytail, showing nicely formed cheek and jaw bones and a slender, graceful neck. There was definitely potential there. Throw on some makeup and a dress, and I bet she'd be a gal any guy would like to have on his arm.

Still, she had that ghetto hardness to her face. It's a look that comes from learning at a too young age that only the strong survive and only suckers trust someone else to help them do it. You can see it in the way the eyes flit about, in the way the body seems constantly tense, in the way the brain always seems to be manipulating a set of odds.

Yet somehow Sweet Thang had slid underneath that tough, cynical exterior. Maybe it was because Akilah's math told her that a white girl with a ridiculous nickname and nice clothes couldn't possibly be out to hurt her. Maybe it was because she was too damn tired to keeping doing all the calculations.

Either way, Akilah's reactions to Sweet Thang were different. She was allowed in, even when most others were not.

After we placed our order and handed back our menus, Sweet Thang looked at me imploringly one last time. I shook my head. She rolled her eyes. I nudged her under the table with my foot. She batted her eyelashes. I crossed my arms. She got the hint.

"So," Sweet Thang said as gently as she could, "what happened?"

Akilah looked down at the table.

"I don't even know. I mean, I know I shouldn't have left them at home alone," she began. "It's my fault. It's all my fault."

Her eyes filled with water again. I grabbed a napkin for blotting. Sweet Thang took her hand.

Over the next hour or so, it all came out—sometimes in a torrent, other times in a tumble. It was one of those interviews that could have doubled as a therapy session. Sweet Thang nodded at all the right times, shushed when she needed to, supported Akilah's every emotional need.

I was just the guy with the pen, furiously taking notes.

As I suspected, Akilah Harris's twenty-four years on this planet had seldom been easy. Her father was never really in the picture. She said she was four when her mother died of a drug overdose. Akilah didn't know what drug and didn't provide many details. But I suppose, to a four-year-old, none of that would have been especially significant.

She had been taken in by an aunt who lived in the Baxter Terrace Public Housing Project, a grim collection of low-rise brick buildings not far from Interstate 280. It was not exactly what you would call a kid-friendly environment.

Akilah explained how she had gotten pregnant for the first time when she was sixteen, and the aunt—who was very religious and therefore very ashamed—basically disowned her. She dropped out of school to support herself and the child. With no other relatives in the area, she stayed with a succession of friends in Baxter Terrace. Then the baby died of a heart defect when it was less than six months old.

Akilah got pregnant again when she was eighteen, which is how she got Alonzo; then again when she was twenty, which is how Antoine came to be. Akilah didn't say anything about the father, which was hardly unusual. Dads didn't always stick around in that part of town.

Really, it seemed like Akilah had only caught one break in her young life. She managed to find a decent job. She said it was at University Hospital, and it "paid good"—which probably meant she was pulling down $30,000 a year, including overtime. That didn't go very far in most parts of Northern New Jersey, one of the most expensive areas of the country to live in. But to a kid from Baxter Terrace, it could still feel like a lot of money.

And, naturally, the first thing she wanted to do was get the hell out of Baxter Terrace.

But that's where things got complicated. About four years ago, not long after Antoine was born, she got connected with a guy—she was kind of vague about the details—who, in turn, connected her with another guy—she described him as "a Puerto Rican guy"—who, in turn, ushered poor, orphaned Akilah Harris into her very own home.

"It was a chance to raise my children somewhere else besides Baxter Terrace," she said. "I had to do it."

For a while, it worked out fine. Then, suddenly, she couldn't afford it anymore. Sweet Thang—a guileless creature with the kind of naïveté that only the young possess—asked a few follow-up questions about how such a thing could even be possible and seemed genuinely confused. I would have to explain it to her later. Akilah Harris had gotten slammed with a pernicious form of subprime mortgage.

People hear the term "subprime" and get confused, because

the "sub" makes it sound like it's some kind of good deal. It's not. The "prime" refers not to the rate but to your status as a borrower. If you've got five years of perfect credit and a steady job, you qualify for a prime mortgage at a reasonable rate. Being subprime meant that something about you was less than perfect and you were going to get charged a rate that only barely failed to qualify as loan-sharking.

Except, of course, they didn't start out that way. Many of the subprime loans that floated around the ghetto a few years back had had introductory rates far below what the permanent rate would be. It made an otherwise unaffordable house suddenly fall into just about anyone's price range. For a while. Then—surprise!—the real rate kicked in. Just like that, you went from 4 percent interest to 12 percent interest and your monthly payment doubled overnight.

The Puerto Rican man probably told Akilah—and countless other dupes—not to worry about the interest rate reset. After all, it would only take a year or two before they had enough equity in the house to refinance to a regular loan.

And that was true—as long as credit remained easy and the housing market stayed supernova hot. For a while, it did. I had written about Newark neighborhoods where the average home price, driven primarily by real estate speculators, was doubling every two years.

The only problem is, nothing like that lasts forever. When the global credit crunch hit and the easy money stopped flowing, the bubble that was Newark's real estate market experienced a big, messy burst. And people like Akilah Harris, who were led to believe the good times would never end, were finished. The foreclosures came in huge waves.

Some people figured out pretty quickly their days among the landed gentry were over and accepted it graciously, slinking back to the apartments from which they came with their credit scores in shambles. Others tried to do short sales or loan workouts, hoping to emerge with the shirts on their backs—and often nothing more.

And then, every once in a while, there's a real hardhead, like Akilah. She was so determined to hang on to her house—in the face of a financial reality that dictated otherwise—she got herself another job. It was a second-shift job cleaning floors at a pallet-making company.

She just couldn't find any second-shift child care—not for anything she could afford, anyway. And with her mother dead and her aunt refusing to be part of her life, she had no family to leave her sons with. So each day, she worked at the hospital from 7 A.M. to 3 P.M., picked up the boys from daycare, brought them home, and put them in her bedroom with the TV on.

She left them snacks. And then she locked the door "so they couldn't get in no trouble."

Which is why, when that fire started at 9 P.M., they had no hope of escape.

Akilah finished up the details of how the previous evening unfolded for her. None of her neighbors knew she worked a second job or where it was, so no one from the fire department—or the police department or child protective services—had been able to notify her about what had happened. She was just walking back from work a little after 1 A.M. when she saw all the fire trucks and cop cars still jamming her street.

A neighbor collared her before she could get to her house, explained what happened, and convinced her she would be arrested for child endangerment if the cops found her. Akilah spent the night weeping on the neighbor's floor. When she awoke in the morning, the authorities had finally left. She went back to her house to collect some of the things that hadn't been destroyed in the fire and get some items for her boys' funeral.

That's when we found her.

"I know I should have just let the police take me, but I just wanted to spend a little bit of time in the house," she said. "I just felt like, I don't know, like it was the only place I could be close to my boys. I knew I hadn't been there for them in life so I wanted to be there for them in death. Maybe that sounds stupid, but that's what I was thinking."

Akilah sighed.

"So that's my sad story," she said.

It was, I had to admit, an extraordinary interview. I couldn't believe she had shared so much with such brutal candor. Most people couldn't be that honest with themselves, much less with two strangers.

At the same time, she was an orphaned only child who worked sixteen-hour days and didn't seem to have a soul in the world she could count on. She was probably just desperate for someone to listen.

And in two newspaper reporters, she had found a more than receptive audience. Sweet Thang had been mopping tears off her own face for most of the last hour. My eyes were dry, though I felt like my insides had been cleaned out by a canal dredger.

"What do you think the police are going to do to me?" Akilah asked.

The question had clearly been addressed to me, the white guy with the tie.

"It depends on how hard-assed the prosecutor's office feels like being," I said. "If you had other children still in your care, there might be pressure to get the kids removed from you and put in foster care. And to make sure you never got them back, the prosecutor might throw the book at you—child endangerment, negligent homicide. But as it is, they might not feel the need to go after you as much. Do you have a record?"

She shook her head.

"Well, that'll help," I continued. "There's a possibility if you cooperate with them, they'll let you plead to something that'll give you probation and nothing more."

"I deserve to go to jail," she said, without hesitation. "For what I did? I hope they send me away for a long time."

I hoped they didn't. I'm not saying I wanted to nominate Akilah for Mother of the Year. But throwing this young woman in jail wasn't going to solve much of anything. I seriously doubted the state of New Jersey could mete out a punishment more severe than the life sentence of pain and regret she had already received for losing those two boys.

And ultimately, what was she really guilty of? Of making a tragically poor decision about child care, sure. But beyond that? She was a single mother who wanted to raise her children someplace other than the projects and had been too unsophisticated to avoid the usurious scumbags who preyed on that desperation.

The real villain here was that industry of scumbags. It started with that "older man," whoever he was, whose job it had been to hustle fresh meat for the Puerto Rican man, whose job it was to sign them up. But it didn't stop there. Next were the lending executives, who were underwriting the borrowing with impossibly reckless loan products, approving mortgages for people who obviously did not have the means to pay them back. Then came the investment bankers who were bundling and packaging those bad loans into securities that were somehow rated AAA, which proved to be the lipstick on the proverbial pig.

Some of those Wall Street crooks—the ones that didn't get bailed out—got a little bit of comeuppance when those securities were suddenly worth pennies on the dollar. The crooks on the street? The Older Man and the Puerto Rican man? They were still out there, finding new ways to enrich themselves on the misery of others.

And while I couldn't stop them from doing it, I could at least hit them with the only weapon a newspaper reporter had: public embarrassment. The Older Man's role in the whole thing was probably a little too tangential to go at him, presses blazing. But the Puerto Rican man, if I could find him, was a nice target. A story with the headline "Sleazy Bastard" above it would do just fine.

"Tell me a little more about the Puerto Rican man," I said. "You keep a phone number for him? A business card maybe?"

She shook her head.

"Do you remember his name?" I asked.

"It was like . . ." She groped around her memory for a second or two, then gave up. "I don't know."

"What did he look like?"

"He wasn't tall or nothing, but he was built," Akilah said. "He had a goatee he pet all the time, like it was his cat or something. He was dark skinned, for a Puerto Rican. He was bald . . ."

She paused to try and think of more, but nothing was forthcoming.

"About how old?"

"I don't know. Forty? Fifty?"

Or more. Or less. To twenty-four-year-olds, I think any age over thirty-five becomes a blur.

"When was the last time you saw him?"

"Not in a long time."

"Can you think of anyone who might know more about the guy?"

"I mean, you can go into the projects and ask around. People there will probably remember him."

I nodded. They probably did remember. Whether they would tell a cracker like me was another issue.

"Did you keep any of the paperwork?"

"I never got no paperwork," she said.

That was probably not true. But it didn't matter. That's why the Founding Fathers, in their infinite and righteous wisdom, created the blessing that is public records: so reporters like me could snoop around.

The county kept copies of mortgages down at the courthouse. And while that would only provide me the name of the lender, not the mortgage broker, I could work backward from there. Because while I had no legal rights to Akilah's closing documents—which are not public record—Akilah did. I could gently assist her in getting the necessary papers from her lender. Problem solved.

I'd have my sleazy bastard in no time.

Our breakfast long since demolished, I threw a tip on the table, then paid our bill at the register up front. As we walked back to my car, tears started rolling down Akilah's cheeks. Naturally, that set Sweet Thang's waterworks going, too. They both hopped in the Malibu's backseat, leaving me to chauffeur us to Akilah's place. I felt sort of like a white Morgan Freeman driving a black Miss Daisy. Except in this case, Miss Daisy kept wiping her runny nose on her shirtsleeve.

When we arrived, Sweet Thang hopped out with Akilah. They swapped cell phone numbers, then hugged. Sweet Thang watched Akilah disappear inside the front door, then climbed back in the front seat.

"I told her she could stay at my place tonight if she wanted," Sweet Thang said.

"That is such a bad idea," I said as I got us under way.

"That girl has *nothing* and I have a foldout couch in my apartment," Sweet Thang countered. "It's the Christian thing to do. Don't you ever ask yourself what Jesus would do?"

I was tempted to tell her it was a moot point: Jesus came along about 1,950 years before foldout couches. But I didn't want to turn this into an argument about religion—or convertible furniture—so I tried to put a halt to it.

"I'm going to pretend you didn't just invite a source to spend the night," I said. "And you're going to conveniently forget to mention this to anyone back at work. Fair?"

"Whatever," Sweet Thang spat.

I realize I may encourage a slight blurring of the line between reporter and source, but there still is a line. I find a good rule of thumb for journalism ethics is to think of what the headline would be if another newspaper decided to write about how you covered a particular story. JOURNALIST SHOWS SYMPATHY TO MOURNING MOTHER is something I could live with. JOURNALIST HARBORS FUGITIVE FROM JUSTICE didn't have as nice a ring. I hefted a large sigh.

"What?" Sweet Thang said.

"Nothing."

"Come on, what is it?"

"Nothing."

"Don't 'nothing' me," Sweet Thang scolded. "If you're going to be my mentor, we need to have open lines of dialogue. Communication is the most important part of any relationship. We have to be able to share our thoughts and feelings."

I was suddenly having a flashback to my last serious relationship. She had moved into my cozy little bungalow in Nutley and had taken to redecorating it room by room. Then she decided to redecorate me. She wanted me to put product in my hair. And wear flatfront pants. And pay more attention to men's fashion magazines than I did to my fantasy football team. And, above all else, she wanted me to *share* my feelings, and *share* my problems, and *share* my fears.

I'm not saying I'm one of those emotionally constipated men who doesn't have a clue what's going on between his ears. At the same time, there are certain areas where a man has to be able to set his own agenda. Hair product is one of them. So, finally, I shared with her. I shared that no matter how many times she asked, I wasn't going to join her for a manicure. She left me soon after for some guy at her advertising firm. You can probably find them at a nail salon right now.

"Hel-LO?" Sweet Thang said. "Feelings?"

"I feel," I said, measuring my words, "that it's a bad idea for you to have this woman sleeping at your apartment. I know this is hard to hear, but for all we know, Akilah is a nutbag who decided she didn't want to be a mom anymore and burned down her own house with her kids locked inside."

"Do you really think that's what happened?"

I didn't. But I still planned to have Sweet Thang call the hospital and the pallet company to verify her employment, just in case.

"That's not the point," I said. "The point is, we just don't know. So not only is it a bad idea professionally to have a source living with you, it could be unsafe personally, as well."

She turned to face me, smiling wide.

"That's sooo sweet of you," she said. "I knew you were the best mentor ever. I can't wait to tell Uncle Hal what a sweetheart you are and that you're looking out for me. I know he'll totally appreciate it."

I clenched the steering wheel with both hands and drove. Sweet Thang was playing me like a Stradivarius, which is probably what she had done to every Y chromosome she had come across since puberty. All I could do was remind myself once again that she was the female equivalent of the Strait of Magellan: thin, beautiful, and treacherous.

During the final few blocks to the office, she kept babbling about how wonderful I was. It wasn't until we pulled into the *Eagle-Examiner* parking garage I was finally able to get a sentence in.

"Okay, here's the plan," I said, mindful of Szanto's admonition to keep Sweet Thang away from the computer keyboard while any meaningful writing was going on. "First of all, give me your cell number."

"I have two," she said. "Which one do you want?"

"You have two cell phones," I said, mostly out of disbelief.

"Yeah, I talk a lot"—I noticed, believe me—"so sometimes I run out of battery before I have the chance to recharge."

"Two cell phones," I said again. "First, allow me to scoff at you."

I made my best scoffing noise.

"Okay," I said, "now I'll take those numbers."

I file all work-related numbers last name, first name. So I saved these in my phone as "Thang, Sweet" and "Thang, Sweet 2."

I gave her my number and she programmed it in her phone. Uh, phones.

"You program all your numbers in both phones?" I asked.

"Hell-OOO, what if the other one is out of batteries?" she asked.

Good point. Absurd but good.

"Okay, I'm going to start transcribing notes"—and write the beginning, middle, and end of the story—"and I was hoping you could take a trip up to the county courthouse and get a copy of Akilah Harris's mortgage for us."

"No problem," she said, smiling sweetly. "I'll do anything you ask."

She held my gaze a beat longer than was necessary. Somewhere in my lower body, I felt a twitch.

I bid Sweet Thang farewell, wiped my suddenly sweaty brow, then went back up to the newsroom to search for a cold shower.

Instead, I found the one thing that worked faster:

"Crrrtrrr!" Szanto bellowed as soon as I was within radar range.

I walked into his office and sat down to find him munching a mouthful of antacid tablets—berry flavored, by the scent of things.

"Whtdgt?" he asked.

I took that for "what do you got?" and plunged forward, telling him how the intern almost got her neck slit, then about Akilah Harris and her remarkable story. It was a narrative so moving I felt my throat constricting at several points during the retelling. I touched on every tragedy that had shaped her young life, emphasizing that while her tale was unique, it was also achingly typical of the struggle faced by many working poor. I concluded that sharing her story in a thoughtful manner would offer a real insight into our local community and do our readers a tremendous service.

Szanto sat quietly as I spoke. He even stopped chewing his antacid. I felt like I was really reaching him. I was drilling through that hardened, old-time newsman's shell and reaching that fundamentally decent inner core that remembered a good newspaper was ultimately about real people and their stories. And when I was done, there was only one thing he could ask:

"Can we strip the story across the top of tomorrow's front page?"

No, wait. That wasn't it.

"Come again?" I said.

"I said, 'What about the effing space heater?'"

"Sal!" I exploded. "Haven't you just been listening to me? This is human tragedy. Who cares about a damn space heater?"

Szanto clenched his fists.

"I sent you out there to get a simple story about a space heater," he said.

"And I came back with something ten times better. Even Brodie is going to see that. We'll have another chance to write space heaters next week. Come on. This is good stuff and you know it."

Szanto released his fists and instead channeled his stress into grinding his teeth.

"Well," he said at last, "could you at least *mention* the possibility of a space heater? I'm not saying you have to put it in your lede. Just sneak it into the nut graf somewhere."

"Oh, for the love of . . . are you serious?"

Of course he was. Szanto and serious were like fruit flies and ripe bananas.

"Fine," I huffed.

"Good. Now, I think we can make a run at A1"—that's what we called the front page of the newspaper—"but I want you to write it hard."

"What do you mean, 'Write it hard'?"

"I mean, spare me the slant about the poor woman from the ghetto victimized by the larger forces of social injustice."

That, of course, is exactly what I planned to do. And Szanto had been my editor long enough to know it.

"Are you really that hard-hearted?" I asked.

"Oh, I've got a heart of fluffy dryer lint," Szanto said. "I'm just saying, let's not let her completely off the hook here. The fact is, nobody forced that woman to sign a mortgage she couldn't afford. And nobody forced her to compound the error by getting a second job instead of just getting rid of the place. And you want to tell me she couldn't have tried a *little* harder to find somewhere to put those kids? Let's remember, the victims here are those two little boys."

Valid points, all. And in absence of a good counterargument, I pouted.

"Come on now, you can still make it read pretty," Szanto said, and suddenly was rooting for something on his crowded desk. "Just remember the story is about this."

He slid that day's paper across the desk and patted two fingers on the pictures of Alonzo and Antoine.

They were two happy little faces, each with sharp features—like their mother—and a set of eyes that captivated me the way they had Sweet Thang earlier in the day. They were eyes that glowed with hope, love, and happiness. They were the eyes of two little boys who'd never hurt anyone or done anything to deserve this. They were the eyes of the innocent.

"It's about those dead little boys and all the people who failed them," Szanto finished.

I nodded. He was right, of course—just as I had been right about the space heater story being bunk. But that was a good editor-reporter relationship. You had to keep each other honest.

"Fine," I said, then summoned my best parting shot: "But if you screw with my lede I'm going to have Sweet Thang complain to Uncle Hal. And then you'll *really* be sorry."

Szanto grinned, then shoveled in a fresh mouthful of antacid tablets. I retreated to my desk and started pounding on the keyboard. It was two-thirty in the afternoon, which meant I had enough time to craft a lovely story—but not enough time to dawdle. Our deadline for first edition isn't until 8. But Szanto would start hovering over my shoulder by 6, if not sooner.

I was just starting to settle into the story when "Thang, Sweet" popped up on my cell.

"It's not here," she said breathlessly. "The mortgage. It's not here."

"What do you mean it's not there? It has to be there," I said, annoyed she couldn't complete such a simple reporting errand.

"I know, but it's not."

"What address did you use?"

She repeated the number on Littleton Avenue that she and I had both seen earlier that day.

"You went to the Register of Deeds and Mortgages, right?" I asked.

"Yeah, and I typed 'Akilah Harris' into the computer, and nothing came up. Then I searched by address, and nothing came up. Then I looked up the block and lot number and searched under that, but nothing came up."

I sighed and peeked up at the clock. It told me I didn't have time to run up to the courthouse.

"So I flirted with one of the male title searchers and got him to help me," Sweet Thang continued. "He was this total stoner, and stoners don't usually go for me, because I've got more of that wholesome look, you know? Anyway, he couldn't find it on the computer so he looked up the deed and got the recording date. Then he went into the books with the hard copies. He didn't know where the book was and he was going to give up, so I flirted with him some more. Finally, he found it. The book had been misfiled. And then when he got to where the mortgage was supposed to be, he said it had been ripped out."

"Ripped out?"

"That's what he said. Then I had him show it to me. There was a space where it should have been. But it jumped from page 177 to page 195. He said it was totally weird and he had never seen anything like it before."

"Yeah, me neither," I said.

"Then I asked one of the office clerks, and he was this nice guy at first, really helpful. Then he went away for a little while, and when he came back he was all weird with me. He said it wasn't there and I had to leave."

I frowned.

"Did the clerk know you were a reporter?" I asked.

"Yeah. He was really nervous about that. He practically kicked me out. He was just like, 'You have to leave. I'm sorry, you have to leave.'"

I frowned some more. Perhaps if I thought about it, I could produce a perfectly reasonable, perfectly innocent explanation for why documents pertaining to a scandalously predatory loan were missing. But nothing was coming immediately to mind.

Something wasn't right.

Primo had been one of the first Brazilians to arrive in Newark during the late 1980s, never realizing he was in the vanguard of what eventually became a substantial migration.

His father, a well-respected civil engineer, begged Primo not to go, trying to reason with him. Primo was also an engineer. With his father's connections, and with Brasília in the midst of a building boom, there would be plenty of work for many years to come. Why leave for a country where he knew no one and lacked the proper credentials to continue in his chosen field?

Primo was adamant. The father threatened to disown the son. Primo told him to go ahead. He was twenty-seven years old. He wanted a fresh start in America. He was leaving behind everything—his job, his wife, even a small child. He told his wife he would send for her just as soon as he got settled.

But that was a lie. Upon arriving in America, he severed all contact. He changed his name. Then he changed it again. He learned how to manipulate the American system to give himself multiple identities, none of which were truly his own.

He settled in the section of Newark known as the Ironbound, so named because it was surrounded by railroad tracks on all sides. It was almost entirely Portuguese back then, but that was not a problem for Primo. They spoke the same language. And even though the Portuguese knew he wasn't one of them—his accent was different, his skin darker—they tolerated him.

Primo took whatever job he could find at first. He parked cars at a garage in downtown Newark during the day. He bussed tables at a Portuguese restaurant on weekends. He lived in a cold-water flat above a jewelry store, making a deal with the store's owner living where he lived rent-free in exchange for sleeping in the store at night with a pistol.

With virtually no expenses beyond food, Primo saved every penny he could. After a few years, he had enough to purchase an old row house, free and clear. He quit his restaurant job, spending every night and weekend for three months turning the dilapidated house into a tidy-looking home. He took some shortcuts, but only the kind a building inspector would notice. Then he bribed the building inspector. Before long, he sold the house for a handsome profit.

It was a start.

Primo bought another house, then another. He bought shrewdly, being careful not to overextend himself, always working harder and, most of all, smarter. He bid on houses that appeared to be worthless—the ones that looked like they were about to fall over—then used his engineering knowledge to prop them back up. It was amazing what you could do with a few two-by-tens, nailed in just the right spots.

And in a town like Newark, with its aging wooden housing stock, there were plenty of falling-over houses for him to buy. He continually reinvested the profits from his successes, taking only a bare minimum out for his living expenses. Most of the time, he just threw down a sleeping bag in whatever house he happened to be fixing up at the moment, dozing with a loaded gun next to him just in case any neighborhood vagrants got ideas.

Soon, he had more houses than he had time for. So he hired a team to work for him. They were all fresh-off-the-boat Brazilian immigrants who, under Primo's tutelage, could prop up a house and primp it for sale in just weeks. As Brazilians continued arriving throughout the 1990s, Primo's workforce grew. Two teams became four teams. Four became six.

He was slowly building an empire.

CHAPTER 2

People sometimes ask me how I write, whether I favor a particular method or technique. I try to tell them writing is an individual process and that one person's system probably won't work for someone else. But if they persist, I usually tell them the truth. For me, the essence of writing comes down to one simple thing:

Frequent urination.

The first thing I do upon sitting down is hit the caffeine. Usually it's Coke Zero, but sometimes, in the early morning or later at night, I go for tea. I'll drink Diet Pepsi if I have to, but only under desperate circumstances. I never drink coffee. I may be the only journalist in the world who despises coffee.

After consuming my caffeinated beverage of choice, I switch to noncaffeinated—usually water, to avoid dehydration. Then I jump back to the caffeine. I continue this alternating pattern until the writing is done.

The end result is that I pee like I'm about to run the Kentucky Derby. Once I get going, I can't last more than about twenty minutes without a trip to the loo.

Maybe that sounds like an annoyance, but I've found it to be an essential part of the writing process. It's during these many trips to the bathroom that the magic happens. Turns of phrase leap into my head, transitional sentences mysteriously appear, narrative structure makes itself apparent. The pee flows out, the words flow in. I'm not sure if this is some kind of cosmic balancing act—I try not to think about the physics behind it—I just know it's happened too many times to be mere coincidence.

Clearly, I wouldn't recommend this method for anyone with urinary incontinence. And it does come with some limitations: instead of worrying about writer's block, I fret over sewer capacity; I could never consider a job as a foreign correspondent in Europe because the pay toilets would bankrupt me; and with longer articles, I end up getting so overcaffeinated I shake like an eighties hair-band drummer.

But I have come to accept over the years that this is how I do things. Some writers hunt and peck. I piss and peck.

Akilah Harris's story was a twelve-flush job—more than I thought it would be, but by no means a record. When I was through, I decided to give Sweet Thang the lead byline. I figured it would help get her noticed in the office for something other than her breasts. Byline politics—who got them, whose name came first, who was appearing on A1, and who was getting buried on C5—were a constant source of chatter in the office. That, of course, was the only place people talked about bylines. I'm quite confident that the vast majority of our readers skipped right over them.

But for the small percentage who actually paid attention, the next day's story would start "BY LAUREN MCMILLAN AND CARTER ROSS." A lot of veteran staff members would have put their own names first, under the thinking that she was an intern—thus deserving of secondary status—and hadn't actually written the thing herself. But I just felt even though I had been the one putting the words on the page, Sweet Thang had made the greater contribution to the story by getting Akilah to open up the way she did.

Besides, the quotes were what carried the story. The opening quote was perfect: "I know I shouldn't have left them at home alone," Harris said. "It's my fault. It's all my fault."

What made it perfect was that it would keep Szanto off my ass. It established that Akilah was taking responsibility for the tragedy. Once she blamed herself, I could get on with the business of blaming everyone else.

It also set up the question that would hopefully pull the reader through my prose: what happened in this young woman's life that led her to this rather desperate position, forcing her to abandon her young children? I took the narrative right up to this morning, her decision to make one final trip to the house and her reasons for doing so. Which set up the final quote:

"I just felt like it was the only place I could be close to my boys," Harris said. "I knew I hadn't been there for them in life so I wanted to be there for them in death."

In the business, that's what we call a kicker quote—and a fine one, at that.

By the time I was done, Sweet Thang had been back from the courthouse for a while. To keep her busy, I had put her on fact-checking duty. Generally speaking, one's ability to check facts exists in an indirect relationship to one's rate of publication. Those yawning, indolent sloths at monthly magazines can—and do—spend weeks fact-checking. At weekly magazines, they still have the luxury of a few days. At daily newspapers? It's mere hours. If we're lucky.

It was one fundamental vulnerability in any newspaper's attempt to get it right on deadline. A source who lied convincingly could sometimes snow us. Fortunately for us, most of your hardcore liars—the real pathological ones—lie about lots of things. And you only need to catch them once for it to set off those alarm bells that indicate you should look sideways at everything else they said.

There was not much about Akilah's story that could be verified one way or another. A spokesman for the hospital said she wasn't an employee of theirs, but she still might work there—she could be employed by any number of cleaning services that had contracts with the hospital. The pallet company, which didn't like the idea of its name going anywhere near a story like this, refused comment. But I suppose that was to be expected.

By the time Sweet Thang was done with those phone calls, I had a draft for her to read before I filed it.

"Oh, my goodness, this is soooo awesome," she gushed after she finished. "You are totally going to have to teach me how to write like this."

"It's really nothing," I mumbled false-modestly.

"Nothing?" she said, a little too loudly. "How could you say *nothing*? It's totally brilliant—the way you work in all the important facts along with all those great details, the way you use the quotes, the way it flows so perfectly. I couldn't write it that well in a week and you did it in, like, two hours."

I often find it difficult to accept a compliment gracefully, so I just kept my mouth shut like the strong, silent cowboy I am and gave my best it-warn't-nothing-ma'am shrug.

"No, really, I want to know how you did this," she demanded.

I debated telling her about the frequent-urination method but decided such advanced concepts in fluid dynamics were better left to the professors at Princeton. So I gave my other standard writing advice:

"Writing is like a muscle," I said. "The harder you work it, the stronger it gets."

I immediately regretted the metaphor.

"I bet you've got the biggest muscle of anyone I've ever met," she gushed.

I coughed uncomfortably.

"Well, I'm going to file this thing now," I said, glancing at the clock. It was 5:45, which was getting to be the time of night when the acid in Szanto's stomach compelled him to start demanding copy.

"Oh, definitely," she said. "And thanks for giving me the lead byline. You totally didn't have to do that."

"You earned it. Without that interview, we wouldn't have had a story."

"That's so sweet of you," she said, then added in what was intended to sound like an afterthought: "By the way, some of the interns are getting together at McGovern's after work for a quick drink or two. You want to join?"

"Sure," I said too quickly. Then, in the second it took me to consider the implications, I added, "I'll try to stop by."

"Cool," she said, giving me a little wave as she departed. "See ya."

Sweet Thang wasn't gone from my desk for more than fifteen seconds before Tina Thompson roared into the same spot.

Tina is our city editor. At most newspapers, the city editor is some frumpy bearded guy named Bruno. At our paper, it's Tina, a too-hot-for-her-age thirty-eight-year-old with curly brown hair, a penchant for short skirts, and abs you could play checkers on. Her hobbies include yoga, jogging, and keeping me in a permanent state of confusion.

We were clearly . . . something. I liked her intelligence, her wit, her sarcasm. And did I mention her abs? We always enjoyed our time together. She obviously cared about me. She even saved my life once—long story.

But I couldn't accurately say Tina and I were an item, because it had never been consummated by the appropriate adult gymnastics. It was difficult to speculate whose fault that was. There were times when I had clearly been invited to show her my floor routine but stumbled on the way to the mat. Other times, I participated in the warm-ups then withdrew my name from consideration before the competition began. It all made for a relationship that had never gotten past the preliminaries.

It was just complicated. What Tina wanted out of me was not companionship, commitment, or even recreational sex. She wanted insemination. Having spent most her life as a career-driven alpha female, Tina had recently decided she was going to try motherhood. And she was sufficiently type A in personality that she didn't feel like wasting time with the whole dating-cohabiting-marrying paradigm. She didn't want to fiddle around with anonymous sperm donors, either. As she explained it, she wanted her baby's daddy to be smart, above six-feet tall, and have light-colored eyes—but didn't want it to be some lanky, green-eyed homeless guy who managed to convince a fertility clinic he went to Stanford. That left her with six-foot-one, blue-eyed, Amherst-educated me.

She promised it was a no-strings-attached deal. She even offered naming rights. But I was still unsure about it. On the one hand, I had what Mr. Darwin would describe as the male imperative to spread my seed. On the other hand, I was a little conflicted about someday having to explain to Carter junior that his mother had been interested in me primarily for the fifty-fifty chance I'd pass on my bone structure.

Like I said, it was confusing. As was the fiercely territorial look she had on her face as she approached.

"Just stop it," she hissed.

"Stop what?" I said, trying to summon my best innocent face.

"Oh, Carter," she mocked Sweet Thang's voice in a violent whisper. "You're so wonderful. I want to write just like you."

"What did I do?" I said, perhaps too defensively.

"Oh, Carter," she continued in the voice, "you're such a great writer. Why don't you have drinks with me and then come over to my place and *write* for me all night long?"

"Oh, come on."

"Writing is like a *muscle,* Carter? And which muscle is she supposed to think you're bragging about? Your trapezius? Why don't you just pull her into the supply closet and ask her to play Seven Minutes in Heaven?"

"Now you're just being silly."

“Am I? Or did I just see her give you *the little wave*?”

“That? That was not the little wave. That was just . . . a wave.”

She closed in and clamped her hand on my chin, lifting my face for closer inspection.

“I thought so,” she said, the whisper getting even angrier. “You have *glitter* on your cheek.”

“So?” I said, wiping both cheeks quickly.

“So Sweet Thang was wearing makeup with glitter in it. Is that just a coincidence?”

“Glitter has been known to become airborne,” I pointed out.

Tina stuck her fists into her side, glared at me for a moment, then stomped off. Three strides into her stomping, she turned around and jerked her head, like I should have known I was supposed to follow her. I trailed after her. It was either that or get scolded in front of the entire newsroom.

She went into the (thankfully empty) break room and was ready for me with an ambush when I entered.

“She’s hitting on you,” Tina hissed.

“Is not.”

“And you’re *flirting* back!”

“Am not!”

“I heard her saying you gave her the first byline on that story. You want to tell me if she was dump-truck ugly with an ass she couldn’t fit through an elevator door you would have done that?”

“She earned that byline—”

“Liar!”

“And besides, if her ass was that big she never would have fit in the booth at the restaurant and we never would have gotten the interview.”

“Don’t change the subject.”

“I’m not sure I know what the subject is.”

“The subject is that every male under the age of ninety in this newsroom has been following that girl around with drool pouring out their mouths for the last month, and you, of all people, are not going to join them. It's improper, it's unseemly, and it's gross. She's a child."

I raised my right hand like I was taking the presidential oath of office and said, "I have absolutely nothing but the purest of intentions toward that young woman. And I have no indication her feelings for me are anything besides professional admiration."

"You are and always have been a *dreadful* liar, Carter Ross. You've been screwing her with your eyes ever since she got here."

"I don't even think I said hello to her until this morning."

"And let me guess, you let her tag along with you all day long because, what, you're deeply concerned about the quality of instruction she receives during her internship?"

"Szanto told me to work with her," I said, still sounding far more defensive than I intended.

"Oh, sure. Did Szanto also tell you to jump in her lap the moment she asked you out for a beer after work?"

Couldn't exactly dispute that one. Tina sighed and waved her arms in the air.

"Look at you! You can't even defend yourself! Of course you want to have sex with her. She's twenty-two. She's got helium balloons for tits. I should probably be worried if you *didn't* want to have sex with her, because it would mean you were dead from the waist down, which would mean you're absolutely no use to me. All I'm saying is, if you sleep with her, don't even think about sleeping with me. I'll find some other guy with good breeding potential to get me knocked up."

With that, Tina stormed off.

I looked at my only friend in the room, the Coke machine. "Did you get all that?" I asked it.

The machine hummed back at me.

"Just to review," I said. "A woman who has expressed exactly zero interest in a conventional monogamous relationship just berated me for flirting with an intern. Can you figure out what to make of it?"

The machine hummed some more.

"Yeah," I said. "Me, neither."

Before I could make it back to my desk, I was interrupted by a strangling sound coming from Szanto's office. It sounded vaguely like my name, so I stuck my head in.

"You looking for me?"

"Where is it?" he asked.

"By 'it' do you mean the beautiful story I have crafted that you cannot wait to put on A1?"

"Something like that, yeah." Szanto said.

"Just about to file," I assured him.

"Good. You got a quote from the mortgage company, right?"

I looked down at my shoes and tried desperately not to look sheepish.

"We, uh, had a little problem there," I began.

Szanto didn't wait to hear the rest. He burst out with a long string of language that would have made my grandmother cover her ears, finishing it with, ". . . and I told you to write it hard. We can't tell this sob story where we make the predatory lender the bad guy and not reach out to the bad guy and give them the opportunity to tell the other side."

"I know, I know," I said. "I had Sweet Thang run up to the courthouse and pull the mortgage. But it was missing."

"Missing?"

"Yeah. She said the computer file didn't exist, and when she went to look for the hard copy, it wasn't in the books. So we don't actually know who the mortgage company is."

Szanto considered this news for a moment as he gulped some coffee out of a large Dunkin' Donuts cup he had been reusing for weeks, judging from the stains on it. He frowned at the coffee, like it had just told him to lose weight and stop smoking.

"This coffee is crap," he said, then took another large swallow. He frowned again.

"Well, we can't run the story without talking to the mortgage company, the broker, or someone to give it some balance," he said. "I'm holding it."

Holding a story means it's not going to run in the next day's paper. While that may not sound like such a devastating thing, it's remarkable how quickly something that's been held for a day becomes stale. It doesn't actually lose news value to the outside world. But it does lose buzz within the building. By the next day, the cabal of editors who make the decision about where to place stories in the paper feel like they've already been hearing about your story for an eternity. And given their attention spans—think: salamander—they get bored quickly. So even though it would still be new news to readers, it's treated like old news by the editors. What is surefire A1 material on Day One becomes back-of-the-book fodder on any day thereafter, and the next thing you know your brilliant narrative is just filling space above ads for assisted living facilities.

"Aw, come on, don't do that," I said. "What if I was able to find the guy who sold her the mortgage and get a comment from him?"

Szanto grimaced. "I told the future ex–Mrs. Szanto I wouldn't be home late tonight," he said.

There were already two ex–Mrs. Szantos. And with the way he treated his wives—giving them about as much care and attention as most people give their rental cars—it was pretty much assumed there would be more.

"How about this: if I can get the broker by eight, we run the story. After eight, it holds. Deal?"

"Fine," Szanto said.

"Great," I said, peeling out of his office before he could modify the arrangement.

I looked at the clock on the wall—6:07—and was actually feeling pretty good about things until I got back to my desk. That's when I sat down and realized there was only one way I was going to find the goateed, shaved-headed, so-called Puerto Rican man: Go to the Baxter Terrace Public Housing Project after dark.

Don't get me wrong, going to the projects any time of the day wasn't exactly my idea of fun. There were certain dangers constant to Newark's rougher projects—junkies were not known for keeping stringent track of time, and a junkie that needed money for a fix was always unpredictable. But at least during the day there were normal people out in the courtyards. Old ladies sat on stoops, kids played ball, mothers watched their babies. The dealers were still around, sure, but the regular folks could maintain at least a modicum of social order. It didn't matter how hardcore a gangbanger was, he still respected a grandma—his own or someone else's—sitting on a stoop.

But then, after dusk, the old ladies, kids, and moms would go inside, fully surrendering the turf to more insidious elements. The dealers. The gangs. The vagrants. People whose interests clearly tended toward the antisocial. There something primeval about what the darkness did to a city like Newark.

About the only thing I had going for me was the element of surprise. Absolutely no one expected to see a well-dressed white man striding confidently into the middle of that environment. Sometimes I could actually see guys startle as I rounded a corner. As long as I kept moving—and didn't stay long enough for them to recover from shock—I really had nothing to worry about.

Or at least that's what I kept telling myself as I went down to my Malibu and got it rolling in the direction of Baxter Terrace.

Slated for a demolition that was forever being delayed for one reason or another, Baxter Terrace was among the last of Newark's bad, old projects—a relic of the failed experiment that was high-density public housing. When it was first built in the 1930s, people clamored to get into Baxter Terrace. It was segregated, of course—blacks lived on one side of Orange Street, whites on the other—but desired by both races. Tenants were chosen only after careful consideration by the tenants' association.

After moving in, the residents—all of whom had jobs and made timely rent payments—were responsible for much of the maintenance. They cleaned the hallways and stairwells. They swept the sidewalks. They kept gardens full of flowers. The Newark Housing Authority, which owned and managed the properties, watched closely, evicting anyone who failed to toe the line. A resident who left for work without cleaning their dishes might come home to a note from the superintendent warning them not to let it happen again: dirty dishes might attract bugs.

It's difficult to say whether the housing authority or the tenants were more responsible for the decline from that golden era of public housing. But sometime during the late 1950s, the quality of the tenants began slowly declining, with more on public assistance—and fewer who cleaned, planted gardens, or paid rent—every year. Management became less conscientious about the white glove inspections, which allowed tenants to become even more slovenly. The housing authority fell further under the sway of City Hall, which was becoming increasingly corrupt, and many of the cleaning jobs were of the no-show variety.

Plus, as fewer tenants paid rent, the housing authority had less of a budget for maintenance. And once you start to let things slide in a high-density housing situation, they go in a hurry. The rats, mice, and roaches get a foothold almost instantly. The garbage piles up. The small leaks turn into big ones.

The tenants' association complained as things got worse, and the bosses at the housing authority eventually got tired of hearing it. So they busted up the tenants' association.

That meant the tenants were no longer picking their own neighbors, which brought even more decline in the quality of the people moving in. Rent collection dropped further, which meant even less money for maintenance. And the tenants—who no longer had any collective voice or empowerment through which to improve conditions—stopped caring about the buildings, which only strengthened the various negative feedback mechanisms already in place.

Which was how you ended up with stairwells that smelled of urine, booze, and rat droppings; hallways that hadn't seen a mop in years; and apartments where the humans fought an ever-losing battle with the pests that had taken up residence.

Perhaps the most apt description of Newark's housing projects I've read came from *No Cause for Indictment,* a book by Ron Porambo about the Newark riots, which described the projects in the late 1960s: "If never visited, these dwellings cannot be imagined. Once seen, they can never be forgotten."

And, if anything, the last forty years had only made them worse.

I parked my Malibu at the fringes of the projects, then plunged into the haystack to begin looking for the needle. It had been more than three years since Akilah Harris encountered this guy. He could be anywhere by now. Or he could be around the corner.

My entrance into the courtyard caused a small stir among the lookouts. I could tell because in the middle of February, in the dark of night, Baxter Terrace suddenly sounded like an Audubon Society refuge—birdcalls being the latest in urban drug-selling counterintelligence.

As had been explained to me by a dealer I got friendly with not long ago, the old alert system was very limited in what it allowed. If a lookout saw something that didn't look right—whether it was a cop or just a well-dressed white guy like me—he did the same thing: he yelled "cops" or the radio code for an officer, "five-oh," and everyone scattered. The guy sitting on the stash was forced to abandon his perch, making it vulnerable to being swiped by anyone who might have seen where it was hidden.

Birdcalls allowed much more information to be imparted to other members of the operation, without the visitor being aware of what was being communicated. So while a crow's harsh cry could harken the arrival of a member of the city narcotics unit—a significant threat—the sweet song of a chickadee might signal an officer who was merely escorting a social worker to an appointment, allowing business to continue in guarded fashion. Someone like me, a stranger on unknown business, might warrant a whippoorwill's call.

Where exactly a city kid learned what a whippoorwill sounded like, I have no idea. But these kids were nothing if not resourceful. It makes you wonder what they could have accomplished under different circumstances.

And now I needed their help. If anyone would know my mortgage hustler, it would be the drug hustlers who worked the same turf, albeit different clientele. My only other alternative would be to knock on doors until I found someone who knew the guy. But given what you often found behind those doors—the frightened, the aged, the mentally ill, the belligerent, the chemically addicted—I would be better off trying to work the dealers than to waste time on trial and error.

As I pressed farther into the courtyard, the birdcalls quieted down to a mild chatter. By now, everyone who needed to be aware of my arrival had been apprised. And yet, while they obviously knew where I was, I couldn't see them. It was too cold for anyone to just be hanging out. I dug my hands into my pockets and kept peering into the darkness.

Finally, two figures emerged from one of the corner buildings. I took my hands out of my pockets—no need for them to think I was armed—and walked toward them. They were both late teens from the look of them. One was tall and slender, with a head full of thick braids jutting from under a stiff-brimmed black cap. The other was shorter, with a hooded sweatshirt pulled over short-cropped hair.

"Hey," I said. "I'm sorry to bother you guys. I'm a reporter with the *Eagle-Examiner*. I'm looking for . . ."

They walked down the stairs just as I was approaching them, brushing past me wordlessly, staring straight ahead like I didn't exist.

"Look, I'm not a cop," I said, following them. "I'm just a newspaper reporter working on a story."

"Nah" was all the one with the braids could say. And even that was muffled.

"Guys, I just need a little help here," I said.

"Ain't no snitch," the one with the hoodie said.

The no-snitch mentality—which had long been the rule for dealing with law enforcement in the projects—had been expanded in recent years to encompass all outsiders. And reporters were most certainly included. It was, quite frankly, a huge pain in the ass. My intentions were almost always benign—in this case, I was trying to track down a lender who may have preyed on poor people—but convincing a hardened no-snitcher of this could be impossible.

More than anything, it just pissed me off. It wasn't because it made my job harder. Okay, it was partly that. But it was mostly because the no-snitch mentality—and the decline of law and order it brought—had been almost as destructive to the community as the drug trade.

"You're a moron," I said once they were out of earshot.

Or at least I thought they were. Apparently, not all of today's youth have ruined their hearing with loud music.

"What you say?" Braids said, turning around and stopping.

He looked more surprised than anything. I hadn't really intended to create a confrontation with this kid—especially when I didn't know how many friends he might have nearby—but there was no backing off now. By himself, he wasn't much to be afraid of. It helped that I outweighed him by about thirty pounds.

"You're a moron," I repeated, walking toward him. "I'm trying to do a story that will help shine light on a scumbag who preys on people from the projects. But you're such an ignorant moron all you're worried about is snitching."

Braids and Hoodie were momentarily speechless. They clearly had not expected anything resembling aggression out of the mild-mannered newspaper reporter.

"Damn, yo, he just called you *ignorant*," Hoodie said.

"Oh, you're ignorant, too," I said, drawing in even closer. "Because you know where all this no-snitch crap has gotten you? As a black man in this country, you're six times more likely to be murdered. But, wait, it gets even better, because as a young black man living in an urban area, you're thirty times more likely to be murdered. Congratulations."

I knew the first factoid to be true. I made up the second one. But I didn't think there was much chance these guys were going to call me on it. At the moment, they were just gawking at the strange white man who came into the projects to spout numbers from the Bureau of Justice Statistics.

"So go ahead," I finished. "Keep not snitching. I just want both of you to remember this conversation so that when I write a story about one of your funerals someday, I can find the other one and say I told you so."

From an outsider's perspective, I'm sure what I was doing would not seem particularly wise: picking a verbal fight with two young men who were quite possibly involved in the local drug trade, quite possibly armed, and quite possibly ready to call in reinforcements who could quite possibly separate me from my face.

But I had a hunch that wasn't going to happen. You really only got yourself in trouble in the projects if you were so strong as to be a threat or so weak as to be a target. As long as you existed somewhere in the murky middle, you were okay.

Besides, Braids and Hoodie were basically kids. And it's not hard to keep kids a little off balance, especially if you're telling them something they've never heard before. People don't turn off that natural curiosity until they're further into adulthood.

I glared at them a little bit, just to let my last statement sink in, and finally Hoodie broke the standoff. By laughing.

"Damn," he said. "You one crazy nigga, you know that?"

I chuckled.

"That has to be the first time anyone has called me *that*," I said.

They both laughed.

"What's your story about anyway?" Braids asked. "You said someone is messing with people in the projects?"

"Yeah, a Puerto Rican guy who sells people crooked mortgages."

Braids and Hoodie just looked at each other blankly, then at me.

"He's sort of short and squat," I continued. "Shaved head. Wears a goatee. Probably drives a nice car—an Audi, maybe a Mercedes."

"I ain't never seen nobody like that," Hoodie said.

"Only people who drive cars like that around here are . . ." Braids paused, not wanting to say too much.

Hoodie filled in the blank: "They're people you already know. You know?"

In other words, they were pushing something with a little more kick than subprime mortgages.

"You ever see people around here selling mortgages?" I asked.

"Depends. What's a mortgage?" Hoodie asked.

I suppose I shouldn't have been shocked by the question. Why would a black kid raised in public housing—a kid reared in a family that had probably been in America for ten generations without owning a stick of property—know what a mortgage was?

"It's . . ." I didn't know where to begin. "Never mind. Okay, forget the Puerto Rican guy. You know someone named Akilah Harris?"

Braids and Hoodie exchanged glances again. But this time they were a lot more knowing.

"Maybe," Hoodie said. And suddenly I realized they were both smirking.

"What's so funny?"

"Nothing," Braids said.

They stood there, grins widening. Obviously, Akilah was known in these parts. That was hardly surprising. Akilah was only a little older than these two. They had probably grown up with her.

"C'mon," I said. "Spill."

"I ain't saying nothing," Braids said, holding his hands in the air.

"Why you want to know?" Hoodie asked, obviously curious. "You making a story about her?"

"Her house burned down," I said. "There were two kids inside."

"Damn!" Braids said.

"Yeah, I heard about that," Hoodie said. "Someone was saying it was on the news."

Despite the tragedy of the situation, they were still smiling. Something about Akilah Harris was humorous to these guys, though I couldn't imagine what. I tried to think like a teenaged boy. What made them laugh? Toilet humor. Fart jokes. But how would that be connected with Akilah? It just wasn't coming to me.

"What's so funny?" I said.

More smirking.

Finally, Hoodie couldn't help himself. "You sure there were only two kids?" he said. "I figured she would have had, like, six by now."

Braids busted up laughing. "With, like, eighteen different daddies," he added, which made them both laugh harder.

Of course. The only thing teenaged boys found funnier than fart jokes was sex. And apparently Akilah Harris was known to be generous in that department.

"So she's a ho," I said.

"She's like the biggest ho out here," Braids confirmed.

"Is she sleeping with someone in particular?" I asked.

"Akilah? Shoot, who *hasn't* she slept with?" Hoodie said. The boys yukked it up again and I laughed along with them, even though—if I started thinking like a mature adult for a moment—none of this was really all that amusing. I let them giggle themselves out, then tried to push the conversation away from the topic of Akilah's promiscuity.

"From what I'm told, she moved out of here about three years ago," I said.

"Maybe, I don't know," Braids said. "You still see her sometimes. She visits her mom or something."

I could feel my brow creasing. "I thought she was an orphan," I said.

"Akilah? Hell, no. She got a mom," Braids said. "Her mom and my mom are like cousins. I mean, they ain't blood. But they best friends."

"Are you sure that's not her aunt? I thought her aunt raised her?"

"Naw, that's her mom," Braids said. "Whoever told you she don't have a mom don't know what they talking about."

Lying was more like it. Those alarm bells in my head were starting to ring from one ear to the other. It's possible the rest of Akilah's story was true, that she only made up the orphan part just to engender a little more sympathy. But reporters quickly learn lies are like cockroaches: where there's one, there's bound to be others.

I was already starting to feel embarrassed I had been so taken in by her saga. Akilah had Sweet Thang and me figured out from the moment she saw us—a couple spoiled white kids who would bite on the hard-life-in-the-black-city cliché, chew it up, and swallow every last morsel.

"And you say her mom lives around here?" I asked.

"Yeah, she right over there," Braids said, pointing two buildings down. "Third floor. Right side. You can ask her."

"I will," I said. "Believe me, I will."

I considered trying to take down names and phone numbers for Braids and Hoodie in case I had any more questions. But they weren't exactly quotable sources on the subject of Akilah Harris. And the chances I would get a real answer out of either of them was so remote, I decided not to bother. So I thanked them for their time and started walking toward Akilah's mother's apartment.

On the way, I had a quick phone call to make.

"Szanto," grunted a voice on the other end.

"Hey, it's Carter," I said. "Can the Akilah Harris story for tomorrow."

"Why?" he said, half gargling with a mouthful of coffee.

I told him what I learned, along with my guess that there were probably other aspects of the story that couldn't be verified.

"Yep, smells like garbage day at the fish factory all right," Szanto said. "Let's kill it."

As I walked through the gaping front entrance of Akilah's mother's building—whatever door was there had been ripped off long ago by neighborhood pharmaceutical salesmen—it occurred to me I could probably just drop the whole thing. Akilah Harris was no longer a gripping human interest story or a victim of tragic exploitation. She was a liar whose negligence killed two children. From a news standpoint, that made her a lot more run-of-the-mill: your basic two-faced criminal, not someone worthy of reader sympathy.

But there was something telling me to keep digging on this one. Was I outraged Akilah would dare attempt to mislead a gifted investigative journalist such as myself? Hardly. Was I just curious what else she made up? A little.

No, it was the missing mortgage record. Things like that didn't just happen by accident. Someone wanted something covered up. I didn't have the slightest idea who or what. But reporters love cover-ups only slightly less than they love their own mothers—more if their mothers don't cook well. Whisper the word "cover-up" in a noisy room full of reporters, and I guarantee we'll all stop and turn our heads to listen. There's just something about cover-ups we can't resist. And it seemed worthwhile to waste a little more time trying to figure out this one.

Besides, it beat researching manufacturer's specifications on space heaters.

I reached the third floor, turned left, and found a door with "Harris" typed on a small, plastic piece of tape. From somewhere inside, *Entertainment Tonight* had been cranked to a volume that ensured that local corpses were now fully aware of the latest starlet to check into rehab due to "exhaustion."

I knocked, wondering if it was even possible the sound could be heard above all the smugness coming out of the television. I waited.

Apparently not.

I knocked again, harder. This time I heard someone stirring inside. Feet shuffled up to the door. Then nothing. I had the feeling I was being examined through the peephole, which always made me slightly uncomfortable. I mean, do you smile? Look serious? Stick your eye real close and try to look back? What is proper peephole etiquette anyway?

An angry black woman inquired, "Who is it?"

"I'm a reporter with the *Eagle-Examiner,* ma'am," I yelled, trying to be heard above the television. "I was just hoping to ask you a few questions."

"It's after dark," the voice said.

"I'm aware of that, ma'am, but . . ." I began.

"I don't open my door after dark."

"Ma'am, I'm going to slip my business card under your door right now so you can see I'm Carter Ross from the *Eagle-Examiner*."

"I don't care if you're Ed McMahon and I may have won a million dollars, I don't open my door after dark."

I rolled my eyes—could she see that through the peephole?—and groped around in my head for another approach. It was hard to work my charm through a steel door, even harder when I had to compete with Mary Hart's breathless report about the weight loss secrets of Hollywood Hunks. I couldn't concentrate.

"Do you think you could turn down the TV so we could talk through the door?" I asked.

No response. I had the distinct feeling she had gone back to her couch.

"Ma'am?" I pleaded. This was getting pathetic. I knocked again.

"I told you, I ain't opening the door," she shouted from somewhere inside the apartment.

"Could I call you?" I asked.

"No," she said.

Of course not.

"If I came back in the morning, do you think you could talk with me?"

"You can try."

The emphasis was on the "try," which was not particularly encouraging. And, sure, I could try. But it would probably just delay the inevitable. I decided if this woman was meant to talk to me, it was going to happen now. I just had to push a little harder.

"Ma'am, I'm working on a story about Akilah Harris," I hollered. "I understand you're—"

Before I could finish my sentence, I heared movement inside—it sounded like a chair slamming into linoleum—followed by a strangled cry.

"Go away!" she wailed. "I don't want to hear that name! Don't you say that name to me! Go away!"

She kept yelling, but her voice had gone something beyond hysterical, so it was impossible to make out what she was saying. Between the shredded vocal cords and the uncontrolled crying, it was pretty clear the name Akilah Harris had been enough to put Mrs. Harris into distress.

And I wasn't the only one aware of it. From downstairs, I could hear footsteps coming my way. A matronly black woman in slippers and a faded floral print housedress huffed up the stairs, froze me with a look of pure disgust, and brushed past.

"I just wanted to talk to her," I said defensively. "I didn't mean to—"

But she was not there to hear my excuses. She entered Mrs. Harris's apartment without bothering to knock. The door had been unlocked all along.

An open door. In the projects. Who knew?

From within the apartment, I heard the new woman comforting Mrs. Harris, whom she called "Bertie." For a while, Bertie kept crying and moaning unintelligibly. After enough shushing, she calmed down. There was dialogue between the women, though it was too muffled to hear.

And, for whatever reason, I just kept standing in that hallway of that hellhole housing project, hoping a big reset button would descend from the ceiling so I could press it and get a do-over on this whole encounter. Why had I pushed her so hard? Clearly the woman was agitated. No one in that state is going to suddenly settle down and cooperate with a reporter. In the morning, when she was calm, she might have talked to me.

As I cursed my lack of patience, the woman in the housedress reappeared.

"What are *you* still doing here?" she said, spitting out the word "you" like it burned her mouth.

"I just—"

"She don't want to talk none," the woman assured me.

"I know, but I—"

"She don't want to talk."

"I just wanted to apol—"

"And I'm telling you, she don't want to talk."

The woman crossed her arms and glowered at me, daring me to lob up another feeble rejoinder so she could smash it back in my face. It was Olympic verbal volleyball. But while she was Misty May-Treanor and Kerri Walsh, I was the lightly regarded team from Liechtenstein.

"So what you're saying is, she don't want to . . . doesn't want to talk?" I said.

"That's right," the woman said. "You best be moving on now."

"Okay, I get it," I said, then reached into my pocket for a business card. "Could you please just tell her I'm sorry I upset her so much? It was never my intention."

The woman accepted my business card without comment, and I took that as my opportunity to leave with at least some shred of dignity intact.

I arrived back in the newsroom in time for a treat: a copy editor catfight.

Newspapers are full of strange animals, but the copy editors just might be the oddest of all the birds. A lot of them work a 6 P.M. to 2 A.M. shift, so they're nocturnal. They are sometimes awkward socially, which is why they didn't become reporters. And nearly all of them claim to be expert grammarians—and are not afraid to get into the occasional scrap over language or usage.

This one appeared to feature Marjorie, a tall, storkish woman with a voice like a foghorn against Gary, a small, nervous man with a somewhat legendary standing among his fellow copy editors. Gary was reputed to have memorized every word of the paper's style manual, our Bible governing everything from capitalization to punctuation to spelling. Most of the copy jocks didn't test him—except, apparently, Marjorie.

". . . not the point," Marjorie was booming as I entered. "I'm sure that's what the style manual says. I'm saying, in this case, we shouldn't apply the style manual."

"You can't argue with the style manual," Gary countered. "It's not called the 'suggested' manual or the 'do this if you feel like it' manual. A lot of thought was put into every entry and it's not up to us to change it on the fly because it suits our needs."

"It's not about *my* needs," Marjorie said. "It's about the readers'."

I walked over to another copy editor, a younger guy named Evan, and asked him for a translation.

"We've got a Buster Hays special: the fifty-ninth anniversary of the Battle of Sunda Strait, told through the eyes of some fossil from Linden who claims to have been a pilot," Evan said in a hushed voice.

Buster Hays was himself a fossil: a cranky, crusty contrarian who should have retired eons ago, except he loved to stick around and remind the younger generations how much better things used to be. Among his specialties were World War II anniversary stories, which he did with special zeal. So, unlike most papers—which dutifully did the fives and zeros of the big ones, like D-day and Pearl Harbor—we did the threes, sixes, and sevens of just about every significant (and insignificant) military encounter of the time period. It was fairly useless from a journalistic standpoint, unless you happen to think there's news value in the fast-fading memories of old guys rambling about details they were probably getting mixed up in the first place.

But, much as I hate to admit it, readers loved the stuff. Buster had at least a four-year backlog of future anniversary stories, all generated from reader letters he received in response to previous anniversary stories.

"So what's the dispute?" I asked, keeping my voice down so as not to interrupt Gary and Marjorie's blowup.

"Buster wrote the guy from Linden served in the Air Force," Evan told me. "I don't think they called it the Air Force back then."

"That's right! They didn't!" Gary said, somehow picking up on our whispers over Marjorie's booming. "From July 2, 1926, to June 20, 1941, it was known as the Army Air Corps. Then on June 20, 1941, it was renamed the Army Air Forces and it stayed under that name during the battle in question. It did not become the U.S. Air Force until September 18, 1947!"

"I'm not disputing that," Marjorie interjected. "I'm saying if we put in the paper this guy from Linden was part of the Army Air Corps—"

"Army Air Forces," Gary interrupted.

"Fine, whatever," Marjorie said. "As I was saying, if we write he was in the Army Air Whatever, the Army part is going to confuse the vast majority of our readers who came of consciousness well after the aforementioned name change was made."

I always wondered if readers knew how much we fought for their supposed interests. Many an impassioned argument in the newsroom was based on what was best for "the readers." It was ironic in at least two ways: one, most people in the newspaper business have at least some disdain for readers, because the ones we hear from with the greatest frequency are confused octogenarians calling in to complain we weren't giving enough ink to President Truman's new jobs proposal; and two, most of the readers whose rights were being so highly cherished were going to take that day's paper, briefly check the weather and the Yankees box score, then use it to potty train their puppy.

"So we should be factually incorrect to make it easier on the readers?" Gary said. "I don't know if I'm ready to bend to the lowest common denominator that way."

"Well, aren't you just standing at the gates of Western Civilization, holding back the Huns," Marjorie countered. "We're a daily newspaper. We're supposed to be written at a level eighth graders can understand. You think an eighth grader is going to care about alterations in military nomenclature made before their parents were born?"

"It's in the style manual," Gary replied.

"I don't care about the style manual," Marjorie shot back.

The air suddenly left the room. Gary looked stricken. At least three copy editors blanched. I expected one of them might need smelling salts.

"Don't . . . don't *care*?" Gary said.

Marjorie looked to her left and right, saw she had lost all support, and started backpedaling like Galileo at a Vatican wine party.

"Well," she said. "I suppose we might get calls from military historians if we just wrote 'Air Force.' So I . . . I guess we'll do it your way."

The other copy editors exhaled. Gary straightened slightly, making himself a fraction taller in victory.

"Very good," he said.

The catfight over, I was just about to walk away when Evan stopped me.

"Carter, you got a second for a small question on your story?"

"What story?" I asked.

"The one about the mom in the fire."

"That story isn't running."

"Sure it is," Evan said. "It's going A1, above the fold."

"Oh, crap," I said.

"What's the matter?"

"We're about to strip a lie across the top of our newspaper."

* * *

I charged toward Szanto's office, knowing full well he'd still be there. It was after eight, the time by which he assured the future ex–Mrs. Szanto he'd depart. But I'm sure she knew that to be a meaningless promise. Newspaper spouses eventually learn to act as if they live on Central Time while their partners are Eastern Standard: Szanto's 8 o'clock really meant 9.

The moment Szanto saw me steaming toward him, pained expression No. 42—which starts as a tight grimace around the eyes and spreads—washed across his face.

"What the hell?" I demanded.

"What?" he said, though he knew full well what.

"I thought you killed the story."

"I did."

"So why is it—"

"It wasn't my call," he said, spreading his hands as if to absolve himself of responsibility.

"I don't understand."

"Brodie saw 'space heater' high up in the story and his Willie started throbbing," Szanto said.

It was long-standing *Eagle-Examiner* tradition that when Brodie liked a story, he was described as having a hard-on for it—or an erection, or a woody, or any number of the infinite variations to describe male sexual arousal. Why this usage evolved was lost to history. But the resulting imagery was seldom pleasant.

"I don't care if he printed it out and dry-humped it on the conference room table so everyone could watch," I replied. "How can we run that story knowing what we know?"

"Brodie said we could just take out the part about Akilah being an orphan. He said it was probably a misunderstanding that could be easily explained, and it was no reason to kill a story about the very important subject of space heater malfunction."

"But I didn't get a quote from the mortgage company," I said. "What about getting the other side of the story and all that happy hooey?"

Szanto looked at me through tired eyes.

"We didn't mention the name of the mortgage company anyway," he rationalized. "So it's not like you've maligned its reputation."

I stared at Szanto as he fingered the cigarette he planned to light just as soon as he could run to the back stairwell where he—and untold scores of others—illegally smoked during the wintertime.

"So you agree with him?"

"I didn't say that," Szanto said. "I said it was his call. Look, you wanna argue with Brodie's stiffie, you go ahead. Me? I don't want to get poked in the eye."

Neither did I. Brodie was a basically pleasant old man, but his management style did not involve toleration of open dissent. If he hadn't made up his mind about something, he would stay quiet and listen to the discussion that ensued among lesser editors. But his decisions, once made, were notoriously final. I could storm into his office and make all kinds of noise, but it wasn't likely to do any good. I'd have better luck trying to turn the ocean tides with a teaspoon.

"Fine," I huffed. "But when we have to run a correction, it better not say 'due to a reporter's error.' This isn't on me."

Szanto didn't answer, choosing to end the conversation by turning his attention back to his computer screen and grumbling something too consonant-heavy to be understood.

That left me stuck in a curious spot. On the one hand, I was off the hook. I told my editors I had deep misgivings about a story. They ignored me. Woe to them.

But that was small comfort. I took a great deal of pride in getting a story right, or at least trying my damnedest at it. It went straight to the core of perhaps my deepest journalistic value: that the truth exists, and that it's my job as a reporter to find it.

I realize that flies in the face of the moral relativism that has become so popular on campuses and in highfalutin big-think magazines, where the professors and editors will have you believe there is no such thing as the truth, only stories told from different perspectives. They'll spin that marvelous bit of postmodern logic that says there are no absolutes and therefore we cannot possibly judge anyone else's beliefs. And they'll tell you journalists are hopelessly flawed creatures incapable of escaping their own innate biases long enough to ever approach anything resembling impartiality.

To which I reply: fiddle-faddle.

I'm not saying it's simple to find and tell the truth. It takes a great deal of hard work, intellectual honesty, open-mindedness, and a willingness to keep listening to people even when your gut is telling you they're full of it. Then it involves drilling through the layers of one's cultural assumptions and prejudgments, all the way down to the mushy middle of all of us, where I believe there's a basic humanity that tells us what's right and what's wrong. If we as writers apply that code—without the anchors of agenda or ideology—we can lift our prose to something that can be called the truth. It's the very best of what journalism can and should be.

So to have a story running under my byline that I knew was suspect? It made my guts twist. I never wanted to be one of those writers who skimped on the facts simply because they got in the way of a good story. And it pissed me off, that's what I was going to look like if Akilah's story blew up in our faces—all because of Brodie and his space heater vendetta.

I went back to my desk, pondered what I might do with what remained of my evening, but couldn't bat down my ire at the executive editor. Really, the man had left me only one option: go to McGovern's and get drunk enough to start making bad decisions.

McGovern's was your basic, beloved dive bar, from the ancient laminate floor tiles all the way up to the prehistoric corkboard ceiling. As an Irish bar that somehow survived white flight, it was legendary in Newark generally and among Newark newspapermen in particular. Many a generation of our trade had made it their first (and often last) stop after work to soothe the edges of a hard day on deadline with a few (and often more than a few) adult elixirs.

Long before it was our hangout, the guys from the *Newark Evening News*—the afternoon paper that once dominated the state, before its demise in the early seventies—used to hang out there, too. And somehow I hoped that if and when the *Eagle-Examiner* was ever replaced by some other news-gathering media, which looked increasingly likely given the dire shape of newspaper advertising revenues, those future journalists (or content providers, or information aggregators, or whatever they'd call themselves) would gather at McGovern's as well.

By the time I arrived, the tables at the far side of the bar were filled by a few pitchers of Coors Light—why do kids drink that panther piss?—and a handful of *Eagle-Examiner* interns. The only one I knew that well was Tommy Hernandez, who was now in his second year as an intern with us. Only twenty-three, Tommy was one of the best natural reporters we had, a guy who knew how to hit the streets and find a story. He was still technically an intern—it's how we got away with continuing to underpay him—but he had been given a promotion recently and was now our second reporter on Newark City Hall, a great gig for someone his age.

Tommy was the only son of the world's strictest Cuban immigrant parents and he still lived at home, which made it all the more amusing his folks didn't have the slightest clue he's gay as Elton John's eyewear collection. They just thought he had a lot of male friends who dance well.

"There you are!" Tommy sang out when he saw me. "Someone was loooooking for you."

"Oh, yeah, who's that?" I said, sitting down and fumbling

with a salt shaker so I could pretend I didn't care who or what he was talking about.

"Oh, you know who," Tommy said, then switched into his best Sweet Thang impersonation: "Oh, my goodness, don't you think Carter is such a good writer? Isn't he just amaaaazing? Isn't he sweeeeet?"

"Oh, stop," I said.

"Oh, I will. She won't," Tommy said. "That girl has a bad case of Carter Ross Fever."

I turned to the other intern sitting with Tommy, a young Korean woman named Mi-Ryong Kim who, in our brief interactions, always acted like she was afraid of me.

"The problem, Mi-Ryong, is that Tommy thinks he's cute when he exaggerates. And he's not."

Mi-Ryong giggled at me.

"She has a crush on yooouuuu," Tommy taunted.

Ignoring Tommy, I kept talking to Mi-Ryong: "How much has he been drinking?" I asked. "He's blitzed, right?"

She giggled some more.

"Sweet Thang wants to have your baaabies," Tommy continued.

"Do you think we should get him a cab?" I said. "I mean, he's so plastered he's delusional."

Mi-Ryong, though still giggling, was starting to look uncomfortable, so I turned to Tommy.

"I'm going to go get a beer now," I said. "And if you don't cut this out by the time I get back, I'm going to get some of the rougher guys in this bar to reprise *Brokeback Mountain* on you. And I'm not talking about the scene in the tent."

I went to the taps, casting a fleeting look around to see if Sweet Thang was elsewhere in the bar. She wasn't. I ordered a Yuengling and scanned to the left. No Sweet Thang. I got my beer, tossed down a fiver—more than enough for a drink and a tip at a place like McGovern's—and looked to the right. Still no Sweet Thang.

I'm not sure why I cared. Shacking up with Sweet Thang qualified as a genuinely bad idea. On the Personal Destruction Scale, it ranked somewhere between riding a broken motorcycle in the rain and piloting one of those superlight airplanes that have to be assembled from a mail-order kit. I should have been thrilled that she wasn't there, because it meant at least one of us came to our senses. And yet, being a typical guy, I still wanted to be wanted. An evening of having a lovely young creature like Sweet Thang extolling my many great features was just what the ol' ego needed. I scanned the place one more time on my way back to the table, but no.

"You can stop looking for her," Tommy said when I returned. "She isn't here."

Mi-Ryong had already shoved off, so I dropped the I-don't-care act. There was clearly no fooling Tommy

"Where'd she go?" I asked.

"She got a phone call and all of a sudden she was in a hurry to leave," Tommy said. "I'm guessing it was someone hotter than you. Jealous?"

"Hardly," I said, taking a long sip on my beer.

"You should stay away from her," Tommy said. "She's bad news."

"What makes you say that?"

"Gay intuition," Tommy replied. "She just seems like she'd get a little stalkerish."

"Right," I said.

"Besides, Tina would cut your dick off," he added.

"Yes, there's that, too," I conceded.

Tommy and I settled into a typical after-hours reporter conversation—basically talking about the various ways the business was dying and how the people running it were hastening the demise—for another beer and a half. Then Tommy, who had clubs to get to and boys to see, announced it was time to go, and I figured it was time for me to do the same.

Except, unlike Tommy, the only boy I was going to see was my cat, Deadline. He and I shared a small house with a tiny lawn in Bloomfield, one of those great northern New Jersey towns that lacks in neither population density nor attitude.

Deadline and I previously lived in Nutley, another well-lived-in New Jersey bedroom community known for its concentration of Italians and, not surprisingly, its phenomenal pizza. We enjoyed it and planned on staying for a while. Then a source of mine blew up our house—he and I had some artistic differences over my work—and Deadline and I decided we needed a change of scenery.

My Amherst friends urged me to join them in paying way too much to live in way too little space on that small island just on the other side of the Lincoln Tunnel. But I liked having a dandelion or two to pull and, besides, Deadline was scared of those big New York City rats. I had first looked for a place in Montclair, a town made trendy about fifteen or twenty years ago when a small enclave of artists and writers discovered it. Unfortunately, the stockbrokers heard it was trendy and mounted a hostile takeover, meaning a guy on a reporter's salary could no longer dream of affording the real estate. So Bloomfield it was.

Deadline was asleep in my bed by the time I got home, so I tiptoed in, careful not to wake him. If he doesn't get his twenty-two hours of shut-eye a day, he gets ornery. I read the new Michael Connelly on my nightstand until the other side of midnight, when I finally wrenched it out of my hands. I was just drifting off, or at least it felt that way, when suddenly my cell phone was ringing.

I looked at my clock. Six-fourteen A.M. What kind of sick, depraved, thoughtless person calls a reporter at 6:14 A.M.?

I looked at my cell phone. "Thang, Sweet," it said.

"Hello?"

"It's gone," Sweet Thang sobbed. "My necklaces, my bracelet, my earrings, my jewelry box, it's all gone."

At first, Primo paid little attention to the ancillary service industries that coexisted alongside his. He fixed up houses. That was enough.

But after a few years, as he began doing the development side of the business by rote, he became increasingly aware of—and annoyed by—the people making money off his hard work: the real estate agents taking their six percent, straight off the top; the lawyers with their exorbitant hourly rates; the title searchers, appraisers, and home inspectors, each charging their ridiculous fees; the mortgage brokers with their commissions, which became even richer with the more exotic subprime loans.

Parasites, all of them. Primo did the work. Primo took the risk. Primo made the sacrifices. All so they could get fat?

No more, Primo decided. He was not going to let those untold thousands of dollars slip away with every house he built. So, much like the robber barons of the nineteenth century, who expanded their businesses vertically until they controlled every aspect of production, Primo began spreading his reach.

He opened a real estate agency and gave it all his listings. He lured some young lawyers away from their firms and paid the start-up costs for them to hang out their own shingle—in exchange, of course, for a healthy kickback on all the business he sent them.

He founded a title search company, a home inspection agency, an appraisal business, a mortgage brokerage. He even opened his own pest control business, because state rules required a house be certified termite-free before a certificate of occupancy was issued.

Primo did it all. He was a complete, one-stop shop for home purchasing. His customers, who were eager to jump into the late 1990s/early 2000s real estate market and start making easy money, were thrilled he streamlined it for them. They happily shuffled from one link in Primo's chain to the next, and Primo profited at every stop.

It made the whole system so simple to manipulate. After Primo fixed up some dilapidated dump, he'd recruit some greedy-yet-naïve investor and put him through the system. Primo's real estate agents would make the house seem like a steal—the myth of the old lady who lived there forty years and meticulously maintained it was a favorite. His appraisers would inflate the price using bogus comparables and a generous tape measure. His mortgage brokers were trained in the art of fudging a loan application, overstating the buyer's wages and rental income, and then selling the buyer on some dreadful subprime loan with a sweetheart introductory rate that made it all seem affordable.

And then the lawyers would tie a neat bow around the whole package. Each house was rehabbed and sold by a different limited liability company, or LLC. Each service enterprise was fronted by a different LLC as well. Primo had so many different LLCs—all with different postal addresses, all with fictitious names as their corporate agent—it was sometimes hard just to come up with new names for them.

Each believed it was independent, thus avoiding any conflict-of-interest laws. Each was encouraged to find as much outside work as it could, adding to the air of their legitimacy. But each answered to only one man, and that man was Primo.

CHAPTER 3

Between the melodrama in Sweet Thang's voice and the unsightly number on my clock, it took me a few moments to parse her first utterance. And, in true Sweet Thang fashion, she was frantically piling more words on top of the initial ones, creating a verbal traffic jam that was causing extensive delays in the non-E-Z Pass toll lane that was my early-morning brain.

Somewhere in the midst of a detailed description of all the items on her charm bracelet—just after the "oh-so-cute sombrero" she got on a trip to Puerto Vallarta and during the "darling little gondola" her father brought her back from Venice—my overloaded ears got the message to my slumbering vocal cords that it was time to wake up.

I shoved aside Deadline, who had taken his half of the bed out of the middle, and willed myself to sit up.

"Slow down, slow down, slow down," I begged. "Your jewelry is gone?"

"I already said that!"

"I know, but I just now understood it," I said. "Don't you know what time it is?"

"What does *that* matter?"

"It's"—I looked at the clock again—"six-nineteen A.M. This is not an hour of the day when I function."

"But I'm in crisis!" she whined. "And Akilah is gone."

"Wait, Akilah? As in Akilah Harris?" I asked. "What does this have to do with Akilah Harris?"

"Weren't you listening?"

"I thought we already established this: no."

"I just told you, Akilah spent the night . . ." she said.

I said a word that would need to be bleeped on network television, then added several more. But Sweet Thang, unheeding of my profanity, had already set her mouth back to the races.

". . . I was at the bar last night, waiting for you—I don't want you to think I just stood you up for no reason—and I got a call from her. She said she didn't have anywhere else to go and I couldn't just turn her out on the streets. So I picked her up in Newark and drove her back to my place in Jersey City . . ."

"You did not. Oh, my God, you did not."

". . . and I just felt like after her hard day, she shouldn't have to sleep on my pull-out couch, because it's kind of lumpy in spots and the mattress is kind of thin because it has to still be able to tuck in when it's in couch mode . . ."

"I can't believe this," I was mumbling, entirely to myself. "I can't effing believe this."

". . . so I told her she could sleep in my room. Because I have this Select Comfort bed. You know, that's the kind with the sleep number on it? And I told her if she wanted more firm she could dial a higher number, and less firm she could dial a lower number. My Gram Gram got it for me for graduation; it's totally the best present ever, because it's like having your own personalized, individualized bed . . ."

"This just is not happening," I continued. "Even you're not this dumb."

". . . so I let her borrow some pj's—and I heard that, it's not dumb to be generous, it's Christian—and she seemed to be settled in just fine. I went into the living room and pulled out the couch and was watching reruns of *The Hills* and she was dead asleep. I mean, I heard her snoring and everything . . ."

"Just let me know when I get to say 'I told you so,'" I interjected.

". . . and then I went to sleep—not yet, by the way, let me finish—and in the morning I got up and she was gone. And so was all my jewelry. I have one of those jewelry boxes that's sort of like a little armoire, with little cabinet doors you can swing open and the little knobs on it, you know? It's really cute. Anyway, I leave it out on my dresser, which is where I like to keep it, so I can see my jewelry when I get ready in the morning and envision how it's going to look with my outfit . . ."

"Of course you do."

". . . also, I hate tangled jewelry, it drives me IN-sane. So the way I lay it out, with the earrings on their trees and the necklaces on their stands and the bracelets arranged in chronological order of when they were given to me and the rings laid out alphabetically by color? Well, that and the jewelry box, it kind of takes up most of the dresser. But when I came in just now, the dresser was bare. And the jewelry box was gone. And Akilah was gone. And I don't care about most of the stuff—it's just stuff, after all—but I really, really have a sentimental attachment to that charm bracelet. It just reminds me of all the places I've been and all the things I've done and I've had it since I was a little girl and it's pretty much my most treasured possession."

She hesitated, and not knowing how long it would be before she actually came to a full pause, I interrupted.

"So, to sum up, your stuff is missing . . ."

"Primarily my charm bracelet, yes."

". . . and you called . . . me?" I said, laying on the incredulity as thickly as possible. "Shouldn't you call the police? Or your insurance company? Or, hell, Zales or something?"

"I can't."

"What do you mean?"

"I told you already. It wouldn't be Christian. I can't do that to Akilah."

"I'm sure Jesus would have reported the crime," I said.

"I'm sure He would have turned the other cheek."

"No, Jesus Christ would have thrown His weight around with the Jersey City Police Department to make sure they were looking into it, maybe even used His influence with the Hudson County Prosecutor's Office," I said. "You need to read the Old Testament more. Sometimes God gets good and pissed off and it only makes sense His only begotten son would be a chip off the old block."

"Don't blaspheme," she said curtly. "And I am absolutely not, under any circumstances, going to tattle on Akilah."

"*Tattle?*" I spat. "What's next? She didn't commit larceny, she's just a bad sharer?"

"That poor girl has enough troubles in this world. I am not going to add to them simply because I have been deprived of a few material possessions."

"So, again, why are you calling me?" I asked.

"Because I didn't"—I could practically hear her lower lip begin quivering—"I didn't have anyone"—cue the sniffles—"anyone else to call," she finished, and began bawling.

But, of course, she was still talking.

"I'm"—gasping inhale—"scared and I"—shuddering exhale—"don't want to be"—tiny stifled sob—"alone."

Over the next six tearful minutes, we agreed that I should drop everything else I was planning on doing, not pause for breakfast, take the briefest of showers (I won that battle despite a fierce onslaught of whimpering), and come over to her apartment.

It wasn't exactly what I planned for my morning, but there's something about the weeping, frightened, vulnerable female that this particular Heroic Male simply cannot ignore. Saddle the gallant steed, shine the armor, locate the damsel, and Mrs. Ross's boy will always ride to the rescue.

Mrs. Ross's boy is a sucker that way.

I was shaved, showered, and dressed in fifteen minutes—no real man needs more time than that—and out the door in sixteen, pausing only to make sure Deadline had enough food to maintain his inactive lifestyle.

As I backed down the driveway, I briefly glanced at the newspaper loyally waiting for me on the front porch and felt a pang at leaving it there. Long before I started writing for one, starting the day with a daily newspaper was a cherished habit. I was raised to believe it's just one of those things a decent, educated citizen does. Then it became my profession, and it became a kind of necessity: the reporter who doesn't know what's in the paper is not a very good reporter. I once had an editor who was known to quiz people as they came in the door to make sure they had read that day's edition before they arrived at work. For me, reading the paper in the morning is like religion.

But then I reminded myself religion is all about being comfortable with hypocrisy and I kept driving. I'm sure there wasn't anything so dire in there that couldn't hold until after my white knight routine was done.

I made good time to Sweet Thang's place, which was in the increasingly fashionable Newport section of increasingly fashionable Jersey City. She had given me the apartment number (12J) and her door pass code (90210—she assured me she wasn't too young to have watched the show by the same name in reruns), and I soon found myself riding up a mirrored elevator to the top floor of a rather swank apartment building.

When Sweet Thang answered her door, she was still in her bedtime attire, which consisted of boxers, a ribbed tank top, and lots of creamy, perfect, youthful skin. She had a fresh, soapy smell and greeted me with a hug that made me a little lightheaded.

"Oh, my goodness, thank you so much for coming over," she murmured as she gave me one last squeeze, then released me. "It makes me feel like a thousand times better just to have you here. I can't tell you how totally gross and violated I feel right now. I mean, I'm still not going to tattle on her to the police but, ewwww! How gross is it to have someone just come into your house and take stuff! Like, I would have totally given her some money if she asked for it, didn't she know that? It's just soooo uncool and—"

I put a finger to my lips and made a shushing noise.

"Sorry," she said quickly. "I know. Babbling. Stop now."

Her place was spacious, nicely furnished, and, I immediately surmised, not possibly affordable on her $500 weekly intern's salary. If the ample square footage didn't tip me off, the commanding view of Manhattan did.

"Nice place," I said as I trailed her from the small foyer into the living room, where the foldout couch was still unfurled.

"I just painted in here," she said. "Do you like the color? It's from the Ralph Lauren Urban Loft collection. It's called 'Sullivan.' "

"Do you call it 'Sulli' for short?" I asked.

"No, but I think I'll start," she said, smiling.

"You're lucky they let you paint it yourself. I've heard of places like this where they make you use whatever contractor the landlord prefers because they're afraid the tenants will be too sloppy."

"Well, my dad owns the building," she said.

"Oh," I said. I'd figured Daddy was loaded. I didn't realize he was *that* loaded.

She added quickly: "I pay him rent, though."

Market rate, I'm sure. She flopped down on the bed, propping herself on one elbow and stretching out her gorgeous, bare legs underneath her. She left room for me to sit on the bed.

I chose a nearby chair.

"Does your dad own other buildings?" I asked, not sure if I wanted to know the answer.

"A few. Real estate is just a hobby."

"And his day job is . . ."

"Investing."

"Riiiight," I said.

"Don't do that," she snapped.

"What?"

"You're making assumptions about me!" she said. "I only told you he owned it because I thought you wouldn't make assumptions."

"I wasn't making—"

"I'm not a spoiled little rich girl," she said. "I've worked for what I've gotten."

"Okay," I said, but apparently wasn't convincing.

She eyed me.

"Look, everyone has a dad," I said. "Yours happens to be filthy rich and friends with a guy who runs a newspaper. You don't need to apologize to me for having advantages in life. I'd only hold it against you if you *hadn't* done something with them. I didn't exactly start this race in last place myself."

"Thanks for understanding," she said, and we bonded for a moment, just a pair of hardworking spoiled little rich girls—even though the only real estate my parents owned was a two-story colonial.

"So you can say it now," she said.

"Say what?"

"That you told me so."

"Well, I guess I did," I said. "But I have to admit I'm feeling a little responsible for what happened, because I didn't quite tell you everything."

"What do you mean?"

I guided her through my discovery of Akilah's nonorphan

status, finishing it off with how I tried to get the story yanked but was overruled by Uncle Hal's space heater fetish.

She pouted.

"I thought we were working on the story together," she huffed. "You were going to have them pull the story without telling me?"

"I was planning to tell you everything at the bar," I said. "But I guess I got there right after you left to pick up Akilah."

"Oh."

"About that . . ."

She rolled over on her stomach, smothering her face in her pillow. I couldn't help but admire her tight little ass as she loosed a muffled scream and kicked her legs in a minitantrum.

"Ahh hhhann oooeee ahh ddiii daaa," she said.

"Come again?"

She lifted her head: "I can't believe I did that."

"You want your lecture now?"

She nodded and fixed me with a big blue-eyed gaze.

"Okay," I began. "It goes like this: as a reporter, you're going to be constantly tripping on people who need help—sometimes a lot more help than you can possibly give them. You will, of course, care about them. That's good. That's human. But remember, it's not your job to save them and you couldn't if you wanted to. It's your job to write about them. If someone else decides to save them after that? Bully for them—and bully for you, because your words obviously inspired someone.

"Otherwise? Lay off. You have to remember these are people who have been failed by a whole lot of folks in their lives, and one or two goodhearted acts by a stranger isn't going to turn things around for them. You won't last six months in this line of work if you make all the problems you see your business. Got it?"

She nodded again, blinking the big blue eyes several times.

"End of lecture," I announced. "Now, why am I here again?"

"I was hoping you might have a few ideas how I could get my charm bracelet back."

I started shaking my head and was about to launch into an explanation of how thoroughly improbable that was, when I heard the gallant steed whinny, reminding me sometimes the Heroic Male has to conquer long odds to fulfill his quest.

"Oh," I said, sighing, "I guess I've got a few."

My first idea was breakfast. I waited for Sweet Thang to shower and dress, failing miserably at filtering out the inappropriate thoughts floating through my head as she did so. I resisted the urge to sift through her things as she got ready, though I couldn't help but marvel at the general *Martha Stewart Living* feel to her place. Every paint color appeared to have been deliberately picked and matched with some other fixture or accessory in each room. It was an impressive display of decorative genius—if a bit sickening.

Sweet Thang emerged from her bedroom in a light blue knit dress, and I tried to pretend like I didn't notice how nicely it clung to her. We left her apartment and made our way to the nearest diner, which in the great state of New Jersey is never more than a few blocks away.

I went with the pancakes, always safe. Sweet Thang surprised me by ordering a No. 2—two eggs, two pancakes, two sausages, juice, toast, and coffee—and surprised me even more by finishing it. Breakfast, she explained between bites, is the most important meal of the day.

As we chewed, I formulated our strategy. Someone had to go see Bertie Harris, our only firm connection with Akilah. And, after the first impression I made the previous evening, we would be better off if the someone wasn't me. I'm sure she and Walter the Beemer would make quite an impression at Baxter Terrace.

My assignment would involve a visit to Reginald Jamison, one of my best sources for all things hood related. He made a surprisingly good living selling silk-screened T-shirts out of a storefront on Clinton Avenue. Everyone called him "T-shirt Man," which was then shortened to "Tee." I was probably one of the few people who came into his store who knew his real name was Reginald.

Tee and I had gotten to know each other a few years back when I did a story that cast him in a favorable light as an entrepreneur. We had been buddies ever since. I liked having a guy plugged into the streets. He liked the novelty of having a white friend—in some parts of Newark, it was almost like keeping an exotic pet.

Tee was about 250 pounds of muscle, tattoo ink, and braids, all of which gave off the impression he was one tough gangsta, a front he maintained when it served him. In reality, the dude was about as hard as a roll of Charmin. He had a wife he doted on (mostly because she'd kick his ass if he didn't). And he had a sentimental streak that was even wider than his biceps. I once caught him watching a bootleg DVD of *Love Actually* in the back of his store.

As a businessman, he was strictly legit. Still, he grew up with most of the illegitimate businessmen in the area, so he was well acquainted with the city's informal economic infrastructure and didn't mind sharing his contacts now and then.

By the time I made it to Tee's place, it was about ten o'clock.

"Aw shoot, Whitey's here, hide the weed!" Tee crowed when he saw me.

"C'mon," I said, "since when does white man need to actually see the weed before he makes an arrest? You know I'll just plant it on you later if I have to."

"Good point," he said as we shook hands, then slipped into his exaggerated white man's voice: "To what do I owe the pleasure of your appearance, Mr. Ross?"

"I got a hypothetical question for you," I said.

"Yeah, but it probably ain't all that hypothetical, right?" he said, switching back to his normal voice.

"Well, let's just say you're a citizen of Newark who has recently come into a substantial amount of jewelry and you want to liquidate your holdings," I said. "Is there a merchant in the city who provides such a service without probing too deeply into the origin of the items in question?"

"Now, why you think I know something like that?" he said in a fake rage. "Why is it anytime Whitey needs to know about stealing stuff, he come see his black friend, huh? Because that's all the black man is good for, huh? How come you're not coming here to ask me my thoughts on municipal bonds?"

"Because I'm not in a high enough tax bracket to take advantage of the benefits of munies," I answered.

"Oh," Tee said. "Well, in that case, yeah, I know the guy you gotta see."

"Who?"

"This is off the record, right?"

"Of course."

"Well, allegedly"—"allegedly" is one of Tee's favorite words—"you go see Maury."

"Maury?"

"Yeah, that's the name of the pawnshop. The dude who own it ain't named Maury—it's named after some Jewish dude who owned it a thousand years ago. But people still call him 'Maury' anyway. Everyone in the hood knows: you got some stuff, you need some cash, you go to Maury."

"And he's, uh, not known to ask many questions?"

"Most of the rest of the pawnshops make you fill out all kinds of paperwork, do this ninety-day waiting period thing, all that. Maury is known to be a little less strict with his bookkeeping," Tee said, then added, "allegedly."

"And if I strolled in, asked for Maury, and inquired about some particular jewelry?"

Tee laughed.

"He'd assume you're a cop and suddenly get real hard of hearing, you know what I'm sayin'?"

"I do. So what's my plan?"

"Well, break it down for me here. What are we dealing with?"

I told Tee the whole sordid tale of Akilah and Sweet Thang, finishing with my frantic 6:14 A.M. wake-up call and the small amount of culpability I felt in the whole mess.

"So you got yourself some tasty little honey and you're trying to get her stuff back?" he cooed. "Oh, that's sweeeet."

"Yeah, I'm just made of cotton candy. Do you think you can introduce me to this Maury character?"

"Oh, I don't actually know him," Tee said. "I just know him by reputation."

"So you know someone who knows him?"

"Let me make some calls," Tee said. "I'll holler at you later?"

I was about to answer when I was interrupted by the sound of Beethoven's Fifth Symphony coming from my pocket.

"That's my editor," I said. "Like the ringtone?"

"Remind me to download you some LL Cool J."

"That's, what, a drink or something?"

Tee just shook his head and muttered, "White people."

I waved at Tee as I left his store and went into the street to answer the call.

"Good morning, sunshine!" I said.

"Tell me you got something," Szanto barked.

"Tell me what you're talking about."

"Windy Byers," Szanto said, exasperated. "Brodie somehow thinks there's a Pulitzer somewhere in this. He's got a boner that could win him the county pole vault championships."

Wendell A. Byers Jr.—nickname: Windy—was a Newark councilman. He was a bit of an idiot and lot of a blowhard, the kind of guy who had the habit of talking when he should have been listening. I had met him enough times that a picture of him appeared in my mind. He was African-American, but he straightened his salt-and-pepper hair, which was brushed back across his head. He was in his fifties, but the weight he carried made him look older. And he had one of those meticulously groomed, pencil-thin mustaches, and it was etched across his fleshy, flaccid face.

His father, Wendell senior, had also been a Newark councilman. And that, apparently, was enough for the citizens of the Central Ward, who had been sending someone with that name to represent them for the last forty years or so. As a result of this honor, Windy Byers spent a long and thoroughly undistinguished political career being driven around in a city SUV, pretending he was important. It was unclear what the citizens got out of the deal.

"Uh, I'm sorry, what's happening with Windy Byers?" I said.

"He's missing. Didn't you read the paper this morning?"

I cursed my lousy karma: of all the mornings to not glance at the paper before I left. I thought about offering any number of creative excuses—most of which would have required knowledge of viruses that cause temporary blindness—but decided on the truth instead: "No. I kind of had a little emergency this morning."

"You want to tell me what's more important than a kidnapped city councilman?"

This was not going to be easy.

"Sweet Thang's charm bracelet," I answered. I was glad Szanto couldn't see me, because I was grinning like an idiot and it would have driven him berserk.

"Come again?"

"You know the story Sweet Thang and I wrote yesterday?"

"Yeah. It got bumped off A1 by the Byers story and buried on the county news page—not that you would know because you didn't read the paper. Anyway, what about it?"

"Well, you may or may not be aware, but Sweet Thang is a rather kindhearted young woman and she, uhhh . . ." I paused, groping for the right words. I had hoped to have this little mess cleaned up before anyone needed to learn about it. Sweet Thang was going to have a hard time living this down. And I was going to have a hard time explaining it in a way that wouldn't have Szanto shotgunning Tums.

"Have I not made it clear I'm in a hurry this morning?" Szanto barked.

"Sweet Thang let Akilah Harris stay at her place," I blurted. "And sometime in the middle of the night, Akilah stole Sweet Thang's jewelry and took off. I've been trying to get it back."

I could practically hear the new hole being torn in Szanto's stomach.

"Are you serious?" he asked.

"I am."

"And this is what you've been doing with your morning?"

"I have."

What followed was a rant spiked with language you are unlikely to hear from your local librarian. He strongly suggested that I, as his investigative reporter, ought to stop worrying about the missing jewelry and start worrying about the missing councilman.

Then he hung up.

"Nice chatting with you," I said to the empty phone line.

I sighed. I knew exactly how this was going to play out. I would be assigned to put together some kind of Sunday piece that Told the Real Story—or however much of the Real Story we could assemble between now and then. In the meantime, it was Tuesday and we, as a newspaper, would spill countless barrels of ink during the coming days, covering every detail of the life and perhaps-death of Windy Byers, all the while pretending he was something other than a hack local politician who had ridden his father's half-good name to a long and undistinguished career in service to the public/himself.

I wasn't keen on canonizing him like that. On the bright side, at least I wouldn't have to get a space heater reference high up in whatever I wrote.

My first step in this whole process was, of course, to do what

I should have done first thing this morning: read the paper. I hopped in my Malibu and started looking for one, which was harder than you might think. This being Newark, we couldn't keep newspaper boxes on the street. Otherwise, for seventy-five cents, some homeless guy—sorry, Housing Challenged American—was going to break in just as soon as we filled the box, swipe all thirty copies, and sell them on the street for reduced rates, netting himself the fifteen dollars he would need to keep his belly full of Wild Irish Rose until the next morning. What we did, instead, was cut the petty larceny out of the equation: we hired the homeless guys directly and put them to work selling the paper for us.

On the street, the *Eagle-Examiner* was known as "The Bird." People who delivered or sold it were known as "Bird Flippers." I think all involved enjoyed the double entendre.

Still, after the morning rush hour, most of the Bird Flippers had already made enough money to be happily inebriated the rest of the day, so it took a little while before I found one still manning his post.

I tossed him a buck, told him to keep the change—the last of the big spenders, that's me—and settled in to have a look.

As Szanto said, the disappearance of Wendell A. Byers Jr. was stripped across the top of A1. It was obviously late-breaking, and the layout person—who was either too rushed or too lazy to redesign the entire front page—had simply swapped out the Akilah Harris piece in favor of the Byers news.

The story appeared under the byline of Carl Peterson, our night rewrite guy. When Peterson first came to the paper, his approach may have charitably been called "new journalism." Now it was just called overwriting. He stuffed his copy with adverbs and adjectives, filling the small spaces left in between with clichés. He wrote how the disappearance of the "beloved Central Ward councilman" and "scion of a Newark political dynasty" was being treated as "a deeply suspicious event" by police who "strongly suspect foul play." The councilman's wife, described as "thoroughly overwrought with anxiety," reported her husband's absence Monday evening, setting off a "city-wide manhunt" in which "concerned constituents" were being enlisted.

The only problem with Peterson's prose was disentangling the facts from the compositional exertions. And in this case it was especially difficult because Peterson didn't seem to have many facts beyond: *(a)* the honorable councilman failed to return home to Mrs. Honorable Councilman; *(b)* she called the cops; and *(c)* the police had at least a half-cocked notion something untoward had happened. There was no mention of what led police to that conclusion, or whether there had been any ransom demands, or whether he had even been kidnapped in the first place.

Not that I blamed Peterson for the lack of information. As night rewrite man, he was hostage to whatever dispatches he got from reporters (usually not much for a deadline story like that) and whatever the Newark police felt like telling him (usually even less).

I drummed my fingers on the steering wheel. There were so many ways this thing could go—involvement with the mob, involvement with a girlfriend, involvement with a girlfriend who was herself involved with the mob. Without at least some hint of a direction, I'd be like Fred Flintstone in his boulder-wheeled car: moving my legs a lot but not really going all that fast.

I needed a cop to whisper something in my ear. And the cop that immediately came to mind was Rodney Pritchard, a homicide detective I became friendly with a while back. I had written a blow-by-blow story of how he tracked down and apprehended a fugitive wanted for murdering his wife. Pritch caught the guy so unawares he actually answered the door to his apartment hideout while eating a piece of jerk chicken—allowing Pritch to deliver the once-in-a-career line, "You're under arrest, now drop the chicken."

My story made Pritch mildly famous, helping to launch him on a long winter of law enforcement awards banquets. So now we were the kind of buddies who tell each other secrets. Or at least that's what I hoped as I dialed his number.

"Yo, Pritch, it's Carter Ross," I said breezily. "What's shakin'?"

"Sorry, you got the wrong number," Pritch said, then hung up.

I was just about to drop Pritch from my Secret-telling Buddies List when he rang me back.

"Sorry about that," he said in a hushed voice. "It's *hot* around here."

"So what's going on with this Byers thing?"

"I don't know, man, you tell me," Pritch said. "I mean, who the hell just takes a councilman? You have to be either very pissed or very dumb."

"Who's handling the case"

"Fellow named Raines caught it."

"He any good?"

"He's okay."

"Would he talk to me off the record? Tell him I won't quote him, but I'll find lots of ways to make him look like a dogged and heroic investigator in print."

"I don't think it would matter," Pritch said. "Raines isn't in it for the newspaper clippings. He's pretty by-the-book. I'll be honest with you, he's so straight, I don't even think I can ask him for you."

"Fair enough. What about you? You hearing anything? Water-cooler talk?"

"What have we told you guys officially?"

"That all of Newark is playing a game of Where's Windy and your guys seem to believe he didn't just wander off to Florida for the weekend without telling anyone."

"Well, we got a good reason for believing that."

"I'm listening."

"We found blood in his house," Pritch said.

"Really," I said as I grabbed a notebook and started scribbling. "Like, a lot of blood?"

"A little blood, from what I hear."

"How little? Are we talking 'oops, I cut myself shaving' or 'oops, a samurai left his sword in my head.'"

"Probably closer to the shaving accident," Pritch said. "But I don't know a lot of people who shave in the foyer of their house, and that's where we found it."

"Is it definitely his?"

"We don't know. Labs aren't back yet. But who else's could it be?"

Anyone's. Cops were so short on imagination sometimes.

"By the way," Pritch said. "You didn't get this from me, right?"

"Of course not. I don't even know you," I assured him. "What is the current thinking on why anyone would feel like stealing Windy Byers?"

"It's too early. Our guys either don't know or ain't sayin'. Between you and me, I don't think they have a clue."

"But it doesn't sound like some botched robbery or something?" I said. "I mean, you take a councilman, it's because you meant to take a councilman, right?"

"Well, I've heard his laptop was missing. But it was just the laptop. I've had too many cases where people report one thing 'stolen' and then it turns up somewhere later."

"Sure," I said. "So we're told the wife reported him missing. What's her deal?"

"From what I hear, she was out at some church group thing on Sunday night," Pritch said. "She comes back home and her husband isn't there, but she doesn't think anything of it. She just thinks he's out at a political event or something. Then the next morning she wakes up to an empty bed and calls us."

"Our story said she called Monday night."

"Yeah, we probably just told you guys that so you wouldn't jump all over us for not calling you about it earlier. The public information office does stuff like that all the time."

Didn't we know it.

"Anyone think the wife has something to do with this?" I asked. "You know, she found him cheating, killed him, got rid of the body, then reported him missing?"

"That's a theory."

"Is it the official theory?"

"I don't know," Pritch said. "Look, I gotta run. I'm crouched in the stairwell talking to you like you're the girl I keep on the side. And I just don't like you that much."

"All right. Do me a favor and keep your ears open. I owe you lunch."

"You owe me more than one," Pritch said, then hung up.

My next call was to Tommy Hernandez, our fabulous gay Cuban intern. Since Tommy was now one of our City Hall beat writers, Councilman Byers was one of his responsibilities. General rule of thumb in journalism: if one of your key sources vanishes suspiciously, you're going to be busier than a paisley top with plaid pants.

He answered after half a ring.

"Hey, I'm in Byers's neighborhood," Tommy said, not bothering with salutations. "Come meet me here."

"Got cross streets for me?"

"It's on Fairmount, just north of South Orange Avenue," Tommy said.

It took six minutes to get from Tee's neighborhood to the scene and only a few seconds to figure out which house belonged to the councilman. If the police tape didn't clue me in, the TV trucks parked out front did. I parked, got out, and had a look around.

The councilman's neighborhood had clearly seen better days.

Uh, make that better centuries. I'm sure sometime around World War II it had been a great little place to raise a family. Now, after decades of mortgage redlining and highway construction, absentee landlordism and slumping schools, the GI Bill and white flight—and all the other things this country allowed that led its suburbs to prosper at the expense of its cities—there were only faint memories of what had been.

The slate sidewalks, once a smooth runway for baby boomers' strollers, were now a jagged moonscape of broken rock. The elm trees that once lined the street were down to a few straggling, struggling survivors, creating a more desolate effect than if they had all been chopped down.

The same could be said for the houses. Some had long ago been flattened and turned into vacant lots. Others looked so unkempt, unwanted, or abandoned you only wished they would have a sudden meeting with a wrecking ball. Then there were a few that defied the odds and, with regular painting and maintenance, had aged gracefully. It only made me more wistful, wondering what the street would look like if it had just been cared for a little more through the years.

And you could blame the federal government, whose policies helped create this mess. Or you could blame the whites, who turned and ran when things started getting tough; or the blacks, who let it get even worse; or the schools, which warehoused urban kids instead of educating them; or the churches, which too often had their doors closed when they should have been open; or the economy, which no longer provided the kind of factory jobs that made a city go; or, well, take your pick.

It was everyone's fault. And no one's fault. And I wondered if I would ever live to see the day when the sidewalks were smooth, the street was shaded by trees, and the houses all had fresh paint.

None of which was going to get my story written. So I started going up and down the block until I found Tommy, dutifully going door to door, talking to neighbors. I caught him coming down the steps of a sagging old duplex, having just been shooed away by someone's great-grandmother.

"Do you shop in a catalogue that's called 'Old and Boring' or do you go to normal places and it just turns out that way?" Tommy asked. "I mean, khaki pants, blue shirt, red tie. Was that your boarding school uniform or something?"

Tommy was not a big fan of my fashion sensibilities, which he accused of slipping into a coma sometime around 1997.

"Oh, it takes many long seconds of work each morning to look this dull," I assured him. "How's the canvassing?"

"The usual," Tommy said, waving toward the houses. "It happened at night and these are all old people who wouldn't dream of going out after dark. They didn't see anything."

"And they keep their TVs turned up high to drown out the sound of the sirens," I said, nodding in the direction of University Hospital. "So they didn't hear anything, either."

"You got it."

"Well, if it makes you feel better, I got a little bit of scoop for you," I said.

"That the cops found blood in the front entrance?" Tommy replied. "Yeah, I know."

Of course he did. Tommy was that kind of reporter.

"Who told you?" I said.

"One of the guys in the Crime Scene Unit hangs out at some of the same clubs I do, if you get my drift," Tommy said, grinning mischievously.

"Ah," I said. "But, let me guess: this is not well-known among his colleagues at the Newark Police Department?"

"At work, he's so far in the closet you'd think he survives by eating hangers," Tommy said. "But he's definitely one of mine."

Tommy and I started walking back up the block, toward an encampment of TV cameras.

"So what's your theory about this so far?" I asked. "Did Windy Byers run off with his girlfriend?"

"His boyfriend maybe," Tommy said.

"Boyfriend?"

"Oh, don't act all shocked," Tommy said. "Sometimes I think half the brothers in Newark like it on the down low."

Sex "on the down low," as it is known, involved otherwise straight, mostly married black men who get together under the pretense of masculine activities (poker, beers, bowling, whatever) and have sex with each other. I didn't know how much of it to believe, but it was a never-ending source of gossip in Newark: who did what with whom and where, who pitched, who caught. It was never confirmed by firsthand knowledge—no one ever admitted being involved—but it was not unusual to hear it whispered that a guy liked it on the down low. And if anyone would know, it was Tommy.

"Okay, so why did his boyfriend kidnap him?" I asked. "Was he afraid Byers was going to go public or something?"

"Oh, I have no idea," Tommy said. "I just always heard stuff about Windy Byers doing it on the down low with one of his council staffers. So . . ."

Tommy's voice trailed off. We were nearly within earshot of the TV news foofs, who were standing around in a pack, preening.

"What's this, a superficiality convention?" I asked.

"No, Matos is going to make a statement," Tommy said.

Matos was Newark Police Chief Felix Matos. And sure enough, when I looked closer, I saw the preeners had congregated around a small podium that had been crammed with microphones, each with their ridiculous little logo box attached. Yes, indeed, I was in for one of the most useless events in all of journalism: the made-for-TV press conference.

I'm not going to say I loathe local TV newspeople, but if one of them were on fire and I had a full bladder, I'd still run off and find a urinal.

It's not that they're bad people, per se. On a one-on-one basis, most of them are quite likable. It's their business that went bad. Regardless of the medium, newsgathering organizations always play on that fine line between informing and entertaining. If you walk it properly, there's a nice balance: hard-hitting investigative stuff mixed with breaking news tossed alongside human interest features—and, of course, the comics. Some meat. Some potatoes. Some veggies. Some ice cream. Good meal.

But somewhere in the race for ratings—that great quest to find and titillate the lowest common denominator—local TV news had crossed a threshold where the desire to entertain swamped the need to inform. Some of the old-timers mourned it. The younger generation didn't seem to know any better. They were trained to go somewhere, get their sound bites, find their visuals, acquire the bare minimum of information needed to do a stand-up, and then get out. Giving people ten-second blurbs and quickly flashed images may satisfy some simian urge to marvel at shiny things. But I'm not sure it served any real purpose beyond voyeurism.

Mostly, I found it abhorrent that people still called them "journalists," because that's not really what they were. Any group of people who collectively worried about their hair that much could not truly be classified as journalists. They were performers.

And press conferences—which had once been meant for the press and the press only—had become more like public performances, what with the all-news channels often carrying them live. Everyone was cognizant of being on stage, under the glare of the klieg lights and the eye of the wider world, and acted accordingly. The reporters asked questions meant to show how smart they were or demonstrate how beautiful they sounded. The sources, leery of verbal slipups, stuck to the script, which reduced them to automatons whose words and actions would seldom get them confused with real human beings.

The actual conveying of information—or, heaven forbid, real

understanding of an issue—was, at best, a byproduct of the whole show. If you, as a reporter, wanted such things, you had to wait until the lights went off and the cameras were being packed up and hope you could get your source alone for a real conversation, however unlikely that was.

But I could tell from the way the chief's motorcade of SUVs pulled up to the press conference—lights flashing, sirens blaring—that wasn't going to happen this time. This was all about the show. The chief rolled out the passenger side of his truck in full dress uniform and made great display of placing his hat atop his full head of dyed-black hair, about which he was infamously vain.

Behind the chief, disembarking from the rear door, was a woman who had to be Rhonda Byers. She had a matronly, thick-ankled look about her and was dressed in a proper, slate-gray churchgoing suit and high heels that just had to be killing her feet.

She was quickly joined by a black man with no discernible neck, who took her arm. They were flanked by police officers, who helped her wobble toward the makeshift podium. The cameras ate it up, of course—the stricken wife, bravely doing what had to be done for her missing husband.

The cops finished steering Mrs. Byers toward the microphones, where she stood, still holding on to Mr. No Neck's arm.

"Who's the guy Mrs. Byers is leaning against?" I asked Tommy.

"Denardo Webster," he said.

"And that is . . ."

"Windy's chief of staff," Tommy said.

Matos strode up to the microphones, appropriately grim-faced, clutching a photo and a small note card, because apparently he couldn't remember his lines.

"It is my unfortunate duty to report the disappearance of Councilman Wendell A. Byers Jr.," Matos read from his card. "Mr. Byers was last seen in his home Sunday night around sixteen hundred hours"—you had to love it when cops used military time—"by his loving wife, Mrs. Rhonda Byers. We have reason to suspect a crime or crimes may have been committed and we are asking the public's help in locating Councilman Byers. Anyone who sees this man is urged to call our tips hotline."

With his hand trembling just slightly, Matos held up a picture of Byers. The cameras zoomed in. It was marvelous theater.

"There is no cause for the general public to be alarmed, as we believe the councilman's disappearance may have been politically motivated." Matos continued reading. "We are currently investigating whether a crime or crimes occurred and are bringing the full resources of the Newark Police Department and the Essex County Prosecutor's Office to bear in our investigation."

Matos put the card in the breast pocket of his jacket, then half turned his body so he could look at Rhonda Byers.

"Mrs. Byers would now like to make a brief statement," he said.

This was the moment the cameras were really waiting for, of course. There was no better sound bite on a missing person story than a distraught family member pleading for the return of their loved one, especially when they started blubbering all over the place and needed comforting. Big, emotional displays always played well at six and eleven.

But Mrs. Byers wasn't going to give that to them. She was actually quite composed under the circumstances.

"Thank you for coming," she said, in a voice that came across as strong, even authoritarian. "I would like to make a public plea to anyone who has seen my husband or anyone who knows anything about his disappearance: please, please help us bring Wendell home. He is a husband and a father and he needs to be back where he belongs, serving his community. Thank you."

With that, she stepped away from the podium. I had to admit, I was impressed. She had natural stage presence and the practiced delivery of someone who was accustomed to addressing a large group. I could instantly imagine her speaking before her church congregation, telling parishioners that the Ladies' Fellowship Group was holding its Tuesday night Bible reading on Thursday this week. And unlike her husband, who would have babbled on and made something of a fool of himself, she knew how to stand up, say what needed to be said, then step aside. She was clearly the brains of the Byers family.

Matos took back the podium.

"At this time," he said, "I will take any questions . . ."

The hairdos all shouted at once; a perfect beginning to a question-and-answer phase was a breathtaking exchange of non-information, delivered in fluent copese.

Was the councilman forcefully kidnapped?

"It's too early in our investigation to answer that question. All I can say is we have reason to suspect a crime or crimes may have occurred."

Why do you suspect that?

"We have information to indicate foul play was involved, but I can't get into specifics at this time."

Why do you believe it was politically motivated?

"We are not ready to discuss possible motives at this time. But we want to stress we believe there is no danger to the general public. Our officers are investigating any and all leads and are developing more information as the investigation progresses."

Do you believe the councilman may have been harmed?

"We have not reached any conclusions on that subject. I have to stress, this is an ongoing investigation."

How is the family doing?

"The councilman's family is doing a lot of praying. No more questions please."

Always good to end with God. Matos stepped quickly away from the podium. The cameras immediately swarmed Rhonda Byers to get the footage of her being escorted away by No-Neck Webster, which was perfect: it gave Tommy and me a chance to get the chief on the side for a little off-camera time. But the chief was striding quickly toward his SUV and didn't appear to be in the mood to stop.

"Chief, I'm told you guys found blood at his house," Tommy said in a low voice so the clueless TV people couldn't hear it.

"You didn't get that from me," Matos said, still walking.

"You gotten any ransom demands or anything like that?" I asked.

"If I did," he growled as he climbed into his SUV, "I sure wouldn't tell *you*."

He slammed the door, and the truck quickly pulled away.

I was about to find an excuse to depart—maybe something about how hanging around TV people makes me nauseous—when my phone provided me one. Beethoven's Fifth began its signature "du du du duuuuuh" in my pocket. Tommy raised an eyebrow at me.

"Szanto," I said. "A man like that needs his own ringtone."

"A man like that needs a haircut and eyebrow tweezing," Tommy corrected me.

"Well, that didn't come with the phone, so the ringtone will have to do," I said. "Give me a shout later, okay?"

"Got it. Buy yourself some ties that are a little less Republican in the meantime, okay?"

I smiled and flipped him off as I walked away, then brought the phone to my ear.

"*Eagle-Examiner* reporter Carter Ross here," I said, oozing cheer. "How may I help you?"

"One, stop being a wiseass," Szanto retorted. "Two, I want you to find that charm bracelet."

"Excuse me?" I said.

"I want you to get Sweet Thang her charm bracelet back. That's your new assignment."

"Ooookay," I said. "I'm officially confused here. I thought I was supposed to be investigating the disappearance of a public official."

Even over the phone, I could hear the sound of molars mashing against each other. Szanto made a noise that came from somewhere deep in his chest and began speaking deliberately.

"Sweet Thang called Daddy. Daddy called Brodie," he said. "You figure it out."

"And Windy Byers?"

"Wherever he is, he can wait."

"Boss, do you really—"

"Dammit!" Szanto exploded. "If you don't find that charm bracelet, you're going to be covering Girl Scout meetings in Hunterdon County for the rest of your career! Are we clear?"

And naturally he hung up before I could answer.

"Once again," I said, "nice chatting with you."

I went back to my Malibu to think for a few minutes, trying to help my brain ease through the shift to my new assignment. Ordinarily, one of the things I like about my job is that I never know where a day is going to take me. I just wish this day could make up its mind.

I rang Sweet Thang's cell phone—the first one, not the second one—to see if she was making progress but got her voice mail, on which she sounded even more bubbly than in real life, if such thing was possible.

"Hey, it's Carter," I said. "Call me."

Then, because I didn't know what else to do—and because it was only around the corner—I scooted over to Akilah's burned-out house, just to snoop around.

I climbed the front steps, thinking of all the hopes Akilah once had for the place, all of which had burned up along with those two precious kids. There was no telling how much of what Akilah had told us was a lie—twenty percent? fifty? seventy?—but there had to be at least some shred of truth in her story. She had made a grab for the American Dream, and somewhere along the way it became a Newark Nightmare.

"Hello?" I said as I entered. "Anyone here?"

There wasn't, of course. But I had to check, in case squatters had moved in already. As a rule, squatters are like large spiders: they frighten you a little bit, but chances are they're a lot more scared of you than you are of them. They were, by and large, harmless.

With the coast clear, I proceeded upstairs, where I was looking for . . . what exactly? I didn't know. I was hoping I'd know when I found it.

Assuming the floor didn't collapse on me first. And given the structural damage the house sustained in the fire, that was always a possibility. So I walked as gingerly as possible. The first doorway I encountered appeared to lead to a guest room. It was fairly well toasted, and the furniture had been tossed—the fire department often turned things over to make sure there were no embers hiding underneath.

The children's bedroom was pretty bad, too. And I could feel my throat tighten when I saw the boys' bunk bed. They should have spent a childhood in that room, whispering all their hopes to one another with the lights out—the older boy in the top bunk, the younger boy on bottom—figuring out the world one hushed conversation at a time. I walked out of the room quickly, hoping the sick feeling in my stomach would subside.

It didn't, mostly because my next stop was the master bedroom, Akilah's room, which looked like it had been the scene of an inferno. The ceiling had been painted black by smoke, and the fire burned clear through to the roof in spots. The side of the room closest to the street was particularly charcoaled.

Akilah's bed was strewn in several pieces—again, fire department handiwork—but the dresser with the TV the kids had been watching was basically untouched. In the far corner of the room, I saw an empty bag of Cheetos. Akilah had mentioned she left the boys with snacks. So that was their last meal. A bag of Cheetos.

As I mulled over the injustice of that, something else occurred to me: all the rooms had been burned to some degree. I had covered enough fires in my career to know that was unusual. Accidental fires start in one place—a short circuit in a wall, a cigarette butt in a couch, a toaster in a kitchen—and the damage spreads out from that central spot. In this case, the damage seemed to be all over, like it had started in multiple places at once.

Which meant this fire wasn't an accident.

Arson. Of course it was arson. I thought about my first impression when I saw the house, how surprised I had been to see it wasn't a ratty old tenement, like all the other Newark fires I wrote about. The new houses seldom burn. I should have known then it was arson.

The only real question was who struck the match. Akilah Harris? I knew she was a liar and a thief already. Still, it was a pretty big leap from there to murdering your own kids, right? But if not her, then who?

I was so lost in my thoughts, I almost didn't hear the noise coming from downstairs. A door opening? Footsteps?

I went quickly to the top of the stairs.

"Hello?" I shouted.

No response. But I did see a quick glimpse of someone stealing out the back door. It took me a moment to process it—perhaps a moment too long—but then it struck me:

It was Akilah Harris.

For years Primo concentrated on home rehabs. It was what he knew, what he was good at. He had his scam. He worked it. The money flowed.

But it wasn't enough. It was never enough. Primo always found himself yearning for more, but he was ultimately hamstrung by economics: the exponential growth in his business was only possible for so long. Without outside money, he could keep five, maybe ten, houses going at any time. Any more than that and he started having cash flow problems.

It was all about financing. Merely reinvesting his own profits was only going to get Primo so far. Major developers needed major financing—big loans that allowed them to leverage thousands of dollars of assets into millions of dollars of liquidity. It was their lifeblood.

The problem was, no one with serious cash was looking to throw money at someone like Primo. Home rehabbers were seen as unshaven hicks in pickup trucks, fly-by-nighters who might just chuck it all and go fishing. Their trade was considered grubby, unglamorous, and, most damningly, untrustworthy.

No, the venture capitalists and investment bankers were looking for the new home builders. They wanted the beautiful renderings of the four-hundred-thousand-square-foot mixed-use retail/residential projects with the 240-unit condominium project next door. They wanted 3-D models complete with the little cars in the parking lots, four-color brochures printed on glossy paper, builders who had corporate offices and a professional feel. They wanted something they could sell with a straight face to their clients.

Yes, Primo had to get into new construction if he was to be taken seriously. Still, it was a very different business from rehabbing. And it brought with it a new layer of complexity. There were permits, licenses, a thousand different codes and guidelines governing everything from sewer hookups to the width of a stairwell tread.

It was all new for Primo. The rehab business was almost totally unregulated: it was virtually impossible to draw up any kind of ordinance that reined in the activities of a professional house flipper yet still made it possible for Joe Fixit to do renovations on his house. Legally, you couldn't write a law that separated the two.

New home construction was different. Especially in a crowded state like New Jersey, every aspect was regulated and then overregulated. And it could quickly get you wrapped up in more red tape than you'd ever seen. In Newark's City Hall they used industrial-sized spools of the stuff.

Some folks liked to blame the City Hall workers for this, perpetuating the myth of the lazy government employee. But that was absurd, akin to blaming a single tree because you couldn't get through a forest. The truth was, Newark had been ruled by a succession of political machines for decades. Blacks, Italians, Irish, Jews—they all took their turns. And each machine contributed its own patronage hiring, adding one civil service position at a time until it created a bureaucracy that had become baffling even to the bureaucrats.

It frustrated Primo endlessly at first. But then he finally figured out the secret: to get through it, you needed to have a friend on the inside, someone who could pick up a phone and get the governmental mountain to move with a single word.

The only real issue was making sure you found the right friend.

CHAPTER 4

I descended the staircase in three long strides and a jump, hitting the landing with both feet and bolting out the door. If I had given it a second's thought, I probably wouldn't have gone after her. Much like the proverbial dog chasing the car, I wouldn't know what to do if I caught her.

But I wasn't thinking at that point, just reacting. I burst into the backyard, which was small and fenced in on three sides. Akilah had chosen to go over the back fence and was just getting down the other side.

"Akilah, wait!" I shouted, which was probably stupid. If she felt like talking to me, she wouldn't be making like this was the Urban Steeplechase World Championships. She sprinted through a narrow alleyway toward the front of the houses on the next street.

I tore off after her, more or less throwing myself over the back fence, showing all the grace of a wounded elephant. I landed awkwardly, stumbling as my ankle buckled but, thankfully, did not give way. I was able to right myself, then follow her down the alley into the next street.

I emerged in time to see Akilah rounding a corner and set my legs churning. In a game of chase, she had some advantages: this was her neighborhood, not mine; she was younger and thinner;

and she was probably more motivated. But I still had longer legs and kept in decent enough shape from my regular—okay, semiregular—workouts that I could run a six-minute mile. So I knew I could reel her in. Eventually.

But I soon realized this wasn't going to be a footrace, rather hide-and-seek. As I rounded the next corner, I caught a fleeting glance of her turning into a hulking brick apartment building. I followed her through a propped-open door into a large once-impressive lobby with marble floors and a chandelier hanging overhead. Straight in front of me, up a short flight of steps, was an elevator. But the numbered lights above it told me it was already on the fifth floor. No way Akilah had managed to go up that far in the fifteen seconds she had been inside.

Stairs. She had gone for the stairs. I found them to the left of the elevator shaft and shoved open the door. I could hear someone several flights away, running upward, panting.

"Akilah, I just want to talk," I yelled as I launched up after her, taking steps three at a time. I could tell I was gaining ground. From above me, I heard a fire door opening. But which one? Fourth floor? Fifth? My thighs were burning by the time I got to the fourth floor and peeked out into the hallway. No Akilah. I went back to the stairs and galloped up another flight, leaning out the door for another look. This time I spied Akilah's small body disappearing out a window at the end of a hallway onto a fire escape.

She took the time to shut the window, which was getting stuck on the layers of flaking paint that all but inhibited its function. I reached the windowsill, heaved the glass back open with one shove—it's not my fault I'm bigger and stronger than her—and rolled out.

I was surprised to find her still on the fire escape when I got there.

I was somewhat less surprised to find she had pulled a knife.

I righted myself. We were perhaps ten feet apart. The knife

didn't scare me too much. But being five stories up sure did. The platform was made of that metal grating you can see through—I *hate* that stuff—and I fought a brief wave of panic as I realized I was sixty feet in the air on a rickety fire escape that probably hadn't passed inspection in my lifetime.

"Don't come closer," she said wildly, slashing the air with the knife. "I'll cut you."

"Easy, easy," I said. "Just take it easy."

The knife was a threat but, truthfully, not much of one. Akilah weighed perhaps a hundred pounds and had a wingspan at least a foot shorter than mine. In order to really hurt someone with a knife, you have to either catch them off guard or overpower them physically—neither of which was going to happen here. Still, I didn't want to get too close, putting us at something of an impasse.

"Stay right there!" she shrieked. "Don't come no closer."

"Okay. It's okay," I said, trying to make my voice sound calm. "No one's going anywhere. We can just talk."

"You don't know nothing," she said. "You don't know nothing about my problems. You don't have a clue."

"Just relax, honey," I said. But she wasn't listening.

"This guy, he's coming to get me. He burned down my house and now he's trying to kill me just like he killed my babies."

"Akilah, I've got no idea what you're—"

"He's crazy. Just crazy. He killed Boo. He killed my babies. He killed them! He killed them!"

"Akilah," I said forcefully. "Listen to me: I'm not going to hurt you. I just want Sweet Thang's jewelry back, okay?"

I thought that would relax her—the docile white boy was only on a crusade for a harmless little charm bracelet. Instead, she stared back at me in something beyond horror.

"You work for him!" she shrieked. "Oh, my God, you work for him!"

She turned and tore off down the fire escape, jumping down

the steps instead of running down, shaking the entire structure in a way that made the bottom of my stomach feel like the top. A headline immediately flashed in my head: EAGLE-EXAMINER REPORTER PLUMMETS TO DEATH WHILE CHASING CHARM BRACELET. I gripped onto the side of the building, scratching at the brick to get a handhold, sure the entire rig was going to peel off the side.

But it held. Meanwhile, my panic cost me several seconds. By the time I recovered and willed myself to look down—did I mention I *hate* those see-through grates?—Akilah had reached the end of the fire escape and, not bothering with the ladder, leaped the final dozen feet down to the alley. She hit the ground and rolled, like a seasoned stuntman, then popped up quickly and rounded the corner.

I thought about going after her. I could have probably chased her down again. But then what? She threatens me with the knife, she raves some more, we reach another impasse.

"Akilah!" I yelled in desperation. "I just want the charm bracelet!"

But she was already gone.

I inched over to the window, tossed it open, and happily rolled back inside, grateful to once again have solid subfloor under my feet. I sat down to catch my breath, feeling the lactic acid in my legs. Meanwhile, bits of our conversation—if you could call it that—were playing back through my head.

This guy, he's coming to get me . . .

He burned down my house and now he's trying to kill me . . .

He killed Boo. He killed my babies . . .

You work for him . . . Oh, my God, you work for him!

As I rubbed my thighs and tried to figure out what was going on, I was certain of only one thing: I still had a lot to learn.

When my heart rate finally returned to merely dangerous levels, I lifted myself off the floor and rode down in the elevator—no more stairs for me, thanks. I was back to the warmth and safety of my Malibu when the phone rang. The number that flashed up was listed in my phone as "Office Incoming."

"Carter Ross," I said.

"You are despicable," I heard in return.

"Hi, Tina," I said. "How's the weather where you are?"

"Angry with a ninety percent chance of I'm-going-to-kick-your-ass," she said. "I want you to imagine something. Can you do that for me?"

"I think so."

"Imagine you're in the eleven A.M. story meeting and you're the city editor. You do know what the eleven A.M. meeting is, right?"

"A bunch of editors gather around a conference table and decide how they're going to ruin the next day's paper?"

"You got it. Now, imagine you're the city editor, and a big story has broken in . . . the city. Are you with me so far?"

"I think so," I ventured.

I felt like there was a great horned owl winging overhead and I was a small burrowing animal, trying to scurry through a field, scared out of my wee rodent brain, unsure where or when the attack would come, hoping against hope that I could make it to safety.

"Okay, now you're being a good little city editor, trying to plan your coverage. And you happen to ask, 'What's our investigative reporter Carter Ross contributing to this?' Can you imagine asking that question?"

The bird was circling overhead now, and I felt my weak, furry legs scrambling frantically, uselessly. The field was too big. I was too small. My tail kept getting snagged in the tall grasses. I could hear the beating of wings getting closer.

"Why would I ask a question about what I'm doing?" I said, futilely trying to stall the attack. "Don't I already know what I'm doing?"

"No, you're not Carter Ross. Try to keep up: you're the city editor," she replied patiently, in that kindergarten-teacher voice most women over the age of thirty can summon instantly. "Remember, you have to imagine you're the city editor?"

"Oh, right."

"Okay, good. So anyhow, you've asked this question about Carter Ross. And do you know what the reply is?"

"Am I supposed to know this one?" I asked.

"No, not yet."

"Okay, then no."

Where was the edge of the woods, anyway? Where was my den, my nest, or whatever home I had managed to scrape out for myself with my continuously growing rodent incisors? Did the mouse *ever* win in those nature shows?

"The reply you get," Tina said, sighing dramatically, and now I knew the attack was coming—the owl was swooping down from the left. No, the right! It's too late for Mr. Mouse! Too late!

"The reply," she continued, "is that Carter Ross, the investigative reporter, is off chasing after a young girl's charm bracelet—although, really, he's probably just chasing the young girl. Ha ha ha.

"Now," Tina said, "how would that make you feel, Mr. City Editor?"

The owl's talons closed around my tiny, trembling body and I was lifted off the ground, my meager *eep-eep-eep* cry all but drowned out by the victorious hooting as the owl flapped skyward.

"I don't know," I said meekly. "Since we're pretty clearly talking about you, why don't you go ahead and tell me how it made *you* feel."

"Well, let's see here," she said, sarcastically pretending that she was suddenly considering the question. "As an editor at this paper, I feel it's a pretty foolish waste of resources that we've got major news breaking and you volunteered to go play Superhero getting Sweet Thang's charm bracelet back . . ."

"I didn't volun . . ." I tried to interrupt, but by this point her voice was too loud for her to possibly hear me. She had her prey secured and was bragging to the other owls nearby that she had caught a meal.

". . . and as a woman, I feel pretty foolish for having ever occasionally professed that I may have slightly cared for you. Because if you're that much of an idiot, there's no way you meet the minimum IQ requirement to be my child's sperm donor daddy anyway. So how did it make me feel? Frustrated, sad, and angry. Yes, I would say that would be a start."

Her volume had reached a level where it was no longer necessary to hold the phone to my ear—arm's length was as close as I dared go without risking permanent hearing loss. I kept it there until I was fairly certain the screaming was over.

"Are you done?" I asked.

"Probably not," she spat back.

I sighed.

"Look, Tina, what exactly is this all about?"

"What is *what* about?"

"This whole jealousy thing," I said. "I mean, let's just say—and this is strictly for sake of argument—that I wanted to date Sweet Thang. Or let's say it's not Sweet Thang, because I realize there are complications there. Let's say it's some other woman you don't know and will never meet. So long as it doesn't lower my sperm count, what's it to you?"

There was a pause. Was the great bird considering releasing its quarry? Would I be reunited with my earth-dwelling, grub-eating clan of fellow furry friends?

Uh, no.

"I . . . can't . . . *believe* . . . you," she finally said, enunciating each word like she was teaching an ESL class. "You didn't really just do that, did you?"

"Do . . . what?"

"You just tried to have The Conversation with me *over the*

phone?" she said, capitalizing the *t* and *c* with her tone. "Now it appears you couldn't be my child's sperm donor because you are a less evolved species. Who tries to have The Conversation with a woman over the phone?"

"I, ahh, was just asking a ques—"

"That's it," she declared. "You're taking me to dinner tonight. You can't possibly expect me to have The Conversation at any less than a four-star restaurant. Pick me up at eight."

And that was it. Had I, in fact, escaped? Was I free to continue my burrowing and gnawing? For the moment, I must say I felt safer. Warmer.

Which probably just meant I was already in the owl's stomach.

For whatever Tina's thoughts on the absurdity of my task, I was still under orders to track down a charm bracelet—and, I must say, was getting nowhere in a hurry on my assignment.

Asking Akilah directly was out of the question, unless I was ready to commit to some serious cardio training or, at the very least, buy a stun gun. I tried reaching Sweet Thang on her cell phone—both of them—to see how she was coming along with Mrs. Harris. But when "Thang, Sweet" and "Thang, Sweet 2" went to voice mail, I hung up rather than leave a message, slightly annoyed I hadn't heard from her yet.

Not knowing what else to try, I called Tee to see if he was getting any traction.

"Yeah," Tee said. His typical salutation.

"Hi," I said. "It's your white friend."

"You know, I do have two of them, so you're going to have to narrow it down."

"You're cheating on me? I had no idea. Who's this other honky in your life and why have you never spoken of him before?"

"Well, I don't really consider him all that white. Not like you," Tee said. "He's a bit of a wigga."

"I'm sorry, a wigga?"

"Yeah, a white dude who act like a nig—"

"Got it," I said quickly. "Anyhow, talk to me. Tell me some good news."

"Well, I made some calls."

"And?"

"It look like Maury don't got too many friends. At least he ain't got the same friends I do."

"Oh" is all I could think to reply.

"I reached out to brothers who know everyone, and they still don't know Maury," Tee said. "I mean, everyone knows him, but nobody *knows* him. Not well enough to make an introduction, you know what I'm saying?"

"Yeah, I think I got you," I said. "Well, thanks for the effort."

"Yeah, no problem," he said. And I was about to bid him farewell and hang up, except he added: "How bad you need this jewelry back, anyway?"

I thought about those Hunterdon County Girl Scout meetings with which Szanto threatened me. After the second or third year, the annual cookie sale story was going to get pretty stale. Not even I liked Samoas that much.

"I would say I'm pretty desperate at this point."

"So you got an emergency, huh?"

"I do."

"All right," Tee said. "I didn't want to do this. But if you say it's an emergency, I'll break the glass."

"Shatter it."

"I mean, I ain't got no choice."

"None."

"Okay, I'll get right on it."

"Super."

"Because it's an emergency."

"Absolutely."

"Then I have to."

"Right."

"Okay then. I'm going to do it."

"Fantastic," I said, then just had to ask: "Tee, what are we talking about?"

He paused dramatically.

"I'm going to call Mrs. Jamison," he said at last.

Tee always referred to his wife as "Mrs. Jamison." He tries to lead people to believe he's just being cute. But, really, he's afraid of her.

"And what's Mrs. Jamison going to be able to do?" I asked.

"You haven't met her yet, have you," he said, more as a statement than a question.

"No."

"Wait until you meet her. You'll understand."

"She's that tough?"

"She's so tough she can slam a revolving door," Tee said ominously.

"Well, then I'll be glad she's on our side."

"Meet us outside Maury's in fifteen minutes," Tee instructed me.

"You sure she'll do it?"

"I'm a *man.* My woman do what I *tell* her to do."

"In other words, you already called her and she already said yes," I said.

"Exactly. See you in fifteen. Don't be late. Mrs. Jamison don't like waiting."

By the time I made it to Maury's and parked, Tee was already out front, dressed in camouflage wind pants and a puffy black jacket. Tee is about five feet ten. The woman standing next to him was nearly as tall, with tight blue jeans, a New York Knicks jacket, and her hair pulled back in a tight ponytail. She looked like she could boil water just by staring at it.

"Hey Tee, thanks for doing this," I said, shaking his hand then turning to his wife. "You must be Mrs. Jamison. I'm Carter Ross. Nice to meet you."

I reached out my hand to shake with her, but she left it hanging there like she was trying to figure out if I carried a deadly strain of avian flu.

"So, you lost a necklace or something?" she said. She had a big, resonant voice. I was betting a choir somewhere would have been thrilled to have her in their alto section.

"Well, it's actually a whole lot of jewelry—an entire jewelry box full," I said. "But the one piece I really have to get back is a charm bracelet."

"And this belongs to your . . . girlfriend, is that right?"

Out of the corner of my eye, I saw Tee nodding.

"Yes, ma'am, my girl . . . girlfriend."

"And you're planning on marrying this girl?" she demanded. Again, I saw Tee nodding, this time with more force.

"Yes, yes, ma'am."

"That's good. Because I don't want to be doing no favors so you can get some cheap booty call. I do not condone intercourse unless it is going to lead to marriage. You hear me?"

"Yes, ma'am," I said, then willed myself to sound more convincing. "I'm going to make an honest woman out of her, just as soon as I save up enough money for a nice ring. I don't want to make it some cheap thing. I was thinking two, three carats."

"You hear that, Reginald! He's going to get her a *nice* ring," Mrs. Jamison boomed, backhanding Tee in the gut. Tee's stomach, much like the rest of him, is pretty solid beef. But he still grimaced a little.

"I swear to you, this man, if I hadn't told him exactly what to get, he would have gotten me a ring out of a cereal box," Mrs. Jamison continued, then stuck out her left hand so I could inspect it. "As you see, he came though in the end, didn't you, baby?"

She gave Tee a quick, full-lipped kiss. Tee appeared grateful he wasn't getting smacked again.

"C'mon," she said, as she headed toward the entrance. "Let me do the talking."

Maury's Pawnshop, Check-Cashing, and Payday Loans was what you might expect from a hock shop buried deep in a Newark neighborhood, only more disgusting. In front of the semishattered glass door were three concrete steps, each crumbling at the edges. A WE'LL BE BACK sign with a clock face on it was attached to the inside of the door, but the plastic hands had been ripped off, leaving one to guess when, if ever, someone might return; or, for that matter, why they'd want to.

Inside the cramped waiting area, I got the distinct impression little about the place had been updated since the original Maury opened shop—sometime shortly after he returned from the war, judging from the décor. It had that Norman Rockwell feel to it, except this was the version Rockwell painted when he was old, bitter, and off his antidepressants.

The faux wood paneling had several fist-sized dents in it. The linoleum had been scuffed straight through to the plywood floorboard in spots. In one corner, there was a gumball machine without a lid—and, therefore, without gumballs. The chrome-framed chairs bolted to the floor in the middle of the room had all lost their arms, and their seat cushions had taken a beating through the years. On the wall, a poster produced by the American Pawn-Owners Association—featuring a smiling, Stepford Wife–looking woman saying, "We buy and sell your finest previously owned merchandise"—had been thoroughly and profanely vandalized.

The only things I guessed were not purchased by the original Maury himself were the NO WEAPONS ALLOWED, EXCEPT FOR SALE sign and the two-inch-thick bulletproof glass that now covered the space between the countertop and the ceiling. The glass apparently worked, because I counted six bullet-sized pockmarks peppered across the front.

Behind the glass, a pudgy, indolent-looking Hispanic guy was engrossed in a Mexican soap opera, the kind whose plotline seemed to consist almost entirely of buxom women showing their cleavage to swarthy men with well-groomed mustaches.

"Excuse me," Mrs. Jamison said, and not timidly. Still, the man didn't budge. His full attention was fixed on a woman wearing a red dress that showed off approximately seventy-five percent of the total surface area of her breasts.

"ExCUSE me," Mrs. Jamison said again, this time loud enough to penetrate the bulletproof glass. The man tore his eyes away from the screen and turned toward us. A small piece of Plexiglas covered a circular cluster of airholes that served as the only means of communicating with the outside world. He slid it open to better hear us—not that Mrs. Jamison had trouble projecting.

"Hi, sugar, what's your name?" Mrs. Jamison said.

The man looked alarmed—this was not how his interactions with customers typically began—but he answered, "Pedro."

"Pedro, I'm here to see Maury," Mrs. Jamison informed him.

"Who are you?"

"You tell him Mrs. Jamison is here to see him."

She said it so matter-of-factly—as if Maury would know exactly why she had come calling—that Pedro got off his chair and went into the back room. Mrs. Jamison rested her elbow on a small ledge in front of the bulletproof glass, quite secure in her ownership of the space around her.

I scanned the store a little more. The glass was divided into four cubbyholes—two for clerks and two to display some of the wares for sale—a mix of guns, electronics, and some serious bling.

Tee once explained to me that bling served a dual role in the hood. It was a status symbol, of course. But it was also a form of insurance, a means to sock away money during the good times so you were never flat busted when things went bad. Example: a guy flush from some gainful venture lays out $9,000 for a secondhand diamond necklace. He does this so he can enjoy and display the fruits of his success. But he also acquires it in case his next venture goes bad—that way he's got seed money to start all over again. Sure, Maury or his numerous competitors might only give the guy a $7,000 return on his "investment." But that's a worthwhile deal for our urban entrepreneur. And, best of all, his safety net is never farther away than his neck.

Tee, who seemed to be reading my mind, muttered, "Man, some nice insurance policies here."

"Reginald!" Mrs. Jamison said sharply. "We didn't come here to shop."

"I was just lookin'," Tee said, chastened.

Pedro returned and mumbled, "He's no here."

I was about to call balderdash on Pedro—how could you say he's not here when you spent three minutes talking to him?—but as soon as I drew the breath to speak, Mrs. Jamison put her hand on my arm. She was in control of this situation.

"Pedro, you and I have just met, but I fear we're off to a bad start," she said in a voice that perfectly straddled the line between calm and scary. "Surely, a man of your intelligence understands all men must build relationships based on mutual trust. When you betray that trust so early in a relationship, it really makes me question your decency as a man. Is that really how you want to be known, Pedro? Is that what you want put out into the universe?"

Pedro's eyes were starting to grow wide. I wasn't sure how much of the actual language he was absorbing. But, as linguists have repeatedly proven, nonverbal cues are every bit as important as verbal ones in conveying meaning. And Mrs. Jamison's non-verbals were nearly as loud as her verbals.

"Now," she continued, "you have a mama, don't you, Pedro?"

Pedro nodded.

"Did your mama raise you to lie to another woman like that?"

Pedro shook his head.

"Okay, Pedro, then let's try this again. I'm here to see Maury, and I ain't going nowhere until I do. So why don't you run back to that little room and tell him that."

She made a shooing motion with her hand. Pedro's feet stayed rooted, but the uncertainty was all over his face. Did he defy his boss? Or piss off this crazy lady who was babbling in that scary voice about who-the-hell-knows-what?

Mrs. Jamison gave him some gentle nudging.

"Pedro, I don't want to have to raise my voice. Believe me, you do *not* want me to raise my voice," she said. "So let me make this clear to you: you're in that little box right now. But you're going to have to come out eventually. And when you do, I'm going to rip you in half with my bare hands."

Without pausing, Pedro slid off his chair and walked quickly toward the back room.

The man who emerged from the office moments later was not Pedro. It had to be Maury. He was a tall, gangly middle-aged black man who appeared to have stepped straight out of 1981, with a head full of Jheri curls—in all their greasy, ringletted glory—and a smile that included at least three gold-capped teeth. I wondered, amid all this pawned merchandise, if the caps were previously owned, too. I also wondered where he kept his Rick James albums.

He opened the Plexiglas.

"I'm told by my assistant there are some unruly customers out front?" he said, but he had a fairly prominent lisp, so it came out as, "I'm told by my athithtant there are thome unruly cuthtomerth out front."

"You must be Maury," Mrs. Jamison said.

"That'th what people call me."

"I'm Mrs. Jamison."

"Yeah? Tho?"

Maury peered at us over the top of his dark glasses, Jheri curls just barely brushing against the jacket of his purple—yes, purple—three-piece suit. Underneath was a pressed white shirt with a banded collar, a perfect accent for an outfit that might be described as priest-meets-pimp. I couldn't see what he was wearing on his feet, but I was guessing there were some two-toned shoes down there. Maury was clearly a man with that kind of style.

"You have a piece of jewelry that belongs to this gentleman's fiancée," Mrs. Jamison said. So now Sweet Thang was my fiancée? Tina was going to love that.

"Who thaid that?"

"I'm saying that."

"And who are you again?"

"I'm Mrs. Jamison."

Maury pondered that for a moment, pointed at me, and asked, "Who'th he?"

"This is Mr. Carter Ross. And his fiancée is very unhappy her jewelry was stolen from her."

"Thtolen!" Maury said, as if the mere concept repulsed him.

"Allegedly stolen," Tee interjected.

Mrs. Jamison glared daggers at him.

"What?" he said. "Until something is proven in a court of law, it's just an allegation."

Mrs. Jamison's glare had upgraded to machetes.

"A'ight," Tee said. "I'll shut up now."

Maury wasn't focusing on either of them but rather on the oddity in the room. The white man.

"You a cop or thomething?" he asked.

The question, while clearly tossed in my direction, was handled by my self-appointed spokeswoman, Mrs. Jamison. "He's a newspaper journalist," she said. "He is a top, top editor at the *Eagle-Examiner.*"

Sure I was. Why not? If I was engaged to Sweet Thang, I might as well be a top, top editor. Whatever that was.

"Yeah?" Maury said, sounding impressed.

"Yes and, sugar, believe me, if he don't like you, he'll write an exposé blowing your whole operation out of the water," Mrs. Jamison said. "They'd put your picture in the paper and everything."

I tried to look serious, like I was already planning out how the front page would look. It was, of course, patently unethical to abuse my position as a newspaper reporter to threaten someone like this. But Maury didn't seem like the kind of guy who was going to write a letter of complaint to *Columbia Journalism Review.* And, besides, technically it was Mrs. Jamison abusing my position. That subtlety, I rationalized, absolved me of any wrongdoing.

"Tho what'th thith jewelry I'm thuppothed to have?" Maury asked

"It's a charm bracelet."

I thought I saw some recognition wander briefly across Maury's face.

"I'm not thaying I have anything like that," Maury said. "But if I did, when would I have acquired it?"

"This morning," Mrs. Jamison said.

Maury turned toward the back room and shouted, "Manuel! Manuel, get me that thtuff from earlier today."

Pedro appeared from the back room and said something in Spanish.

"Yeah, yeah, that thtuff," Maury said, and Pedro disappeared again.

"Manuel?" Mrs. Jamison spat. "He told me his name was Pedro."

"It ain't neither," Maury said. "Jutht like my name ain't Maury. You got to keep your ammo-nimity in thith line of work."

I grinned at the apparent mispronunciation and wanted to

ask if he also had to keep his "anonymity," but it wasn't my place to intercede.

"Pedro, you have a truthfulness problem," Mrs. Jamison shouted after him. "We're going to have to talk about that."

Maury again focused his attention on me.

"I mutht thtate for the record, Mr. Roth, thith ethtablithment doeth not traffic in thtolen merchandithe. But there are thome unthcrupulouth people in thith world who may mithreprethent the originth of thome itemth and take advantage of my generouth nature."

Mrs. Jamison arched her right eyebrow, crossed her arms, and let out a perfectly skeptical, "Uh-huh."

"Now, how would you dethcribe thith thtolen merchandithe?"

Again, a question for me. But this time I was going to have to come up with an answer. I had meant to get more specifics about the bracelet, but Sweet Thang wasn't returning my phone calls for some odd reason—where was that girl, anyhow?

So I was on my own. What did Sweet Thang's charm bracelet look like? I knew somewhere in my brain, in the part charged with important tasks like quoting movie passages and song lyrics, there was an excruciatingly detailed description of the charm bracelet—albeit one that was provided between 6:14 and 6:19 earlier that morning, when I was not yet functioning.

I rewound through my day, through my bouncing around Newark, my breakfast with Sweet Thang, my lecherous thoughts while she was in the shower, my hasty nonnewspaper-glancing departure from my own house, my jarring wake-up call, and . . .

There! Just after the jarring wake-up call. I was hearing Sweet Thang's voice in my head now, saying something I wasn't comprehending in the moment. But somehow it had stuck in there, in a small crevice next to the John Cusack *Say Anything* monologue. And I found myself pulling it up with near-perfect recall.

"Well, it's a charm bracelet," I said. "I've never seen it, but she told me about it. Some of the pieces include a sombrero she got in a trip to Puerto Vallarta. There's also a darling little gondola her father brought her back from Venice."

"Excuse me, did you just say 'darling'?" Tee asked.

"Reginald!" Mrs. Jamison scolded. "At least someone *listens* to his woman."

She drew her hand back but did not let it fly. Tee cringed anyway. Maury placed his chin in his hand, giving himself a moment to think about it.

"Thombrero, huh?" he said. "I may have theen thomething like that."

He walked to the back room, Jheri curls bouncing, and returned moments later with a gold charm bracelet suspended between his fingers.

"Thith it?" he asked.

He held it up. It had to be Sweet Thang's. It just looked like something a Vanderbilt coed would own.

"Yeah," I said. "That's it."

"Well, now, thith ith a very rare piethe of fine jewelry we're talking about here," Maury said. "I don't think it'th pothible for me to part with thith piethe for leth than a thouthand dollarth."

"How about you part with that piece and we won't press charges for receiving stolen merchandise," Mrs. Jamison countered. "This gentleman's fiancée is a white girl and she could go to police headquarters and fill out a report and everything. You know how cops like to help white girls."

Maury considered this a moment.

"Hundred buckth."

"Twenty."

"Done," Maury replied, and started hitting numbers on his cash register.

Just like that, I happily parted with a portrait of Andrew Jackson, and Maury slipped Sweet Thang's charm bracelet through the revolving box in the bulletproof glass.

Maury pointed a finger at me.

"Don't try coming back for the retht of it," he warned. "I thtill have to be able to make a living, you know."

Some living. The sheer sleaziness of the place finally overwhelmed me, so I just waved at him as we walked out the shattered front door. He didn't have to worry about me coming back.

I bid the Jamisons farewell, thanking Tee for his assistance and promising his wife one last time I would make an honest woman out of Sweet Thang just as soon as I could find her an engagement ring that would shame the Hope diamond.

As I drove back toward the office, I turned on my radio, tuning it to an all-news station to see if any of my colleagues in the media had learned anything useful about Windy Byers. I didn't have to wait long for the story, which led the top of the hour. The announcer referred to Byers as the "beloved Newark councilman" who hailed from a "Newark political dynasty" and so on. I love it when the radio guys just read from the newspaper. Sometimes you can practically hear the newsprint crinkling under the microphone. The station cut to a clip of the Matos press conference, going for the sound bite about how the Byers family was doing a lot of praying.

I flipped the radio to FM and felt myself frowning. Having successfully retrieved Sweet Thang's charm bracelet—great journalistic triumph that it was—I now presumed I would return to real, actual reporting on the Byers story.

And I didn't know where to start. Reporting can be a bit like exploratory surgery, except you perform it wearing oven mitts and a blindfold. Sometimes you're not even sure what part of the body to cut open. As a general rule, you never know where you're going until you've already been there. I often wished I could start at the end, having already acquired all the necessary hindsight. It would save so much time.

When I arrived in the newsroom, it had that big-story buzz about it. Editors who normally sauntered around like they had no place to go were walking with alacrity. Reporters who might ordinarily be leaning back as they gabbed with sources on the phone were hunched over, hard at work. Buster Hays, resident dinosaur, had three Rolodexes open at the same time, pulling out business cards that were probably older than I was. The forever-silly Tommy Hernandez was staring at his computer screen with a fold between his neatly trimmed eyebrows, perhaps the first time I had seen so much as the slightest crease in his otherwise unworried countenance.

And the beauty of our newsroom was that, like most newsrooms, you could see it all unfolding before you. There were no walls, no partitions, no cubicles to wreck your view—just tightly clustered islands of desks stretching over a sea of open space.

I marched over to mine, which was against a far wall, an auspicious spot whose principal advantage was that it allowed me to see the enemy (editors) approaching from a good distance. My desk had once been used by an old-time city reporter who chain-smoked like Chairman Mao and, as legend had it, quit his job because he refused to comply with the new policy when the newsroom finally went smoke-free in the mid-nineties. The desk sat empty for years after that—to aerate, I assume—but when I moved in, there was still an ashtray sitting atop. I don't smoke, but I kept it there, in memory of my predecessor and as a monument to a bygone time in the history of our industry.

Sadly, the computer sitting on my desk was roughly as old as the ashtray. No one knew the exact age of our terminals: they already qualified as antique when I started at the paper; by now, the only way anyone could figure out how long they had been there was through carbon dating. We were assured they would be replaced just as soon as advertising revenues rebounded. In other words, we had a long wait.

As my machine clicked and rattled to life, I began playing

around with various Windy Byers theories, seeing if I could find one that fit. The police chief said they thought it was "politically motivated," but I was having a hard time digesting that one. Byers was a hack who had been in the game long enough that he knew how to play by the rules and avoid pissing off important people. He had no policy initiatives that could have engendered anyone's ire. It wasn't like he had unpopular or dangerous ideas inasmuch as I'm not sure he had ideas, period.

I could much more easily believe this was the result of some romantic entanglement. But if the spilled blood was to be believed, Byers's disappearance was not a peaceful one—which ruled out the run-off-with-the-girlfriend/boyfriend scenario.

Then again, there was nothing yet to say the blood belonged to Byers. For all we knew at this point, it had another owner. Perhaps Byers was not the kidnapped but the kidnapper, having belted someone over the head, dragged his victim out of the house, and gone on the lam until he could concoct a cover story.

In other words, the blindfold and oven mitts were firmly in place. So I did what any good reporter does when facing such uncertainty: I procrastinated by checking my e-mail.

It was, by and large, the usual mix of urgent messages from our hyperactive HR department (send in your vacation pictures for the company newsletter!); press releases I would never read (the office of a congressman from New Orleans sent me three or four a day because I once wrote a story that contained the word "Louisiana"); and come-ons from that seemingly massive group of African princes who needed but a small loan to claim their long-lost fortunes (doesn't it always take $50,000 to become a multimillionaire?).

I nearly turned away without reading any of them. Except there was one message, which claimed to be sent by "Concerned Citizen," that stood out. It had the subject line "keep digging." Curious, I clicked twice and read:

ms. mcmillan and mr. ross,

i saw your story today in the eagle-examiner on that woman with the two kids. theres a reason you couldnt find the mortgage. there are things going on at the courthouse which if i told you you wouldnt believe. keep digging and youll find it.

im sorry i cant give you my name. but i could get fired for talking to you and i have kids to feed and i need this job.

signed,

a concerned citizen.

I leaned back and reread it. As a reporter, you get anonymous mail all the time. Much of it is nonsensical, rambling, Unabomber-style stuff good for a laugh—and not much else. But every now and then you get something like this that sticks to your ribs. You learn to separate the credible from the crazies, primarily by judging grammar and spelling. Other than the aversion to apostrophes and the e. e. cummings approach to capitalization, this one wasn't bad.

Mostly, it brought back the things that had been gnawing at me since Sweet Thang first called me from the courthouse. Where was that silly mortgage? Who made it disappear? And, perhaps most important, why?

I lifted my eyes from the screen and realized I had allowed myself to get a little too engrossed, which meant I didn't notice Sal Szanto huffing toward me. And now it was too late: 245 pounds of pear-shaped, middle-aged Italian-American editor was already standing over me, close enough I could smell the stale coffee on his breath. So much for being able to see the enemy coming.

Szanto was one of those editors who didn't believe in leaving his office, except in cases of emergency or lunch. As it was now past lunchtime, it could only mean he was in crisis.

"Did you get it?" he asked, without prelude, with an urgency that just made it impossible not to mess with him a little.

"Hi, Sal, nice to see you," I said. "There's something different about you. Did you switch antacid brands?"

"Yeah, yeah. I'm wearing a different deodorant, too. It's called Garbage Guard. They tell me it works great, so why don't you cut the garbage and tell me whether you got the bracelet or not."

"Yeah, I got it."

"Did you give it to her?"

"Not yet."

"Why the hell not?" he demanded.

"Here," I said, fishing the bracelet out of my pocket and dangling it in front of him. "Why don't you give it to her? Go ahead. Be the hero."

Szanto turned to look in the direction of the intern desk pod, a place from which Sweet Thang was, of course, still absent.

"Where is she?"

"I think you're beginning to realize why I haven't given it to her yet," I said.

Szanto swung back toward me, annoyed, what little patience he had long since spent. I don't know what it was, but the more frustrated he got, the more I enjoyed screwing with him.

"Do you know where she is?"

"I assume she's off somewhere looking for her bracelet."

"Did you call her cell?"

"No, Sal, I sent smoke signals which were then relayed by drummer-messengers perched on a series of hilltops," I said. "It's the newest, most sophisticated method of communication yet devised. I don't think humankind will ever come up with anything better."

Szanto drew breath as if he was going to let me have it, then stopped himself.

"Look," he said, sinking into a chair next to me, releasing a huge cloud of java-tinged exhaust. "I just need you to help me out here. You know how fixated Brodie gets about certain things, right?"

"I do."

"He's like one of those little dogs, the little white ones with the black splotches that want to hump your leg all day long," Szanto said. "What do you call those?"

"Jack Russell terrier?"

"Exactly. He's a Jack Russell terrier. And right now, I'm just a lonely ankle, and I've had this dog's tiny little schlong banging into me all day—bang, bang, bang, bang. I mean, can you imagine what kind of day that is?"

"Don't even want to."

"No, really, you don't. Trust me," Szanto said. "Anyhow, the whole reason Brodie is giving me this undue attention is this bracelet. Apparently, Sweet Thang called her daddy crying, and her daddy called Brodie and asked for a favor, and with everything else going on, Brodie still thinks I have nothing better to do than to make sure he can do a favor for his buddy. So if you could please, please just get this girl her bracelet back, and tell her to call her daddy, who can then call Brodie, you'd really be doing *me* a favor."

"Okay, I'll do it just as soon as she walks in the door," I assured him, then turned my attention toward my computer screen, which is International Body Language for "we're done with this conversation and now you can go away."

Except Szanto was acting like he didn't understand it.

"Not soon enough," he said.

"Huh?" I said, still keeping my head down.

"You got to go find her."

"Excuse me?" I said, and looked up at him, trying to effect my best vacant stare, as if I didn't know who he was or what he was talking about.

"Find her. Find Sweet Thang and give her that bracelet."

"You've *got* to be kidding me."

He didn't reply, just grinned—one of his four smiles for the year, so he must have been serious.

"You're not kidding me."

He shook his head.

"Sal, I sent Sweet Thang off on what is probably a dead-end reporting errand to Baxter Terrace," I said. "I called her, at least twice. I don't know why she's not answering her phone. Maybe she stopped at the mall and decided to buy the entire Nordstrom shoe department on her way back in. But she'll be back any second. And when she gets here, I'll give her the bracelet."

Szanto shook his head again.

"Not good enough," he replied. "Look, the sooner you get that bracelet to that girl, the sooner my half-hourly e-mails, phone calls, and just-checking-in visits from Brodie stop. And I just can't take him. I can't take any more of that today."

He clasped his clubbed fingers together in a pleading gesture. His eyes were big and wet, and in a moment of weakness—brought on by an awareness of the abuse I piled on him and a small amount of guilt that at least one of his stomach ulcers probably had my name on it—I agreed.

"Okay." I sighed. "Fine. I'll call you the moment I hand her the bracelet."

"Thanks," Szanto said, raising himself with a grunt from the chair next to me. He clapped me affectionately on the shoulder—another quarterly event—then walked away.

Before committing myself to another Baxter Terrace jaunt, I dialed Sweet Thang's numbers one last time. Both went to voice mail.

I looked at the time on my phone, which read 2:13. She and I departed Jersey City around nine-thirty. If she drove straight to Baxter Terrace, she would have gotten there no later than ten. That meant Sweet Thang and her buoyant personality had spent more than four hours in one of the nation's most depressed public housing projects. It sounded like a reality show gone horribly wrong—instead of *Dancing with the Stars*, it was *Prancing in the Projects.*

There was no telling what had kept her there all that time. It was daylight, so I wasn't concerned about her well-being. Well, okay, I worried about it a little. Mostly, I was just curious: What had she been doing all this time?

I filled my drive thinking about the possibilities. As I walked through the courtyard toward Bertie Harris's apartment, I heard a series of birdcalls—a macaw, a chickadee, and an osprey. Okay, I'm making that up. But it sounded like different birds than last time.

Going through the open portal of Bertie's building, I hiked the three flights up to the landing where I had been so thoroughly stonewalled the night before. I raised my fist to rap on the door but then paused mid-strike, having heard a noise from inside. What was that? Was it . . . laughter? I paused, just to make sure. Yes, laughter, the deep, chuckling kind you hear from two long-time friends who know just how to get each other going.

I also smelled something powerful enough to overcome the natural stench of the projects. Was it . . . baking bread?

I thought about eavesdropping a little more, but I just had to know. I knocked.

"I'll get it," I heard Sweet Thang call.

She opened the door, looking delighted—if a little surprised—to see me.

"Oh, my goodness, hi!" she bubbled. "It's so great of you to come over. We're having the best time! Come on in. I'm just making some banana bread."

I stepped over the threshold feeling a little uncertain, given the rebuke I had experienced the last time I visited. But no, everything had changed. There would be no screaming, no hateful glares, no slamming of furniture. Sweet Thang was here. Baking was happening. A transformation had taken place.

Especially when it came to the apartment's occupant, who was sitting at a card table in the far corner, a coffee mug in front of her, smiling pleasantly. She was older, but it was always hard to tell with black women. I was thirty-two and already had wrinkles. She'd probably be in her casket thirty years from now and still not have any.

As a skilled observer of the obvious, I concluded this had to be Bertie Harris. She and Akilah had the same cheekbones, the same lean build, the same no-nonsense ponytail, the same dark coloring.

"Mrs. Harris, I'm Car—" I started.

"I know who you are," Bertie replied agreeably.

"I'm sorry abou—"

"I know you're sorry about last night. And I'm sorry, too," she said. "Lauren explained to me how it is for a reporter on deadline. You was just trying to do your job."

This had to be the easiest reconciliation in the history of human relations. I ought to have Sweet Thang do my advance work more often.

"Well, please accept my apology all the same," I said.

"You're right," Bertie said to Sweet Thang, who was in the kitchen, "he *is* cute."

"Told you," Sweet Thang chirped back.

As I blushed, Bertie took a sip from her coffee, utterly comfortable with my presence. I tried to relax, still feeling like I didn't quite belong, not wanting to screw up whatever it was Sweet Thang had done to build a trust with this woman.

I wasn't going to sit down until offered a place (we cute boys have manners), nor was I going to take off my jacket (we cute boys aren't presumptuous), so I sneaked a furtive glance around the apartment (we reporters are nosy). The furnishings—a small couch, a recliner, a coffee table, and that folding table—were older and a bit worn. But I had certainly seen worse.

The television that had been blaring *Entertainment Tonight* was still playing but with the sound down. It had to be at least a forty-two-inch screen, which surprised me a little. You don't see many of those in the projects—sad to say, but nice belongings usually get stolen within a week of their arrival. That the TV was still here either meant it had just arrived; the local addicts were too lazy to steal from the third floor; or, more likely, Bertie Harris was so well regarded around here no one messed with her.

In the pictures that were scattered about the place, I saw Akilah with what appeared to be some older brothers and sisters—again, so much for the lonely-orphan story.

"I'm going to leave it in there another few minutes," Sweet Thang announced as she came back into the room and took a seat at the folding table. "The middle is still just a little gooey."

"Mr. Ross, you better marry this girl if you have any sense," Bertie said. "It's not every day you find a woman who can bake."

"Wait until you taste it first," Sweet Thang said.

"I don't need to. I can smell it. It's wonderful."

"I was just lucky you had some soft bananas," Sweet Thang replied. "My recipe doesn't work unless they're good and ripe."

They kept bantering about the subtleties of perfect banana bread and I could only watch in amazement. Here was this woman in the midst of a family tragedy; a woman who, just last night, would have thrown me out her window if she had the strength. Yet she and Sweet Thang were instant buddies.

That was Sweet Thang's gift, one I didn't necessarily have but could at least recognize and appreciate in a fellow reporter. She made people *want* to talk to her.

One of the few traits that I've found universal among *Homo sapiens* is the desire to be understood by other *Homo sapiens*. It's a need that translates across every racial, gender, and socioeconomic barrier. Whether you're talking about the CEO or the janitor, the congressman or the undocumented immigrant, people just want to be listened to. It's why we talk so damn much.

Most of the time, we harbor the suspicion no one is really

paying attention. Or, if they are, they still don't get it. But every once in a while, we bump into someone like Sweet Thang, the rare person who actually makes us feel heard.

I must have been smiling as they jabbered, because Sweet Thang interrupted my inner monologue with a question:

"What's so funny?"

"Nothing," I replied. "I'm just glad you girls are having fun."

"Oh, we've been having a blast," Sweet Thang assured me. "It was just so lucky I came over when I did because it was Bertie's turn to host mah-jongg, but she was short a player and I was able to step in."

"I thought about canceling the game, what with everything going on," Bertie said. "But then I thought it'd be nice to have something to take my mind off things."

My only comment was to Sweet Thang: "You know how to play mah-jongg?"

"My Gram Gram taught me."

"Taught her good, too," Bertie cackled. "She whupped a bunch of old ladies."

"I just got lucky," Sweet Thang corrected her.

"Five times in a row!" Bertie cackled and lightly slapped the table.

She sipped her coffee. Sweet Thang crossed her legs. I was still standing, still feeling like I didn't belong.

"So," I said, "how long have you lived here?"

"Too long," Bertie replied. "You wouldn't believe it, but this was still a pretty nice place when I moved in here. Now?" She shook her head. "It's shameful what this place has become. Every time I hear they want to knock it down, I cheer. They just can't seem to get around to it."

She was finished on that subject and we lapsed into silence. I heard the oven tick and creak as the gas turned on. The volumeless television was on a local all-news station that, at this time of day, repeated the same loop every half hour. I suddenly felt the urge to leave. I didn't know what Sweet Thang had managed to create with Bertie Harris, whether it would help our story or not, but I felt like an intruder. It was time to do what I came to do and make my exit.

"Oh, by the way, Lauren, here's your bracelet," I said, pulling it from my pocket and handing it to her.

"Oh, my goodness, thank you!" Sweet Thang said, fingering the oh-so-cute sombrero from the Puerto Vallarta trip. "I was so worried, I even called my dad. I'm going to text him right now and tell him I got it back."

And then Daddy would tell Brodie, who would stop his Jack Russell terrier impersonation on Szanto, who would undoubtedly be grateful.

"Where did you find it?" she asked, fingers flying.

"Atalittlepawnshop," I replied quickly, hoping Bertie wouldn't pick up on it.

But she did.

"*You* pawned your bracelet?" Bertie asked.

Sweet Thang tossed me a pleading glance, but I lobbed it right back. I didn't know what she had and hadn't told Bertie Harris about her thieving daughter, and it wasn't my place to do so. This was Sweet Thang's deal.

"Akilah stole it from me," she said, finally.

Bertie sighed and set down her coffee cup so she could rub her temples. She closed her eyes.

"You let her stay with you and she stole your bracelet," she said, shaking her head, forcing out a sigh. "You were a good Christian and she was a thief in the night. Oh, Lordy, Lordy, Lordy. She stole your bracelet."

"She didn't mean to . . ." Sweet Thang started. "I'm sure she felt like she didn't have a choice. She needed the money."

"No," Bertie said immediately, forcefully. "Don't make no

excuses for that girl. I been making excuses for her all her life and look where it got us. Akilah has always been a . . . a difficult girl. Lord knows I've tried with her."

Bertie let loose another sigh, this time with a bit of a groan mixed in.

"I took her to church, I made her do her homework, I taught her to have respect. Respect! It was just like I did with my other children, and they all ended up successful. They all got out.

"Her older sister went to college," Bertie continued, shaking her head and counting her children on her fingers as she went. "One of her older brothers went to the army. The other got himself a good job, a union job. But Akilah, she . . ."

"You did the best you could," Sweet Thang said, patting her on the hand and looking at her with those tell-me-more eyes. And the thing was, she really wanted to know. Other reporters got away with faking that sometimes. But that was the essence of Sweet Thang's gift as a reporter. She didn't have to fake it. Deep down, she really did care.

"Akilah had a different father from the other children," Bertie said. "We split when she was young, but she still had too much of her father in her. She was always a wild child, always doing her own thing. You couldn't talk no sense into her. I gave her all the mothering I could and it still wasn't enough."

"She told us she was an orphan, that her mother died when she was young," I said.

"I bet there were times she wished I did," Bertie said. "But I'm still here."

Bertie started sniffling. Sweet Thang retrieved a box of Kleenex. It was like interviewing Akilah all over again—it had that same kind of confessional feel, and there were once again sopping tissues involved. I could only hope this time we weren't being served a steaming load of something that belonged in a cow pasture.

"She got pregnant for the first time when she was sixteen.

I mean, I was raising a daughter in the projects, what did I expect?" Bertie said. "I told my pastor I didn't want to have nothing to do with that child or its mother, but he told me I had to forgive her and so I did. And then that baby died. And it just about broke my heart."

So, at least that much of what Akilah had told us was true, after all. Bertie blew her nose.

"Then she started fooling around with that damn married man," she said, putting her hand across her heart like it was about to give. "We got a saying, Mr. Ross: 'Ain't nothing dumber than love.' And let me tell you, there wasn't nothing dumber than Akilah and that married man together."

She was done blowing her nose for a moment. She was getting angry now.

"I just couldn't take it after that. He got her pregnant"—she said the word with special disdain—"then he got her pregnant again. He had a wife and children, a whole other family, and he kept Akilah on the side, like a whore of Babylon. And she kept having his kids. I just couldn't understand how that man's wife could put up with that monkey business.

"But he's a politician," she finished, shaking her head as if that explained everything.

"Really?" I asked, suddenly more than a little intrigued. "What's his name?"

"Oh, he's . . . oh, now, what's that fool's name? It's . . ." She tapped her head, like it would make it come to her.

"Well, I'll be!" she said, pointing to the television. "That's the man right there."

I looked at the screen, whose forty-two inches were filled by a Missing Persons poster depicting Wendell A. Byers Jr.

Primo was no stranger to bribery, having used it expertly through the years to nourish his home-rehabbing business. When you were talking about home inspectors or appraisers, it was relatively simple. Offer a man a week's salary for something that took him only a few seconds and cost him nothing—something like signing his name to a piece of paper or changing a few figures here or there—and chances are he was going to do it.

For those few who had crises of conscience, Primo made it clear there were painful consequences for not accepting a small gratuity in exchange for a little cooperation. Coercion and persuasion. Stick and carrot. It was a powerful combination, one that allowed a man to rationalize his moral weakness. Primo had yet to find a working man who failed to take him up on his offer.

With politicians, however, it was a different deal. It was a game of finesse, not brute force. These were powerful people, after all. They were not easily threatened.

There was one thing that made it easier for Primo, however. Under New Jersey law, what he and most people would consider a bribe was actually legal. It was called a campaign contribution.

Sure, there were caps on how much one could donate. But those were circumvented easily enough—with all the donors and all the candidates, it was nearly impossible for any law enforcement agency to check where a donation was really coming from. The state's campaign finance laws, intended to be a moat guarding the castle of electoral credibility, were little more than a puddle.

The real difficulty, Primo quickly realized, came in discovering which politicians could be bought for a sizable campaign contribution, and which ones would thank you for your generosity and then lose your phone number as soon as you asked for a favor.

There was some expensive trial and error. And it involved some ass-kissing and attending events Primo didn't particularly care to attend, simply to gain access to the key people. But ultimately Primo had discovered the effort was worthwhile. Because once you got the right person on your side, you could make government do virtually anything for you.

It was all about influence—or, rather, the perception of influence. From a statutory standpoint, an elected leader actually had very little authority over government. Only a few positions within a municipal or state government were political appointments, people who could be hired and fired at the whim of an elected leader. The majority were civil service positions. Firing them was an arduous process.

That might seem to make them difficult to influence. But the thing Primo discovered was that most civil servants didn't truly understand how government worked. And they were paranoid about losing their jobs. So when an important person—or, again, someone they perceived as being important—told them to do something, they usually did it without question, no matter what the statutes might have to say on the subject.

Studies have shown it repeatedly: Human beings are programmed to accept leadership, totalitarian or otherwise. Even in America—land of the free, home of the brave, the country that created the notion of rugged individualism—most people will follow orders they believe are coming from above.

So for Primo, the whole game was about finding someone will-

ing to use his influence to make government work the way Primo wanted it to. He took his time and wasted some donations to find that person.

But, finally, Primo came across a city councilman who seemed willing to do just about anything for cash.

CHAPTER 5

So Akilah Harris was Windy Byers's slam muffin. And Windy was Akilah's baby daddy. And now Windy was missing, Akilah was on the run, and the kids were dead, none of which could possibly be coincidence.

But how, exactly, did it all relate? I gazed at the TV screen, bewildered. Windy Byers stared back at me with his ridiculous pencil mustache and his fat face—but precious few answers. My mind began toying with the possibilities.

Scenario No. 1: Akilah and Windy, the star-crossed lovers, decided to run off together but didn't feel like dragging the kids along. Hence the fire. But that didn't work. One, it made them unimaginable monsters. And while Akilah was a liar and Windy was a dimwit, they just didn't seem like they had that much evil in them. Besides, why would Akilah keep returning to the house if that was the case? And why would she have slept at Sweet Thang's place if she really just wanted to run off with her boyfriend?

No, Windy and Akilah didn't seem to be in cahoots on this one. If anything, it was possible they were both being victimized—after all, there was blood in the foyer of Windy's place, while Akilah's house had been made to double as a barbecue pit. But by whom? Who would want to hurt both of them?

Of course. Scenario No. 2: Rhonda Byers, the councilman's

churchgoing wife, learned of her husband's affair, then parted company with her sanity. She torched the love shack with the bastard children still inside, then sliced up her husband. Now she was reporting him missing in the hopes no one would ever suspect a member of the Ladies' Fellowship Group could go on a homicide spree.

I held up Scenario No. 2 for a moment or two, turned it around a few times so I could look at all sides. And yes, it worked. I thought about her demeanor at that press conference, so self-assured, so preternaturally composed, so unruffled. Shouldn't she have been a little more distraught? Isn't that what everyone did for the six o'clock news?

I'm not saying I would put Scenario No. 2 in the newspaper yet—I still had a lot to prove before I reached that point. But the jealous wife was certainly a dangerous animal, capable of all kinds of nasty. Especially if the wife in question was packed in as tight a box as Rhonda Byers, with her proper suits and her toe-pinching shoes. It tended to make the explosion that much more spectacular when it all came unwrapped.

It would also explain why Akilah was making herself such an elusive figure and would lend some sense to her rant on the fire escape. After all, you're not paranoid if people really *are* out to get you.

I pulled my attention away from the television and turned toward Bertie Harris and her pile of sodden Kleenex. Bertie didn't necessarily have all the answers—it didn't sound like she and her daughter were too close anymore—but she at least had some of them.

"Mrs. Harris, would you mind if I sat down?" I said.

She pointed toward an empty chair. "You can call me Bertie, you know."

I sat. Sweet Thang smiled at me, like she was proud I was now a member of the Call Me Bertie Club. I took off my jacket and draped it around the chair, then sat down.

"I know this is painful to talk about, but it may help me

figure out who killed your grandchildren," I said. "Can you tell me about Akilah and that man you just saw on the screen, Windy Byers?"

"Byers!" she said. "That's the fool's name, Windy Byers. Of course! Lord. You think he had something to do with those poor children?"

"I don't know what to think right now," I said. "You have heard he's missing, yes?"

"What do you mean?"

"He didn't come home Sunday night. His wife called the police Monday morning. That's why his face was on the TV just now. The cops are calling it a suspicious disappearance. A police source told me they found blood in the house. I think he may be in trouble."

Bertie absorbed this news for a moment.

"And Akilah is in trouble, too?" she asked.

"I'm not real sure," I said, not wanting to haul out my Rhonda Byers theory just yet. "But I'm hoping I can take what you know about Windy and Akilah and use it to learn a little more."

"Well, I'm not sure how much I know. Akilah and I weren't real chitchatty about that sort of thing," she said, pantomiming "chitchatty" with her hands. "She knew I disapproved of her sneaking around with a married man. She say, 'But Mama, we in love.' And I tell her, 'Akilah, you can't be saying that about another woman's husband. He ain't yours to be in love with.' But she didn't listen."

"How did they meet?" I asked.

"Oh, I was there when it happened," Bertie said. "He came here campaigning one time—you know, those politicians always come around when they looking for your vote. He was walking around and he took a real interest in Akilah. She couldn't have been no more than eighteen. Can you imagine that?"

Quite easily, I thought, as I sneaked a glance at Sweet Thang in her formfitting knit dress, her perfect, slender legs crossed beneath her. If there was a straight man who wasn't attracted to younger women, I had yet to meet him.

"I didn't think nothing of it at first," Bertie continued. "I thought he was just helping her, like a mentor. He got her a job over at the hospital"—another area where Akilah didn't fib—"and he looked after her. I didn't think there was nothing going on."

"I heard this part already," Sweet Thang told me. "I'm going to check on the banana bread."

She rose from her seat and slid by me, brushing me lightly with her hand as she passed, giving me a little chill down my spine. It made me wonder: if she could do that with a single light touch, what would full-body contact be like?

Bertie Harris brought me back into the conversation before my mind drifted too far.

"Are you going to put this in the newspaper?" she asked.

"I have no idea what I'm going to do," I said, which happened to be an honest answer.

"Well, I guess it don't matter now. You reap what you sow."

I wasn't sure who was reaping or who was sowing in this particular farming metaphor. But if it made Bertie more comfortable talking to me, she could plant a whole field for all I cared.

"So when did you realize they were . . ." I groped for wording that wouldn't seem crude. "When did you start to think they were getting intimate?"

"Well, I should have known before I did. He was always giving her little presents, jewelry and stuff—a real charmer, he was. I'd see her wearing a necklace and say, 'Where'd you get that, girl?' and she wouldn't say nothing. But I knew," Bertie said. "Then she went and got herself pregnant."

I nodded. Yes, that would be a strong indication intimacy had occurred.

"Then he bought her a house," she added.

"He what?" I asked. Jewelry. Jobs. Even an apartment. I had

heard of politicians getting those things for their girlfriends. But never a house.

"Uh-huh. A house. The house that burned down, he bought it for her," Bertie said, shaking her head. "She came home one day and said, 'Mama, me and the kids is moving out. My man got me a house.'"

It was, I realized, one final lie out of the mouth of Akilah Harris. She wasn't struggling under the weight of a mortgage, as she told us. She was getting it for free.

Which was just lovely for Akilah, I'm sure. But I could only begin to imagine how Rhonda Byers felt when—as wives inevitably do—she learned about it. Your fifty-something-year-old husband is not only cheating on you with a twenty-something-year-old-woman, but he has two kids with her and bought her a house.

I'm no expert on the mysterious workings of that alien planet known as the female psyche, but I'll posit that would make any woman pretty damn mad.

Mad enough to kill.

Sweet Thang returned to the living room, looking pleased with her domesticity.

"It's done and it's perfect," she announced. "But we should give it at least twenty minutes to cool."

I hadn't eaten a thing since breakfast. A nice hunk of warm, fresh-out-of-the-oven banana bread sounded delightful. And it was tempting to think that since I was in possession of information no one else had, I didn't need to be in too much of a rush. But I had learned, mostly the hard way, that nothing stays secret too long. And this story was sensational enough—SOURCE: MISSING POL WAS TWO-TIMING!—the New York tabloids would be swarming across the Hudson River as soon as they learned of it. I had to get as much of a head start on the competition as I could. There was no time to dawdle. Not even for fresh baked goods.

"Unfortunately, I think Bertie will have to enjoy it by herself," I said to Sweet Thang. "You and I have to be going. We've got work to do."

Bertie turned to Sweet Thang with a conspiratorial smile.

"Well, the boss has spoken!" Bertie said.

"Oh, he's not so bad," Sweet Thang assured her.

Bertie stood and shuffled toward her new friend.

"I just have to give you a hug," she said, grabbing her, her voice choking slightly. "Thank you so much for listening to an old lady go on like I did."

"Oh, my goodness, it was so lovely meeting you," Sweet Thang said, hugging back. "Thank you for your hospitality."

I stood up and extended a hand as soon as they broke their embrace. "Bertie, it was very nice talking with you," I said as she lightly grabbed my hand for one of those nonshake shakes. "If you hear from Akilah, please give us a call."

"Oh, she don't come around here no more," Bertie said. "We always end up fighting because I always tell her what I think. I know I should be more understanding, but I just can't deal with her and that married man. I just can't."

"You mentioned she had brothers and sisters," I said. "Do any of them have contact with her?"

"I don't know. They wouldn't tell me if they did. They'd know it would just upset me. But if Akilah was going to run to any of them, she would run to Tamikah. That's her oldest sister. She was like a second mother to that child. They was always close."

Bertie gave me Tamikah's phone number.

"That's her home number," Bertie said. "She don't like it when I call her on her cell, so I just call her at home."

"Thanks," I said. "I hope you don't mind if we call you when we have more questions. And sorry again about last night."

"You just be good to this young lady, you hear?" she said.

I assured her I would. And with that, we departed. I waited until we were down the stairwell and out into the courtyard, headed for our cars, before I spoke.

"Holy crap," I said. "That was pretty incredible."

"Which part?" Sweet Thang asked.

"Uh, the part where Windy Byers, the suddenly absent city councilman, had two children out of wedlock and bought a house for his mistress," I said. "I thought that was kind of obvious."

Sweet Thang had this look on her face like the Clue Fairy had not yet visited her.

"I thought we didn't put people's personal lives in the paper," she said.

"We do when they turn up missing under mysterious circumstances," I assured her. "Heck, in this case, we'd do it even if ol' Windy was still hanging around. I mean, he's a public figure. Sure, we might look the other way if a councilman has a quiet little something on the side. But a councilman having two kids with his mistress and buying her a house? That's not just adultery. That's practically polygamy. And it certainly raises hard questions about how he's affording it, which is something a voter has a right to know."

"Oh," she said. She thought for a moment, almost said something, then stopped herself. If she was an NFL lineman, I would have whistled her for a false start.

She paused for another tick, then asked, "So what do we do now?"

"Well, we have one source saying Windy and Akilah were knocking boots, but we need more," I said. "Then we need a law enforcement source to link Windy and Akilah and tell us Rhonda Byers, the scorned woman, is the primary suspect in the investigation."

"She is?"

"Sure she is. Think about it. Windy Byers was unfaithful to

his wife, and not in a small way. Then his girlfriend's house gets burned down and he goes missing. Who else but the wife did it? Let's face it, Windy is probably somewhere off the Jersey shore right now with a weight tied to his leg, slowly sinking to twenty thousand leagues under the sea. Or at least he is if Rhonda has contracted out her work properly."

"But how . . ." she began and paused. Still no visit from the Clue Fairy. "But how are the cops going to figure that out?"

"We're going to tell them."

"We are?"

I sighed. Didn't the journalism schools teach anything these days?

"Of course we are. It's one of the oldest tricks in our bag," I explained, feeling a bit professorial myself for a moment. "We learn something that we strongly suspect is true, but we can't prove it with enough certainty to put in the newspaper—not without major investigative resources and subpoena authority. We just don't have those things. But the cops do. So we tip off the cops, they check it out, and when it comes back that we got it right, they leak us the story as a nice thank-you. We get to run it as a big exclusive. They solve the case. Everybody wins."

"But how do we attribute it?"

"As 'law enforcement sources said,' of course."

"But it wasn't law enforcement sources. It was us."

"Well, yes and no," I said. "It was us that planted the idea, sure. But by the end, it becomes something the cops really do believe. So it's quite accurate to say 'law enforcement sources said.'"

"But isn't that, I don't know, like, influencing the news or something?" Sweet Thang asked. "Aren't we making the news instead of just reporting it?"

"Well, technically?" I said, a bit stumped for how to rationalize it. "Technically, a little bit. It's a gray area, but only slate gray, not charcoal. If our ultimate responsibility is to the public and its right to know important information, and this becomes a way to serve that right? To me it becomes something we're obligated to do."

Not that we brag about it, of course. Tipping off the cops is the sort of thing that could get a newspaper sued in half a heartbeat if, God forbid, we turned out to be wrong and the person in question really was innocent. A lawyer could argue the act of tipping shows malice, a key element in libel cases.

Still, this sort of interplay between the authorities and the newspapers happens all the time. Not long ago, one of our best reporters learned an ex-mayor had a warehouse full of smoking-gun documents. We knew we couldn't get into the warehouse, but the feds could. So our reporter tipped off the feds. They raided the warehouse. We got the scoop the mayor was under investigation. The mayor ultimately went to jail. The feds looked like they were doing their jobs. We stayed well ahead of the competition on the story the whole way because, of course, the feds were feeding it to us. Again, everybody won.

Well, except the mayor.

We reached the outer limits of Baxter Terrace and I walked Sweet Thang over to Walter the BMW.

"So what's next? Do we go down to police headquarters and file a report or something?"

"It takes a bit more finesse than that," I said. "But don't worry about that. I'll handle it."

"Oh," she replied. "What do you want me to do?"

"Why don't you go find Akilah's older sister Tamikah," I said, tearing off a piece of notepad paper and copying down the number Bertie had given me.

Sweet Thang looked uncertain.

"But what do I dooooo?" she whined.

"The same thing you did with Bertie Harris."

"Play mah-jongg with her?"

I laughed because I thought she was kidding. But no, Sweet Thang wasn't smiling. Silly intern. She had all the raw ability in the world but didn't have the first idea what to do with it. She'd learn.

"No. Not mah-jongg. I meant earn her trust, like you did with Bertie," I said. "Once she trusts you, let her tell you the story of what happened with her sister and Windy Byers. Hopefully she'll confirm everything Bertie told us and add a few new bits of information. If we're lucky, Tamikah is Akilah's confidante and knows everything."

"But what if she won't talk to me?"

Sweet Thang pouted. I smiled and patted her on the shoulder.

"She will. People like talking to you," I said. "Besides, if Rhonda Byers really is what I think she is, Akilah is in all kinds of trouble right now. And we're working to get her out of that trouble. Tamikah will see that and she'll want to help us lock up the woman who is trying to kill her sister."

She reached out and grabbed my arm.

"I'm so glad we're working together," she said. "It's, like, just amazing. You know so much. I'm learning so much more from you than I ever learned from any of my professors."

"Well, it's their job to teach you the rules," I said. "You have to know what they are before you know which ones you can break."

She nodded. I pointed down at the goose bumps that were forming on her thighs.

"C'mon, let's get you and your bare legs out of this cold," I said. "Call me later."

"Okay. Bye. Thanks again for everything."

I gave her a little wave—but not *the* little wave—and went to my car, pleased that I'd managed to have an interaction with Sweet Thang that didn't feel sexually charged. Maybe I had just been misreading her intentions all along. Maybe she just flirted because it was how she related to men, and there was nothing behind it. All the incidental contact—the grabbing of the arm, the brushing of the hand—was just because she was a naturally touchy-feely person. She hugged me this morning. She hugged Bertie when we departed. She was just like that with everyone.

And sure, Tina thought Sweet Thang was trying to get me in bed. But just because Tina devoured men like they were Tic Tacs didn't mean Sweet Thang did. She was a nice young woman who was pleased to have found a mentor, nothing more. I vowed to rinse my mind of the dirty thoughts I kept having about her and treat her with pure professionalism for the rest of our time together.

With that decided, I started driving back toward the office and thinking about the best way to approach the Newark police with my newfound knowledge. I put in a call to Rodney Pritchard, who answered on the fourth ring.

"Pritch, I need a favor," I said.

"Don't you always," he replied.

"Yeah, but this time I might actually have something to offer in return. That fellow who caught the Byers case, you said his name was Raines?"

"Yeah?"

"I need a sit-down with him. The sooner the better."

"I told you, man, he's strictly by the book," Pritch said. "He won't talk to a reporter."

"Even if that reporter has a vital piece of information on the disappearance of Councilman Byers?"

There was a brief moment of silence on the line.

"You're not playing me, are you?" Pritch said.

"No, sir."

"Because if you're playing me and you really don't have anything, I swear to God I'll throw you in a cell overnight and tell all the fellas in the lockup we found a Klan hood in your car."

"Pritch, trust me. Detective Raines is going to thank you for introducing me by the time this is over."

"He better," Pritch said. "Let me call you back."

We hung up just as I pulled into the *Eagle-Examiner* parking garage. Once inside the building, I passed Szanto on his way to the three o'clock story meeting—which was basically like the eleven o'clock story meeting in its overall inefficiency, only by now the editors had eaten lunch. He flashed me a thumbs-up. Obviously, Sweet Thang's Dad had gotten the message through to Brodie, who had eased off on Szanto.

"Grrjb," he graveled.

Whatever that meant. I returned his thumbs-up and thought about stopping to inform him of the latest revelation about Windy Byers. But no. That would be a terrific blunder—blunderific, as it were. The last thing you want to do is give your editor a hot piece of information as he heads into a story meeting. Inevitably, he'll share it with everyone at the meeting. And even though your story is only half-baked and not nearly ready to be put in the newspaper, every editor in the building will start running wild with it.

The next thing you know you're being pestered by a page designer who wants help with a graphic, a Web-head who would like a voice-over for a podcast, and a copy jock who wants to sneak a peek at the top of your story so she can start working on a headline. And when you try to explain to them the story might not even be true, they look at you like, "But the managing editor told me about this. It must be true."

So I kept walking. It's one of the trump cards reporters always have: the editors only know what you choose to tell them.

My first thought upon walking into the newsroom was to find Tommy Hernandez so I could share the latest. Whereas you need to be careful with what you tell editors, it generally behooves you to speak freely with fellow reporters. They may have already learned something that can help your story. Or they might be able to take what you've learned and get it confirmed or denied with independent sources, which can be invaluable.

Alas, Tommy wasn't around. So I settled in at my desk and did a quick property records check to see who owned Akilah's house. Sure enough, it wasn't Akilah. Fairmount Avenue Partners LLC—no doubt a thinly veiled front for Windy Byers, who lived on Fairmount Avenue—had purchased the house from Rio Financial LLC for $360,000.

I searched Rio Financial LLC in our business entity database and it led to a name I didn't recognize with a P.O. box in Roseland, which was on the leafy side of the county. It sounded like the typical Newark developer—suburban guys dipping into the city to try to make a quick buck.

Then I searched Fairmount Avenue Partners LLC and, sure enough, the registered agent was one Wendell A. Byers Jr. of Fairmount Avenue in Newark. I could now write with impunity that Windy Byers bought his girlfriend a house.

Satisfied, I leaned back for a moment and then, driven by some impulse I could neither name nor explain, found my fingers back on the keyboard, surfing my way toward Sweet Thang's Twitter page.

The first item was posted at 9:41 A.M., right around the time she and I broke from breakfast. It read: "Update 4 my girlz: CR is still supertasty. I could eat him with a fork. I want to get on him and grind him through the floorboards. LOL!"

It's amazing what you could accomplish in 140 characters or less. In this case, Sweet Thang had suddenly made my throat feel dry. So much for me having misread her. There was now no doubt: a nuclear-hot twenty-two-year-old wanted to sleep with me.

That was good news, right? What guy wouldn't welcome that news?

A guy who knew he was past the age to be banging interns, that's who.

But then I thought: her dad is loaded. And she's gorgeous. So why not just dive in? There have to be worse fates in life than shacking up with a beautiful woman from a rich family, right?

And then I thought: since when do you care about money? Only jackasses—and future divorcées—marry for money or looks. And besides, she's way too young and immature. She doesn't know what she wants. It will end badly.

But then I thought: Did you look at her in that dress today?

And then I thought: but by the time she's ready to have kids, I'll be one of those dads hanging around the playground who is so old no one is sure whether he's a dad, a granddad, or just some pervy guy who likes little boys.

I was somewhere in the midst of countering that argument when, out of the corner of my eye, I saw Tina Thompson coming toward me.

I furiously began trying to get Twitter off my screen, clicking on that little *X* in the upper right-hand corner. Why did I feel so guilty, anyway? I hadn't done anything, had I? I had nothing to hide, right? More pressingly, why was this damn computer taking so long to get the page off my screen? She was getting closer. I clicked the *X* again. Nothing. I clicked on my e-mail so there would be something different on the screen. Still there. *Click*. Nothing. The computer was completely frozen. *Click. Click-click.*

Finally, just as she was sidling up to my desk, I did the next best thing and hit the power button on the front of the monitor. Mercifully, the screen went dark.

"Hey there, handsome," she said, seeming not to notice my computer issues. "How come you look flushed?"

"I was running stairs," I said. "Got to keep the blood moving, you know. Deep vein thrombosis can be a killer."

She looked at me and cocked her head

"I thought that only happened to old ladies on airplanes," she said.

"Well, you can never be too cautious," I said, then went full tilt for the topic change. "Aren't you supposed to be in the three o'clock meeting right now?"

"Oh, I blew it off," she said. "I've got too much to do with this whole Wendell Byers thing to sit around listening to people make decisions that are just going to change by the time we actually have to put the paper out."

"Makes sense," I said. "What are we going with right now?"

"Well, we've got the blood in the foyer and the stuff from the press conference. That and a bunch of react quotes should be enough to carry the paper for tomorrow. Unless you have something new?"

I weighed whether to share what I had learned. I had confided in Tina in the past with this sort of thing and could trust her to keep quiet. She wasn't my editor, after all.

But she was still an editor. So I decided to zip it.

"Nah, not really," I said.

She looked at me and arched an eyebrow.

"You're lying."

"Dammit. How do you *do* that?"

"If I told you, it would ruin the fun," she said. "Anyhow, you gonna tell me what it is or not?"

"I'll pass for now," I said. "It's just a theory at this point, anyway."

"Is the theory that Wendell Byers is being moved out of the way so someone else can run for Central Ward council?" she asked.

"No. Why, whose theory is that?"

"Tommy said that's the buzz going around the streets. He's out chasing it down right now, seeing if it goes anywhere."

That explained why he wasn't in the office.

"You put any stock in that?" I asked.

"It makes as much sense as anything else I've heard," she said. "You know they play politics rough in Newark."

"Yeah, but generally they don't kill you. They just smear your reputation with anonymous flyers about how you're really a gay, white, Jewish Republican."

"Well, it seemed worthwhile for Tommy to look into," she said. "By the way, don't think I've forgotten about dinner tonight."

"Never. I'm still picking you up at eight?"

"I changed my mind. You're not picking me up. I want us to be in separate cars so if you totally blow it, I'll be able to make a big scene and walk out on you."

"Oh. Good to know."

"You're meeting me here at eight-thirty," she said, handing me a sticky with the name and address of a restaurant in Hoboken. I knew the place. It was on the Hudson River with commanding views of the Manhattan skyline. The prices on the wine list looked more like airline fares.

"Dress nicely," she added.

"How nicely?"

"Wear a jacket or they won't let you in. Wear a tie or I won't talk to you. Wear a suit and I just might jump you in the coat closet."

"Got it," I said.

"And don't be late."

"Don't be late," I repeated.

"I mean it. If you're late, I'm going to drag one of the waiters into a supply closet and take out my sexual frustrations on him and you'll miss out."

"Got it," I said again. And she departed.

Just then, cranky old Buster Hays, who sat a few desks away, wheeled his chair around and looked at me scornfully.

"Hey, Ivy," he said. Buster called me Ivy because he apparently thought Amherst was an Ivy League school. My efforts to educate him that it was a proud member of the New England Small College Athletic Conference had, so far, failed.

"You really going to let a woman boss you around like that?" he asked. "You're totally whipped."

Normally I tried to come up with some kind of retort for Buster's mindless zingers. But I couldn't this time.

Not when he was right.

I was about to head back to Twitter—to see what else Sweet Thang had written about that delicious fellow, CR—when my phone rang.

"Carter Ross," I said.

"Hey, it's Pritch," he whispered. "My guy says he'll meet with you on the condition that you consider yourself a confidential informant, not a reporter."

"Hey, whatever works for him. When?"

"How soon can you make it down here?"

"How does 'now' sound?"

"Sounds good. I'll meet you in the lobby at Green Street. Try not to look like a reporter. I'll be the guy who ignores you. But just follow my lead."

"I'll do my best," I said, making toward the elevator.

Newark Police Headquarters, located on Green Street in the heart of downtown Newark, was another one of those municipal buildings that had probably been magnificent at some point in time, back when Newark was a manufacturing powerhouse and the home to captains of industry. Now you had to look hard—and charitably—to see the majesty. But it was still there.

I walked into the building and up to the lobby on the third floor. Rodney Pritchard was waiting there. He saw me, made the briefest eye contact, and started back down the stairs. I followed. But not too close.

He went out the door, took a left, then another left on Broad Street, past City Hall. What were we? Russian spies from Montclair? I walked a little faster so he was within earshot.

"The password is 'Lesbian weasel,'" I said. "But I'll warn you: everything I know you can probably find on Google."

"Stop playing," he said, without turning around. "I'm just doing this the way my man Raines said. He doesn't want to risk being seen with you in the office. I told you, he's by the book."

"He also must be getting pretty desperate if he's meeting with me this quickly," I said. "He doesn't have squat, does he?"

"He didn't tell me either way. But you're probably right."

Pritch crossed the street, walked past a sandwich shop, then took a left turn into a pizzeria, where someone's Italian mama was behind a counter, yelling at the late-lunch stragglers to place their orders. Pritch kept walking into a back room, which at this hour—it was now after three—was empty, except for one man sitting in a corner booth.

"Carter Ross, meet Sergeant Kevin Raines," Pritch said.

Raines was a short, round black man who stored his extra weight in his ass. He was probably in the neighborhood of fifty and dressed in a gray suit, a white shirt, and a black tie. That made him unlike most Newark detectives I met—guys who knew they were going to work long hours and therefore swapped formality for comfort in their clothing choices.

"Nice to meet you," Raines said crisply, in a way that made it clear he didn't believe it.

He had a bland, slightly nasal voice and I was willing to bet most people who talked to him over the phone didn't know he was black. He may have preferred it that way.

I immediately had him pegged. He was the guy who didn't want to do favors for people and didn't like to have them done for him. He was a sergeant because he scored higher on the exam than anyone else, not because he politicked better. He didn't go to the bar after his shift with the fellas. He didn't backslap. He didn't bend rules. He was already at the edge of his comfort zone just by meeting with me.

None of which made him a bad person. I was just going to have to work on expanding that comfort zone and making him a little more pliant if he was going to be of any use.

"All right," Pritch said. "Have a nice time. I got things to do."

Pritch walked out, leaving Raines and me to stare at each other uncomfortably.

"Thanks for meeting with me," I said.

"Detective Pritchard said you had information to offer the Newark Police Department," Raines said officiously.

Yeah, and if he thought I was just going to dump it on the table and leave, he had another think coming. Whether he wanted to think of me as a reporter or not, I was one. And whether he wanted to think of himself as a source or not, I was going to treat him like one.

"Well, let's just slow down for a second," I said. "First of all, I haven't had lunch yet. I'm going to grab something from up front. You want anything?"

I could have held off. But I needed to start loosening things up a bit. I needed to establish we weren't a cop and a reporter. We were just two guys. And some guys require diet soda and pizza to get them through the afternoon. Hell, I might even spill the soda, because that's what guys do.

"No, thank you," he said.

"Some water? Anything?"

"I'm fine."

"Okay, I'll be right back."

I went back into the main room and ordered my slice, which came quickly. Then I went to the refrigerator and selected a Coke Zero for myself and a bottle of water for him. Another important thing to establish: he wasn't making all the decisions here.

I paid and returned to our table.

"I just felt it would be rude to eat this in front of you and not get you anything," I said, sliding the water in front of him.

He didn't touch it. He barely looked at it.

"We are clear that I am not meeting with you because you're a reporter," he said. "Officer Pritchard tells me you have information that may be vital to my case and vouches that your information is probably good. That's all that matters."

"Fair enough," I said. "So I take it you've never dealt with a reporter before?"

"It's against department policy to comment to the media without approval," he said.

"Okay, no big deal," I said as I opened my Coke Zero and took a long pull, making a big show out of savoring its artificially sweetened goodness. Then I picked up my slice and bit off a big hunk, chewing loudly.

Raines looked at the bottle in front of him. It was ice-cold and just starting to get a thin haze of perspiration on it. And to a cop who had probably been going for the last twenty-four hours on excitement and adrenaline—but not much hydration—I bet it was looking pretty good.

He cracked it open and took a sip. I was already starting to wear him down.

I put my pizza back down on the table.

"Okay. Well, just a quick user's guide to dealing with reporters, or at least this reporter," I said, wiping pizza sauce from my chin with a napkin. "First key phrase is, 'off the record.' That means you can tell me anything you want, but I won't put it in the newspaper—unless I get it from somewhere else, of course. As far as I'm concerned, this conversation and every other one we have is off the record unless we explicitly agree otherwise. Okay?"

He nodded.

"Second key phrase is 'not for attribution.' That means I *can* use the information you give me in the newspaper, but I can't attach it to your name as a source. And when I say you're an unnamed source, I mean that in the most sincere way possible. Reporters have gone to jail to protect the identity of their sources and I would do the same."

I had never been tested on that front. And I hoped I never would be. But I also hoped, if some judge ordered me to reveal my source, I'd have the stones to tell him to shove it, then take the contempt-of-court charge and spend some time as a ward of the state. Short of dying for a story—which I certainly *didn't* plan to do—going to prison to protect a source was as balls-out a thing as a reporter could do. And I fancied myself the kind of guy who would do it.

"Finally, I want to make it clear that I'll tell you everything I can to help your case," I said. "But information is a two-way street in my town. And so is trust. You have to trust me that I'm not going to put anything in the paper that will get you in trouble with your bosses. And I have to trust you that I'm not going to get blindsided by some press release announcing an arrest—or, worse, by a story in one of the New York papers that we didn't have first."

His back straightened a little.

"I'm not here to make deals," he said.

"Well, in that case I guess I'm wasting my time," I said, rising from the booth and grabbing my lunch.

I turned to leave like I was going to storm out—though, as storms go, mine was hardly a raging nor'easter. It was more like light, spitting rain on a balmy June day when the sun is still shining and there's only one stray cloud in the sky. I practically had my hand cupped to my ear so I wouldn't miss the sound of him asking me to stay. It was, all in all, a pretty horrible bluff.

Thankfully, he didn't call me on it.

"Hang on," he said. "Just hang on. All I'm saying is, I don't have the authority to make any deals on behalf of the *department*."

I stopped but remained standing.

"Sergeant Raines," I said. "I can tell you're a man of honor and I'm telling you I'm one, too. I don't need a deal with your department. I just need your word that if I help you now, you'll remember me down the road. Is that fair?"

He held out his hand. I shook it, then sat back down.

"Damn," he said, cracking a half-smile for the first time. "You're tough."

"Eh, once you get to know me, I'm easy like Sunday morning," I said, smiling back.

"Oh, now you're talking Lionel Richie," he said, with a sudden burst of enthusiasm. "Now you're talking my kind of music."

Ah, the magic of Lionel: Raines had gone from stony to practically glowing with the mere mention of the former Commodores' front man. I had finally penetrated the outer defenses of Sergeant Raines. It was just me and ol' Kev now, gabbing away. Even his voice had changed—you could actually tell you were talking to a black man.

"Well, hello, it's me you're looking for," I said.

He laughed out loud.

"All right, all right," he said, still chuckling. "You're pretty good. You're pretty good."

We guffawed a little bit more, but I didn't want to push it too far with my newfound buddy. And before he had us booking tickets to see Lionel's next tour, I got back to business.

"So, you got yourself a hell of a case with Windy Byers," I said.

"Tell me about it," he said, shaking his head.

"You've heard about his girlfriend by now, yes?" I asked.

"I heard some rumors, but nothing I really put stock in. He must have kept it pretty quiet."

"Well, she's not a rumor. Her name is Akilah Harris," I said as he pulled out one of those small cop notepads and wrote down the name. "And she's not just a girlfriend. She's practically his second wife. She's had two kids by him."

"Whoah!" Raines said.

"That's not even the best part. Windy bought her a house."

"A what?"

"A house," I said. "It was a little more than two years ago."

“I’ll be damned,” he said.

“But there’s more,” I said. “The house he bought her was the one on Littleton Avenue, the one that burned down with two kids inside.”

“Yeah, I heard about that.”

“I’m pretty sure it wasn’t an accident,” I said.

He nodded and asked, “When did it happen?”

“Sunday night, around nine P.M.”

“Which is also around the last time anyone saw Windy Byers alive,” Raines said, shaking his head. “I’ll be damned.”

“So what do you think,” I said. “Sound like jealous wife gone nuts to you?”

He leaned back and took a swig of his water.

“I certainly haven’t heard a better theory,” he said.

“Okay, so I’m going to go ahead and write that Rhonda Byers is the Newark Police Department’s chief suspect in Windy’s disappearance,” I said, winking.

“Oh, hell no,” he said. “But, strictly, strictly off the record, I like her for this. I really like her. I’ve been going all through Windy Byers’s council career and there’s not a single red flag. And nothing else has jumped out at me. Now maybe there’s a big political conspiracy out there, but I don’t see it.”

“Me, neither,” I said. “What do you make of the blood in his house?”

He flashed a look that was somewhere between chagrined and, well, just a grin.

“You heard about that, huh?”

“I got my sources,” I said, smiling back. “Is the blood his?”

“Don’t know yet. This isn’t *CSI*. Our lab doesn’t turn stuff around during commercial breaks.”

“Fair enough. So where do we go from here?”

“Let me think about it for a second,” he said.

He leaned back in the booth and finished the rest of his water in one long swallow while I chewed my pizza. He crushed the bottle between his hands, screwed and unscrewed the cap once or twice, keeping his attention focused downward. Then he looked up.

"I think I got something you can do for me," he said, then added, "if you're up for it."

"Shoot," I said.

And that's how I found myself heading back to Fairmount Avenue to interview Rhonda Byers.

My deal with Raines was that I would approach Rhonda Byers with questions about the last few days, so I could assemble a timeline of the hours leading up to her husband's disappearance. I'd take careful notes, of course—that's sort of what I do—and then I'd call Raines and we'd compare the story she gave me to the one she had already given Raines, searching for the kind of inconsistencies you usually find when someone is pulling a story off the fiction shelves of their brain.

For Raines, it was a way to grill a suspect without her realizing she was being grilled—or that she was a suspect. It also allowed him to sidestep or at least delay the rather prickly task of accusing a councilman's wife of a felony.

For me? It was a good way to make sure the lead investigator on the biggest crime of the year kept taking my phone calls. And it might even give me something useful for the paper.

I was glad I didn't have Sweet Thang in tow, because I didn't feel like explaining that, once again, I was walking a very fine ethical line. Should I be doing a cop's work for him? Of course not. But it's not like he asked me to slap cuffs on Rhonda Byers. He just wanted me to talk to her, which is what I do for a living anyway. So what's the harm in sharing a little information with my newfound source when it might lead to greater understanding of a story?

Besides, Sweet Thang was a bad fit for this particular task in at least one other way. For as good as she was at getting people to talk, I don't think Rhonda Byers was going to be in the mood to spill her heart to an attractive younger woman, i.e., the kind of woman who stole her husband. There had been enough bodies dropped in Newark already.

As I drove back toward Fairmount Avenue, I called Tommy. It was mostly a courtesy. This was his beat, after all, and he deserved to know what was happening.

"Hey, what's up," he said, without the usual Tommy zip in his tone.

"That's all you got? 'What's up?'" I asked. "No snappy rejoinders about how my clothes make you think of Alex P. Keaton from *Family Ties*? No catty comments about how my family ought to organize a hairstyle intervention?"

"No. I just don't have the energy to point out the obvious right now," he said, heaving a melodramatic sigh.

"Oh, come on, what's wrong? Boy troubles?"

"I wish. I'm going over ELEC documents."

ELEC was the New Jersey Election Law Enforcement Center. Every candidate and political group in the state has to file reports stating where they get their money and what they do with it. Most politicians give the bare minimum of information—you'll see line items like "$28,350 . . . Miscellaneous expenses"—while staying (pretty much) within the law. Usually, the only worthwhile thing we get from ELEC reports are donor lists filled with names of individuals and businesses that are getting rich off government contracts. And, this being New Jersey, bribery of this sort is not only prevalent but legal.

Still, wading through the reports takes time, concentration, and the ability to resist butting your head into your computer while you wait for another PDF document to load.

"ELEC reports," I said. "What's the matter, you having trouble sleeping?"

"No, I've just been looking into everything about big, fat old Windy I could find and I wanted to make sure I was thorough."

"Tina said you were on the streets, running down some rumor?"

"Yeah, that's what I told her," he said. "I just knew if she saw me in the office she'd keep bothering me. So I'm sitting in a coffee shop, doing it on my laptop. Don't tell her."

I felt a surge of paternal pride: my little intern Tommy had already learned the virtue of lying to his editor. Sniff. They grow up so fast.

"Oh, your secret is safe," I assured him. "I was just calling to give you a heads-up. I'm going over to Rhonda Byers's place."

"Oh, okay," he said. "What's happening there?"

I told him what I had learned about Windy's extracurricular activities and their unintended consequences.

"And you think Rhonda Byers did all that?" Tommy asked when I was all done.

"Yep," I said.

"Really? Rhonda Byers?"

"You don't buy it?"

"Well, I don't know. I mean, I'm sure you're right. It's just . . . I just—"

"Spit it out!"

"She seems so nice."

I laughed at him. Apparently, grasshopper still had much to learn.

"No, I'm serious!" he protested. "I met her a bunch of times at council meetings. I think she's the only one besides me who goes to all of them. She's not over-the-top friendly or anything, but she's always very kind to me. She explains things to me all the time when I don't get them. She probably has a better idea than her husband what's actually going on in this city."

"Yeah, I already figured she was hogging most of the IQ

allotted to the Byers household," I said. "But to me that makes it fit even better. A smart, with-it woman like her learns that her idiot husband is two-timing her in the biggest way possible. Can't you just see her losing it?"

The line was quiet for a moment as Tommy considered it.

"No," he said at last. "Not really."

"Well, you got a better idea for what happened?"

Another pause.

"No. Not really."

"Well, there you go," I said as I pulled up in front of the Byers residence. "I'm off to the black widow's web. Wish me luck."

The TV trucks had all departed the Byers's neighborhood—off to find Shocking Things You Might Not Know About Your Deodorant, no doubt—and the crime scene tape that had been stretched across their front gate was now flapping in the late afternoon breeze. It was only four o'clock, but the sun was already getting low. The wind rustled some dead leaves as I opened the gate, which creaked as I swung it shut behind me. I was starting to feel like a character in a slasher flick—and not the wily brunette who survives to the end. I was the bubble-boobed blonde who somehow ended up getting killed in her underwear.

And why shouldn't I be a bit queasy? If I was right, Rhonda Byers had killed three people. And even though one of them had it coming, two of them were innocent children. I didn't want to talk to a person like that. I didn't even want to be breathing the same air.

Still, there was a story to be written. So I rang the doorbell. I heard footsteps, then a woman who was probably Rhonda Byers's sister—same height, same build, same bearing—answered the door.

"May I help you," she said without emotion.

"I'm Carter Ross. I'm a reporter with the *Eagle-Examiner* and—"

"She's not here," the woman said immediately, and started closing the door with all due haste.

Under normal circumstances, I'm all for getting a door slammed in my face. It's the sort of thing that lets a reporter know he's still alive. But I couldn't let it happen this time. So I stuck my foot across the threshold before the door could shut.

"I know this is a difficult time for the family," I said, as the door bounced off my shoe. "But we're just trying to make our coverage as complete as possible and I was hoping for her help."

The woman was about to find a new way to tell me to get lost. But then, from an inside room, I heard that authoritarian voice.

"Let him in," Mrs. Byers said.

I was escorted into a dim living room, where Rhonda Byers was sitting on a Queen Anne–style couch with the shades drawn. Her bare feet were propped on a nearby coffee table. She was no longer dressed in the gray suit and uncomfortable shoes. It was now a sweatshirt and jeans. I surmised a girdle had been removed as well.

The room did not have a television, just a lot of shelves packed with books, all of them spine out. She was a reader, obviously. There were knickknacks, but the room didn't feel especially cluttered. I sometimes get my decorating styles a little mixed up, but I was fairly certain the room would qualify as Victorian. Except it wasn't your charming Aunt Beverly's Victorian, where all the little baubles have stories behind them. It was your stern Aunt Helga's, where everything had a brittle feeling, like you couldn't move anything—not even the air—or something would break.

"Mrs. Byers, Carter Ross from the *Eagle-Examiner*," I said.

She offered no greeting, smile, or handshake, which was fine by me. I didn't particularly feel like returning any of them.

"We're writing a story about the hours leading up to the

councilman's disappearance," I continued. "I was hoping you could fill in some blanks for me."

She looked at me with the same expressionless face her sister wore.

"Mr. Ross, I'll be honest, I don't want to talk with you, just like I didn't want to go on television today," she said, without much enthusiasm. "But the police tell me that media attention is good, because it will help them find Wendell. So I'll do what I can."

Okay, so that's how she was going to play it: the dutiful wife sacrificing herself to bring her poor husband back home. I could roll with that.

"I'd like to go through the final forty-eight hours before he disappeared," I said. "It would start Friday evening. What were you and Mr. Byers doing that night?"

During the next hour or so, she went over everything, and I drilled her on every inane detail. It was a long succession of political fund-raisers, pancake breakfasts, civic association meetings, high school basketball games, and so on. It was the sort of thing you expected from a local politician—the hobnobbing with the moneyed set, the glad-handing with the constituents, the seeing and being seen. Windy was a man on the go.

But, strikingly, he wasn't on the go with Mrs. Byers. At every stop on Windy's itinerary, I kept asking where she was. And she always seemed to be somewhere else—reading at home, or at a church function, or at her sister's house. She admitted she had no idea where Windy was at certain times, or that she had only learned where he had been after the fact. She often was uncertain about when events began or ended. She never seemed to be able to offer an exact time when her husband arrived back home.

It gave me the window I felt I needed to see if I could bait her a little.

"You and your husband didn't seem to spend much time together," I offered.

"We were both very busy," she said, trying to dismiss it easily.

I didn't let her.

"I know this is difficult to talk about," I pressed. "But I have to ask: Were there problems between you and Mr. Byers?"

Rhonda glanced nervously at her sister, who had been sitting in the room quietly listening.

"I . . . I wouldn't say problems . . ."

She was faltering, if only slightly. This was my chance to see if I could start playing with the dials on her thermostat and add a few degrees to that icy blood of hers.

"Well, what would you say then?"

"Is it . . . is it really necessary to bring my . . . my marriage into this? Into your article?"

"At this point, everything is relevant," I insisted. "I don't mean to be rude"—actually, I did—"but I have to ask the question: Is it possible your husband was having an affair?"

Finally, the sister exploded.

"How does that matter?" she demanded. "The man's been kidnapped!"

"It's—" I began but was drowned out.

"You have a lot of nerve—"

"Jeannette, I'll handle this," Rhonda insisted.

Jeannette leaned forward as if she was going to object some more, but Rhonda held up a hand, "I'll handle this."

"Young man," she said, turning toward me, having already cooled herself back down. "Can we talk off the record?"

"Sure," I said, and put down my pen, which up to this point had been waving furiously.

"Are you married?" she asked.

"No."

"Well, Wendell and I have been married for twenty-eight years," she said. "After a while it gets . . . well, it's not like I thought it would be."

"How so?" I asked, and resisted adding, you mean on your

wedding day you never envisioned murdering him in cold blood and making it look like he disappeared?

"I don't know how it happened, but we drifted apart," she said. "We were in love when we were younger. I really believe that. But it was always hectic, with me chasing after the children and him in politics. After the kids were out of the house, I thought it would get better because we'd have more time to spend together. But it got worse. He did his thing. I did mine. Separate worlds."

"So why not divorce him?"

"I don't know," she said, sighing and looking away. "I think you have to be angry with someone to go through all the trouble of getting a divorce. And I couldn't summon enough feeling for him to hate him that much. But to say we had a marriage anymore?"

She shook her head.

"Yet I'm told you always went to the council meetings," I said. "Why?"

She stopped and thought for a moment.

"I guess I found it interesting," she said. "That was maybe the one area where we still shared a common interest. We could talk about that. I'd like to think he . . . I guess I think he valued my opinion on those matters."

Uh-huh. Probably Windy was like Tommy. He needed Rhonda to explain stuff to him.

"But other than that, you barely saw each other?" I asked.

"That's true," she said, shaking her head again. "I can't believe I'm saying it, but it's true."

"So, and again I hate to be rude"—no, really, I didn't—"but is it possible your husband has met someone else and is off with her somewhere right now? It happens, you know."

Yes, Mrs. Byers, your husband just ran off. No, Mrs. Byers, I'm sure you didn't do anything untoward. Wasn't that the illusion she wanted the world to believe? Isn't that the story she hoped I would buy? The offer was on the table. All she had to do was take it.

But she didn't. Maybe she was too smart to be that obvious.

"I . . . I don't know," she said. "I'm so . . . More than anything, I'm sad for him. I worry he's gotten himself in trouble. I just hope he's all right."

She looked at me and blinked, like she was trying to keep tears from tumbling out her eyeballs. Maybe she was. She was so convincing, I actually believed her for a moment.

God, I felt like a cub reporter. Where was my cynicism? My natural suspicion? That little voice in my head that told me to distrust everything I heard? What was I, going soft?

"Do you think you have enough for your story?" the sister asked, finally taking control of the situation.

"Enough for now," I said, because we had been at it for an hour and I wanted to leave while I still had my disbelief.

"Then I think it's time you go," she said. "My sister has been through too much already."

And this time Rhonda didn't object.

Neither did I. Short of a tearful confession—which Rhonda Byers was far too cagey to give me—I had gotten what I came for. Raines and I could go over everything now. It was time to leave.

I bid the Byers sisters farewell and led myself to the door, with Jeanette close on my tail. As I walked through the foyer, I lingered slightly, pretending to fumble with my jacket until I saw what I was looking for: a big, smudgy streak of blood, about two feet long and as obvious as a snake on a sidewalk, on the molding near the floor.

It seemed odd Rhonda Byers hadn't cleaned it up yet. Perhaps the police had instructed her to leave it undisturbed, in case they needed to do more testing. I was glad they did because it gave me the chance to study it.

I'm no forensics expert, but it looked like the kind of smear you'd get if you were dragging a bloodied body out the door.

Primo cultivated his relationship with Councilman Wendell A. Byers slowly, having learned from other failures not to push too far too fast.

The important thing was to keep the initial favors small: a phone call to the city engineering department to prod them for an approval; or a letter to the water authority to speed up a permit for a sewer hookup; or an introduction to a fellow council member, with a few kind words about Primo as a developer.

All the while, Primo kept the contributions coming. A Newark council campaign was a surprisingly expensive endeavor. Sending out mailings, making local media buys, maintaining campaign offices and staff, printing posters and lawn signs—it all added up. Even a longtime incumbent like Byers had to shell out $250,000 or more to hold his seat. What's more, keeping a healthy campaign fund in between elections helped fend off the wolves. Would-be candidates weren't keen to challenge a well-financed opponent.

So the need for cash was constant. And Byers was no different from most politicians in that he hated fund-raising—the glad-handing, the overpromising, the grubbing for money from friends. That's where Primo came in. The more money Primo gave, the less Byers had to raise himself. It was easy and, above all, it was addictive.

Any candidate would enjoy having to spend less time with his hand out.

Once Byers was hooked on the money, the size of the favors steadily grew. And it became more quid pro quo. Do this, I'll give you that. Influence for sale. And beyond the help in navigating the city bureaucracy—which saved numerous headaches—was the real golden goose. Land.

In a place like Newark, city-owned land was abundant. For many decades, owners who fled to the suburbs—or absentee landlords who decided to cut their losses—simply abandoned their properties rather than continue to pay the taxes on them. After a few years of nonpayment, the city would seize the property. After a few more years, when whatever structure left on the property had been vandalized beyond the point of repair, the city knocked it down.

It all had the effect of making the city of Newark far and away the largest owner of empty, developable land within its own boundaries. For a long time, the land was essentially worthless. But then, as Newark's building boom began in the late nineties and then picked up momentum after the turn of the millennium, it rapidly began increasing in value. And, under statute, the sale of this land was the purview of the city council, which had to approve all deals.

For Primo, this was the real benefit of having a councilman in his pocket. Generally speaking, if one councilman wanted a land sale approved, his colleagues would stay out of the way and allow it to happen. Professional courtesy ruled.

Again, Primo started small, with a parcel here or there, then built up to larger chunks of contiguous land. With the way Primo had his business set up—in an endless chain of seemingly unconnected LLCs—no one even realized Councilman Byers was always recommending sweetheart land sales to the same person.

It allowed Primo an abundant supply of nearly free land on which to build houses. And in the most densely populated state in

America, where land was always at a premium, it gave Primo an enormous edge on the other developers. It was basic economics. Getting one of your chief raw materials for virtually nothing did wonderful things for the bottom line.

Primo paid for the privilege, yes. But the cost was nothing compared to the benefit.

CHAPTER 6

As I drove back toward the office, I could feel one of those wiggling, niggling suspicions trying to work itself free from deep underneath my skullbones. Except, of course, the moment I became aware of it, my conscious brain began doing a little dance all over it. Whatever small hint of genius may have been forthcoming was stomped back down, hopefully to resurface at a later time.

Clearly, it was something about Rhonda Byers. Had she been too cool? Or too melodramatic with the near-tears? Had she given away anything I hadn't noticed?

Nothing came to me. And Kevin Raines wasn't going to be any immediate help—his cell phone went straight through to voice mail.

"Sergeant, it's your confidential informant. Give me a call when you have a moment," I said, then left my number.

By the time I got back, it was six o'clock and there was some serious typing going on in the newsroom. Tommy looked like he was holding a staring contest with his computer screen. Tina had her shoes off and feet curled underneath her, a sure sign she was rewriting someone's lede. Buster Hays was banging on his keyboard with his usual vigor—having been raised on a manual typewriter, he still hit the keys like he was making sure his letters stood out nice and crisp.

I had barely sat down at my desk when Sweet Thang slid up to me and sat in an empty chair across from me, smiling. Somehow, despite a long day, she still smelled fresh and soapy.

"Oh, my goodness, I had the most amazing afternoon," she gushed. "And I'm actually talking about the part after I left you. I mean, the part before that was great, too. But then it got better. Well, I mean, not better better, but really good, you know? You won't believe what I learned."

This was the first time I had seen her since I read her Twitter post, with all its CR consumption and floorboard grinding. I wondered if she put it there in the hope I'd trip across it, because it would embolden me to make a move. Or maybe she just figured it was one little tweet, and since I wasn't following her, I'd never see it.

Or maybe I should get this silly girl out of my head, especially when she was right in front of me, still babbling in my direction at speeds faster than the human ear was trained to perceive. I was already four or five paragraphs behind.

"I'm sorry, I'm sorry," I said. "I wasn't paying attention. Could you start over again?"

She shook her head and rolled her eyes—like, what was my problem?—then went back to full speed ahead.

"I was SAY-ing, I couldn't get a hold of Akilah's sister. So I didn't know what else to do and I didn't want to bother you, because I bother you enough already, you know? So I tracked down the guy who sent us that e-mail instead."

"Uh, what e-mail?"

"The concerned citizen e-mail. Didn't you get a copy?"

"Oh, right," I said. With everything else going on, I had just forgotten about it. "How'd you track him down? It was anonymous."

"I thought it was pretty obvious," she said.

"Sorry. Still not with you."

"Chuck—sorry, concerned citizen—said something in his message like, 'I know why you couldn't find the mortgage.' And I'm like, hel-LOOO! We never mentioned that we couldn't find the mortgage in the story. There are only two people who knew that. There was that title searcher, but I'm sure he was too busy getting stoned to read the paper. And then there was that clerk guy. So I went and found him."

"Oh," I said, impressed. "I thought he was worried about losing his job. How did you get him to talk to you?"

"I just flirted with him," she said, like it was the most obvious thing this side of making toast.

"Oh, right," I said. "Flirting."

"You don't think that's bad, do you?"

"No. Flirting is good."

She flashed me a knowing smile.

"Anyhow, Chuck—his name is Chuck—was all nervous at first. He was like, 'I can't talk to you.' And then I flirted with him a little more and he was like, 'I meant I can't talk to you *here*.' "

"Well done," I said.

She smiled quickly. "Hold off on your compliments until the end. It gets better."

"Sorry," I said, but she was already going.

"So we agreed to meet outside the courthouse at four—I accept your apology, by the way—and take a walk. At first he was like, 'I can't tell you, it's too deep, you can't handle the truth, blah, blah, blah.' So he was like, 'You have to guess, and if you guess right I'll tell you.' I couldn't guess it, but he told me anyway."

"Why, more flirting?"

"No, actually we were sitting on a bench at that point so I kept crossing and uncrossing my legs."

"You realize you're pure evil," I said, but couldn't stop myself from grinning.

"Well, I thought about what my journalism professors would

say about it. And they would probably tell me all the reasons I shouldn't do it. And then I thought about what *you* would say about it. And I knew you would tell me all the reasons I should. So I thought about what would ultimately have the greatest public benefit and I decided you were right."

"I am," I assured her. "Just remember to use your powers for good."

"I will, don't worry. Anyhow, Chuck said that his boss came up to him this one time and told him to erase this mortgage from the computer. Chuck said he didn't want to do it, but the boss told him if he didn't do it, he'd just find someone else who would, so it was like he didn't have a choice. Chuck thought the orders were coming from somewhere up high—someone with a lot of pull."

I nodded.

"Anyhow," she continued. "Chuck said he had sort of forgotten about it, but when I came along and couldn't find a mortgage, he thought I was just being a ditz at first"—imagine that—"but then he looked into it and he realized it was the mortgage he had been told to erase. Ex-CEPT he didn't totally erase it. He wiped it from the computer but kept a hard copy and put it in a folder in his house."

"And so you accompanied him back to his house to get it?" I prompted.

"Well, he said he just moved, so he wasn't quite sure where it was. But he said he'd look for it when he got home."

"Wonderful," I said. "So why did he think he was erasing it?"

"He said he didn't know, but he got the sense it was political or something."

Of course it was. If you're Windy Byers, you're probably quite keen to make sure no one discovers you've bought a house for your girlfriend. So you yank some strings in the clerk's office and get the mortgage removed lest it fall into the hands of your political enemies.

Or, worse, into the possession of a nosy newspaper reporter who knows a document like that would allow him to take that juicy little tidbit—something that would otherwise fall into the category of nasty rumor—and put it in print.

Sweet Thang started bouncing up and down in her chair like a third grader who has been told she must wait five minutes before going to the bathroom.

"So what now?" she asked. "What now? What now?"

"Well, first, can I compliment you?"

She pretended to think for a moment. "Yes, you may."

"Great work tracking down this guy."

"Thank you," she said, with a smile that would have graded flawless on the diamond clarity scale.

"Okay, onward. You still have that phone number for Akilah's sister handy?"

"Yeah, right here," she said, using it as an excuse to wheel her chair next to mine, allowing our knees to brush. The girl was a master at creating incidental contact.

"Bertie said it's a home number, which turns out to be a nice break for us," I said, turning to face my terminal. "It means we can do a reverse lookup and see where she lives."

My computer screen was dark for some reason, so I pressed the power button. As the monitor warmed up and the image snapped into focus, I suddenly remembered why I turned it off in the first place. But, by that point, it was already too late. There on the screen, in brilliant 256-color, 1024-by-768 pixel resolution, was Sweet Thang's Twitter page.

I glanced at her out of the corner of my eye to see if she had noticed, hoping I could click it away before she got a good look. But no, she was peering at it curiously, head tilted, like it was something she had seen before but couldn't quite place.

Then I watched as recognition crashed across her face. And it wasn't a small, gentle-lapping wave. It was one of those tsunamis that wipes an entire Indonesian fishing village off the map.

"Oh. My. Goodness," she said.

Her blush started from the jawbone, then progressed upward, going from her cheeks all the way to the top of her forehead, filling every available inch of skin in glowing crimson.

"Yeah," I said, not knowing what to say. "I, uh, sorry about that. I didn't mean to, uh, you know, leave it on the screen like that."

Sweet Thang was, for perhaps the first time in her life, stunned to silence.

"I was just sort of wasting time and one click led to another," I explained. "I didn't mean to pry. I just . . ."

I could tell she was rereading the post to check if it was as bad as she remembered. And, of course, it was probably worse.

"I didn't realize . . ." she started, then stopped. "I thought you . . . I didn't think . . . You're not following me or . . ."

"It's Twitter," I said apologetically. "Anyone can read it, even if they're not one of your followers. Facebook is the one where people need to have permission to see stuff you've written."

"I know, but . . . I . . ."

"If it makes you feel better, I didn't read any of the other ones," I said.

She buried her face in her hands and moaned softly. "I'm soooo embarrassed," she said into her palms.

"It's not a big deal," I insisted.

"It's like one of those bad dreams where the entire school has read your diary," she said.

I decided to skip the lecture about how you have to assume when you type something that it could be read by anyone—one of the great perils of modern Internet living—and instead just said, "Sorry."

"I think I might die."

She whirled around and walked away without saying another

word. I sneaked a glance to my left and right to see if anyone might have noticed—an intern turning a shade just short of purple might tend to attract attention. Thankfully, it appeared to have been strictly for my benefit.

I returned my focus to the screen and clicked the *X* on the upper right corner of the window. This time, naturally, it went away immediately.

Then I got back to my reverse lookup. Tamikah's number was unlisted. But that was hardly a deterrent. Few people are careful enough with their telephone numbers to keep them out of the hands of a reporter who knows what he's doing. The LexisNexis database has millions of unlisted numbers. Even something as seemingly innocent as voting records is a great place to get numbers—no one thinks about it, but if you fill in the "phone number" blank on the registration form, you've just made your digits part of the public record.

So it took about thirty seconds to find where Tamikah—last name Dunwood—now resided. It was an address in South Orange, a street I vaguely recognized as being near Seton Hall University, wedged up against the Newark border.

And while perhaps that made it sound like the Newark girl hadn't made it very far, that wasn't the case. Now that East and West Berlin are unified, there are few starker borders in the world than the one between the New Jersey municipalities of South Orange and Newark. Literally, you can be driving through the hood, on a litter-strewn street lined with tenements and bodegas; then you blink, and you're in suburbia, with neatly trimmed landscaping and seasonally appropriate lawn decoration. Drive maybe half a mile farther and you're in a historic part of town, dotted with million-dollar houses and fancy imported cars.

Yet the two worlds almost never collide. It's not about race—South Orange is actually thirty-five percent African-American. It's about caste. The Newark–South Orange line might as well have a sign that says, "Now entering upper middle class."

So Tamikah was now a long way from Baxter Terrace. I Googled her address, then clicked on the satellite view. I zoomed in as close as it would go and, I swear, I could see a plastic Santa in one of the neighbors' yards.

Then I typed the address into our property-tax database. The house was owned by Ryan and Tamikah Dunwood. It was 2,250 square feet, four bedrooms, one and a half baths, set on a 50-by-150 lot, and assessed at a very nonprojectslike $549,500.

And it was soon going to be visited by at least one *Eagle-Examiner* reporter. Maybe two, if the other one ever recovered from a potentially terminal case of Twitter-induced mortification.

After a few more minutes of document snooping on Tamikah Dunwood revealed little more of use or interest, I was revisited by Sweet Thang, who returned from her brief sojourn looking refreshed, considerably less flushed, but chastened.

"Let's not talk about it," she said quickly.

"Fine with me," I said, to her visible relief.

I knew, at some point, we would have to deal with the fallout from my accidental discovery. You didn't just drop a bomb like that into the middle of an acquaintanceship—let's not call it a relationship—and expect everything to magically reassemble itself as it had been before. There were now bits and pieces of emotional shrapnel all over the place. Cleaning up the mess could take a while.

Still, for the time being, it seemed only pragmatic to ignore the eight-hundred-pound tweet in the room.

"So, moving on," I said. "It turns out our friend Tamikah lives in South Orange. Would you like to pay her a visit?"

"Does South Orange mean we can take Walter this time?"

"Yes," I said. "South Orange is definitely a more Walter-friendly kind of atmosphere."

"I'll grab my keys."

"Meet you out front."

Two minutes later, we were waiting for the elevator, staring at the numbers as they ticked toward our floor, stewing in an uncomfortable conversation lag where neither of us knew what to say. It was awkward, but I discovered there were benefits to having Sweet Thang in sheepish mode: it was much quieter.

We rode down the elevator. In silence. We walked out to the car. In silence. And we made it to South Orange with only the smallest of small talk—a few passing comments about traffic and weather.

We pulled up outside the house, which appeared to be your basic side-hall colonial with yellow clapboard siding and neatly clipped shrubbery. The driveway was short and led to a detached two-car garage. I could see a hint of a swing set in the backyard.

I disembarked from Walter's passenger door. With Sweet Thang trailing, I walked a few paces on a concrete pathway, then up four steps to a small front porch. I rang the doorbell.

It was answered by, of all things, a white guy. He wore the unofficial business-casual uniform of the greater New York metropolitan area: black shoes, dark charcoal gray pants, light blue button-down shirt.

I instantly wondered how he and Tamikah met. I was even more curious how the rest of the Dunwoods felt the first time Ryan brought her over for dinner.

"Hi! Can I help you?" he asked. He said it to me but wasn't looking at me—he was too busy giving Sweet Thang a thorough up-and-down.

"Hi, we were hoping to talk to Tamikah Dunwood," I said.

He turned and shouted, "Tammy, honey, there are some people at the door for you."

Oh. So she was Tammy now. I guess she left Tamikah back in the projects.

The guy turned his attention back toward Sweet Thang, his eyes shifting busily back and forth between her legs and torso.

Then a little girl who was maybe four or five ran up and grabbed his thigh. She was unmistakably mixed race, with the light chocolate skin of a black girl but the straight brown hair of a white one.

"Daddy, I'm *hungry,*" she said earnestly.

"I know you are, sweetie, so why don't you eat your chicken?"

"But I'm hungry for *brownies.*"

"After you eat your chicken, then you can have brownies," he said, ever the model of fatherly patience.

He patted her head as she ran away, gave a "what can you do?" shrug, then cleared out of the way as his wife came to the door.

"Hi, how are you?" said Tammy/Tamikah in a tone that was friendly but not overly so.

Instant first impression? It was Clair Huxtable from *The Cosby Show.* And no, I'm not the kind of white person who thinks any African-American they meet looks like a black celebrity (because, as the whispered saying goes, "they all look alike"). No, Tammy Dunwood really *did* look like Clair Huxtable.

She certainly didn't look like Akilah. I know they had different fathers, but there wasn't even the slightest resemblance from their shared mother. Tammy was at least half a head taller, and while certainly not overweight, she was more rounded, without all Akilah's sharp angles. Her hair, also straight—though perhaps straightened—was just below her shoulders.

She was dressed like she had spent her day in an office cubicle somewhere on the other side of the Hudson River.

"My name is Carter Ross; this is Lauren McMillan. We're reporters with the *Eagle-Examiner.*"

I waited for her to have that flash of recognition, like she knew why we were here. But it wasn't forthcoming.

"Okay?" she said, drawing out the *y* until it sounded like she was asking a question.

"We're working on a story about Akilah," I said.

And that's when I got the reaction, the one that seemed to

ask, *Oh, Christ, what is it this time?* Her face went ashen and her voice dropped an octave.

"I have two young children and I don't want them to hear this," she said in a low voice. "Can we please talk outside?"

She didn't wait for an answer, just closed the door behind her and folded her arms, mostly for warmth. The temperature was in the thirties and she wore nothing beyond a thin silk sweater over her blouse.

"What is it?" Tammy asked.

"Have you seen the stories about her in the paper?" I asked.

"I'm sorry. We get the *New York Times*. What stories?"

Sweet Thang and I shot each other looks. Tammy had no idea what had happened to her two nephews. It seemed impossible: it was in our paper, it was on the local news; even if she did not consume any of those media sources, someone she knew did. Even if her mother hadn't called her—and, apparently, she hadn't—wouldn't her neighbors or coworkers have said something? Then I remembered there was no way for an outsider to know that Tammy Dunwood from South Orange was in any way related to Akilah Harris from Newark.

Especially if Tammy never mentioned she had a little sister. Or that her real name is Tamikah. Or that she grew up in the hood.

I considered the best way to break the awful news about her nephews but concluded there was no good way. So I dumped it on her. I dumped it like the big steaming, stinking load it was.

"There was a fire at your sister's house Sunday night," I began. "Your sister wasn't home, but your nephews were."

Tammy's hand flew to her mouth, but an "Ohgod" escaped before it got there.

"I'm sorry to say they didn't make it out," I said as Tammy's eyes went misty. "We spent some time with Akilah the morning after the fire, and she told us she was an orphan with no family and had no choice but to leave the children at home alone because she couldn't find child care."

"Oh, Akilah," Tammy moaned softly.

"We didn't know she was making up parts of the story, so my partner here took pity on her and let your sister spend the night," I said, gesturing to Sweet Thang as I talked about her. "But Akilah ended up running off in the middle of the night with Lauren's jewelry.

"Then we located your mother, who obviously confirmed Akilah wasn't an orphan," I continued. "Your mom told us about Akilah's affair with Windy Byers and about the house he bought for her. She said Akilah might still be in contact with you and gave us your number. We were hoping you could fill in some blanks for us or possibly even help us locate Akilah."

The dumping complete, I let Tammy have a moment to sift through it. I glanced over at Sweet Thang, only to become aware she was shooting me a dirty look. I cocked my head quizzically, which only made the look dirtier.

And then I got it: maybe, possibly, I had been a little brusque. You don't just waltz into someone's otherwise fine life, introduce yourself, and then add, oh, by the way, we heard your sister is a big sloppy mess and, oh yeah, you've also got two fewer nephews to shop for at Chrismastime.

Tammy was reeling from the news, more in shock than anything.

"I . . . I'm not sure, I . . . I don't know . . ." Tammy began, and I sensed our time on her porch was about to become quite short. But before Tammy could fully get the sentence out of her mouth, Sweet Thang leaped to my rescue.

"I'm so sorry you had to hear it like this," she said, shooting me one more disgusted glance. "We thought you already knew. You must be just devastated right now."

Tammy turned her attention to Sweet Thang.

"You . . . you let . . . you let my sister stay with you last night?"

Sweet Thang nodded.

"It wasn't a big deal," she said. "He shouldn't have told you."

"No, it's just I . . ."

Tammy closed her eyes, brought her hands to her temples, and began massaging them. There was some kind of unseen battle going on between her ears. I didn't know what exactly it was about. But I could tell she wasn't winning.

Finally, she looked up at us.

"The last time my sister and I spoke—this was a week or two ago—she told me she was in danger of losing the house and asked me if she and her boys could come stay with us. And I told her no. Can you believe that? A perfect stranger"—Tammy waved toward Sweet Thang—"was willing to take her in, but her own sister wasn't."

Sweet Thang started rationalizing for her. "In some ways it's simpler for a stranger. You must have a lot of history with her I don't have."

"Oh, we've got history," Tammy said. "I don't even want to start talking about that. You'll be bored to tears, but I'll be the one crying."

"It's not easy with family," Sweet Thang said. "Sometimes you're harder on your own family than you are on a stranger. It's natural. We judge the people we love a lot harsher."

"No, that's not it. You know what it is? And, I'm sorry, I don't even know you, but I'm just going to tell you this. What did you say your name was? Laura?"

"Lauren, yes."

"Lauren, here's how it is when you grow up where I did and then you leave. People back home—my family, everyone—think that because I went to college and live out here now, I must be living in some rich la-la land. Well, you know what? This isn't Shangri-la. It's South Orange. My husband and I have two children and we're struggling to make ends meet just like they do back home, we're just doing it in a place that doesn't smell like piss.

"But anytime someone gets in trouble, it's always, 'Go to Tamikah, talk to Tamikah, she's got money, she'll help you out.' But I don't. And I can't. I'd have half of Baxter Terrace sleeping in my basement if I didn't draw that boundary. And even though I know I need to draw it, I still feel guilty."

"But you've got your own family to worry about," Sweet Thang countered. "You have to do what's right for them. I understand that completely."

"I bet you understand a lot right now. My sister stole your jewelry. So, congratulations, you're part of the club now."

"It's nothing, really," Sweet Thang said. "Honestly."

"I still feel terrible about that and . . . you know what? It's cold out here. Would you like to come inside?"

Sweet Thang smiled pleasantly. In less time than it had taken me to completely screw up this interview, she had completely unscrewed it. Like I said, the girl had a gift.

"That would be delightful," she said.

Tammy walked inside ahead of us, asked us to sit in the living room, then went into the kitchen for some quick negotiations with Ryan the Devoted Husband with the Wandering Eyes. Within moments, there were excited noises and suddenly two little girls were scrambling into their jackets, rushing past us out the front door. Dad trailed close behind.

"Cold Stone! Cold Stone!" the younger one sang as she ran out into the driveway for what was obviously an impromptu trip to a nearby Cold Stone Creamery.

"Bribery," Tammy explained as she reentered the living room. "I just wanted us to be able to talk without those little ears around. They don't know about any of this sort of stuff and I want to keep it that way."

"How old are they?" Sweet Thang asked.

"Emma is four and Gracie is six."

Which meant they were the same ages as Alonzo and Antoine. They were cousins who lived perhaps three miles apart. Yet their lives could scarcely have been more different.

"They're adorable," Sweet Thang said.

"They're also a handful, but thank you," Tammy said, sitting down and smoothing her pants. "So I think I've figured out why you're here. It's Windy Byers, isn't it? I heard about him. You think Akilah has something to do with his disappearance?"

"We're not sure," I said honestly.

"You don't think she kidnapped him or something, do you?"

"No, nothing like that," I said. "If anything—and this is just a hunch at this point—I think Windy's wife may be involved. It's possible she learned about the affair and went out for revenge, burning down Akilah's house and having her husband killed."

Tammy put on a confused face.

"But why would she do that now? She's known about the affair for years."

"She has?" I asked. Now it was my turn to be confused.

"Oh, sure. I don't want to say she condoned it. But Akilah made it sound like she knew about it and was more or less okay with it. Or maybe resigned to it is a better way to say it."

"Huh," I added, ever the eloquent speaker.

"But, in any event, I don't even think it matters anymore. They broke up. Or, I should say, Akilah broke it off with Windy. So why would Mrs. Byers go after Akilah now?"

Why, indeed.

I stared stupidly around the Dunwoods' living room for a moment, as if the answers were somehow tucked neatly behind their Pottery Barn furniture. If Windy and Akilah weren't an item anymore, that might suggest these two events—a bonfire on Littleton Avenue and a kidnapping on Fairmount Avenue—were not connected after all. But if that was the case, why was Akilah running around Newark saying everyone was after her?

"I'm still trying to sort all this out, and I know you are, too," I said. "So do you mind if we start at the beginning?"

"Not at all."

"Okay, your mother told us Akilah and Windy met about six or seven years ago, is that right?"

Tammy looked up at the ceiling for a moment. "That sounds about right," she said.

"And, I'm sorry, but I have to ask: what exactly would bring a fifty-something-year-old councilman and a teenaged girl from the projects together anyway?"

"I can't tell you the number of times I've asked myself that same question," she said. "I think for her it was the power—and the money, of course. I mean, he got her a job. He gave her nice things. She called him 'Boo' or some ridiculous pet name like that. She felt special that someone so important would sneak around to be with her. And for him? Who knows? I mean, you know that family comes from the projects, too, right?"

"Really?"

"Oh, yeah. The Byerses and Baxter Terrace go way, way back. Both the boys were raised there. I think their mom, she's dead now, but she kept living there right to the end. So I think, I don't know, this is just me guessing here, but for people like us—people who made it out of the projects—there's a lot of different ways to deal with it. Me? I got out and stayed out and I don't particularly like to go back.

"But for some people—maybe it's just guys, I don't know—it's like a point of pride. They still want to keep coming back around the old neighborhood. They say it's to keep it real, but I think they just want to show off. And I think some of them also keep a taste for project girls. Windy, he married up—I think Mrs. Byers's daddy was a doctor or something—but the word around Baxter Terrace was that he always liked to have a girl who was a little more down home that he could visit. So there he is, the big shot, coming back to Baxter Terrace. And there she is, the pretty young girl. It happens."

And Windy was far from the first politician in our nation's history to have it happen to him.

"So that's how it started. How did it end?" I asked.

"Well, he cut her off," Tammy said. "She broke up with him after he told her he wasn't going to pay for that house anymore."

"Why not?"

"I don't know. I don't know if he was suddenly having money problems or if his wife wasn't letting him do it anymore or what. But one day he just came over and said, 'You have to leave.'"

"Even after he had two children with her?" Sweet Thang interjected.

Tammy looked at Sweet Thang for a long moment, then cast her eyes downward and said softly, "They weren't his."

Oh.

"She told everyone they were his. I think she even tried to convince herself they were his. She liked the idea of the boys having a councilman for a father. But even before they split up, I started making noise about how she should go after him for child support. Make it legal, you know? She said she didn't want the fuss, but I was going to hire a lawyer. Then she finally told me they'd never pass the paternity test. I guess Windy wasn't always around, so there were other men. Please don't tell my mother. She's ashamed enough as it is."

"We won't say anything," Sweet Thang said.

Right. Mum's the word. We may end up printing it in a newspaper and distributing several hundred thousand copies of it. But we won't tell Mom.

"So Windy kicks her out," I said. "Then what?"

"Well, she came to me asking if she could stay with Ryan and me, and we—I—I just couldn't. She was so mad. And she was saying how she had no place else to go. I told her she could get an apartment on her salary at the hospital, but she said there was no way she was moving back into some cold-water flat. When she left here, she was talking about how she was going to pay the mortgage herself."

Tammy shook her head, like she was still in disbelief.

"I told her she wasn't making nearly enough at the hospital," Tammy finished. "But she didn't want to hear it. She said she'd find a way."

"That must be where the second-shift job came in," I said. "She told us she was working at a pallet company, cleaning floors or something."

"And that's why she wasn't home for those little boys when that fire started," Tammy said. "So if I had just"—Tammy started losing her composure—"if I . . . I . . ."

She couldn't finish her sentence. The guilty tears dripped down both sides of her face. Sweet Thang dove in to console her.

Meanwhile, I was starting to realize much of what we heard from Akilah—which I previously dismissed as one long fabrication—was really just a series of small twists on the truth. She wasn't an orphan in the real sense of the word, but she was estranged from her mother and cut off from her sister. And she was struggling under the weight of a pretty hefty mortgage after all.

At the same time, my casting of Rhonda Byers as the vengeful wife was starting to look rather implausible. If Rhonda was of the mind-set to go after Akilah, she would have done it years ago—not now, when the affair was over. And if that was the case, Rhonda probably had nothing to do with her husband's disappearance, either.

Then that thing that had been trying to wiggle and niggle its way out of my brain finally surfaced. It was that big, obvious blood smear. If Rhonda Byers was trying to hide a crime, wouldn't she have been smart enough to clean it up before the police arrived?

So, to review, I had a missing councilman who threw around his weight to hide the existence of a now-torched love shack. And the former occupant of that love shack, the councilman's secret girlfriend, was convinced the perpetrator of those crimes was now after her.

And I still didn't have the slightest idea what was really going on.

It took a while to mop up the tears, meet the kids when they got back from ice cream, then say our good-byes. By the time we returned to Walter, it was starting to spit rain at us. It was also far later than I thought.

"Dammit," I said, looking at Walter's clock, which read 8:04.

"What is it?" Sweet Thang said.

"Damn, damn, damn," I replied.

"What's happening?"

"I, uh, I'm going to be late for something," I answered.

"Something important?"

I looked over at Sweet Thang, with her bouncy blond curls and cute button nose, and I just couldn't bring myself to explain that her tasty CR had a date with the city editor. I told myself it was because I didn't want to break her heart. But if I was being more honest, it's because I was a typical, despicable guy, and even though I knew I should have absolutely nothing to do with Sweet Thang, I still wanted to keep my options open.

"It's, uh, just a dinner with a friend," I said.

Except it wasn't just dinner with a friend. It was a dinner at a four-star restaurant with a dress code. I looked down at myself. I was presentable, with my white shirt and my half-Windsor knotted tie. But I didn't have a jacket. I needed a jacket.

I did some math as Sweet Thang pulled away from Tammy's house and headed back toward Newark. It was going to take at least fifteen minutes to get back to Newark. From there, it was another fifteen minutes back to Bloomfield to grab a jacket out of my closet. It would take at least thirty minutes to get from there to Hoboken. At that point it would be after nine, even if I could find parking quickly. There was just no way I could be more than half an hour late for a date—at least not with a woman like Tina.

Okay, different plan: Bloomfield was ten minutes away. If I had Sweet Thang stop off there, I could run in and pick up my jacket. Then it would be fifteen minutes to Newark to get my car and only another fifteen minutes to Hoboken, if I got cute with the speed limit and decided to make some red lights optional. That would get me there only about fifteen minutes late. Anyone would forgive fifteen minutes. Hell, that was just being fashionable.

"Actually, would you mind stopping at my house in Bloomfield on the way back?" I said, as the rain picked up in intensity. "I'm a little pressed for time and I need to grab something."

"No problem!" she said enthusiastically.

"Great," I said. "Just get on the parkway and I'll guide you from there."

As Sweet Thang headed for the Garden State Parkway, I pulled out my phone and texted Tina: "Unavoidably detained. Running late but on the way. Wait for me."

I shoved my phone back in my pocket, then settled into Walter's passenger side seat. Sweet Thang had the radio on and was lightly singing along to some vapid pop song.

"So, Tammy seemed really nice," Sweet Thang said between verses. "I just felt so badly for her because I know what it's like to . . ."

She kept yammering on, but I wasn't paying much attention. I threw in an "uh-huh" and "oh" every once in a while to at least pretend I was paying attention. Mostly, I was focused on the green Ford Windstar in front of me, which was inching along the entrance ramp to the parkway at precisely the same speed as the red

Honda Civic in front of it, which was creeping like the white Mitsubishi Gallant farther up, and so on.

What was taking so long? Sure, it was raining—pretty hard now, actually—but why wasn't the ramp moving? Where were all these people going anyway and how could it possibly be more important than my potential booty call with the ravishingly hot Tina?

Then, in the distance, I got a glimpse of the parkway itself. And there it was, 8:12 at night, and all four of its northbound lanes were a sea of red brake lights reflecting on puddles of water. The only thing moving was the puddles as more rain fell on them.

It took another six minutes just to get on the road, and I watched despairingly as the number on Walter's clock grew larger. Sweet Thang was jabbering about something now—her recent trip to Turkey? The turkey sandwich she ate for lunch? I definitely heard the word "turkey" thrown in—and I kept trying to recalculate my various ETAs until they stopped having any meaning.

Then, at 8:31, I got a text from Tina: "UR late."

I immediately fired back: "Stuck in traffic."

Less than a minute passed before I received: "Not my fault. U close?"

I winced and tapped out: "Not really. Very sorry."

This time it took a little longer to get: "Pulling waiter into supply closet now. Good night."

I quickly texted: "Rain check?"

Her reply: "You suck."

I sighed, buried my phone back in my pocket, and stared out at the brake lights of a disco-era Oldsmobile Cutlass.

"Something wrong?" Sweet Thang asked.

"Yeah, my friend had to cancel dinner," I said. "I was supposed to be there"—I looked at the clock—"four minutes ago."

"So? Won't your friend wait for you?"

"I guess not."

"That's not a very good friend," Sweet Thang said definitively.

And maybe it was the way Sweet Thang said it—like it was one of life's fundamental truths—but the more I thought about it, I decided she was right. Who cancels on someone when they're four minutes late? What kind of friend is that?

It's not really a friend. It's a control freak of a woman who is playing games and messing with a guy's head. And who needs that? Not me. Not anymore. No, I needed something simpler in my life.

I reclined a bit in my seat, no longer stressed about traffic or worried about Tina's wrath. Walter's heater was working with quiet efficiency, and I savored the warmth of the car and the smell of the leather seats. I glanced over at Sweet Thang, who was again singing along to the radio, unbothered by the nasty weather, the long day, or any of the small inconveniences of life. She was just happy. And wasn't it pleasant to be with someone who was happy?

"So it looks like I'm free for dinner," I said. "What about you? You hungry?"

We decided that on such an inclement night, dining in was better than going out. And since my place was closer than her place—and we were headed in that direction anyway—we chose my place. Shortly after reaching that conclusion, the parkway started moving again, as if the Traffic Gods themselves wanted us to make good time.

My house is what Realtors would call "cozy," but only because "so small you can vacuum the entire thing without having to change plugs" doesn't fit as well on a multiple-listing service entry. But I liked it just fine. After all, it was just me and Deadline. And Deadline didn't like to travel too far for the litter box.

As a modern bachelor, I shop on an as-needed basis and keep nothing beyond the bare essentials in my refrigerator: beer, processed cheese, salsa, and, possibly, milk (for morning cereal).

Anything else will grow a beard and be applying for credit cards by the time I get around to throwing it out.

My freezer is a different story. The freezer, I have discovered, is the key for the on-the-go single guy such as myself, because you can keep things in there for months and not have to worry about it looking like a breeding ground for penicillin. Meats. Sauces. Side dishes. Entrees. They're all in there, all premade. And they're all frozen while still fresh. That's the mistake most people make with their freezers. If you toss in leftovers because you know they're about to turn, a couple months in the deep freeze is not going to make them perk up. You have to put some love in your freezer if you expect it to love you back.

After we dashed inside, dodging raindrops all the way, I did a quick freezer raid and—rejecting options that would require some assembly—came away with sausage lasagna and half a baguette. I tossed them both in the oven, lit some candles (another modern bachelor must-have), and opened a bottle of red wine.

Sweet Thang was checking out my living room, which also doubled as my family room, sitting room, great room, and TV room. She cooed at Deadline, who was pressing himself against her leg, in something near rapture. I've heard of people judging new acquaintances based on how their pets respond to them—because, after all, if *Fluffy* likes you, you must be okay.

That wouldn't work with Deadline. He accepts affection indiscriminate of the source. A masked, knife-wielding assailant could break into my home and hack me into a dozen pieces as I slept. But if he stopped to rub Deadline behind his left ear on the way out, Deadline would be purring so loudly you'd think someone started a lawnmower in the next room.

"Your cat is soooo cute," Sweet Thang said. "What's his name?"

"Deadline," I called out as I puttered around, getting things just right.

I can't say I was actually trying to seduce Sweet Thang or was even cognizant of how my actions might be construed. At a certain point in time, when you've been dating long enough, some gestures just become automatic. Like the candles. Or the iPod playlist with just the right music (my rule: no Barry White. It looks like you're trying too hard). Or remembering to bump up the thermostat a few degrees. It becomes like a dance you know so well you can just lose yourself in the song and let your body react to the rhythm. Especially once the wine starts working.

So I wasn't considering the ramifications when, after dinner, I invited Sweet Thang onto the couch with another glass of wine. And I wasn't thinking when I sat within arm's length of her and we talked about old relationships and the wisdom we gained from how they'd gone wrong. And I wasn't paying attention as I started absentmindedly tracing the outline of her cheek with my hand as she spoke of a particularly heartrending breakup.

But the next thing I knew, we were kissing. And sometime after that, her dress became a floor decoration. More garments soon followed it there. The breathing got urgent. The blood got pumping.

And then, just when things were about to get interesting, I heard five words that drained all the blood out of me: "I've never done this before."

She what?!?

I pulled away abruptly.

"What do you mean?" I said. "You don't mean you're a . . ."

I couldn't even spit out the word—"virgin"—because it was so thoroughly inconceivable. Sweet Thang? A virgin? What about all the dirty talk about floorboards and whatnot? The ability to flirt information out of people like a hot double agent? The light brushes with the hand that made my arm hair stand straight?

For that matter, how was it possible a body like hers had gone through high school and college without some guy being clever enough to put it to the use nature intended?

But there she was, nodding at me earnestly.

"It's not like I ever planned it this way," she explained. "It just sort of never happened. I didn't want to be the girl who hooked up at prom. And I didn't want to be the girl who gave it up for some frat boy after a mixer. And I didn't want to have some bar hookup with a guy who was going to give me a fake phone number. And, I don't know. It's not a big deal."

But I knew better. No matter what she said, it was a Very Big Deal. I'm not saying Sweet Thang needed to be a blushing virgin on her wedding night. But I was just old-fashioned enough to think her first time ought to be a little more special than re-heated lasagna on a rainy Tuesday night in February.

I had no business being her first. I was attracted to her physically, but I didn't really like her in that way, and I had finally reached a maturity level in my life where I knew the difference.

Besides, at a certain point, a guy gets too old for deflowering virgins. I just didn't have the energy to deal with the drama of the newly plucked, the guilty phone calls to Mother, the recriminations when the relationship went sour.

"I'm sorry," I said. "I thought you were . . ."

Don't say "more experienced." Don't say "well traveled." Don't say anything.

"It just wouldn't be right," I finished.

I half expected her to convince me it was—she probably wouldn't have to try that hard—but I think she realized it wasn't right, either. So we began the awkward task of disentangling our mostly naked bodies, collecting the various pieces of clothing strewn about the room, and assigning them to the proper owner.

"I'm going to go," she said after she was dressed, going up on her tiptoes to kiss me on the cheek. "Thanks for being a gentleman."

She let herself out. Deadline walked over to me and brushed himself against my leg.

"Come on, cat," I said. "It looks like there's going to be plenty of room in the bed tonight."

* * *

At risk of sounding like a spokesman for the Republican Party's sex education platform, I will say this on the subject of intercourse and the morning after: for all the times I've regretted having sex with someone, I've never once regretted *not* having it. As I woke up the next morning, I realized the previous evening had been another example to prove the rule. Had I sullied virtuous young Sweet Thang, I'm sure I would have felt like Carter the Conqueror in the moment. But I would have inevitably felt like a scallywag by the next dawn.

Instead, as my eyes fluttered open and I briefly replayed the previous night's adventure, I felt good. Honorable. Noble, even. As I showered, dressed, and poured myself a bowl of Apple Cinnamon Cheerios, I felt even better. Not even the low cloud cover and the threat of more 34-degree rain could wreck my mood.

No, only one thing could do that. And it came from my cell phone.

"Duh duh duh duuuuuuuuhhh."

Beethoven's Fifth. Sal Szanto. I put down my spoon.

"Good morning," I said.

"For you it is maybe," Szanto said. "Windy Byers turned up."

"Really? Is he talking?"

"I doubt it. He's dead."

Usually, the news of another human being's demise elicits some reaction in me, even when I barely know the deceased, as was the case here. But a brief search of my emotional state revealed very little feeling for Windy Byers, one way or another. I never thought he was a particularly good guy, and nothing I'd learned over the past three days improved my estimation of him. His death did not register as any great loss to the city, state, or nation, nor as any great shock.

"Where'd they find him?" I asked.

Szanto rattled off an address on Avenue P in Newark, a place in a vast industrial maze in the East Ward, not far from Newark Airport.

"What was he doing there?"

"Not breathing, apparently."

"Come on, you know what I mean."

"At this point, you know everything I know," Szanto said. "We just got a tip on this. Get your ass out there."

He didn't have to tell me time was of the essence. We had tipsters, but so did everyone else. As the home team, we still had a little bit of an advantage on the media horde that was about to descend on Newark. But it wouldn't last long. I had to move. Now.

I tossed out my Cheerios, grabbed a Pop-Tart, and dashed out the door . . . only to remember my car was still in the parking lot at the *Eagle-Examiner*.

"Crap," I said to my empty garage.

I briefly took stock of my situation, which was admittedly dire. I could call a cab, but that could take half an hour or more—Bloomfield was just suburban enough that you couldn't run out to the street and hail one. I could call a friend, but that wasn't guaranteed to be any faster. I could steal a car, but . . . oh, right, I wouldn't know how to steal a car if my collection of pleated pants depended on it.

Suddenly, the solution came to me in the form of that ancient-but-still-running commercial that ends, "Enterprise, we'll pick you up." In my head, I could summon the ridiculous image of a rental car gift wrapped in brown paper, motoring toward someone's house. It always made me wonder: with brown paper covering everything but the windshield, how did the driver get into the car in the first place? And wouldn't it be a little dangerous to drive?

But I didn't have time to ponder such weighty issues. I dashed inside and quickly entered into negotiations with my local Enterprise franchise. I stressed to the lady on the phone that transaction speed—not make, model, or the presence of an onboard navigation system—was my primary concern. She nicely dispatched a driver who arrived in a car that, much to my relief, came without packaging. Within fifteen minutes, I was on my way to Avenue P.

Despite my ambivalence on the subject, I had been provided with a nav system anyway. So while I was reasonably certain I knew the way to Avenue P—I had done a piece about illegal drag racing there a few years back—I tapped in the address just to see if the computer knew a quicker way.

Soon, an alluring female voice was telling me my destination was, of all things, an Enterprise rental car location. It must have been an off-site facility of some sort, spillover from Newark Airport.

As Nancy—I decided to call my nav system Nancy—guided me ever closer to my destination, I began to suspect our hot tip had not, as Szanto might have hoped, bought us time over the competition. Not when I could hear news helicopters hovering overhead.

On the ground was more bedlam. Avenue P was a long, straight stretch of road with only two outside access points, at the top and bottom—which is why the drag racers loved it. From atop a highway ramp, I could already see an armada of news vans had created a small media city at the south end, where the police had erected a barricade that could stop a tank brigade. Certainly, I could join them . . . if I felt like spending my entire day in the cold to learn nothing more than what I could have gotten staying in bed and watching local news.

Ignoring Nancy's advice, which would have led me straight into the gaping maw of that information oblivion, I took an end run around to the north side, snaking through the marshland past an abandoned movie theater and a variety of small warehouses and scrap yards. I was pretty confident the boys from the networks wouldn't know about this way. Homefield at least had some advantage.

At the top of Avenue P there was a much smaller police presence—just a single patrol car and two officers who looked like they didn't particularly want to be standing outside on a raw February morning.

"Hey," I said, rolling down my window as one of them motioned me to halt. "What's going on?"

"Police investigation," the officer said.

"Oh," I said. "I'm just returning my rental car."

"How'd you end up over here? You get lost or something?"

"Nancy told me to go this way."

"Who's Nancy?"

"My nav system," I said. "From the sound of her voice, she's pretty hot."

The guy stared at me like I had been given an extra helping of idiot at birth, which is pretty much the effect I was going for. He stepped away from my car for a moment, turned his back, and got on his radio. As an ethical reporter for a legitimate news-gathering agency, I cannot misrepresent myself in order to gain information or access to something. If the cop asks me whether I'm a reporter, it's pretty much game over.

But if he doesn't ask, I don't exactly have to go volunteering the information.

He turned around and leaned on my window.

"Can I see your rental agreement?" he asked.

"Sure!" I said brightly, and reached for the packet that was still sitting on the passenger seat next to me. He took a cursory glance at the paperwork, handed it back to me, and waved me through without a word.

Primo didn't wrestle much with the decision to kill Councilman Wendell A. Byers. It was just something that, when a certain set of facts presented themselves, became the only course of action.

It began with an argument about a silly house. Primo knew he never should have sold Byers that house, knew it would complicate a business relationship that was already tricky enough. Byers probably should have known better, too. But, ultimately, each man had his weakness. For Primo, it was greed—one more customer to buy one more house. For Byers, it was lust—he liked the idea of having a house for his latest piece of ass. Primo never understood it, but it somehow made Byers feel important.

So the deal was struck. Then it went bad. And, naturally, Byers couldn't see it was his own fault. He blamed Primo, who pointed out Byers should have known what he was getting into. That's when Byers started getting belligerent. And once he started uttering those threats—"I'll cut you off . . . I'll tell everyone on the council you're a bad actor . . . no more land for you . . . you're finished in this town"*—Primo knew he had to act. He had worked too hard to get where he was to have this bozo councilman wreck everything.*

It would mean finding a new councilman to bribe, yes. But there were nine of them. Surely one of them would be amenable—perhaps even Byers's replacement.

So, no, the decision wasn't hard. Killing Byers and getting away with it? That was the difficult part. Primo knew the police would investigate a dead councilman with great vigor. He had to make sure none of the suspicion would land on his doorstep.

At least officially, there was no relationship between the two men. Primo had always been careful to ensure there was no paper trail that could tie them together. Any investigator looking for one would only bump into Primo's seemingly unconnected archipelago of LLCs, none of which led directly to the man himself, and to campaign contributions that would have appeared to come from all over. Primo used aliases for everything. Even Byers didn't know Primo's legal name.

The real danger, Primo knew, was Byers's penchant for blabbery. The man was a human leak, incapable of keeping his mouth shut. What if he told someone about his arrangement with Primo? What if there was something in Byers's personal files? What if he'd told his little whore everything during their pillow talk? It could get messy.

Primo had to make sure there were no loose ends.

CHAPTER 7

After turning onto Avenue P, I drove slowly past a sprawling auto body shop, an impound lot, a small fabricating plant—the industrial underbelly of America. About midway down, Nancy told me, "Turn right."

"Anything you say, sweetheart," I said.

I half expected Nancy to reply "Don't patronize me, dear," but she stayed quiet as a gate swung upward and I entered the green and white wonderland that was Enterprise's off-airport facility.

Inside was a jumbled chaos of official vehicles, marked and unmarked, from Newark police to New Jersey State Police to FBI—a circus of men in dark-colored windbreakers. It was tough to tell if there was a ringmaster for all the madness. From an outsider's perspective, it just looked like a lot of people with short haircuts running around trying to look important.

I couldn't imagine what they were all doing there. Properly deployed, it was enough law enforcement manpower to tackle at least two dozen unsolved murders. Instead, they were all focused on one lousy councilman.

Following the lines that told me where to return my car, I pulled to a stop under an awning at the direction of a very distracted man in a puffy jacket that had CHECK-IN in block letters on the back. He kept looking at the vast parking lot to his left where, about two football fields away, all the short haircuts were focusing their attention. With his handheld computer, he scanned a bar code on the back driver's side window. If it seemed odd to him someone would return a car a mere half hour into the rental, he didn't say anything about it. Of course, that might be because he never actually looked at me.

"Shuttle to the airport is that way," he said, tearing off a receipt and waving vaguely toward the main building.

"Thanks," I said, taking the receipt and making a show of walking in the proper direction until I was out of his line of sight, when I began making my way back toward the parking lot.

Dressed in my black peacoat, dark pants, and rubber-soled dress shoes—and with my own short haircut—I looked coplike enough that no one was stopping me. That was the nice thing about so many different agencies being out here: everyone would just assume I belonged to someone else.

Plus, there was something about the news helicopters overhead—there were now three of them—that added to the general sense of mayhem. I could have been leading around a tiger tied to a piece of dental floss and I'm not sure anyone would have given me a second glance.

As I got closer, I saw most of the action was buzzing around a red Ford Taurus. The parking spots around it had been cleared out and an ambulance, lights still flashing, was parked nearby. That meant the councilman's corpse was still on the premises, perhaps still in the car.

I kept walking toward it and got to within about twenty yards, where a perimeter of yellow crime scene tape had been erected. I thought about ducking under it—inasmuch as no one had stopped me so far—but didn't want to risk it just yet. So I went over to a huddle of guys, all of them black or Latino, dressed in jackets that said either CHECK-IN or CLEANING on the back.

There seemed to be one guy in the middle who was commanding the floor, so I went over to eavesdrop.

Except as soon as they became aware of my presence, they all turned and looked at me.

"Hey, fellas," I said.

Several of them nodded, then one of the cleaning guys eyed me and asked, "You a cop or something?"

I could guess the typical car cleaner at the Newark Airport Enterprise facility was probably making about $8.85 an hour and might have had a run-in or two with the law that left him unfond of those sworn to protect it. So I smiled and said, "Not exactly. I'm a reporter with the *Eagle-Examiner.* I'm probably not supposed to be here. So keep it quiet, okay?"

The cleaners grinned, happy to keep my secret and eager to help.

"He's in the red car over there, the senator or whatever," one of the check-in guys said. "He's still in there. They haven't moved him yet."

"Really," I said.

"Eddie is the one here who found him," another said, pointing to the guy who had been in the middle of the scrum when I came up—a short, weathered-looking Latino.

"No kidding," I said. Eddie smiled proudly at me, showing off a mouth at least three teeth short of a full deck. I stuck out my hand: "Carter Ross."

"Hey," he said, not bothering to take his glove off as we shook.

"What's your name?"

"Oh, Eddie . . . I mean Edgar . . . Perez . . . but they call me Eddie," he said.

Eddie Perez grinned again. There hadn't been a lot of visits to the dentist in his past, but he sure seemed friendly.

"So what time did you find him?" I asked.

"Man, I don't know, it was like six . . . six-thirty . . . My shift start at six, you know? And it was at least an hour in, so like . . .

seven . . . seven-thirty. I don't know. Yeah, seven-thirty . . . eight."

Well. That was precise.

"And what, he was just sitting in one of the cars?"

"Yeah, man, I was doing Row Q, you know, going through, making sure there wasn't no trash, making sure they got the gas in them, you know? And I get to this one car and I can tell someone left something in the trunk because it's riding low back there."

"Tell him about the roast beef sandwich," one of them prompted.

"Yeah, yeah, man," Eddie said. "I went around to the trunk and it smelled a little bit, you know? Like you leave a roast beef sandwich in the car for a couple days and it starts to smell, you know? And people, they do this all the time. The check-in guys are supposed to inspect the trunks, but sometimes they get busy, you know?"

"Right, sure," I said, like I had ample experience cleaning gamy roast beef sandwiches out of rental cars.

"And, man, I open up the trunk thinking I'm going to find someone's suitcase and a sandwich or something. And there's this guy all curled up in there, where the, uhh . . . you know, the thing . . ."

"The spare tire?" I asked.

"Yeah, man, where the spare tire is supposed to be. Except it wasn't no spare tire in there, it was this guy."

"Tell him about the nails," another one said.

"Yeah, man, he had these nails sticking out his whole body, you know?" Eddie said.

"Nails?"

"Yeah, it was like someone took a nail gun or something and went bam, bam, bam, bam. There had to be like twenty, thirty, fifty nails in him, you know?"

I immediately got the image of Windy Byers, his corpse riddled with metal spikes, curled up in the wheel well.

What a way to go.

* * *

Eddie recounted the end of his story, calling me "man" at least seven more times and saying "you know" at least a dozen. But the gist of it was that he went to report the presence of an existentially deprived passenger to his boss, who called the authorities, who came streaming in ever more massive numbers. They interviewed Eddie at some length until they finally realized he was just the guy who cleaned the car and, man, he didn't really know nothin', you know?

In truth, Eddie had probably reached the end of his usefulness to me, as well. He had given me some great bits of what we in the business call "color"—those little details that make a story jump off the page. There was a big difference between a lede that read "Newark Councilman Wendell A. Byers was found dead yesterday at a car rental facility near Newark Airport" and "A cleaning man at a car rental facility near Newark Airport made a gruesome discovery in Row Q yesterday morning, when he found the nail-riddled corpse of Newark Councilman Wendell A. Byers rolled up in the trunk of a red Ford Taurus."

I thanked Eddie for his help, but as the group broke apart, I sidled up to one of the check-in guys, a black guy with short-cropped hair.

"Hey, you mind helping me with something real quick?" I asked.

"Sure, boss, what's up?" he said, in a perhaps Jamaican, perhaps Haitian, definitely Carribean accent.

"You got one of those little handheld computers?"

"Yeah, boss," he said, pulling it out of the pocket of his puffy jacket.

"What can you tell me about this car," I said, rattling off the license plate number to the red Ford that had become Windy Byers's impromptu hearse.

He did some typing, working quickly on the small keyboard

with his thumbs, the only flesh exposed on his otherwise gloved hands.

"It was rented from location oh-one-five—that's here—Sunday at 7:42 P.M. by . . ." He stopped at the name. "Don . . . Donaa . . ."

"Spell it for me," I said.

"First name D-O-N-A-T-O," he said.

Donato. Got it.

"Last name S-E-M-E-D-O."

Semedo. Donato Semedo. What kind of name was that? Italian? Spanish? I didn't dare pull out my pad to write it down, so I did my best to burn it into my memory. Donato Semedo. Donato Semedo.

"Does that thing give you the renter's address?"

"Yeah, boss," he said, tilting the computer so I could see it.

It was on Hanover Street in Newark. I didn't know the street but could guess it was in the Ironbound, which was a German enclave back when all the streets were being named.

"Thanks," I said, thankful to have found such a helpful check-in guy. "That thing tell you anything else?"

"Rental insurance declined," he said. "It doesn't say nothing about the return. He must have just dumped it here."

That explained why the cleaner was the first to find the body.

I might have pushed for more, but I sensed an attack was coming from lower middle management. A man with straight, mousy brown hair, too-big-for-his-face glasses, and a very unfortunate mustache was approaching fast from the direction of the main building. His jacket was embroidered with JEFF on it.

And Jeff looked very excited.

"Excuse me, sir, are you with the police?" he asked.

"No," I said, and was not inclined to volunteer more than that.

"Well, this is not a public area," Jeff said. "And I can't have you walking around talking with employees. I'm going to have to ask you to leave."

"What's wrong with talking? It's a free country."

Good comeback. For a fourth grader.

"I'm going to have to ask you to leave," he said, unmoved by my patriotism.

I briefly considered whether there were any legitimate grounds by which I could protest. But ultimately I was better off bringing as little attention to myself as possible. If the authorities became aware a reporter had been traipsing around their crime scene, they might get persnickety and hit me with trespassing or disturbing the peace or loitering or one of the other charges they typically reserve for young black men hanging out on street corners.

Better to escape relatively unnoticed.

"So you're saying I have to leave?" I asked.

"Yes, sir."

"Okay, no big deal," I said. "Which way to the airport?"

Jeff not only showed me the way to the shuttle but escorted me there, stood next to me with his arms crossed until it came, then made sure I was onboard with the door closed and the shuttle moving.

There were only two other passengers with me, a pair of airport-bound business travelers who had seen my prisoner of war treatment and were nervously clutching their luggage, like I was about to steal it. We passed the police barricade, and as we inched along through the narrow channel between the TV trucks, I decided it was time to join my people. I walked up to the driver and said, "You can drop me off here."

"Here?" the guy said.

"Yeah, I just remembered I'm afraid of flying," I said, quickly pulling a twenty-dollar bill out of my wallet.

"Hey, whatever works for you, pal," the guy said, taking the bill as he pulled the bus to a stop and opened the door.

I disembarked next to a cluster of print reporters, one of whom happened to be Tommy. He stared at me blankly for a second, like I was a strange new life-form crawling out of the sea, then broke himself off from the pack.

"Are you coming from where I think you're coming from?" he asked. He had to shout a little bit to be heard over the thumping of nearby helicopter rotors.

"Yeah," I said, with a perhaps-too-cocky smile.

"How did you get in there?"

"I happen to be a big fan of Enterprise rental car. They pick you up, you know. What's going on out here in the media mosh pit?"

"Nothing. It's just a lot of pretty boys worrying about their appearance too much. It's like I never left the club from last night."

"What have you been told so far?"

"Again, nothing. They haven't even officially confirmed that it's Windy Byers in there. You ask them why the road is closed and all the spokesman says is it's a police investigation. For all we know at this point, this whole thing could be for some wino who died of exposure."

"Oh, it's Windy all right."

"How do you know?"

"I talked to the guy who found him," I told Tommy, then filled him in on all I learned on the inside.

When I was done, Tommy didn't comment on my genius as a reporter, thank me for providing such great details for the next day's story, or compliment me on my brilliant—albeit accidental—ingenuity.

Instead, he said, "Donato Semedo of thirteen Hanover Street, huh?"

Tommy took a few steps farther away from the other reporters. I got the hint and followed him over to the edge of the road, which bordered on a small, forlorn patch of marshland. A faint breeze stirred the dried stalks of pampas grass.

"There's something weird going on," he said.

"Speak, young Tommy."

"Remember how I told you I was going over those ELEC documents?"

"Yeah, the Election Law stuff. I thought you were just punishing yourself."

"I was. But then, I don't know. Windy's donor list was strange. I kept coming up with all these Portuguese names. I can't be sure, I think one of them might have been Donato Semedo. It sure sounds Portuguese."

"Portuguese? I thought maybe it was Italian or Spanish or something."

"No, it's definitely Portuguese," Tommy said. "It seemed like all of his donors had these fresh-off-the-boat immigrant names. And they all had addresses in the Ironbound. And I just couldn't figure it out. Why would the Central Ward councilman get all this money from people outside his district?"

"Beats me. Why?"

"I still don't know," Tommy said. "It was something I was going to look into a little more the next time I got the chance. Then this came up. But now you're telling me Windy has been kidnapped and killed by someone named Donato Semedo and, well, fill in the blanks."

"I suppose we could go pay a visit to Donato Semedo and find out."

Tommy pointed to the line of news trucks.

"Well, you can," he said. "I have to stay here and babysit."

"Oh, right," I said, and was about to bid him adieu and head in my own direction, except I realized I had no means by which to do so. Unless I felt like walking back to the office.

"Of course, I don't have my car with me," I said. "I'm going to need to hitch a ride somehow. Anyone else from our place here with you?"

"Just Tina," he said.

"Tina?" I said, and the mere utterance of her name brought a surge of guilt, even though I had no cause. "What's she doing here?"

"She was on her way to the office when she got the call about Windy and she knew she could get here before anyone else. Not that it mattered—the police had already plugged up the road."

"Where is she now?"

Tommy signaled his ignorance by shrugging. So I pulled my phone out of my pocket and dialed her.

"Tina Thompson," she semishouted over the sound of the helicopters.

"Hey, it's your favorite reporter, where are you?" I asked.

"I'm about a hundred feet away from where you and your boyfriend are having your little chin wag," she said. "I was going to come over, but I didn't want to intrude. You two make a cute couple, by the way."

I looked to my left, then to my right, then back to my left. With all the people and confusion, I didn't see her. Then finally I spotted her walking toward me, waving.

She looked terrific, as usual. She was not particularly dressed up—just black slacks and a plain black leather jacket—but Tina was one of those women who didn't have to try too hard. Her hair was up in a ponytail. Her cheeks had a rosy glow from the cold, like she was just coming in from a jog. As she got closer, she even appeared happy to see me.

"Sorry I didn't wait for you last night," she said. "To be honest, I was still at the office when you texted me and I was looking for an excuse to cancel anyway. It was a long day and I was too tired for a night out."

"Oh," I said. "And here I thought you were pissed at me."

"What made you think that?"

"The part where you texted me that I sucked."

"I was just kidding," she said, then added as an aside to Tommy, "He's such a girl sometimes."

"Not in bed, I hope," Tommy said.

"I wouldn't know," she replied.

"Still?" Tommy inquired.

"He keeps wasting opportunities."

"A tragedy."

"Tell me about it," she said.

Tina crossed her arms and shook her head, her eyes rolling. Tommy consoled her with a pat on the shoulder.

"Are you two finished?" I asked.

"Yeah, I guess so," Tina said. "So what have you been up to this morning anyway?"

I gave her the same spiel I had given Tommy but this time finished with how I needed to mooch a ride off her.

"So, wait, where is your car again?" she asked when I was done.

"It's at the office . . . I had Enterprise pick me up there," I lied quickly, because I didn't particularly feel like explaining why Sweet Thang had taken me home the night before. Tina has a dirty mind. She might jump to conclusions.

"Anyhow, let's get going," I continued before she sniffed out my untruth. "Come on. Time's a-wasting. Chop-chop. Head 'em up and move 'em out."

"Okay, okay, take it easy," Tina said, then turned to Tommy. "I assume you've got this covered?"

"It's pretty easy when nothing's happening and nothing will," he assured her.

And we were off. Tina drives a Volvo, making her perhaps the only childless woman in American who does. But she often reminded me it was only temporary—the lack of child, that is, not the Volvo. It was a wonder she hadn't already installed the infant seat.

I typed "13 Hanover Street" into her nav system, which had a male voice—Nancy, wherefore art thou, Nancy—and the address turned out to be a short distance away. As we drove into the Ironbound and began snaking through its tight streets, I filled the time telling Tina about some of my previous day's discoveries, from my chat with Detective Raines to my meeting with Rhonda Byers to the realization, thanks to Akilah's sister, that Mrs. Byers probably wasn't our black-hatted villain after all.

And then we pulled up to Donato Semedo's residence—or what was supposed to be his residence, anyway. But it wasn't. Not unless he lived on the third baseline: 13 Hanover Street was a small neighborhood softball field.

Not that it was any great surprise. If you were planning to dump a body in a rental car, you probably weren't going to give your real information.

"Are you sure you remembered the address right?" Tina asked.

"Yeah, definitely. It was Dan Marino and Dartmouth College," I said.

"Come again?"

"Dan Marino was a football player who wore number 13. Dartmouth College is located in Hanover, New Hampshire. That was my mnemonic."

"Oh, of course," she said sarcastically. "So what now, Dan Marino?"

I leaned on my palm and looked out at the empty softball field, then said, "I wish I knew."

Tina declared she was needed back at the office, which seemed like a fine place for me to be, at least until I figured out something better.

As we drove toward the newsroom, we artfully avoided the conversation—or, rather, The Conversation—we needed to have about our future and plotted strategy on Windy Byers instead.

"Why don't you type up the stuff you got this morning and we'll put it online," she concluded as we got off the elevator. "No sense in saving it for tomorrow's paper—the whole world might have it by then."

"No problem," I said, and we went our separate ways.

As soon as I walked into the newsroom, I saw Sweet Thang and noticed she was putting great effort into not looking at me. It was a rather dismal performance. Her desk naturally pointed her in the direction of mine, so she had to turn her body away at a strange angle to avoid facing me.

I decided to spare her the agony. She had too many months left on her internship to sit that way the whole time. It would be bad ergonomics. So I went over to the chair next to her and noisily lowered myself into it. She started blushing the moment I sat down, even though she was still pretending to give all her concentration to the morning paper.

"Hello," I said, finally.

"Oh, hi," she said, lifting her face a little bit toward me but still not meeting my eye. "I didn't even see you come in."

Up close, she looked even more pathetic. Her hair was still a little wet, making her blond curls droop. Her shoulders were slumped and she wasn't sticking out her chest like she normally did. She was wearing pants, which was unusual—Sweet Thang was more of a skirts and dresses kind of gal—and a bulky sweater. There may have even been a sports bra underneath.

More than anything, she came across as embarrassed, like she had been scolded. And I was a little surprised to discover my primary thought toward her, which used to involve things you only see late at night on Cinemax, was now something more like pity. Or maybe it was just concern. I wanted to protect her.

"Are you all right?" I asked.

"Ohimjustfinethankyou," she said, a little too quickly.

"Come on, what's wrong?"

"Nothing."

"Lauren," I said, and when I used her real name, she made eye contact for the first time. "It's okay. Whatever happened last night, it's fine by me. It was maybe going to be something, but it wasn't. It's not a big deal."

"You're not . . . mad at me?" she asked, gazing up at me with what the romance writers would call imploring blue eyes.

"Mad at you? No."

"Not at all?"

"Not at all."

"Good!" she said buoyantly. "I have a present for you."

"You do?"

"Two, actually!"

"I can't wait."

"The first is, I couldn't sleep last night, and I felt bad you never got to taste the banana bread I made for Bertie. So I made you some. I used buttermilk. I hope that's okay."

She reached into her bag and extracted a Saran-wrapped loaf so large she needed two hands to grip it.

"Oh," I said, surprised more than anything.

"Don't worry. This isn't bread with strings attached. It's just friendship bread," she added.

"Right. Friendship bread. Thank you."

"The second gift," she said, reaching into her bag and pulling out a stapled document, "is this."

She handed it to me. My eyes scanned the first page, which I immediately recognized as a mortgage—mostly because the word MORTGAGE was written at the top.

"Chuck called me this morning," she said proudly. "He found it in a filing cabinet last night. I went over to the courthouse on my way in and got it from him."

"Great work," I said, glancing up at her to see a proud smile form on her lips.

I turned my attention back to the document. The mortgagee was, of course, Wendell A. Byers Jr. The mortgagor was a bank from Indianapolis. The mortgage amount was $324,000. But it was when I got to the part about the interest rate that things got, well, interesting.

The rate was a mere 3.15 percent. I went to an online mortgage calculator, which told me that made the monthly payment about $1,400. That, plus an escrow payment—call it $500 for property tax and $100 for homeowners insurance—brought the total payment to $2,000.

It was a sweetheart deal. And I would imagine Windy, who was paid $80,000 a year as a Newark councilman, plus whatever work he could boondoggle on the side, could swing $2,000 a month.

But as I read further, I saw it didn't last. The initial rate was just for thirty-six months. For the remaining 324 months, I had to refer to something called the "adjustable rate rider," which was attached hereto in Exhibit B.

Lawyers always make things so clear.

I turned to the back of the document, where Exhibit B told me that the rate was "LIBOR plus 8.99 percent." Like I said, clear as mud.

"Do you know what LIBOR is?" I asked Sweet Thang, who did not attempt an answer.

"Do me a favor," I said. "Go over to Buster Hays and ask him. He's the kind of guy who knows this sort of thing. But don't tell him I'm the one who wants to know. He'll give you a hard time."

Sweet Thang went over to Buster who, as one of the legions of older men enamored of her youthful beauty, was all too happy to help. They had a brief conversation—Buster was lit up like Christmas Eve the entire time, the horny old goat—and Sweet Thang returned.

"It stands for London Interbank Offered Rate," she said.

"That really doesn't help me."

"It's an index," she explained. "It has something to do with an average of a bunch of things and I guess it's something bankers worry about a lot."

"Okay. So LIBOR plus 8.99 means . . . what?"

"Well, he said the LIBOR fluctuates, but lately it's been below two percent," she said.

That meant once the introductory rate on Akilah's house expired, the new interest rate would reset to somewhere around 11 percent. I turned to my mortgage calculator and typed in the new number. The monthly payment was now more than $3,000—more like $3,600 with the escrow factored in.

I went back to the beginning of the mortgage and looked at the dates. The reset, I realized, had happened December 1.

Windy Byers's booty call had just gotten a lot more expensive.

It was the great Nora Ephron, penning lines for the Carrie Fisher character in *When Harry Met Sally,* who observed that everyone thinks they have good taste and a sense of humor—and not everyone could possibly have good taste and a sense of humor.

The same could be said in the sad-but-familiar case of Wendell A. Byers. Everyone thinks they're smart enough not to get swindled in real estate deals—and, clearly, not everyone is. Certainly not Windy Byers.

It turns out that the all-powerful councilman was not much different from so many other Americans at the peak of the subprime boom: he allowed himself to be sold an overpriced house with a bad loan, and then, when the financial feces hit the fan, he got stuck with it.

I laughed.

"What's so funny?" Sweet Thang asked.

"Windy Byers," I said. "Getting suckered by a teaser rate, then panicking when it runs out. I guess keeping a woman on the side suddenly wasn't as fiscally sound, so he told her to take a hike."

"Do you think that's what happened?"

"Well, only two people know for sure, and one of them is now a corpse stinking up a rental car," I said.

"And the other . . ." Sweet Thang began.

". . . is Akilah Harris," I finished. "Think you can find her?"

Sweet Thang looked down at the desk.

"But where do I—" she began whining, and I cut her off.

"Let me rephrase: you have to find her. You've got her cell number. She slept in your apartment two nights ago. You're best friends with her mom. You're pretty tight with her sister, too. If anyone can locate this girl, it's you. I know you can do it."

"You really believe in me?"

"Absolutely," I said.

She grabbed a notepad off her desk, stood up, stuck her chest out like the proud young woman she was, and walked out of the newsroom—leaving me alone with a massive loaf of banana bread.

I walked to the break room, grabbed a plastic knife and paper plate, and sawed off a nice slice of mid-morning snack. I took it back to my desk but had barely gotten the first bite in my mouth when Tina was standing in front of me, scowling at what remained of the loaf.

"What the hell is this?" she demanded.

"It's . . . it's friendship bread," I said meekly.

"And what the hell is that?"

"I don't know. That's what Sweet Thang called it."

"*Friendship bread?* That little sorority girl is giving you something called *friendship bread*?"

"I suppose some would call it banana bread. Would you like some?"

"All that refined sugar and bleached flour?" Tina mocked. "I think not."

"Come on. Bananas have potassium. And there are nuts, too—think of all the protein."

Tina narrowed her eyes at me further. I felt like she was reading the bottom line of an eye chart that was printed on the inside of my skull.

"You were with her last night, weren't you?" she said at last. "That's why you couldn't make our dinner."

"No," I said, unconvincingly.

Lips pursed, Tina stared me down.

"I told you, I got caught in traffic," I said. And strictly as a matter of fact, that was true: at the time our date was canceled, I was caught in traffic.

"I know when you're lying," she said, in a low, scary voice that suggested demonic possession had just occurred.

"I'm aware of that. And it terrifies me."

"And you want to tell me you weren't with Sweet Thang last night."

"I never said that."

"Aha!" she shouted, like the courtroom lawyer who had just scored a major point on cross-examination.

"I was with Sweet Thang at an interview, then got caught in traffic on the Garden State Parkway on my way to see you," I said, which was all true. I just didn't feel like it was the right moment to add: then I nearly deflowered the girl and only stopped short when I was tripped by my conscience while rounding third base.

"All I'm going to say is: beware of women who bake for you," she said, and stalked off.

Nearby, Buster Hayes rose from his chair and made a whipping sound as he walked away.

"Oh, what?" I said, but he had already made his point.

I turned to my computer and began my search for the mysterious Donato Semedo. One bogus address aside, I didn't expect finding him would be difficult. For a reporter who knows his way around public information databases, people with unusual names are a treat. The Robert Johnsons of the world can kill you, but give me a Donato Semedo and I'll be able to tell you whether he wears boxers or briefs within a few keystrokes.

Except, as it turns out, for this particular Donato Semedo.

He didn't vote. He didn't get speeding tickets. He didn't own property. He didn't have a credit card. He didn't have liens against him. He never declared bankruptcy. He wasn't a registered sex offender. He didn't have a criminal record. He never served time in a state or federal prison. He was not a public employee or retiree in the state of New Jersey. He was not licensed to provide medical care, dental care, massage therapy, or child care.

Half an hour in, I was starting to give up hope and run out of databases. Then I remembered one more, a database of last resort in more ways than one: the Social Security Death Index.

Sure enough, I found Donato Semedo. Born January 27, 1917. Died July 8, 1987. Last residence: Newark, New Jersey. Card issued: New Jersey. He was probably some nice old Portuguese man who doddered around the Ironbound without bothering a soul, then had his identity stolen once he departed this mortal coil.

The question—who was Donato Semedo?—ceased to matter. It was now: Who was pretending to be Donato Semedo?

As I leaned back to ponder that question, I became aware my friendship bread was under attack.

"I'm starving," Tommy said as he hacked off a piece with my plastic knife. "Do you mind?"

"Not at all," I said. "I thought you were babysitting the New York press corps."

"I was. Buster Hays took over for me," Tommy said, carefully transferring a slender slice to his plate. "He said a scene like that was no place for a little girl like me."

Tommy lifted the bread to his mouth, then paused. "I swear, one day I'm going to stick my foot up his ass so far he's going to be able to taste my Tod's."

"Tod's . . . those must be . . . shoes?"

"You are so straight it hurts," he said as he chewed. "Oh, my God, this is so good! Who made it?"

"Sweet Thang."

Tommy stopped mid-chew. "You know you have to be careful of women who bake for you," he said. "They're all crazy."

"Why does everyone keep saying that?"

"Cuv ith twue," he said, through a full mouth.

"How would *you* know?"

He swallowed and smirked. "Actually, I don't. But I bumped into Tina and she told me to come over here and say it."

"Evil," I said. "Anyhow, I ran down our friend Donato Semedo. It turns out he's dead at the present time."

"Let me get this straight: they let a *dead guy* take out a rental car, but they make me wait until I'm twenty-five?"

"I know. What a country."

Tommy chewed some more. The refined sugar and all that other bad stuff didn't give him pause. Then again, his metabolism hadn't turned thirty yet. Just wait.

"So did you say Donato Semedo showed up in one of your ELEC reports?" I asked.

"I think so, let me check," he said, and went to retrieve a notepad from his desk. "I started writing down all the names that didn't look like they ought to be giving money to a Central Ward councilman. Yeah, here it is. Semedo comma Donato."

He held up the pad, as if it was evidence.

"So here's a thought," I said. "If Donato Semedo is a dead guy, what's the possibility some of the other names on that list are also dead guys?"

"I'd say it's a good possibility," Tommy said.

"You mind if your notebook comes over to my desk and plays for a little while?"

"Okay. But no unhealthy snacks and no scary movies."

"Got it," I said as he handed it over.

I started by running the names on Tommy's list through the

voter rolls. Anyone who was engaged enough in the political process to make a donation ought to be registered to vote, right? True, it wasn't going to be perfect. Some names were too common—Jose Silva being the Portuguese equivalent of John Smith. And since some of these people would presumably be foreign born, they might not have earned the right to vote.

But that was where the death index again came in handy. And I started getting hits. Inacio Barbosa. Dead. Martinho Fortes. Dead. Cornelio Moniz. Dead. Desiderio Ronaldo. Dead.

Within half an hour, I had more than a dozen confirmed cases of daisy-pushing donors who had, in a fit of posthumous generosity, given roughly $50,000 to candidate Wendell A. Byers Jr. And, beyond those I could say with confidence were deceased, there were at least another two dozen whose mortality could be considered suspect. All told, the haul of potentially dirty money in Byers's campaign coffers was over $100,000.

I went to Tommy's desk to return his notebook.

"Your notebook played well with others," I said. "But he has a lot of naughty names in him."

"Yeah, what's up with that?"

"Well, this is just a guess, but most of the time when you have bogus campaign contributors, it means someone is trying to circumvent contribution limits. The classic way of doing it is, say I'm president of a company that really needs a road-paving contract and I want to throw fifty grand at the mayor. I can have my company give so much—the dollar amount always changes, but it's around ten grand—and I can give my ten grand personally. But I'm stuck after that. So I enlist a bunch of my employees, hand them each ten grand, and instruct them to make a generous donation in their own name."

"Okay. So if you can have living employees do that, why enlist the nonliving?"

"Because, matey," I said, affecting a pirate brogue, "dead men tell no tales."

"Ah, pirates," Tommy said wistfully. "To be stuck aboard a ship full of men out at sea for months at a time."

Before I could jog Tommy out of that little fantasy, my cell phone rang.

I recognized the number as belonging to Detective Sergeant Kevin Raines.

"Hello," I said. "Is it me you're looking for?"

"Yeah, hey," he said quickly. "It's Raines."

"What, no props for the Lionel reference?"

"I'm a little busy. I just realized I never returned your call from yesterday. How did things go with Mrs. Byers?"

"I can give you the play-by-play if you want, but I'm pretty sure that's a dead end. We paid a visit to Akilah's sister last night, and she told us Mrs. Byers has known about the affair for a long time—and besides, the two lovebirds split up several weeks ago. At the moment, I'm more interested in Donato Semedo."

"Hang on a sec," he said. "How the hell do *you* know about Donato Semedo? We haven't told anyone about that."

"What do you think I do here, sit around playing with myself all day waiting for you guys to tell me what's going on?"

"Well, no, but—"

"You know he's dead, right?"

"You mean the original Donato Semedo? Yeah, we figured that out," Raines said.

"Know anything about the guy pretending to be Donato Semedo?"

"Yeah, he's short, broad, and favors hats that keep his face hidden from security cameras."

"He also favors nail guns from what I hear," I said.

"Goddammit. Now how the hell do you know *that*?"

"Sometimes a reporter just knows things," I said. "Did you also know that he made a contribution to Windy Byers's most recent reelection effort?"

"Yeah, so?"

"Well, isn't that illegal, Officer?"

"I got a murder on my hands," Raines said. "You think I care about a campaign finance law violation?"

"But don't you think it's interesting that there was a connection between Byers and the guy who killed him?"

"Maybe. I'm still trying to get basic forensics done at this point. I don't have time for all that Oliver Stone stuff right now. But if that's really flipping your skirt up, go talk to Denardo Webster."

Denardo Webster. The name rang a very soft bell, then I placed it: Windy's chief of staff, the no-neck guy who escorted Mrs. Byers at the press conference.

"He'll probably play dumb at first, but don't let him. He knows what's up," Raines continued. Then, before disconnecting, he added, "I can't believe I'm saying this to a reporter. But if you learn anything, let me know."

I thanked him and turned to Tommy.

"See if you can find anything that ties all these names together, other than a predilection for taking long dirt naps," I said. "I've got an errand to run."

The constituent services office for Central Ward Councilman Wendell A. Byers was located on Springfield Avenue, just a few doors down from African Flavah, my favorite breakfast spot. And while I was tempted to visit Khalid and spend some quality time with his pancakes, that would have to wait.

My last act before leaving the office was to type the name Denardo Webster into our public employee database. It told me he was being paid $72,253 a year for his services. This, of course, gave me questions to ponder as I drove. Did a Newark councilman actually have a staff that needed chiefing? And what, exactly, did he do all day that was worth $72,253?

I suspected the answer would be: not much.

The office was a small storefront with impressive decal work on the glass door. The crest of the Newark City Council and Windy's name were outlined in gold. The view inside was blocked by metal shades, which were lowered and drawn. Underneath the decal, taped to the door, was a handwritten sign that said APPOINTMENT'S ONLY. NO DROP IN'S PLEASE.

I tried not to let the wanton apostrophe abuse grate at me as I pulled on the door. It was locked. I pressed the doorbell and, as I waited, fought the urge to rip the paper off the door and scrub out the offending punctuation. I hit the button a second time and, finally, heard it buzz open.

I found Denardo Webster sitting in full recline, his feet propped on a desk. Up close, he was even bigger than he had seemed at the press conference: my height but probably twice my weight. Back in the day, he had been someone's defensive tackle—or someone's bouncer. And even now that he had allowed himself to go soft, I got the impression he'd be handy to have around if you needed someone to lift a piano.

Not that he was working all that hard at the moment. An extra-large Styrofoam container of fried chicken and French fries sat on his rather generous lap. And he was about halfway through demolishing every grease-soaked morsel. The boss was dead, but it apparently hadn't spoiled this guy's appetite.

"Can I help you?" he said in a deep, thick, syrupy voice.

"I'm Carter Ross with the *Eagle-Examiner,*" I said. "You must be Denardo Webster."

He took a bite of chicken and sat there, stoically, staring at me as he chewed. He swallowed and wiped his mouth with a napkin before answering.

"You got an appointment?" he asked.

"No," I said impatiently. "If I had known Councilman Byers was going to die today, I surely would have made one. But it kind of caught me by surprise."

More staring. The feet were still on the desk.

"I can't help you if you don't have an appointment," he said.

Without exerting too much effort, he leaned slightly forward and grabbed a toothpick, then began cleaning his right front tooth.

"Okay," I said, trying to keep from losing my mind. "Could I please make an appointment for, say, right now."

"Can't," he said. "I'm on my lunch break."

He chomped down on the toothpick with his back molars and reclined further.

"As a matter of fact," he continued. "I'm going to have to ask you to leave. I'm on my lunch break. The office is closed right now."

"You're kidding me, right?" I said, close to yelling.

He looked at me impassively. Even the toothpick, which he lazily shifted from side to side, was moving slowly.

I considered my options. Strangling the guy was one of them. But that wouldn't ultimately get me the information I needed, and, besides, I'm not sure I could locate his neck, much less choke it.

Trying to intimidate him with a damning article about bureaucratic inefficiency—what *did* he do for his seventy-two clams a year anyhow?—didn't feel like it would motivate this guy much, either.

Then, magically, wonderfully, I heard Tommy's voice in my head: *I just always heard stuff about Windy Byers doing it on the down low with one of his council staffers.*

I glanced around the office. There didn't appear to be any other council staff besides the chief. Then I looked at the massive man stretched out before me and wondered, was it really possible? This guy and Windy? You'd be talking about more than six hundred pounds of man love rolling around on each other. Could it be?

Only one way to find out.

"Look, I know you and Windy liked to do it, okay?" I said.

As soon as I said the words "do it," the toothpick dropped out of his mouth. And I knew it was true. Congratulations, Denardo Webster. I now own you.

"His wife knew about it, too—Windy told her," I lied. "She and I agreed that it was best kept out of the newspaper—no sense in dragging out something that would just hurt a dead man's reputation. But if you don't cooperate with me, you give me no choice . . ."

"Just take it easy, take it easy," he said, the molasses suddenly gone from his vocal cords. "Let's just be cool, okay?"

I looked at his desk and saw the picture of a middle-aged woman and a pair of chunky little boys who favored their daddy. Yeah, I definitely owned him.

"Oh, I can be cool," I said. "But I need some answers, and I don't plan on waiting for an appointment to get them."

"Okay, okay, yeah, sorry about that. It's just I get people coming in off the street all day long and—"

I held my hand up to stop what would otherwise be a stream of excuses. "Don't worry about it," I said, and pulled out my notebook. "Tell me about Donato Semedo, Inacio Barbosa, Martinho Fortes . . ."

I could have continued, but there was not the slightest bit of recognition on his face.

"I got no idea who those dudes are, I swear," he said.

"They all made pretty sizable campaign contributions to your boss," I said.

"Oh, oh, yeah, yeah, I know what you're talking about," he said. "But, I swear, I never met them. I don't know who those dudes are."

"I'm sure you don't. They're all dead."

He looked at me quizzically.

"Yeah?"

"Them and at least a dozen others. All dead people. All giving money to Windy Byers."

"No foolin'," he said.

I nodded.

"Look, all I know is, this dude came in all the time and gave me an envelope with cash in it," Webster said. "Then he'd hand me a piece of paper with the name of the donor. I don't know if it's someone who's dead or alive. I just write it down in the logbook, because Windy, he likes to put it in this computer file he has."

"Computer file?" I asked, my interest piqued. "You mean, like an Excel spreadsheet?"

"Yeah. Whenever I got cash, Windy wanted to know so he could put it in his laptop."

"Why in the world would he want to log illegal campaign contributions in a spreadsheet?"

"Maybe he didn't know they were illegal," Denardo said.

Even though Windy had never been the quickest draw in the saloon, I'm not sure even he could have been that willfully ignorant. He had to know the money was dirty. Then again, perhaps he hoped that if he logged it in his Excel file—then reported it for all the world to see on those ELEC reports—it would have the effect of cleaning it. It would at least give him some plausible deniability if he was ever investigated. Okay, so maybe he wasn't as dumb as I thought.

"Do you have a copy of the file?" I asked.

"Naw, I didn't do any of the computer stuff. I just did pen and paper. When the Spanish dude gave me cash, I wrote him a receipt. Then he'd leave. That's all I know."

"Tell me about the Spanish dude," I said.

"I don't know. He's not the boss or nothing. He's just a . . . a runner or something."

"He got a name?" I asked.

"We never got real friendly."

"What's he look like?"

"Oh, man, he's like . . . I don't really look at him, you know?" Webster said. "He's a Spanish dude. Kind of a little dude like those

Spanish guys are. Sometimes he's got tools on his belt. I think he's like a construction worker or something."

"What kind of car does he drive?"

"I don't know." Webster pointed to the drawn shades. "I can't see the street from here."

"How often does he come in?"

"Pretty regular. Every couple of weeks. Sometimes more, sometimes less."

"When was the last time he was here?" I asked.

Webster reached into his desk, pulled out an account book, and leafed to the last page in which there were entries.

"Last week," he said. "On Tuesday. I remember it was around lunchtime."

That narrowed it down at least a little. Though I suspected his definition of lunchtime was rather generous.

"How much did he give?"

"Ten grand."

"Where does it come from?"

"I don't know, I swear. Please."

I concentrated on Denardo's pudgy face, searching for any kind of twitch or eye shift that might suggest artifice. But all I saw was an earnest, bordering-on-desperate gaze in return.

"No clue who his boss is?"

Webster shook his head. "Look, man, I swear, I ain't clownin' you or nothing. If I knew, I'd tell you. I just don't know. Windy, he did his own thing and I did my own thing, you know? It wasn't like we told each other everything."

"Okay," I said, getting ready to leave. "I'm sure I'm going to have more questions. I'll call you. What's your cell number?"

He gave it to me and added, "We're cool, right?"

"Well, that depends. You're not going to give me a hard time again, are you?"

"No way, man," he said. "Anything you need. No appointment necessary."

* * *

As I wandered back out to Springfield Avenue, I knew I needed to find the mysterious Spanish dude, who was probably either Portuguese or Brazilian, given the names he toted on those little pieces of paper.

I got back in my car and sat there hoping maybe, somehow, the Spanish dude would just drive up and park in front of me, with his envelope stuffed full of cash, and tell me everything—who he worked for, what the money was about, why it resulted in Windy needing to be dead. I could have the story written by five o'clock.

But that wasn't going to happen. He was never coming back. And the chances that someone on a bustling avenue might have rememebered one random Hispanic guy who pulled up on the street every couple of weeks and went into Windy Byers's constituent services office? Slim.

If only there was a camera in the office. But I'd looked. No camera. I stared out at the street some more, watching the traffic scoot along, looking at the buildings, reading their signs, waiting for inspiration.

And then I saw what I needed. High atop the three-story brick building that housed African Flavah, there was Khalid's bulletproof camera, safe inside its little cage, bolted into the concrete.

I hurried into the restaurant to find Khalid in his normal spot: behind the counter, standing at the grill underneath an institutional-sized oven hood, cooking twenty lunches simultaneously, the orders for which he somehow kept in his head. Frankly, Khalid's occupation was my idea of eternal damnation. But Khalid once told me he could do it happily, ten hours a day, every day of the week—which is what he pretty much did. He opened at five every morning, when the airport porters and construction guys started drifting in, and kept the grill roaring until three in the afternoon, when the lunch crowd finally died down and he closed up shop.

"What's going on, Cousin Carter?" he boomed as soon as he saw me out of the corner of his eye.

He called me "Cousin Carter" because his grandmother was half white—German, I think. He figured that one-eighth Caucasian blood must mean we're related somehow.

Then again, if you go back far enough, aren't we all?

"Cousin Khalid," I returned. "How you been?"

"Blessed. I've been blessed."

I watched as he displayed his virtuosity on the grill, mesmerized by his ability to juggle eggs, sausage, hamburger, potatoes, French toast, fish, grilled cheese, pancakes, and bacon.

"So, trust me when I tell you I have a good reason for asking," I said. "But tell me about that security camera outside."

"Uh-oh," he announced to the other customers sitting at the counter, none of whom looked like me, "the white man is here playing PO-lice. We all in trouble now."

"What are you talking about?" I said, playing along. "You're part white."

"Yeah, but only a small part. That means when the PO-lice come, they gonna leave one-eighth of me alone, but the other seven-eighths is gonna be gettin' its ass kicked."

His audience cracked up. In truth, the frequency of police misconduct was exaggerated in the hood. A lot of it was just people telling stories, misrepeating versions of rumors that they themselves had greatly embellished. But it did happen on the rare occasion, and it only took one legitimate incident to lend credibility to all the loose talk for years to come.

"So with that camera, you keep tapes or anything?" I asked.

"Sort of, hang on," he said. He said a few things in Spanish to one of the guys taking orders, who immediately assumed Khalid's post behind the grill.

"Come on," Khalid said, walking through a door marked EMPLOYEES ONLY and into a small office. A newish computer sat on a cluttered table, and he parked himself in front of it.

"This is actually pretty cool," he continued. "They got these companies that want to charge you a billion bucks a month for monitoring, and then a billion more to store your data. But I figured out how to do it on this computer for free. The stuff you can do with wireless now is incredible."

How about that: Khalid, short-order chef and closeted computer nerd.

"How much does the outside camera see of the street?" I asked.

"It's pretty high up, so it sees a lot. Here, let me show you," he said as he started fiddling with the mouse.

A few clicks later, I was looking at a reasonably wide angle view of Springfield Avenue, including the sidewalk outside the entrance to Windy's place a few doors down.

"How long do you keep the data?"

"Oh, I got like a month's worth. I got a big-ass hard drive and the way I got the camera set, it only takes a picture every six seconds. That makes the file sizes smaller, so I can keep it for a while before I got to throw it out for space."

"So if I wanted to see a week ago Tuesday, around lunchtime, could you do that?"

"Yeah. Hang on a sec," he said, and clicked some more. He opened a file folder with the appropriate date, then started choosing among data files that were labeled by time: "00:01–03:00," "03:01–06:00," and so on. He selected "12:01–15:00" and clicked.

"What are we looking for?" he asked.

"I'm not sure. But I'm hoping I'll know when I see it."

The full-color footage was relatively decent quality—several steps above the grainy black-and-white stuff you see on the news whenever there's a convenience-store robbery—though the one-frame-per-six-second shutter speed made it like watching TV on jittery fast-forward.

After a few minutes of seeing nothing promising, I started feeling bad for Khalid, who had a restaurant to run. I assured him I could handle it by myself. He gave me a brief primer on how to work the controls before going back to his grill.

Over the next twenty minutes of footage—which covered about two hours' worth of real time—there were one or two images that made me stop the tape and take a closer look. But nothing really seemed like what I was looking for.

Then I finally got a hit.

I watched it a few times all the way through, then started going frame by frame.

Frames 1–4: A small, white pickup truck—New Jersey license plate JNM 89V—pulls up outside Windy's office.

Frames 5–7: The truck, now parked, sits still, with the driver inside. It's impossible to tell what he's doing—listening to a good song as it finishes up?—or whether he's idling or has cut the ignition.

Frame 8: The driver, small statured and brown skinned, probably Hispanic, gets out of the truck. He's wearing a black baseball cap pulled low over his eyes, a bulky sweatshirt with the hood off, and jeans. I don't see any tools or tool belt. But he looks like a guy who might be a contractor of some sort.

Frames 9–11: The man walks to the front door of Windy's place. It's hard to tell for sure, but it looks like he's moving with a certain amount of urgency.

Frames 12–15: I don't actually see him ring the bell—that part must have happened in between six-second interludes—but he's standing outside like he's hit the button and is waiting for Denardo Webster to get off his plentiful rump and buzz him in.

Frames 16–31: The man disappears inside. Traffic continues moving up Springfield Avenue in that herky, jerky style.

Frames 32–33: The man reappears and walks back to his Datsun.

Frames 34–35: The truck pulls away.

Figuring six seconds per frame, the whole transaction lasted three and a half minutes. I briefly tried to figure out how to do a screen grab and e-mail myself some of the key images, but that was beyond my technical abilities. So I did the next best thing, printing out several of the frames on a nearby ink-jet.

I reemerged from the office to find Khalid in his favorite spot, in front of his grill.

"I think I found what I was looking for," I said. "Thanks more than you know. I gotta run."

"All right," Khalid announced. "The PO-lice is gone, everyone can relax now."

Most of them seemed to know Khalid was kidding. But a few of them gave me the stink-eye just in case.

I was fairly certain I had found my Spanish dude—or, more important, his license plate. But there was one man who could confirm it for me, and he was just a few doors down, still working through his chicken and fries.

"What's going on, my friend?" Denardo Webster asked as soon as I had been buzzed in. Yeah, we were friends. Sure. Blackmail makes everyone fast pals.

"I think I found your Spanish dude on some surveillance camera footage," I said, laying my printouts on his desk. "This him?"

"Yeah, yeah, that's the guy. Damn, that's definitely him. He's always wearing that hoodie, too. I forgot about that. Don't matter how cold it is, he just wears that blue hoodie."

"This picture jog anything else in your memory about him?"

"You know, I don't think I ever heard that little dude say more than like two words all the times he came in here," Webster said. "I don't know if he spoke much English."

"Got it. Anything else?"

He thought for a second, then shook his head. "Here's my card," I said. "If anything else comes to you, call me."

"You bet."

By the time I walked out the door and got in my car, I had already dialed Rodney Pritchard's number.

"Pritchard," he answered.

"I need a quick favor," I said.

"It'd better be quick," he said. "I got a date with a ham sandwich."

"Can you run a plate for me? New Jersey JNM 89V."

"Yeah, hang on," he said, and I heard him typing. "It's a 1991 Datsun. You must be hanging out with the rich and famous again."

"Yeah, I saw Paris Hilton driving it."

"Well, it's registered to Hector Gomes. DOB 1/16/74."

He gave me an address on Van Buren Street in Newark.

"Thanks Pritch," I said. "I—"

"I'll say it for you: you owe me."

"I do, indeed," I said. "Enjoy that sandwich."

"Mmphhll," he said, then hung up.

I started the Malibu and did a quick illegal U-turn back in the direction of Van Buren, which was in the Ironbound. I was about halfway there when my cell phone rang and "Thang, Sweet" flashed up on the screen.

"Hello, darling, how have you been?"

"I've been great," she whispered. "I found Akilah. I'm with her right now, but she doesn't know I'm calling you. So shhh."

"Good news," I whispered back, even though I probably didn't need to. "Where did you find her?"

"I texted her and told her I forgave her for stealing my jewelry and if she needed anything she could always call me and I would still be her friend. She called me like thirty seconds later."

"Awesome," I said. "So, what'd she have to say about her ex-boyfriend?"

“Oh, she confirmed everything. She said she and Windy dated for a long time and that he bought her the house, but then a little while ago he came and told her he had to sell it because he couldn’t afford it anymore. She said she got that second job because she was going to try to work out a deal with him where she paid the mortgage herself.”

“Why didn’t she just tell us that the first time we talked to her?” I asked.

“She said she still loves Windy, even though they broke up, and she knew if it got out he had an affair it could hurt him politically and she didn’t want to get him in any trouble.”

“That’s nice of her,” I said. The loyal, loving ex-girlfriend. How come I always got the vindictive ones who mailed back my favorite sweatshirt in ribbons?

“I think she knows who killed Windy,” Sweet Thang whispered with extra fierceness.

“Really? Who?”

“She’s hinted at it a couple times, but she won’t tell me. She says she doesn’t want to put me at risk, whatever that means. I can’t get her to . . . Hang on, she’s coming, call me right back.”

Sweet Thang hung up. I dialed her number.

“Hello!” she said in a chipper, much louder voice. Obviously, our phone call was now with Akilah’s full awareness.

“Hey, Lauren, it’s Carter,” I said.

“Oh, hi, Carter!” Sweet Thang said, as if we hadn’t spoken in years. She put the phone down for a moment and announced to Akilah, “It’s Carter. Remember my colleague Carter?

“How *are* you?” she asked.

“Oh, I’m just ducky,” I said. “Where are you guys right now?”

I could hear Sweet Thang cup the phone.

“He wants to know where I am. Is it okay if I tell him?” she asked Akilah, who must have signaled her assent because Sweet Thang brought the phone back to her mouth and said: “We’re back at Akilah's house, just getting a few things. I'm helping her move into a Red Cross shelter."

I was about to tell her that sounded like a fine idea. But before I could get the words out, I was interrupted by Sweet Thang's loud, piercing scream.

Then the line went dead.

The abduction of Wendell Byers went as smoothly as Primo could have hoped, aided in no small part by Byers's own lack of guard. The fool was convinced being a councilman made him invincible, as if elected officials didn't bleed like everyone else.

Byers was so unsuspecting, Primo probably could have done the job himself. But Primo brought two men along, just in case. They were pros from New York, rented thugs. They went through the front door—unlocked—and found him in the study, typing on his laptop. He was, naturally, outraged at the intrusion. But his blather only lasted so long. One of the thugs clunked him on the head with a paperweight, opening a small gash in his scalp. The other bound him with an electrical cord. Together, they dragged him out of his house while Primo, having nothing else to do, grabbed the laptop.

It had been an afterthought, taking the computer. Later, when a broken Byers started whispering secrets, Primo realized it had been a brilliant bit of criminal intuition.

But first Primo had to do the breaking. They tossed Byers in the trunk of Primo's sedan, then brought him back to the warehouse. When Byers came to and found himself tied to a chair, he was indignant at first, filling the room with his how-dare-yous and you'll-pay-for-thises. It was typical Byers bluster, and Primo wanted to silence it.

So he took his nail gun, grabbed Byers by the wrist, and shot a nail into Byers's right hand, actually pinning it to the wall behind him. The man yelped with pain, cursing Primo loudly and profanely—as if it would do any good.

There was still too much fight in Byers. So, slowly, Primo took it out of him. He positioned a clock in front of Byers's eyes and informed the councilman that he would be leaving the room for ten minutes. Then he returned and punched a nail in Byers's forearm.

Primo knew the anticipation of pain was almost as excruciating as the pain itself. So he kept returning every ten minutes, wordlessly shooting a nail into another part of Byers's body, then departing. After forty minutes, Byers stopped cursing him. After an hour and a half, Byers was more than ready to talk. After three hours, Byers was begging to talk. But Primo waited until four hours passed before he chose to listen.

That's when it came pouring out of Byers—all the answers to Primo's questions, everything Primo needed to bring this messy arrangement to a neat conclusion. Whenever Primo decided Byers was being something slightly less than a hundred percent forthcoming, he left the room, announcing he would return in ten minutes. Sometimes he left the room even when Byers was cooperating. It kept Byers's fear at the appropriate level.

Eventually, the councilman began growing weak, slipping in and out of consciousness. So Primo finally finished him off with a few nails to the head. By that point, Primo had already learned everything he needed to know.

Other than the laptop—which Primo already possessed—Byers had left behind just one piece of evidence that could prove troublesome for Primo. But Primo could take care of that quickly enough.

CHAPTER 8

There is something about the female scream that juices my body chemistry. Probably it's hardwired, a remnant of the days when my more hirsute forebearers clung together in nomadic bands wandering an inhospitable planet. Back then, a woman's scream meant someone was about to be sabertooth tiger lunch. Or something like that. Whatever it was, I suddenly found myself wired on adrenaline, with my heart pounding and my body primed for large-motor activity.

My hands were shaking, but I managed to force my fingers to call Sweet Thang back, on the off chance it was nothing—like a big spider scared her and made her drop her phone.

But my call went straight to voice mail and, besides, I knew this wasn't arachnid related. Sweet Thang had made that kind of noise when Akilah jumped her and put a knife to her throat. It was an I'm-in-trouble-come-help-me-now-don't-dawdle-please kind of scream.

I pulled a screeching U-turn, the kind that involved jumping a curb because the road just wasn't wide enough, and sped toward Akilah's house. As I blew through a series of red lights—I thought they were orange, Officer—I called my favorite detective sergeant, in hopes of getting some reinforcement.

"Raines here."

"I think Akilah Harris knows who killed Windy," I said. "And I think the killer is after her."

"Whoah, whoah, whoah, slow down. What happened?"

I relayed what Sweet Thang told me about Akilah knowing more than she let on, then told him about the scream.

Raines was unimpressed.

"All you really know for sure is that your colleague's cell phone doesn't work," he said.

"Come on, you've got two young women in trouble, probably kidnapped or worse," I said, feeling a little frantic that I couldn't impress on him the gravity of that scream. "Can't you put out an amber alert or something?"

"I can't put out an amber alert because someone yelled just before her cell phone battery conked out," Raines replied. "We would need confirmation an abduction had occurred. And besides, amber alerts are for kids, not adults."

I knew that, of course. I also knew, thinking as a levelheaded cop—and not an easily addled newspaper reporter—he was right: I had a strong hunch something was wrong, but little more than that.

"If you can get a witness to say they saw a forcible abduction, we've got a different scenario on our hands," Raines continued. "Otherwise, you got nothing."

"Can you at least ask a squad car to meet me at the house? Something?" I begged. "For all I know, it's a hostage situation and they're still holed up inside."

"Fine," Raines said. "I'll ask patrol to send a car over. But I'm a little busy, you know? I got a pretty major investigation here, and I'm going to have to ask you to lose this number if you keep bothering me with half-baked hunches."

He hung up before I could reply.

Continuing to drive as if traffic signals were mere suggestions, I contemplated my next move, concluding quickly I didn't have one. I couldn't exactly charge into Akilah's house, guns blazing.

Not when the the most dangerous weapon I had in my car was nail clippers.

Thankfully, I arrived at Akilah's simultaneously with a white and black Newark patrol car. Two cops, a tall black man and a short Hispanic woman, got out. I waved to them.

"We were told we got a possible DV," the guy said. "You the one who called it in?"

DV. What's DV? Oh, right: domestic violence. Why would Raines tell them it's a domestic violence?

"Yeah, that's me," I said. "I was talking to a colleague of mine on the phone and I heard her scream like she was in real trouble."

I could tell the guy thought I was wasting his time and was doing his best to suppress an eye roll.

"And she's in *there*!" the female cop said, pointing to Akilah's burned-out shell of a house which, admittedly, didn't look very domestic at the moment.

"Yeah," I said. "Her name is Lauren. There's a woman with her named Akilah."

"What's the guy's name?" the male cop asked.

"I, uh, I don't know."

More barely restrained eye-rolling.

"All right," he said, then turned to his partner. "We'll check it out. You stay here."

The cops walked up to the front door—or, rather, the hole where it used to be—and entered. I braced myself for the sound of gunshots, or another scream, or something. But the cops came out two minutes later. The guy looked perturbed.

"There's no one there," he hollered from the top of the porch. "You sure they were in that place?"

I was about to answer when I was interrupted by a lady standing on the stoop of a three-family house two doors down.

"They left," she said, in an African accent. She had a brightly colored shawl wrapped around her shoulders, and I could guess from the slippers on her feet she didn't want to leave her spot. The male cop took the lead and walked toward her.

"Who left, ma'am?"

"Two women, three guys," she said. "They got in a black car and drove away."

I felt the adrenaline rush renew itself.

"See? They were kidnapped," I said in a voice that sounded more like yelling than I wanted.

The male cop shot me an annoyed look that said, *Shut it*.

"Could you please describe the women?" he asked.

"One was a pretty white girl, blond hair. The other was small, dark. She was pretty, too, but she looked like a mess. I had seen her before. She lives in that house, but I don't know her."

"Now what about the men?" he asked.

"I didn't look that hard."

"Did it look like they were being forced into the car?" the cop asked.

She thought for a moment

"Maybe. Maybe not. The little dark one was crying. But they walked to the car and got inside."

Something unintelligible squawked on the cop's radio, which he had attached to his belt. Whatever it was, he was suddenly in a hurry to leave.

"All right. Thank you, ma'am. You can go back inside."

The cop started walking toward his patrol car.

"What!" I said. "That's it? You're not going to do anything?"

"You heard her. She said they weren't abducted."

"She said she wasn't sure. There's a difference."

I panned my eyes toward the female cop, just to see if there was a chance I'd be able to prevail on her softer, female side . . . except, apparently, she wasn't into that stereotype. She seemed more concerned her hat wasn't sitting straight as she walked toward the squad car and paid little heed to my discussion with her partner.

"She said one of the women was crying," I pleaded. "Doesn't that mean anything to you?"

"My wife cries all the time," he replied as he got back into his car. "I'm sorry, sir, we have to go."

As he pulled away, the shriek of the tires on the pavement made it all the more emphatic: the police were not going to help me on this one.

Better sharpen those nail clippers.

Not to denigrate Officer Friendly's interrogation techniques, but I felt there was a little more to be learned from our eyewitness, so I jogged up to the African woman's house, climbing the steps to her sagging front porch. There were three doorbells. I rang all three.

A window to my left cracked open.

"Yes?" a voice asked. It was the African woman.

"I'm Carter Ross. I'm a reporter with the *Eagle-Examiner.* Do you mind if I ask you a few more questions about what you just saw?"

"Hold on," she said. Soon, she was standing with the front door slightly ajar. She didn't ask me in, which was fine. I didn't have time for hospitality.

"Yes?" she said again.

"I'm worried those two women may be in trouble," I said. "Can you tell me a bit more about the men you saw them with?"

"I'm sorry, I didn't get a good look."

"Please try."

She closed her eyes and concentrated for a moment.

"Well, two of them were large. They were young," she said. "The other was old. He wasn't very tall, but he looked like he had muscles, like a weight lifter."

She paused.

"He had a beard, a, what do you call it," she said, opening her eyes and drawing a circle around her mouth with her finger. "A goatee."

Short. Built. Goatee. It seemed like a description I had heard before.

"Racially, was he white, black?"

"I would say . . . Hispanic."

"And how would you describe his hair?" I asked.

"He didn't have any. His head was shaved."

That cinched it for me. Akilah and Sweet Thang had been kidnapped by the so-called Puerto Rican man, the one Akilah said sold the mortgage on her house. I had dismissed him as being a product of her imagination, just another piece of her intricate fabrication. But really he was like everything else in Akilah's world: twisted slightly, for storytelling purposes, but basically real.

It also fit the rough description of the man who had returned Windy's corpse at Enterprise—Donato Semedo, or whatever his name was—whom Raines had described as short and broad.

"How long ago did they leave?" I asked.

"About ten minutes ago," she said.

In other words, right after I heard Sweet Thang's scream. He probably marched them right out of the house. It was a bold move—a kidnapping in broad daylight—but I supposed if Akilah knew something about the murder of Windy Byers, the killer would take some big risks to be rid of her.

And anyone who happened to be with her.

"And you said the car was black?"

"Yes, long and black. Like the cars the men drive to pick people up at the airport."

"A livery cab?"

"Yes, a livery cab."

"Thank you, ma'am, you've been very helpful," I said, slipping my card through the door opening. "Please call me if you think of anything else."

I trotted back to my Malibu, wondering how I could track down a single black livery cab in a city where ten thousand of them came to pick people up at the airport every day.

I had no shot.

At this point, my only connection to the Puerto Rican man was Hector Gomes of Van Buren Street. I had to get to him, fast, with what resources I had.

I made two phone calls. The first was to Denardo Webster. My picture was helpful, but he was the only one who really knew what Gomes looked like. I told Webster about the abduction and instructed him to meet me at Gomes's house just as soon as he could get his feet off his desk.

My second call was to Tommy, who would be helpful if there was, in fact, a language barrier to surmount.

"Hey, can I pick you up outside the office in five minutes?" I said. "I think Sweet Thang is in real trouble, and I may need your Spanish or maybe even some fake Portuguese."

"Okay," Tommy said. "I've been figuring out some real interesting stuff with these dead donors, by the way."

"Great. You can tell me on the way."

Once again, I made the Malibu do things the good people at Chevrolet never intended, which might have bought me an extra minute or two. I jammed the brakes to noisy effect directly outside the building, where Tommy was waiting.

"What's going on?" he asked as he climbed in.

As I tore off toward the Ironbound, I told him about Sweet Thang's bone-chilling scream, my inability to convince the authorities to take it seriously, and the existence of the so-called Puerto Rican man.

"I think I know who he is," Tommy said. "But he's not Puerto Rican. I think he's Brazilian."

"Tell me more."

"Remember how you asked me to check out all the dead donors and see if maybe there was something they had in common?"

"Yeah."

"Well, I was looking at the names for a while, and I wasn't getting anywhere. They were just a bunch of dead guys who lived in the Ironbound and they . . . Red light, red light, red light."

I looked up and saw, sure enough, a traffic light. And it was red.

"Sorry," I said, wearing off a layer of brakepad but managing to get the car stopped just a foot or so over the line.

"No problem. Anyhow, after a while I stopped looking at the names and honed in on the addresses instead. You know, like maybe there was a pattern there?"

"Okay," I said, gunning the car as soon as the light turned.

"And it turned out there was," Tommy continued. "All of the houses had been flipped."

"Flipped?"

"Yeah, you know, bought for a low price, rehabbed, then sold . . ."

"I know what flipping is," I said.

"Sorry. Anyhow, once I caught onto the pattern, it was pretty easy to see. Basically, after all these old people died, their houses had been bought by an LLC—that stands for 'limited liability company,' by the way."

"I know what—"

"I know, I know, sorry. I just didn't know what any of this stuff was before I started covering it. Anyway, it's all these different LLCs, never the same one twice, buying these houses and flipping them for, like, twice the original price or more six months later."

"Okay," I said as we passed under the railroad tracks by Newark Penn Station. "So, to play devil's advocate, who's to say these LLCs have anything to do with one another?"

"Well, they don't appear to, except I recognized one of the names: Bahia Partners LLC," Tommy said. "I remembered from a council meeting I covered not long ago where they were voting on selling some city land to Bahia *Group* LLC. Then I started looking through the council minutes from the last few years—our library has them on file—and I started seeing a few other land-buying LLCs that turned out to have very similar names to LLCs that had flipped properties. There was, like, Amazonas Associates LLC and Amazonas Company LLC, Esperito Santo Investments LLC and Esperito Santo Financial LLC . . ."

"I get it, I get it," I said. "Someone got tired of thinking up new names so they just started recycling the old ones with a small twist on them."

"Yeah, and it turns out they're all names of states in Brazil," Tommy said. "And you'll never guess who was always proposing the land sales to those particular LLCs."

"Oh, but let me try," I said. "Councilman Wendell A. Byers."

"Very good," Tommy said. "You're pretty smart for a guy who thinks khaki is the new black."

I had to slow down once we crossed into the Ironbound and onto Ferry Street, the only road in Newark that is reliably crowded at just about any hour of the day.

As we crept along, I assembled the narrative in my head. A house flipper who wanted to get into new home construction knew it would be handy to have a city councilman in his pocket. So he started using the names of dead people to make campaign donations well above and beyond the legal limit. In return, the councilman supports the developer in making city land purchases, likely at generous rates.

It sounded like your garden variety Garden State corruption. So where did that cozy little relationship go wrong?

I couldn't figure it out. Or, more accurately, I didn't have the time to give it proper thought. Having passed Monroe, Madison, and several other dead presidents, I finally made it to Van Buren

Street. It was one way, the wrong way, so I had to hook around on Polk. He was a better president anyway.

Finally I reached the address, which belonged to a small, wooden-framed, single-family house with no apparent sign of activity.

"Okay," Tommy said. "What now?"

"Well," I said. "Isn't it obvious?"

"Not to me."

"Damn. Me, either."

I looked around for an aging white Datsun and saw it parked down the street, which wasn't especially surprising. If this guy really was a contractor of some sort, he probably shouldn't be real busy late in the afternoon on a raw day in February.

Another car pulled onto the block and I recognized it as a city-owned SUV.

"Let's go," I said. "That's Denardo Webster, Windy's chief of staff."

"And down low lover?" Tommy asked.

"One and the same."

I got out of my car and hailed Denardo, who pulled alongside with his window down.

"Okay, here's the deal: this is the Spanish dude's house," I said, pointing across the street. "We need to figure out who his boss is. Then we need to figure out where the the boss is. And we need to figure it out fast."

"And you're thinking the Spanish dude's boss is the guy that killed Windy?" Denardo said.

"I am."

"All right," Denardo said. "Just do me a favor: when we find this bastard, I want a few minutes alone with him to explain my grief over losing my friend."

He could have all year, as far as I was concerned.

"No problem," I said.

Denardo parked in front of us. He grabbed a city council badge off the dashboard—what was he going to do with that? Table some resolutions? Recommend further study?—and joined Tommy and me.

As we crossed the street to confront an unwitting Hector Gomes, I wondered what we must have looked like to an outsider. There was me, the whitest man in Newark; Denardo, the black man-mountain; and Tommy, a scrawny, nattily dressed Cuban kid.

What an odd trio. Yet here we were, the best and perhaps last hope Sweet Thang and Akilah had at making it to tomorrow.

We reached the front door, and as I considered the etiquette of knocking versus ringing, Denardo lowered his shoulder and barreled into it, grunting as his three hundred-plus pounds connected and splintered the wood around the lock.

"Cheap door," Denardo said as it gave way. "That's the problem with these house flippers. They don't build stuff to last."

Tommy and I followed Denardo as he stormed into the living room, where we found a slightly built Hispanic man dressed in a thin white T-shirt, frantically pulling up his boxer shorts.

"Police," Denardo shouted, waving his city council badge. "Let's see those hands."

The hands shot into the air, and as we all took in the scene before us—the open porno magazine, the box of tissues, the small tent he was pitching in his shorts—we all quickly reached the same conclusion: Hector Gomes had been fondling his love monkey.

"Oh, that's just *un*fortunate," Tommy said.

"Would you look at this little pervert?" Denardo said. "I mean, what's this?"

Denardo picked up the magazine, which had been bestowed with the very subtle title *¡Gigante Tetas!* As advertised, it featured some women whose breasts appeared to have been significantly aided by science. Denardo waved the magazine above his head as if it was evidence of the most heinous turpitude.

"This violates morals laws! There are codes and statutes—you're breaking the Public Decency Act!"

There was no such thing, of course. And if any lawmaking body tried to render illegal what Gomes had been doing, it would have to first build some pretty big jails, because every guy in America would need to be locked up. But this was not a moment to split legal hairs.

"I ought to take you downtown right now," Denardo continued. "Hell, I ought to take you to immigration services. You know they'll revoke your green card for this!"

His erection fast subsiding, Gomes looked miserable. I almost felt bad for the guy. We had just interrupted the best part of his day. But I could also see where Denardo was heading with this, and given the stakes, I wasn't going to stop him.

"But it happens to be your lucky day," Denardo said. "Because we ain't here to bust perverts. We need some information. You think you can play ball with us?"

Tommy couldn't help himself: "Oh, I think it's pretty clear he can play ball."

I brought my hand to my face so Gomes couldn't see the smile. Denardo didn't let it break his momentum. He put one foot on the couch and lowered his face until he was a few inches away from Gomes, who weighed roughly one third of a Denardo. I don't know if Gomes was intimidated. But I was intimidated for him.

"Now, you know who I am, yes?" Denardo said quietly.

Gomes, his hands still in the air, nodded. Obviously, he would have recognized Denardo from the numerous times he had run errands to the Springfield Avenue office.

"And you know who I work for, right?"

Gomes nodded again.

"Okay, now I want to know who *you* work for. I want to know where all that money you've been giving me has been coming from."

Gomes looked at me, then at Tommy, then cast a forlorn glance at *¡Gigante Tetas!* But none of us were going to help him with his dilemma. His boss was obviously a bad dude, a man who would not react kindly to an employee's betrayal; and yet here was this crazed, neckless black man in front of him, spouting off about green cards and other topics that tended to get immigrants, even legal ones, very nervous. Gomes knew he was going have to piss off one of these men. So which one?

But ultimately one threat was only theoretical while the other was directly in front of him, huffing fried chicken breath into his face. Besides, Gomes had been caught, quite literally, with his pants down. He had no will to fight. This was surrender.

He slowly let his hands sink to his sides and then whispered just one word:

"Primo."

He said the name reverently, as if we would know instantly who he was talking about. But Tommy, Denardo, and I just stared at each other stupidly.

Denardo recovered first.

"Who's Primo?" he demanded.

"That's what everyone call him," Gomes said, with the medium-heavy accent of someone who started speaking English sometime after adolescence. "I don't know his real name. No one know his real name."

"In Spanish, *primo* means 'cousin,'" Tommy interjected. "But it can also be a nickname, sort of like 'Buddy.' I'm sure it's the same in Portuguese."

"Well, whatever, he ain't no buddy of mine," Denardo said, then turned back to Gomes. "If you don't know his name, how do he give you a paycheck?"

"Cash," Gomes said. "Everything is cash with Primo. I always gave you cash. Primo do cash with everyone."

"So, what, you ran errands for him?" I asked.

"I'm an electrician," Gomes said, with a small hint of pride. "But sometime he ask me to do things. Primo ask you to do things, you do them."

"What, he threatens people or something?"

"He don't have to," Gomes said. "One time a man try to cheat him on some lumber. He end up floating in the river with three nails in his head. Primo say nothing. But everyone know who kill him."

I immediately thought of Windy Byers rolled up in that car, nails sticking out of his body at odd angles. In my imagination, he had a look of horror on his face, like he could still feel those stainless steel spikes in his brain.

Then I thought of Sweet Thang. I'm sure she told this lunatic she was a reporter. Everyone knows you don't just kill newspaper reporters, right? It makes for bad publicity.

Then again, you don't just kill a city councilman, either.

"Didn't anyone report him to the police?" Tommy asked.

"No one want to mess with Primo," Gomes said. "I should no be talking to you. I am as good as dead now. I will have to go somewhere and hope Primo never find me."

"You won't have to if we can get to him quickly," I said. "He didn't kill a lumber thief this time. He killed a city councilman. There are going to be people who make sure he goes to jail a long time for that. We just need to find him."

Gomes lit up.

"He has an office no far from here," he said. "He do all his business there. Sometime I think he live there. I give you directions."

"Hell no," Denardo said. "You're coming with us."

Gomes acquiesced meekly. He went to grab his pants, which were crumpled on the floor next to the couch, but Denardo put out an arm bar.

"Oh, no, you're coming like that. I don't want you running off."

If Gomes complained, I probably would have let the man have his pants—his dignity had suffered enough for one day. But he just accepted the order. I got the sense the guy was actually happy to be on our side. It didn't sound like Primo was exactly a joy to work for. Guys like that tend not to take classes on enlightened management.

"Let's move it," I said. "We might not have much time."

If we were the odd trio coming in, we were now the ridiculous quartet: the whitest WASP in Newark, the black man-mountain, the queer Cuban, and an electrician in his boxer shorts.

Gomes hopped in Denardo's SUV while Tommy and I followed in the Malibu. As we turned back on Ferry Street, heading away from downtown, I saw Denardo's beefy hand shoot out the driver's side window and stick a flashing light atop his SUV. Then he hit the siren—no doubt installed for all those pressing city council emergencies—and we were soon zooming down the road's middle stripe as traffic swerved out of our way.

We veered off Ferry Street onto Wilson Avenue, zipping through an industrial part of town, underneath Routes 1 and 9 and the New Jersey Turnpike, over potholes large enough to jar loose dental fixtures. We took a tire-screaming left at Avenue P, passing the off-airport Enterprise rental car location where the mysterious Donato Semedo—perhaps aka. Primo—had dumped Windy.

At some point, Denardo silenced his siren, though we were still cruising at speeds that would have put us in good company among the Avenue P drag racers. Then he jammed the brakes and turned down a small dirt side street that may or may not have been marked—I was too intent on tailing him to notice.

The street ran along the side of a vast warehouse, the old-fashioned kind made of painted cinder block. Denardo eased to a halt just before the end of the building and pulled over to the side of it. I followed his lead and soon the four of us were joined in a small huddle between the cars.

“The office is over there,” Gomes said in a hushed voice, pointing around the corner. “It’s on the second floor. There’s a parking lot and some stairs that go up there.”

“Can Primo see the parking lot from his office?” I asked.

“Only if he’s looking,” Gomes replied.

He could only see if he was looking. Thanks, Confucius.

“So what’s the plan?” Tommy asked. All eyes were on me.

“Well . . .” I said, stalling to give myself time to think of something.

“You got two females in trouble,” Denardo said. “I say we bust in. If we jump on this dude quickly, he won’t know what hit him.”

“Yeah, but what if he’s armed?” Tommy asked.

“He’ll only have time to get off one shot, at most,” Denardo said. “There are four of us, so that means three of us will get through.”

I got the sense someone had watched too many action movies.

“Whoah, whoah, whoah,” I said. “This isn’t Little Bighorn. No one is charging into battle to get shot.”

Denardo and Tommy had differing reactions to this: the former disappointed, the latter relieved.

“We need to know what we’re up against first,” I said. “Let me just have a look. I’ll be right back.”

I peeked around the corner and saw a black Lincoln Town Car—the brand preferred by livery cabdrivers and short, squat goateed kidnappers everywhere.

Next to it, I could see a rickety set of metal steps that led to a second-floor office. At the top of the stairs there was a small landing, with a door that had windows on either side. The first story of the warehouse was windowless—just a long brick wall. So I crept along it, staying flush to the building to diminish the chance I could be spotted from above.

I reached the stairs and gently tiptoed up, taking the last few steps on my hands and knees so I could stay below the sightline of the windows, then crawled over to the side of the building. Leaning against the concrete, I stayed perfectly still for a few seconds, just to have a listen. But all I could hear was the wind hitting the dried stalks of grass in the nearby marshland.

Were we too late? Had Primo already done something awful and irreversible? It was possible, but there was no sense lingering on that thought. We had to push forward as if Sweet Thang and Akilah were still among the breathing.

That meant I had to take a look inside. Flattening myself against the building, I quietly eased into a standing position next to one of the windows, then turned and nudged myself, inch by tiny inch, toward the pane. I didn't want any large movements, nothing that might make the metal grates squeak or catch the peripheral vision of someone on the inside. But slowly, achingly, I got my body in a position, and soon my right eyeball was nearing the point where I would be able to see into the office.

And then, with roughly the same volume as a jet plane taking off, my cell phone rang.

I jerked my head back and my hand flew to my pants pocket to silence the phone, but I was too slow—it let out two piercing rings before I could find the correct button.

As I withdrew my hand from my pocket, I could hear my heart pounding in my ears. I braced myself for the office door to fly open and for Primo or one of his goons to come barreling out, gun first. I considered jumping off the landing—it was only one story down. But then what? It was just me and a nearly empty parking lot. I'd be target practice.

I waited, but there was no barreling. No gun. No Primo. I sank back down against the warehouse wall, thankful for soundproof doors or the wind direction or whatever it was that ensured that the county coroner wouldn't be listing my cause of death as "Verizon Wireless LG Flip Phone."

It took me a moment to get my nerve, then I began sliding back toward the window so I could finally have a look inside.

I'm not sure what I thought would be in there—Akilah and Sweet Thang bound and blindfolded, pleading for their lives? Primo cackling while he sharpened a comically large knife? Blood and gore everywhere?—but the first thing I saw was a battered gunmetal-gray desk, heaped with old mail, invoices, and other assorted paper. There was a Chinese restaurant calendar from 2004 taped to the wall behind the desk. A black filing cabinet had been shoved in one corner. In the other corner, a small flat-screen television sat atop a cheap entertainment center. It was sparse, and other than the TV, all the furniture looked like it had been claimed off the side of the road somewhere.

More to the point, there were no people inside, at least none that I could see. They must have been in the warehouse—and the only entrance to the warehouse I could see was inside the office.

I tried the door. Locked. Of course. And Denardo wasn't crashing through this one—it was steel, with a metal lock guard. I focused on the windows instead. They had bars on them, but maybe if I could break through the glass, I could reach around behind the door and unlock it.

Was I capable of punching through a window? I had no idea. It wasn't exactly a graduation requirement at Amherst. There was only one way to find out. I hiked my jacket sleeve down over my hand, made a fist, and threw a hard jab.

I connected—it helps when you're hitting a stationary target—but I'm quite sure it hurt me more than it hurt the window. The pain shot through my hand into my wrist and I recoiled, shaking my arm until the pain stopped radiating. Then I gritted my teeth and tried again, harder. This time, the pain made it all the way to my elbow.

"Dammit," I said.

"You sure make a lousy action hero," Tommy said from the bottom of the stairs, where he, Denardo, and Gomes had assembled to watch my effort.

"You got a better idea?" I said, feeling my battered knuckle throbbing.

"I do," Denardo said. He disappeared around the corner for a second, then came back wielding a large, L-shaped tire iron. He climbed the metal stairs, which rattled and groaned under his weight, then performed a quick appraisal of the window.

"You might want to stand over there," he said, gesturing to the other side of the landing.

I did as instructed. Denardo swung the tire iron with both hands, baseball style. The glass cracked but did not break. It was thick stuff and, apparently, shatter resistant. He hit it again. And again. As the crack in the glass got marginally larger, our chances of being able to sneak up on Primo were getting rapidly smaller. But, at this point, I couldn't think of an alternative. This was our only way in. All I could do was hope Primo didn't hear us.

Denardo bore down on his task, getting some good licks in, grunting at the effort. My phone rang again, but I didn't bother to look at it, nor was I as concerned about the noise. It was now but a soft tinkle compared to the racket Denardo was making.

Finally, he created a small hole in the window. From there, the rest of it came away pretty easily. He cleared away a few shards that clung to the frame, then reached around and fumbled with the door handle until it opened.

"Nice work," I said.

Denardo, who was breathing heavily, went inside, straight to the door that led to the warehouse on the far side. He began studying it.

"This thing is for real," he said. "I don't know if I'd do anything but dent this one."

My phone rang again. Again, I reached into my pocket and silenced it.

"Do you know how to pick a lock?" I asked.

"No. Do you?"

"Yeah, me and all the other kids from Millburn."

"Oh. Right."

"Think our pal Hector knows?"

"Even if he did, you need tools for that," Denardo said. "That boy ain't got nothing but boxer shorts and shriveled balls right now."

We stared at the door a little more.

"We're wasting time," I said.

My phone rang again.

"Why don't you answer that?" Denardo asked.

"It's just the office," I said.

"Maybe they could call a locksmith for us."

Somehow I doubted any reputable locksmith would walk past a shattered window and pick an interior door with no questions asked. Then again, I was starting to feel desperate and didn't have a lot of other ideas. It couldn't hurt.

I fished my still ringing phone out of my pocket. Out of habit, I glanced at the screen before answering it, expecting it would read "Office Incoming."

But it didn't. The words on the screen took me a second to parse. Then I felt another one of those primal rushes of energy.

The caller was "Thang, Sweet 2."

Primo was surprised at how resourceful Byers's little whore had been at eluding him.

Torching the girl's house had actually been Byers's idea—a pointless, pathetic attempt to save his own wretched life. Byers told Primo he instructed the girl to hide the evidence in her house, in a place where no one could find it. So, it stood to reason, destroying the house would mean destroying the evidence. If it took out the girl, as well? All the better.

But the girl hadn't been home when the fire was set. And that bothered Primo. After all, what if the girl hadn't hidden the evidence in her house? What if she kept it on her person? What if she left it somewhere else?

It was a loose end and it kept eating at Primo. He realized he couldn't be sure he committed the perfect crime while the girl—and possibly the evidence—was still out there. So he set about tracking her down and reeling her in. With all the information Byers had given him, it wasn't going to be hard.

Except it was. He came back to the house the morning after the fire, but she wasn't there. He rerented the New York thugs and instructed them to find her. But through the next day, they reported only a series of near misses. They chased her all over the city, they said. But somehow the girl managed to slip by them every time.

Finally, Primo came up with a new plan: stop chasing her. Make her think the heat was off. She would show up again at her house eventually—it was the only roof she had, even if it was burned. And when she did, they would grab her.

So Primo and his men set up surveillance near her house and waited. It took twenty-four hours before their patience paid off. The girl came back, dragging a friend. Primo took both of them—the last thing he needed was another loose end.

Soon it would all be over.

CHAPTER 9

I had forgotten about Sweet Thang's second cell phone. But now it came back to me, vividly: how she kept a spare for when she talked out the batteries on the first one, how I scoffed at her when she told me about it, how I shook my head as I stored both numbers. And now it looked like some kind of brilliant.

"Hello?" I said in a quiet voice.

Dead air.

"Hello?" I whispered again, just a little louder.

The reply was a long, barely audible "Sssshhhhh."

The shush belonged to Sweet Thang, and I felt an immediate and powerful sense of relief just knowing she was alive. I gripped the phone tightly, as if holding it was akin to holding Sweet Thang herself, and if I merely managed not to let go, everything would turn out fine.

The next noise was something like static, perhaps the phone's mouthpiece rubbing against something. Then there was jostling, like the phone was being buffeted as she walked.

I cranked the volume on my earpiece as loud as it could go. Denardo frowned at me curiously. Cradling the phone against my ear, I pulled out my notepad, turned to a fresh page, and scribbled, "It's our girls. Shhhh."

He nodded.

I pressed my ear against the phone and concentrated, trying to pick out some sound I could identify, something that would give me a hint as to her whereabouts. There was nothing but more jostling. Then, suddenly, I heard Sweet Thang, as loud and clear as if she had the phone to her mouth:

"It's not in the bathroom," she said. "Maybe Akilah will find it in the bedroom."

Okay. So they were in someone's residence. And they were looking for something.

"I'm getting tired of this," a male voice replied. It was a little more distant sounding—across a room perhaps—but I could make it out okay. It had an accent that came from well south of the border, if not south of the equator. It was agitiated but also authoritative, the voice of someone used to being in charge.

Primo. It had to be Primo.

"So, tell me, honestly, do you like the paint color in here?" Sweet Thang said. "It's a Ralph Lauren color. They called it 'Sullivan,' but I call it 'Sulli' for short."

"You are talking to me about paint?" Primo bristled. "These gentlemen here are ready to hurt you, badly, and you're talking to me about paint?"

"Paint is important," Sweet Thang replied.

Was it ever. I knew that paint. And I knew where I could find it: Sweet Thang's apartment. It was the color she had just painted her walls.

I speed-walked out the office door, gesturing for Denardo to follow me. Placing my finger over the phone's mouthpiece, I whispered, "We have to get to an apartment in Jersey City as fast as your truck can take us," and recited the address from memory. Then I added: "But no siren."

We couldn't risk the noise. Primo would get suspicious if Sweet Thang's pocket started sounding like it had an ambulance inside it. Denardo rounded up the other two members of our rescue crew. As we hurried toward Denardo's SUV, I held my index finger to my mouth in a shushing gesture so they wouldn't start jabbering, then dove into the backseat with Tommy.

He mouthed the words "Call the cops?" but I shook my head. The police had already failed me once. There was no sense in wasting more time with them. And, more to the point, I didn't need this to turn into an armed hostage situation. Someone else could worry about what laws had been broken later. I just wanted the girls returned unharmed.

"It's not in the bedroom," I heard Akilah saying. "It's got to be in here somewhere. I had it when I came in and I didn't leave with it. Let me check the couch again."

"No!" Primo replied. "There will be no more checking and rerechecking! You will find it. Now."

"But I don't—" Akilah began.

"Perhaps I have not explained myself clearly," Primo interrupted. "You *are* going to give me what I need. The only question is how much you suffer first. Do I have to make you suffer? Do you need to feel pain?"

"But I—" Akilah started.

"I've heard enough," Primo barked. "Gag her, Johnny."

I heard the sound of duct tape—a lot of it—being peeled off a roll. Akilah protested but was quickly silenced.

"Now," Primo said. "Break her arm."

Akilah struggled and grunted, then gave a muted yelp of pain. Sweet Thang protested, "Stop it! Stop it! You're hurting her!"

But that was exactly the point. Even with Akilah gagged, the howls poured through my phone, growing increasingly frantic, crescendoing into something that could only be described as animalistic. It stayed at that bloodcurdling pitch for fifteen long seconds until it finally subsided into soft moaning. Just listening to it was horrible. Tommy, who had no trouble hearing it from five feet away, looked like he was going to vomit.

Akilah was starting to talk. But it was impossible to understand what she was saying. Apparently Primo couldn't figure it out, either, because I heard duct tape ripping and suddenly Akilah's voice became distinct: "My arm . . . my arm . . . Oh Jesus . . . Oh my God . . . My arm . . ."

"Oh, honey," I heard Sweet Thang start to say, but she was cut off by Primo.

"You touch her, you die," he spat. "You scream, you die. You move, you die. Davi, make sure she doesn't move."

"Get your hands off me," Sweet Thang squealed.

"He can put his hands wherever he likes," Primo insisted.

The phone jostled and I missed what came next. Primo was saying something, but it remained unhearable until either Sweet Thang stopped struggling or Davi stopped fondling her.

". . . like that," I finally heard him say. "If you think I can't break someone, look at what I did to your boyfriend. By the end, he was begging to tell me about the thumb drive."

Thumb drive. Thumb drive? As in the computer storage device? The kind you plug into the USB port? Why would someone possibly go this berserk just to get a thumb drive?

Then I got it. The thumb drive must have contained a copy of the Excel spreadsheet Denardo told me about, the one where Windy logged all the illegal campaign contributions Primo made. He obviously made a copy for Akilah, as a kind of insurance policy.

In the hands of, say, the U.S. Attorney's Office, that data file was an indictment, conviction, and twenty-year prison sentence waiting to happen. It would also go a long way to establish motive for a murder prosecution should the Essex County Prosecutor's Office get to it first.

So it made sense Primo would do anything to either possess or destroy that file or the thumb drive that contained it—burn down a house, torture a man, kidnap and kill two women.

After all, that thumb drive represented his freedom.

* * *

The sound of Akilah panting, moaning, or sobbing—or some combination of all three—still filled the phone.

"Now," Primo said. "Are you going to tell me where I can find it? Or is Johnny going to work on that arm a little more?"

There was no reply. Akilah was tough and stubborn, a kid from the projects who'd surely had some scrapes in her life. But I don't care who you are, a broken arm hurts like hell. I didn't know how much more she could take.

"Please," Sweet Thang pleaded through choked vocal cords. "Please stop. Please, she's had enough."

"It stops when she tells me what I need to know," Primo said. "Johnny, gag her again. I don't need the neighbors to hear her screaming."

"Just tell him, Akilah, tell him," Sweet Thang begged.

I heard more duct tape being unrolled, then more muffled agony. Maybe I was just imagining it, but the sound was different from the first time. There was more anger this time. This was the man who had set her house afire, killed her children, and killed her (ex-) lover. I felt like Akilah was finding the resolve, somewhere deep inside herself, not to give him anything.

There may have been some self-preservation at work, too. Because, really, once Primo had the thumb drive, what incentive would he have to keep Akilah—or Sweet Thang, for that matter—alive? They were just witnesses at that point, and why would he hesitate to kill witnesses? He had already killed three people, one of them a public official. Two more bodies on top of that wouldn't change Primo's bet. He was already all in.

I was just figuring this out, but I bet Akilah had already done the math. Now I hoped she could hold on until we got there. We were already approaching the Pulaski Skyway. It wouldn't be far now. Denardo was pushing ninety when he could, but the road had enough other travelers that he didn't get many openings. Five minutes. Maybe seven.

There was still the question of what we would do once we got there. It wasn't going to be physical—there were four of us, sure, but Tommy and I weren't exactly street toughs, and Hector didn't have pants on. Denardo was the only one of us you'd draft for your ultimate fighting team. And he was several thousand chicken wings on the wrong side of being in good shape. We'd have no chance against Primo and his thugs, who were armed and, from the sound of things, ruthless.

But maybe we could convince him it was in his best interests to leave the girls and make a run for it. Hell, I'd buy him his ticket back to Brazil or whatever South American country currently lacked an extradition treaty with the United States.

The phone had gone strangely quiet, to the point where I worried I had lost the call. I studied the display—still connected. I pressed the phone harder against my ear, then plugged a finger in my other ear to block out more ambient noise.

Faintly, I could hear Akilah straining to breathe against her gag. We had crossed over the Hackensack River and were bearing down on the Tonnelle Avenue exit, the one for Sweet Thang's place. Not far now.

Then I heard Primo's voice.

"Let's try this again," Primo said. "I can continue to find ways to hurt you. If you think your arm hurts right now, you can only imagine what it will feel like when I have Johhny here dislocate your kneecaps."

Johnny actually laughed, the sick bastard.

"So, Johnny is going to remove the tape, and you're going to tell me where that thumb drive is. Then this ends."

I heard ripping tape, then Akilah gulping air in between sobs.

"Now," Primo said. "Where is it?"

Akilah was maybe trying to say something, but her own hyperventilating was making it difficult.

"Does Johnny need to do some more convincing? He can be very persuasive, you know."

"No! No!" Akilah finally said, whimpering. "Please . . . please . . . please . . ."

Something had changed again in her voice. The anger was gone. She sounded like a wounded little girl. The imperative to avoid pain at all costs had finally won out. Primo had broken her. She was going to tell him, and the next sound I'd hear is gunshots. We were too late.

"Okay. Where is it," Primo demanded.

"It's . . . it's . . . it's in the jewelry box," Akilah blurted, forcing out the words. "I hid . . . I hid it in her jewelry box."

The jewelry box? As in, Sweet Thang's jewelry box? But that wasn't in the apartment anymore. That was . . .

I put my finger on the mouthpiece.

"Turn around!" I shouted at Denardo. "Now!"

"What the . . . it's a divided highway, man," Denardo said.

"Find a way. We've got to get back to Newark."

Primo had been barking at one of his goons to find the jewelry box, figuring it must have been somewhere in the apartment. But it sounded like the guy was coming back empty-handed.

"Where is it?" Primo asked.

Akilah was battling to catch her breath and couldn't get any more words out. Meanwhile, Denardo barreled down the exit for Broadway, a quirky little left exit that, fortunately for us, was also an entrance ramp on the other side. He hooked around and was soon back on the highway, heading in the opposite direction.

"Where is it?" Primo asked again.

"Akilah, do you mean *my* jewelry box?" I heard Sweet Thang say.

Akilah must have signaled affirmatively because Sweet Thang said, "It's at a pawnshop."

"A pawnshop?" Primo asked. "What the—"

"She stole all my jewelry and pawned it," Sweet Thang explained. "See, after you burned down her house, I felt bad she had no place to go, so I let her stay—"

"Stop talking! You talk too much. I don't care about your stories," Primo said. "Where is this pawnshop?"

"I don't . . . I don't know," Sweet Thang said, her voice rising an octave. "This friend of mine went there and got my bracelet back, but I told him not to bother with the rest of it. He never told me the name of the place. Akilah, honey, please just tell him."

There was silence.

"Akilah, please," Sweet Thang begged.

"Tell me or I break your friend's arm, too," Primo said.

Finally, I could hear Akilah moan: "M-M-Maury's."

"Maury's Pawnshop. I know where it is," a new, deeper voice said. It sounded African-American. It must have been one of the goons, probably Johnny—I didn't know a lot of black guys named Davi.

"I'll go get it for you, boss," Johnny said.

"No," Primo said. "We're all going to get it."

Not if we could get it first.

By my best guess, figuring it would take Primo and his entourage at least five minutes to usher the girls down into a car, we had a ten-minute head start on Primo. Ten minutes to negotiate the release of one jewelry box from one slimy pawnbroker. Having seen how Maury operated—speed did not appear to be among his customer service priorities—I just hoped it was enough time.

"Now, it's just like before," I could hear Primo saying. "One of these men will have his finger on a trigger at all times. If you want to live, you do as I say. If you try to run, you die. If you scream, you die. If that thumb drive isn't at the pawnshop, you die. You understand?"

The answer was inaudible, but the rubbing noises coming through my earpiece told me Sweet Thang was on the move again. Then the sound stopped. I looked at my phone, which was flashing. The call had been terminated. Maybe she went into the elevator.

"I lost her," I said.

"Okay, what the hell is going on? Where are we going?" Denardo asked.

"We're heading to a place called Maury's Pawnshop," I said. "It's—"

"Oh, I know Maury," Denardo said. "Everyone in the hood knows Maury."

I filled in our crew on what I had been able to piece together from my eavesdropping.

"So, basically, we're using the thumb drive as leverage in a hostage negotiation," Tommy said.

"Yep," I said.

"Have you ever negotiated a hostage release before?"

"Nope," I said.

And we left it at that. As soon as we got off the highway and entered Newark, Denardo flipped his siren back on and began an aggressive grand slalom through the city streets. Presumably, Primo would be obeying traffic laws—what with two kidnapped women in the car—so Denardo's maneuvering increased our lead by another minute or two. At this point, every second mattered.

We screeched to a stop outside Maury's, leaving some taxpayer-funded rubber on the asphalt.

"Keep an eye out for Primo," I told Tommy. "Call me the second you see him."

I leaped out of the SUV, charged up the crumbled front steps, and burst through the spiderwebbed glass door that separated Maury's Pawnshop, Check-Cashing, and Payday Loans from the outside world. Inside, the same pudgy Hispanic guy as before—what was his supposed name? Pedro?—was staring at the same overwrought Mexican soap opera. Or perhaps it was a different one. The mustaches looked the same.

I was about to start the whole routine where I asked to see

Maury while Pedro stalled us—a dance that would waste precious minutes—but Denardo, who had decided to follow me in, took a shortcut.

"Yo, Tracy, get your black ass out here," he boomed, loud enough to be heard on the other side of the bulletproof glass. "We got some business to conduct."

"Maury's real name is *Tracy*?" I asked.

"Yeah. Between that and the lisp, he got beat up a lot at recess."

"How do you know him?"

"You been around this city your whole life, eventually you know everyone, one way or another," Denardo said. "My cousin used to date his sister. They all went to West Side back in the day."

Maury emerged from the back, his Jheri curls looking freshly lubricated, wearing a lime-green suit and, of course, sunglasses. Again, I couldn't see the shoes. But I was guessing white imitation-snakeskin cowboy boots. Or perhaps some pointy-toed slip-ons.

Maury slid open the small piece of Plexiglas that covered the airholes and pointed at me.

"You," he said. "I thpecifically inthtructed you not to return here."

"Tracy, shut the hell up," Denardo said. "He ain't none of your concern."

Maury looked a little cowed. I wondered if Denardo had been one of the kids who administered those playground beatings.

"Now," Denardo continued. "You got a jewelry box I need."

"How would you dethcribe thith . . . ?"

"It's the one you took off that little skank Akilah Harris."

"Thkank!" Maury said, like it offended him. "Thuch language!"

"Yeah. Now go back to your little hole and get it."

"Thkank!" he said again, then turned and disappeared into the stockroom.

A minute passed. Then two. I kept glancing at the clock on

my cell phone, watching our time advantage slip by as Maury screwed around. I didn't want to know what this scene would turn into if Primo got here and we still weren't in possession of that thumb drive. Would it become an open auction? Or would he just decide to depress the price by shooting the other bidders?

I looked at some of the guns Maury was selling in his display. But they weren't going to solve anything. Not for me. I had never handled or fired one in my life and wouldn't know where to begin. Mostly, I found myself yearning to be on the other side of that bulletproof glass, safely ogling buxom Mexican women with Pedro.

"You know what you're doing with this thing once we get it?" Denardo asked.

"Not yet," I admitted. "I was maybe going to . . ."

Then I looked at the bulletproof glass again.

"Yeah," I said. "Actually, I think I might. Let's just get this stupid thumb drive first."

Two more minutes passed. I tried to keep myself calm, but that's not easy when you can feel your heart thunking against your chest and are in imminent danger of breaking into a flop sweat. I expected my phone to ring any moment with Tommy telling me Primo was about to walk in.

"You okay?" Denardo asked at one point.

"This is taking too long," I said. "This Primo guy is going to be here soon."

"Yeah, I know," he said. "You sure you can handle him?"

"No," I said.

Not exactly the most inspiring answer. But at least it was honest.

Finally, Maury returned, clutching a jewelry box that, just as Sweet Thang once described it, looked like a miniature armoire, with tiny pocket doors and tiny doorknobs and everything.

"Thith it?" he asked.

"Open it," I said.

Maury swung open the little doors and I saw it immediately, hanging on a string with the necklaces: a blue SanDisk thumb drive, encased in a protective plastic shell.

Denardo looked at me. I nodded.

"I'll give you ten thousand bucks for it," Denardo said.

Maury was so startled, he actually lowered his sunglasses.

"Ten thouthand? Cath money?" he asked.

Denardo reached into his jacket and pulled out an envelope, removing the flap so Maury could see the stack.

"Take it or leave it," Denardo said.

"Deal," Maury replied quickly.

"I'll need a receipt, of course," Denardo said.

Maury just nodded and started gleefully banging on his cash register.

"A receipt?" I asked.

"Well, this money ain't exactly mine," he said. "This is the last campaign contribution from that Primo guy. Normally Windy logged it in to his computer, then took the cash to the bank. But he was killed before he got a chance to do it. I've been carrying it around with me ever since. I didn't know what else to do with it.

"So, as his chief of staff, this strikes me as a judicious use of campaign funds"—he grinned—"and I figured I should get a receipt in case anyone asks me to account for it later."

Denardo began shoving the bills through the Plexiglas.

"Actually, stop for a second," I said, then turned to Maury. "There's one more condition of the sale: we're going to need to borrow your store for a little while."

Maury had no problem with the temporary rental of his store. Heck, for another ten grand, he probably would have sold us the whole damn thing. He buzzed us through the heavy door to the side of the bulletproof glass, then showed us the video screen that allowed us to see what was being recorded by the store's security cameras—there was one inside, one outside. After extracting a promise we not touch the "merchandithe," he and Pedro made themselves scarce while Denardo and I hunkered down to wait for our man to arrive.

It didn't take long. I barely had time to remove the thumb drive from the jewelry box before my cell phone rang. It was Tommy.

"A blue panel truck just pulled up a block away," Tommy said. "Hector tells me it's Primo's."

"Okay," I said. "I'm going to put you on speakerphone. I want you to be my eyes on the street. Tell me what you see."

"Okay," Tommy said, his voice squelchy but distinct. "The truck is parking . . . It's parked . . . There's a man getting out of the driver's side, a big black fellow . . . Now there's a bald guy getting out of the passenger side. He looks South American. It guess that's Primo, yeah? . . . Yeah, Hector says it's Primo . . . The back door is opening up . . . It's Akilah! She's walking with the two men toward the pawnshop. She looks . . . She's in pain, yeah, she's in a lot of pain. She's walking on her own and she's . . . Oh! She stopped walking for a second and the black guy shoved her . . . They're nearing the door, so I'm going to shut up now and . . . They're yours."

Just as Tommy's narration finished, I saw three people appear on the video screen. Then the front door swung open. Primo entered.

It was my first look at the man. He was shorter than I thought he'd be, but broader—if I had to guess his dimensions, I'd say five six, 230. A regular fireplug. Even his fingers were short and thick. His bald head had a square, boxlike shape. His goatee, equal parts salt and pepper, made a neat oval around his mouth. Under a three-quarter-length black trenchcoat, he wore a black V-neck pullover and charcoal-gray slacks. His walk was quick and direct. Maybe it was because of all I already knew about him, but he moved like a killer.

Akilah stumbled in gingerly behind him. Her hair had a bedraggled, slept-in-the-gutter kind of look. Her face was a mess of snot and tears, like an infant who hadn't been tended. Her left arm appeared to be fine. But she was holding her right arm like it was made of tissue paper and would tear at the slightest stress.

Johnny the Goon brought up the rear. He was a big chunk of black guy, but his bulk wasn't nearly as troubling as what was bulging against the pocket of his jacket. As I said, I'm no gun expert. But whatever he was packing looked large enough to put a respectable-sized hole in anything it hit.

Primo walked up to the window and put his meaty hands on the counter. I expected to feel a rush of nerves, but it never came. I was calm, in control, anxiety-free. I was one tough hombre when I was shielded behind bulletproof glass.

"Hi, can I help you?" I said, ever the officious clerk.

"I'm looking for a jewelry box for my niece," he said, still looking around the store, not making eye contact, trying to play nonchalant. "Something nice."

"Aren't you really looking for this, Primo?" I said, dangling the thumb drive in front of him.

At the mention of his name, his head snapped toward me. His body seemed to coil, and for a brief instant, I thought he was going to leap through the bulletproof glass. Instead, his eyes narrowed on the thumb drive, then on me.

"Where did you get that? Who are you?" he demanded.

"I'm just a neighborhood pawnbroker, looking to make a deal with you, Primo," I said. "You give me the two women you've kidnapped, and I'll give you this thumb drive."

He glowered at me.

"How do I know that's the thumb drive I need?"

"Take a good look," I said, pressing it up against the glass. "While you were shooting Windy full of nails, I'm sure this is exactly what he described to you."

From the way Primo was studying the thumb drive, I could

see I was right. He started stroking his goatee absentmindedly, obviously a nervous habit.

"I know what you're thinking," I continued. "What good will the thumb drive do you if there are still two witnesses alive who can testify against you? But here's the thing, Primo: either way, you're going to have to make a run for it. You know that by now, right? It's way too hot for you here. So the question you have to ask yourself is, What do you want to leave behind?

"If you leave behind these two women, all they can do is offer the authorities a vague description of a man whose name they do not know, along with a story about how they were kidnapped. Maybe the police would look for you, maybe they wouldn't. Either way, you fall off the radar screen pretty quickly.

"But if you leave behind this?" I said, pulling the thumb drive back from the glass and waving it around. "This drive has everything. Every payoff you ever gave Wendell Byers. Every piece of land he sold you in return. You've got fraud, corruption, racketeering, and, oh yeah, you become the prime suspect in the murder of a city councilman. So what's it going to be?"

Primo's eyes darted back and forth between me and the thumb drive.

"How do I know you haven't already copied the file somewhere else?" he asked.

I turned to Denardo. "Can you give me that receipt for a second?"

He fished it out of his wallet. I held it up against the glass.

"Because we were only a little bit ahead of you," I said. "If you'll look at the time on this receipt, you'll see we bought this thumb drive no more than five minutes ago. And you'll notice there are no computers here. There's been no time to download this data. This is the only copy."

"Ten thousand dollars," he said, after he was done studying the receipt.

"Funded by your last campaign contribution to Windy Byers," I said.

I thought the irony might sting him. But I suppose literary devices didn't have that effect on everyone.

"Your friends are worth a lot to you, I see," he said.

"True," I said. "But I think we both know this thumb drive is worth a lot more to you."

He actually chuckled slightly and petted his goatee a few more times.

"You are right, of course," he said at last. "We have a deal."

I pointed at Akilah, who had been watching the entire interaction with wide eyes.

"She's the down payment," I said. "Both of you stand against the wall over there and let her come through that door."

Primo nodded and walked backward until he reached the far wall. He jerked his head at Johnny, who had been clutching the back of Akilah's shirt. He released his grip and she tripped toward the door, which I buzzed open. She slid through it quickly, then ran back into the stockroom without a single word of acknowledgment. And that was fine. I needed to concentrate on getting Sweet Thang back. There would be time for hugs and thank-yous later. And I suppose I couldn't blame her for wanting to get as far away from Primo as she could.

"Okay," I said. "The final payment is outside in your blue panel truck. Please go get her."

Primo and Johnny stalked out the door, and I once again saw them on the video screen, walking back up the street.

"You still there, Tommy?" I asked in the direction of my cell phone.

"Yeah, I see them coming out of the store," Tommy said. "They're coming back toward the truck . . . Man, Primo looks pissed . . . Now they're getting in the truck, they're starting the engine and . . . They're on the move."

I felt a surge of confused panic.

"They're making a run for it?" I asked.

"No, no . . . They're turning the truck around . . . Just turning around . . . They're cutting off a Dodge Durango . . . The driver just made a proper Jersey gesture at them . . . They're coming back toward the store . . . And . . . They're pulling up to the corner now."

"Okay, I've got visuals, thanks, Tommy," I said, huffing a lungful of air out of my mouth as the truck appeared on my screen. I didn't realize it, but I had been holding my breath.

Primo hopped out of the passenger side door and left it open. The truck's engine was still running. He was evidently going for the quick exit and I wasn't going to stop him. Bringing Primo to justice wasn't my job. That was the responsibility of the Newark police or maybe U.S. Marshals—if they could find a nameless man with a talent for identity theft. I didn't really care. All that mattered to me was that Sweet Thang would be able to tell her grandchildren about this someday.

And if, at the end of the story, the bad guy got away? Well, that would just be a good lesson for the kiddies that the world isn't always fair.

On the screen, I could see Primo open the truck's back door, then Sweet Thang hopped out. I felt my throat constrict a little when I saw her, looking shell-shocked but otherwise unharmed. I swallowed twice and tried to keep my composure. There would be time for emotion, hopefully in another minute or two. But not yet.

Primo grabbed Sweet Thang by the hair—the cruel bastard—and stomped to the front entrance. Sweet Thang followed awkwardly. Walking while being led by one's curls is not a particularly graceful endeavor.

The front door to Maury's swung open and Primo entered,

dragging Sweet Thang behind him. She turned to have a look at where she was going, then saw me behind the glass.

"Carter!" she yelped.

"Just relax, honey," I said. "It's almost over."

Primo faced me.

"Before I let your woman go, I have to know," he said. "Who are you?"

"I'm a reporter with the *Eagle-Examiner,*" I said, then couldn't resist adding, "I guess you're getting a firsthand lesson in the power of the press."

He let out a disgusted grunt.

"Here's how we're going to do this," I said. "You're going to stay against the wall over there. I'm going to place the thumb drive in this box here and spin it toward you. Then you're going to let Sweet Thang go. As soon as she's through the door, you can come get it."

"No good," Primo said. "How do I know you won't just spin the box back as soon as she's in?"

"Because then you and your goons out there would come in with your guns and trap us in this little box. And I have better things to do than be stuck in here all day.

"Besides," I added. "The truth is, Primo, I want to give you this drive so you can get as far away from here as quickly as possible. Because I don't ever want to see your ugly face again."

Admittedly, it was a fairly juvenile thing to say. And given a little more time, I'm sure I could have done better. But he sneered at me a little bit, so I felt at least moderately fulfilled in that I had launched one quasi-decent insult before he ran out the door.

"Okay," he said. "You first. Put the drive in the box."

I placed the blue SanDisk thumb drive—with all its evidence—in the glass cubby.

"Now spin it," Primo said.

I spun.

"Okay, your turn. Let the girl go."

He released his grip, and Sweet Thang staggered toward the door. I buzzed it open. She burst through, then quickly shut it behind herself.

She was safe.

The first thing she did was kiss me. Softly. On the mouth. With her hands cupped around my face. It wasn't exactly the kiss you'd give your cousin, but we could sort that out later.

Then she hugged me. Hard. All over. Except where the soft warmth of her breasts should have been, I felt something jabbing into me.

Apparently, it was getting her, too.

"Ouch," she said. "Forgot about that."

She started lifting her sweater and I turned the other way—we needed to establish these kinds of boundaries in our relationship—which only made her giggle.

"It's okay. I just need to get my phone," she said, reaching in between her cleavage to grab it. "Those guys took my first phone from me. They just didn't realize I had two of them. Good thing I wore a sports bra today. It turned out to be the perfect hiding place."

"That's where it was the whole time I was eavesdropping on you?"

"Yeah. You've heard of speakerphone? This was boobyphone."

Primo, who snatched the thumb drive as soon as Sweet Thang came through the door, was in the lobby, studying his prize, as if he could read the data if he stared at it hard enough. Finally, he exited.

Not that I was paying him much attention. As I said, he was no longer my concern. I was busy trying to think up some witty, half-lascivious remark about Sweet Thang's clever use of her cleavage.

Then I heard a loud crack. Then another. Then a third.

It was the unmistakable sound of someone firing a gun. And it came from right outside the store.

* * *

On the video screen, I could see Primo facedown on the pavement. The truck had peeled away almost as soon as the gun was fired, its passenger door still open. Davi and Johnny weren't sticking around to defend their boss. There was nothing left of him to defend. A small-but-spreading pool of blood leaked from Primo's head.

Sweet Thang clutched my arm as we watched the life pour out of this man whose real name we did not know.

"Is he . . . ?" Sweet Thang began, then answered her own question.

There was no further sound coming from the street. Gunshots and squealing tires have a way of bringing life to a halt in Newark, as everyone dives for cover and waits to make sure there isn't a retaliatory salvo.

But in this case there would be no return fire.

"Call Detective Raines and tell him Windy's killer is dead. His number is in here," I told Sweet Thang, handing her my phone. "I'm going to go out and have a look."

I exited the safety of the bulletproof chamber, treading softly across Maury's lobby. I could see Primo with my own eyes now, through the cracked glass door. He hadn't made it very far, having fallen just beyond those crumbling steps, his arms splayed at an angle that suggested he died before he hit the ground.

Cautiously, I shoved open the door. I looked to my right, but there was nothing unusual. Then I looked to my left.

And there was Akilah Harris, gun still clenched in her left hand.

Her mouth hung open, her crazy hair blowing slightly in the wind, her battered right arm dangling limply at her side. Her eyes were fixed on Primo like she was in some kind of trance.

I hadn't paid much attention to what she was doing back in that stockroom. But now it was obvious: she found herself a gun—Maury had plenty—dug up some matching bullets, sneaked out a back door, and waited for Primo to appear.

I hadn't cared if Primo got away, figuring he'd eventually either get his or he wouldn't. Akilah didn't want to leave justice to chance.

"You okay, Akilah?" I said.

"I fired three shots," she replied. "One for Boo. One for Alonzo. One for Antoine."

I looked at Primo again. Only one shot had hit, at least that I could see, but it had done the job. There was a large, bloody hole on the left side of his bald head, just behind the ear. If there was an exit wound, I couldn't tell—that side was down. Someone else could do all the forensics.

I walked slowly toward Akilah, who hadn't relinquished the gun.

"He's dead," I said. "It's okay now. You can put the gun down."

She didn't move. I walked a little closer. Still nothing. Soon I was next to her and gently removed the gun from her hand, laying it on the ground. She leaned against me and I wrapped one arm around her, being careful not to put any pressure on her broken side. She put her left arm around me, in a not-quite-embrace, and began a rambling explanation of why she had done what she did.

Some of it made sense. Some of it didn't. But I was able to piece together a few items of interest. She said the whole thing started after Windy told her she had to leave the house and she told him they were through. Windy's attempt at reconciliation, with Akilah listening, had been to call Primo and demand he do something about the mortgage—or the councilman would cut off his supply of city land.

Akilah said Primo lost his mind when he heard that, and made all kinds of threats. Windy knew he was in trouble, knew Primo was dangerous, and gave her a copy of his Excel file on a thumb drive. If anything happened to him, she was to hand it to the police.

But she wasn't thinking about the thumb drive—or anything else—when her house burned down. And when she first met Sweet Thang and me, just a few hours later, she was still under the misbelief the fire was an accident. She only realized otherwise after she heard about Windy's abduction, at which point she was a woman on the run with no place to go.

We stayed in our somewhat-hug until the cops arrived. There was, naturally, a lot of explaining to do. I told them the man lying in the bloody puddle was the man who had killed Councilman Byers, which confused them. Then I told them I was a newspaper reporter, which confused them more. They weren't sure whether to cuff me as a suspect or ask me to leave the crime scene until the public affairs officer arrived.

The explaining got a little easier when my detective pals, Pritchard and Raines, showed up. I laid out everything for them chronologically—from the illegal campaign contributions, to the falling-out between Windy and Primo; from the creation of the thumb drive to all the horrible things Primo did to find it.

And yes, I told them Akilah Harris fired the fatal shot into Primo's skull. I wasn't worried for her. Even if they charged her—and I doubted they would—no jury would convict a mother for killing the scumbag who torched her children, kidnapped her, and broke her arm.

About an hour later, having gone through everything a few more times, Pritch gave Sweet Thang, Tommy, and me a ride back to the newsroom. We were mobbed when we entered—everyone, by that point, had heard some version of what happened—but Tina was having none of it and immediately turned into her own crowd-control unit.

"Everyone back, back!" she shouted. "These three have work to do."

It was, after all, coming up on deadline. I settled down to write and the words flowed quickly. Explaining it to the cops had been a useful exercise in helping me order my thoughts. And besides, I had lived a lot of it.

Sweet Thang stayed by my side the whole time, making useful suggestions here and there. Tommy wrote the section about the campaign contributions and their link to Primo's various LLCs—after all, it was his reporting that discovered it. Then we cobbled it together in a long, hopefully coherent, narrative. By the time we were finished, I was pleased with the story. It hit all the pertinent facts. It read well.

And there was no mention of a space heater anywhere.

ACKNOWLEDGMENTS

Writing is a solitary act, but I can promise you this author doesn't stand alone. So, if you'll indulge me, I'd like to offer my profound thanks to . . .

My Facebook friends—you know who you are—who made me take writing this seriously, because they answered a resounding "yes" when I posted a status update asking, "Does anyone actually read acknowledgments?"

Toni Plummer, my editor at Thomas Dunne Books, whose keen eye is surpassed only by her kind heart; and to the rest of the crew at St. Martin's Press and Minotaur Books, including big bosses Tom Dunne and Andy Martin, marketing mavens Matt Baldacci and Jeanne-Marie Hudson, publicist extraordinaire Hector DeJean, and library guru Talia Sherer.

Jeanne Forte Dube, an agent who has provided me with endless amounts of wise counsel, loving support, and street meat.

Becky Kraemer, my secret weapon, who is underpaid but by no means underappreciated.

Karen Kleppe Lembo, Arlene Sahraie, and all the library scientists out there who make it their passion to connect books and readers.

The booksellers who haven't been afraid to take a chance on

a new author; the ones I've met so far, in stores large and small, make me hope we're still friends when I'm an old author.

The interns. (Those who subscribe to my newsletter know I can't risk saying more—too great a chance it will come back to haunt me.)

The readers who have sent an e-mail or stopped by a book signing to share their thoughts about Carter and his buddies; in particular, Maureen Caouette, who knows how to make good use of a snow day.

The reviewers who have taken the time to read my work critically and engage with the words and characters (but who I cannot name individually, lest I sound like a suck-up).

Friends at Christchurch School, who provide such a supportive community for me and my family and who tolerate us when the kids scream in the dining hall.

Tony Cicatiello, James "Kato" Lum, and Jorge Motoshige, who always let me crash.

Joan and Al, the greatest Meemaw and Papa ever; to Ga, who at 92 still teaches and inspires; to my mother and father, who are my biggest cheerleaders and, if you know them, probably forced you to buy this book (sorry).

Last, and most significant, my wife, Melissa, who is a more supportive spouse, devoted parenting teammate, and loving partner than I possibly deserve. Ask anyone who knows me: I married up.